ALSO BY SARAH READY

Stand Alone Romances:

The Fall in Love Checklist

Hero Ever After

Josh and Gemma Make a Baby

Soul Mates in Romeo Romance Series:

Chasing Romeo

Love Not at First Sight

Romance by the Book

Love, Artifacts, and You

Married by Sunday

Stand Alone Novella:

Love Letters

Find these books and more by Sarah Ready at:

www.sarahready.com/romance-books

Sign up to receive bonus content, exclusive epilogues and more at:
www.sarahready.com/newsletter

Josh and Gemma Make a Baby

SARAH READY

CROWN

W.W. CROWN BOOKS

An imprint of Swift & Lewis Publishing LLC

www.wwcrown.com

Library of Congress Control Number: 2021914218
ISBN: 978-1-954007-18-5 (eBook)
ISBN: 978-1-954007-19-2 (pbk)
ISBN: 978-1-954007-22-2 (hbk)
ISBN: 978-1-954007-21-5 (large print)
ISBN: 978-1-954007-31-4 (audiobook)

To you. Yes, you.
Thank you.

Josh

and

Gemma

make a

Baby

1

*"Anything is possible
if you put your mind to it."*

WHEN I WAS A LITTLE KID, I WORSHIPED JOSH LEWENTHAL, NOW,
I couldn't care less about him, I just need his sperm.

I'll be the first to admit, I have no idea how to go about
getting it, but as my obscenely sexy boss, famed self-help guru
Ian Fortune, always says, *"anything* is possible if you put your
mind to it."

That's my motto for this year. Starting today, January first,
I'm going to believe that anything is possible—that magic can
happen. And after thirty-two years of being average in nearly
every way, magic will be a welcome change.

Josh and I grew up in a small river town a few hours north
of New York City. It's the type of town that has a Christmas tree
in the square, a pumpkin carving contest in the fall, and an ice

cream social in the summer. The houses are cookie-cutter cute, the yards are golf course green, and everybody waves hello. It's a kid-friendly, all-American paradise. My family fit right in.

Josh moved to town with his dad when he was eight. Within days my mom warned me to stay away from him.

"Why?" I asked.

"Because he's not the sort of boy that nice girls play with."

"Why?" I asked again. I was in that "why" phase that all kids go through.

"Because I said so."

Well.

My mom was right. I *was* a nice girl. She dressed me in pink poufy dresses and pigtails to prove it. But instead of listening to my mom I snuck out of the house and went and found Josh Lewenthal. I guess there's a lesson there. Even when I was little I couldn't take "because I said so" as an answer.

I found Josh kicking a ball in his backyard. He told me the reason nice girls couldn't play with him was because he knew how girls got babies in their bellies. To prove it, he smacked a kiss on my mouth. I was terrified for weeks that I was going to blow up like a balloon and pop out a baby. After a month I realized that Josh Lewenthal was full of crap and that my mom had been right.

But that didn't stop me from idolizing him. My brother Dylan and Josh became best friends. And like little sisters around the world I wanted to do everything they did and be everywhere they were.

When I was sixteen my big sister Leah came home from college for Christmas break. Within days she told me to stop ogling Josh.

"Why?" I asked. I was still in the "why" phase.

"Because if he catches you looking he'll steal your underwear."

I didn't know what she meant. "Why?"

"Because he collects underwear for a hobby and pins them on his bedroom wall. He has almost every girl's undies in this whole town. He'll tear them off you and then do things."

Leah lowered her voice to a whisper. "Marie Johnson said his hands are like an octopus's. Everywhere at once."

I was appalled and then intrigued. But, "I don't think he'll want my underwear. Dylan is his best friend. Plus, I'm not really into that kind of thing." You know, being a nice girl and all.

"It doesn't matter," said Leah, full of big sister knowledge. "He just has to look at you and you'll rip your undies off for him. He's that good. An *octopus*, Gemma. You better stop ogling him."

I was skeptical, to say the least.

But six months later, while I was cleaning up my parents' garage after Josh and Dylan's joint high school graduation party, Josh told me he'd miss me while he was in New York for college. Then, lo and behold, he stole my underwear. Metaphorically, of course.

For the second time in my life, I spent another few weeks terrified that I was going to blow up like a birthday balloon and pop out a baby.

After weeks of toe-numbing worry followed by my period and sweet sagging relief, I realized that Josh Lewenthal was not worth my fascination/worship/idolization, that he was in fact an immature/emotionally constipated user.

I didn't see him again for six years.

By the time he came back to town I'd been married, divorced, and was long past mooning over fantasies.

I had an apartment in the city and my current (amazing) job, social media marketing coordinator for acclaimed self-help guru Ian Fortune. And I had goals. Lots of goals.

I mean...today I have goals.

Okay. A goal.

And Josh Lewenthal, the man who knows how to make a baby, is integral to my success.

2

"If you can imagine it,
you can do it."

It all started two days after Christmas when my mom called to remind me about the annual Wieners and Wine New Year's Resolution party. She dialed my work phone and instead of checking the caller ID like a normal person, I answered.

"Ian Fortune, Live Your Best Life Starting Now Enterprises, this is Gemma speaking—"

"Gemma, sweetie. It's Mom."

Across the office, Lavinia looked up from her computer. I could almost see her ears twitching as she tried to eavesdrop. She was hired six months before me, and for years now she has falsely acted like my supervisor.

Lavinia is forty-five, she has steel-gray hair, and a mouth that looks like she popped a lemon in it fifteen years ago and never took it out. She blames me for all printer jams, sagging office plants, and overflowing recycling bins—none of which are my fault. She also blames me for the office fridge running low on lime-flavored sparkling water, which is my fault. What can I say, I'm an addict.

I shrugged at Lavinia and turned slightly away from her eagle-eyed stare.

"Why hello, Mr. erhm...Berners-Lee." I pulled a name from my subconscious that seemed vaguely familiar and probably had to do with the internet. "I'm so glad you called. Yes, I do have a moment to speak about SEO."

I sensed Lavinia tilt her head and run her laser eyes over me.

"Is that snoopy co-worker listening in? Well, sweetie. I was only calling to make sure you are coming to the Wieners and Wine party this year."

Ah. Of course.

Every year, even though I haven't missed a single New Year's day party in my entire life, my mom calls to make sure that I'm coming.

Unfortunately, for the past seven years my mom has also tried to set me up with a different middle-aged, partially balding, pleated pant-wearing single man. This year my brother Dylan warned me that she's invited a fifty-year-old with a toupee for my dating pleasure.

"I actually can't come. Something's happened at work," I hedged.

Mom is the queen of sniffing out half-truths and lies. "You've heard, I'm so sorry, honey. Don't let it bring you down."

This wasn't the response I was expecting. "Heard what?"

I glanced at Lavinia. She was pretending to type, but I could tell she was still listening in. She wore a frown of disapproval. I hunched down in my desk chair and propped the phone against my shoulder.

"Don't worry about it, honey. We all know Jeremy is a bad apple. Just because he has another baby doesn't mean he's happy."

I let out a startled cough and pulled the phone away from my ear. I hadn't heard that Jeremy had another baby. That's three now.

I coughed again and hit my chest. Lavinia started to stand in concern but I waved her off. The last thing I needed was her coming over.

"I'm sure he's miserable wiping up spit up and changing dirty diapers. Just look at your sister, she has four kids and never gets any sleep. Honestly."

I didn't respond. I couldn't. Every time I thought I was over my ex-husband and what he'd done, I was proven wrong. I swung my swivel desk chair around, away from Lavinia's probing stare, and faced the far wall covered in a mural of Ian's motivational sayings.

The words melted into an image of Jeremy holding his newborn baby in his arms. An ache spread through my chest so that I couldn't respond to my mom.

"I'm sure *that woman's* breasts are sagging horribly. And I bet she won't be able to lose the baby weight. Serves her right." My mom always calls Jeremy's wife *that woman*. I don't blame her. I've never been able to say her name either.

After six months of marriage I found them spread eagle, going at it like rabbits on our dining room table. My mom promised that affair relationships never last, but ten years, and apparently three kids later, it seems that I was the interloper, not *that woman*.

"I've invited someone for you to meet at the party," my mom said. "His name is Mort. He's got a wonderful career. Makes scads of money. And better yet, he's mature, only fifty mind you, and he doesn't want kids. Not a one. He's perfect for you, Gem."

"Ah," I managed to squeak out. Apparently, the fifty-year-old toupee wearer didn't have plans for children.

Every year it's the same. I trudge into the Wieners and Wine Party, gorge myself on mini barbecue wieners, lime Jell-O salad mold, and processed cheese balls, wash it all down with boxed wine and try to ignore the assessing stare of my mom's latest "set-up."

It's exhausting.

"Do we have to? Maybe we could...skip a year?"

She didn't respond. I listened as she walked from the kitchen, down the hall, and closed the door to her craft room. I could hear the wreath of silver bells tinkling as she shut the door. Mom went into her craft room whenever she had something to say that she didn't want my dad to overhear. He was retired and liked to sit in the kitchen watching gameshow reruns.

"I saw Mimi Butkis last week. I invited her and her son Gregory to the party."

"I don't want to date Greg Butkis."

"That's the point. Mimi said that..." Her voice got all low and pinched. "Mimi said that it's known around town that you're desperate. No one wants to date a mid-thirties chubby divorcee with questionable fashion sense and a bum uterus. Gregory Butkis might not come to the party. Mimi said he's looking for a wife, not a pity date. I'm sorry, sweetie. I didn't want to tell you this, but Mort's the best you can do."

What?

"What? Why?" I whispered.

And it sort of seemed like the universe whispered back, *because I said so.*

And that was the moment.

That moment. Right there.

The exact moment I realized the entirety of my hometown thought I was a dating pariah, with no prospects, no future, and that even Greg Butkis, used car salesman, sleaze extraordinaire, was beyond my reach.

And honestly, when was the last time I had a decent date in the city? It'd been years. Years. My mom was...right.

Last Monday, Ian said, *if you can imagine it, you can do it.* I posted it with a cute kitten background to all our social media pages. It got nine bazillion likes.

Well, at that moment, when I was on the phone with my mom, I started to imagine a different future for myself.

A future where I didn't depend on horrible hookups, pity dates, or the questionable roll of the dating dice.

Besides, I already rode the marriage boat, it tipped over, capsized, and I nearly drowned. No. In the future I'm imagining, I see me fulfilled, happy, loved, with...a family.

A baby.

She's there in my heart, she's been there so long, like a song that I started singing but was never allowed to finish. I've been waiting for her, and in this imagined future, I see her in my arms. I'm singing her our lullaby.

Ever since the surgeon told me I'd never have children I've been mourning that future I couldn't have. I was still married to Jeremy when I found out. He said he didn't care, didn't need or want kids. Two weeks later he was mating like a monkey on the dining room table. So, it was a moot point. I never followed up or went to a doctor to see what could be done.

But it's been ten years. And unlike when I was sixteen and I dreaded what might come after Josh Lewenthal took my virginity...now at thirty-two, I want a family, a baby. Someone to cuddle, to go on bike rides with, to kiss bruised knees, to lie in the grass and look at clouds with, someone to love. I've been wanting it for years now.

I'd been waiting to find the right man. But unlike the carefree, I've-got-all-the-time-in-the-world dating scenes of my early twenties, or even the post-divorce dating app-fueled manic weekend hookups of my mid-twenties, my thirties have brought...Morts. I've seen it all. Men who are married and hiding it, men on their third divorce, men who live in their mom's basement, men in their fifties having a midlife crisis who want to date a younger woman. All Morts.

I've been waiting for a good man to help make my dreams come true.

But, at that moment, I realized my dream doesn't have to include marriage. Or a man.

Single women have babies all the time. I don't need a fifty-year-old toupee-wearing man to have a future of happiness. I can make a future of happiness for myself.

Maybe, I can have a family. Maybe I can finish singing that lullaby.

I just need an egg, some sperm, and a doctor to help make the magic happen.

I can control my own destiny.

My mom wasn't finished talking. "Josh Lewenthal will be at the party," she said. "Did you know he has his own business? He draws web comics. Isn't that strange? He's moved back in with his dad. He's living in the basement. The poor dear. Coming from a broken home. Be nice to him. You weren't nice to him last year."

"Okay, of course, Mr. Berners-Lee. Thanks for calling, I'll talk to you soon," I said, attempting to cut my mom short.

My mom sighed. "Bye, sweetie. See you in a few days. Wear something nice."

I swiveled around and hung up the phone. Lavinia watched

me from her desk. Her glasses were perched at the bottom of her nose. "Who was that?"

"Mr. Berners-Lee. About our SEO." I grabbed my mouse and clicked it haphazardly.

"Mr. Berners-Lee?" she asked, sounding incredulous.

I looked around the office. No one else was paying any attention.

"That's right," I said. "He had some pointers."

"Tim Berners-Lee had some pointers for you?"

"Yup." I said. "Nice guy."

"Tim Berners-Lee? The *creator of the internet* called to give you some pointers?"

Ugh. That's why his name sounded familiar, I'd just been reading a motivational article about him. "Yup. If you can imagine it, you can do it."

Lavinia rolled her eyes and turned away. Over her shoulder she said, "I never realized he would sound so much like a middle-aged woman."

Across the office, one of the database techies snorted into his hand.

Oh well.

Nothing to say to that.

Besides, I had a goal now.

I clicked on my computer, searched the web and found a reproductive endocrinologist, an infertility doctor, only a few blocks from the office. I booked an appointment online for the next day.

THE WALLS OF THE DOCTOR'S OFFICE WERE PLASTERED WITH thousands of baby photos and a sign that said ten thousand babies and counting. In case anyone was confused, this is a place where they *make babies*. It was a sleek, loft-style brick walled office with a large Georgia O'Keefe reproduction that either depicted a flower, an apricot or the female anatomy. Since I was in a baby making office, I'd go with the third guess.

The nurse on the phone told me to drink lots of water and not go pee before I arrived. Apparently, they needed a sample. So, I took her advice and on the way to my appointment I bought a large latte and a bottle of water and proceeded to chug both in five minutes flat.

Dr. Ingraham, the doctor I had my consult with, was not at all what I expected. After the modern loft décor of the lobby, I expected a trendy nerd kind of guy. Instead, Dr. Ingraham was five foot two, as round as he was wide, and bald. His office looked like an episode of one of those exposé hoarder shows. He sat at his desk barely visible behind stacks of papers, journals, cardboard boxes, and piles of plastic anatomy models —penises, uteruses, eggs, sperm, and more were all tossed about on his crowded desktop.

"How are you? How are you?" he asked. He pumped my hand from across the desk. Then, "What a stupid question. You're infertile, that's how you are. Well don't worry, we'll get you pregnant in no time. Would you like some water?"

"Umm, uhhh, no?"

How did I manage to get a hoarder doctor with verbal diarrhea? This must be why all the other doctors were booked for two months out, while this doctor had immediate availability.

Dr. Ingraham ignored my no and pulled out two bottles of water from a mini fridge under his desk.

I sat back down in my creaky chair and crossed my legs. The latte and the bottle of water had hit my bladder and I really needed to pee. Like, *really* needed to pee.

"I reviewed your file. Stage four endometriosis. Blocked

tubes. You had surgery when you were, what, twenty-four? What else. Ruptured cyst. Good, good." He looked down at the manila file on his desk and somehow made his recitation sound like wonderfully cheery news.

"Twenty-two," I corrected.

"Twenty-two what?"

"I had surgery when I was twenty-two. The surgeon said it looked like...really bad." I winced. I couldn't make myself repeat his exact words. "He said I'd never have children." I admitted the last in a low voice. I hoped Dr. Ingraham would disagree with the surgeon's assessment.

"Ha! They always say that, don't they? Idiots. Blunder-brained morons. Just because the waterslide is closed doesn't mean you can't swim in the pool." Dr. Ingraham squinted at me to see if I appreciated his analogy.

"So my pool is open?" I asked hopefully.

"Ahaaa, ahaaaa," Dr. Ingraham said. "That's what we're here to find out. Water?" He held up the bottle.

"No. No thanks." I waved it away.

He smiled and opened the cap. Then he grabbed a slightly dirty glass and started to pour the water into it. As the water splashed into the glass, my bladder protested. I clenched my legs together.

"Let me explain some fertility concepts to you. Ready?"

I nodded and he started in on his explanation.

"See here. You have a bunch of eggs each month that have the capacity to grow." He grabbed a pile of plastic eggs off his desk and held them up. To me they looked like a sushi garnish.

He flew the eggs through the air like a toy. "These eggs are like a group of people waiting for the subway at rush hour. When the train arrives it's packed and there's only room for one person to squeeze in. Whoever's lucky enough to be standing by the door gets on. Unfortunately everyone else is left behind and they all die." He dropped the model eggs and I watched in horror as they clattered on the desk and knocked against the plastic penis. "But that one lucky egg grows and gets to ovulate. Isn't that special?"

So. Wow.

I tried to listen. I promise, I really, really tried. It was horrifying, and weird and all sorts of stuff, but Dr. Ingraham kept pouring more water into his glass, and taking long, gulping drinks, then talking, then pouring more water. And every time he did, all I could think was how badly I had to pee.

"The sperm have to travel the equivalent of around the world to meet the egg at the end of the tube. Because of that, you need to have millions of sperm at the start so a few can make the journey. We can improve the odds by selecting the strongest, best-shaped sperm and giving them a head start. That's called an intrauterine insemination or IUI. You can't do IUI because your tubes are blocked. Your waterslide is out of order. See?"

Why did he have to keep talking about water?

I nodded my head and squeezed my legs. He poured more water and it made a tinkling sound. It was agony.

Gulp, gulp. Whhhhhy?

Fifteen minutes later, he was still talking.

"If you really want the egg and the sperm to meet, we do IVF. That means picking the best-looking sperm and injecting it into the egg. This is like pushing two kids together at the high school dance—most times it works but sometimes you get rejection." He coughed, then mumbled, "At least that was my high school story."

I gave him a sympathetic wince. But it was hard to concentrate on anything he was saying. I squirmed in my seat and shifted, trying to find a spot where it didn't feel like I was going to burst.

Finally, he said, "And that's the end of the fertility lesson for today."

I blew out a long, grateful breath.

"Any questions?" Dr. Ingraham asked.

"No," I said hurriedly. "When can I start?"

AKA, please, please let me go pee in a cup.

Dr. Ingraham looked incredibly pleased. "I like your enthusiasm. I'll have the nurse get some urine and blood."

Thank goodness.

"Next time, we'll get your partner's semen sample."

"My what?"

Dr. Ingraham flipped through my chart. "Your partner. You checked the box indicating that you have a male partner."

I leaned forward and tried to see my questionnaire, but my bladder gave an outraged spasm and I sat back down.

"Did you check the wrong box? If so, I can describe the donor sperm system. It's fascinating. You see, there's a database that-"

Oh my gosh. And that was when, for the first time in my life, I let my bladder change the course of my fate, and perhaps my life.

"I have a partner," I blurted out. "He has amazing, super-awesome, winner sperm. He danced with all the girls in high school. Never got rejected. Not once. We're good. All good."

There. Right there.

That's the moment when Josh Lewenthal came into the picture, even though I didn't know it yet.

All because I really, really needed to pee.

Minutes later, I felt sweet, sweet relief as I peed into a cup. Then I gave some blood so the lab could run their tests. Finally, I went to the front desk to make my next appointment. And when the scheduling person asked the name of my partner in a bored, couldn't-care-less tone, I started to explain that I didn't really have a partner, that I would have to use a donor.

She pointed to a flyer on the desk called *Anonymous Donor Sperm and You*.

And it's like Ian says, sometimes you can feel fate steering you, because when I saw the flier and the smiling stranger with little illustrated sperm floating around him, I said, "I mean, actually, I do have a partner. Probably. Have one. Yup."

The scheduler rolled her eyes. "What's your partner's name?"

At her prompting, a name popped into my head. My mom had just mentioned him, he was living in his dad's basement, writing web comics, thirty-three years old, no marriage, no girlfriend, no kids, not much of a future really. Probably he'd be happy to help. He was my brother's best friend, sort of like family, at least the kind of family that sleeps on your couch and eats all the food in your fridge. It's almost like I'd be doing him a favor.

The scheduler sighed as I took long, long seconds to consider what I was about to do. Would I? Could I? Should I?

Yes.

I did it.

I lied.

"His name is Josh Lewenthal."

3

*"No one can make you unhappy
without your permission."*

HERE I AM AGAIN. STANDING IN FRONT OF MY PARENTS' HOUSE for their thirty-fifth annual Wieners and Wine New Year's Resolution party. The cold wind bites my cheeks and blows snowflakes past. I pull my wool coat tight and look up at the white colonial still trimmed in Christmas lights and pine-scented garland.

Josh will be here, just like he has been for the past ten years. My mom likes to invite him to all our family events since "the *poor dear* comes from a broken home." She's long forgotten that she warned me to stay away from him.

I swing open the door and take in the familiar smell of the New Year's buffet and the happy noises of family and friends congregating.

"Auntie Gemma!" My nieces and nephew, Sasha, Maemie, Mary and Colin, or "the four horsemen of the apocalypse," as I affectionately call them, race up to me as soon as I step inside. The girls shriek and dance around me.

"Auntie Gemma. What'd you bring us? What'd you bring?" asks Sasha. She's eight and a half years old, the oldest, and the ring leader of their little sibling gang.

"What makes you think I brought you anything?" I ask. I try to hold back a smile. Sasha has bright red curly hair like her dad and gray eyes like my sister. I was there when Sasha was born. She came out with a whole lot of spunk and she hasn't settled down one bit.

"Because you always bring us something," Colin says. He's quiet and serious and the voice of reason among the siblings even though he's only four.

Maemie and Mary, six-year-old twins and troublemakers extraordinaire hold hands and jump up and down. The picture frames on the wall vibrate in time to their thumps.

"Hmmm." I put a finger to my mouth and pretend to contemplate what Colin said. "You think so? Funny thing. I happened to be in Chinatown yesterday and I saw this..."

With a flourish I pull a clear plastic sack from my coat pocket. It's fancy imported candy, the pretty pastel gummy kind in shapes like unicorns, kittens, and sharks. The girls start squealing. Colin's eyes light up.

I hold out the bag. "There are twenty pieces of candy. You each get five. Share, right?"

The kids all nod, promising prettily to share and share alike.

I drop the bag into Sasha's hand.

"Alright. Give me my hug and get out of here," I say.

The girls rush me and nearly knock me over with their enthusiasm. Colin hangs back until I gesture for him and he joins the pileup. I love these little hellions. I was there for all their births, their christenings, and I get to babysit them a night a week. I'm a lucky aunt.

I drop a kiss on each of their heads.

"Love you, Auntie Gemma," they chorus.

"Love you too, kiddos."

They rush back down the hallway into the house. As I'm hanging my coat I hear my sister, Leah, yell from the kitchen. "Candy before dinner? Gemma, I will kill you!"

I grin and unwrap my cashmere scarf. Leah's all bark and no bite.

The sounds of the party drift from the interior of the house, and the smell of barbecue wieners and processed cheese wafts to me. My mom is one of those people who thinks that hosting a fancy party means putting miniature foods on toothpicks and adding chopped vegetables to lime Jell-O. No amount of cooking shows or gourmet food magazines will convince her otherwise.

"Gemma! I thought I heard you. What in the world are you wearing?" I turn from the coat closet and smile at my mom.

"It's a work outfit, Mom."

But she's not listening. She holds up the edge of my knee-length olive green sweater and grimaces. I have on black leggings and chunky shoes.

"Sweetie. You'll never attract a man if you dress like this. Honestly. You look like a lumpy cucumber." She drops the edge of my sweater and gestures at the stairs. "Luckily, I bought you a new outfit. I laid it out on your bed." She shoos me with her hands. "Go on. Hurry up."

"But I'm not trying to attract a man," I tell my mom, secure in my new vision for the future. I don't need a man for my happiness.

She looks past the stairs, down the long hall, then leans in and whispers, "Mort is here. Didn't I tell you? He has a fabulous job. Mimi Butkis told me his house is three thousand square feet, with underground sprinklers."

I stare at her, unable to comprehend what underground sprinkling has to do with me.

"Go on. Go on." She pushes me toward the stairs.

I go. But only because I hear Josh and Dylan laughing from the living room. I realize that if I'm going to approach Josh with my plan, I may as be wearing a new dress while I'm doing it.

OH GOD.

My mom has turned me into a pumpkin. When Cinderella was helped by her fairy godmother, she turned a pumpkin into a fabulous carriage. When my mom dressed me, she turned me from an average-looking woman into a top-heavy gourd.

I walk into the living room and pull at the short orange skirt barely covering my bum. Unfortunately, as I tug at it, the orange fabric around my cleavage drops lower and more of me spills out for everyone to see. I blow out a breath. My mom is five foot three and still as thin as a toothpick. Leah takes after her. Apparently, when she bought this outfit she forgot I'm not built like them.

I somehow picked up all the curves that my mom and sister never acquired and plastered them onto my hips and my chest. I've had double-Ds since I was twelve. And unlike popular opinion that big breasts are great, all they've done for me is give me back aches, make it hard to run, and cause men to speak to my boobs instead of my face.

I wrap an arm over my chest and take little mincing steps into the living room so that the skirt doesn't ride too high.

The party is in full swing. Holiday jazz music plays over the stereo system. There are at least three dozen neighbors, friends, and relatives milling in the living room, dining room and adjoining family room. The white carpet is covered in plastic runners and the furniture has clear plastic wrap over it. My mom covers everything in plastic for the party, so every wine, barbecue, or processed cheese spill can be wiped up and away. The plastic scent lingers for weeks and is a reminder of a party well hosted. In fact, the plastic scent is one of my first childhood memories. That, and Josh Lewenthal's kiss. Speaking of...

I look around for Josh but don't see him in the crowd. No problem. I'll grab some wine and wieners and work my way through the rooms.

I inch to the buffet table and try to scoop some wieners onto a paper plate. It's awkward since I'm still using one hand to keep my breasts inside my orange top, but I manage. I grab some red wine and take a long gulp.

My mom swans over. Her face is flushed and she gives me a wide, encouraging smile. "Gemma. Sweetie. You look beautiful." She's talking in an overly loud fake voice which makes me realize that she's actually talking for someone else's benefit.

I look to the man she's pulling along. He's at least two inches shorter than me, his toupee is like a bright yellow scouring pad, and the buttons on his silk shirt are stretched tight over his sagging waist.

"This is Mort, he recently moved to town from Arizona. He manages golf courses," my mom says triumphantly. She turns and smiles at him. "Mort, this is my daughter Gemma."

The wine that I just swallowed goes to my head and I flush from my cheeks down to my chest.

"Enchanté," Mort says in a fake French accent. He looks down at my chest and doesn't look back up.

"Oh dear. The pimento olives on toothpicks have run low. I'll just grab more," my mom says. She scuttles off to the kitchen.

I clear my throat awkwardly. Mort still doesn't look up. I try to cover more of my chest with the plate full of wieners. It doesn't really work.

"So. How are you enjoying the party?" I ask awkwardly.

Mort shoves a pickle in his mouth and manages to mumble around his crunching. "Mm. S'okay. Food's decent, heh?"

I take another swallow of wine and desperately glance around the room. There's my sister rushing after a seemingly hyper Maemie and Mary. Sorry, sis. My dad is on the other end of the room talking with Father Gibbly, the local priest. My dad sees me looking, catches who I'm talking to, and gives me a sympathetic wince.

"Are you ready for the resolution roundup?" I ask. I'm scraping the bottom of the barrel for a topic of conversation so I can escape quickly and tell my mom I did my due diligence with her set-up.

The resolution roundup is at the end of the party where everyone writes their New Year's resolutions on a piece of paper, folds them up and anonymously puts them in a bowl. Then my dad reads them all aloud. It usually gets some good laughs, but other years it results in marriage proposals or baby announcements. So. It's kind of a big deal.

I inch away from the table and move a step back from Mort. I continue, "I was thinking of writing something safe like, exercise more, lose weight, or cut down on drinking, you know? The usual."

Mort looks at the near-empty glass of wine in my hand and at the pile of mini wieners on my plate. "Heh. I read it takes two weeks to fail at resolutions, not one day, heh? Some kind of record." He chuckles at his joke.

Oh. The flush on my chest deepens. I remember what my mom said. *No one wants a desperate, chubby divorcee.*

"Right. Well, I *am* exceptional in every way." I let out a small laugh, so I don't feel like an utter twit.

Mort's the best you can do.

He chomps on another mini pickle. I swallow the last of my wine. Time to go.

"Well, it was nice meeting you—"

"Heh. Your mother tells me you're looking for an older man. I don't usually fancy dumplings like you. Prefer younger ones too. But I could make an exception. Heh? I heard your garage don't park cars. You don't need to worry, that don't turn me off. I've already parked enough cars."

Huh?

My garage doesn't...does he mean my uterus doesn't work? Are the cars his babies?

He's still looking at my chest.

I clear my throat and struggle to say something. There's a tightness at the base of my throat. I think it's a slew of swear words fighting to get out, wanting to tell Mort where to shove it.

Ian, my sexy, amazing boss, says that people choose how to react to situations. No one can make you angry, uncomfortable, or unhappy without your permission. So right now, I *choose* not to kill my mom from the sheer mortification of this moment.

Thank you, Ian. You just saved my mother.

I cough and finally manage to form words.

"Thank you. I think." But then I shake my head. "No. Not thank you. It's not nice meeting you. It's not nice speaking to you. And I hope I never meet you again. You should leave."

"Now hold on," Mort says, and he finally looks at my face instead of my boobs.

"Leave," I say. I fling my hand toward the hall and the front door. But I forgot that I'm holding a plate piled high with barbecue wieners. They tip and spill all over my chest. The goopy, sticky sauce runs over my skin. One of the wieners lodges in the tight space between my breasts and sticks straight up. The rest of them fall to the plastic runner covering the carpet. They hit with a splat.

Mort lets out a snort and looks at me with a disgusted sneer. "I think I had a lucky escape, heh? It's no wonder you can't keep a man."

He turns and pushes his way through the crowd.

I watch him leave. Hot embarrassment washes over me.

"Gemma, you okay?" My dad has made his way over. He grabs a handful of gold cocktail napkins and hands them to me.

"Thanks Dad. I'm fine." I pluck the mini hotdog from my chest and drop it on the plastic table cloth. I smear the sauce with the napkins and try to wipe it off my breasts.

"Who was it this time?" he asks.

"Oh. The usual. A creep with an inferiority complex and a *fabulous job*." I say the last in my mom's voice. "You know, one who doesn't want any kids." I try to say the last bit in a chipper voice, but my dad sees through it and gives my shoulders a squeeze.

"She means well, your mom. She wants to see you happy."

"I know, Dad."

He gives me a one-armed hug. While my mom has been described as flighty and excitable, my dad has always been seen as level-headed and slow to judge. My nephew Colin takes after him. I'd say I'm a mix of my parents, I'm level-headed until I get an *amazing idea* and then I go after it, whether it's crazy or not.

"Why don't you go get cleaned up. I'll hold down the buffet table," he says kindly.

I look down at my chest and my pumpkin dress. I'm covered

in barbecue sauce, and I imagine I look like some sort of slaughtered pumpkin at a Halloween horror show.

I hurry through the room back toward the hall, I keep my head down and try to slip by the guests unseen. I can put the outfit I arrived in back on. There was nothing wrong with it. No matter what my mom said.

As I'm ducking out of the room I hear a familiar voice. It's Mimi Butkis.

"Did you see Gemma yet? You might ask her on a date."

Against my better judgment I stop walking.

Both Greg and his mom are turned away from me, so they don't see me standing only a few feet away.

Greg shakes his head. "I already told you, the last thing I want to do is go out with Dimmy Gimmy. Jeremy told me the surgeon said the inside of her abdomen looks like a grenade went off. Apparently, the medical resident fainted when he saw it. Plus, Gimmy dresses like a slob, eats like a hoover, and has no self-respect. The divorce wrecked her. She's second-hand goods."

Mimi makes a humming noise, I can't tell if she's agreeing or disagreeing with her son's assessment. "Her mother and I are friends though. Couldn't you go on one date? It'll make our craft nights more bearable. I can tell her I tried."

My chest tightens.

Greg and his mom are blocking my way to the stairs. I don't want to walk past them, but if I want to change out of my barbecue-covered dress I have to. I hunch my shoulders, put my head down and quickly walk past.

"Excuse me," I mutter.

I don't wait for them to acknowledge me.

I hurry down the hall and rush up the stairs.

I try to hold back the tears pressing against the back of my eyes. Gah. Greg didn't say anything I haven't already heard. Not really.

Besides.

I have a goal. A plan. A bright future.

I open the door to my childhood bedroom, then stop in the doorway, stunned.

Josh Lewenthal grins at me from my bed.

4

*"Each of us steers
our own ship of destiny
by following the stars
in our heart."*

JOSH IS ON MY BED.

What the heck?

It's like he has some sort of super-psychic power that lets him know when a woman needs him. I think about him stealing my undies all those years ago and I realize that yes, he probably does have a secret power. Some sort of man radar —mandar.

We haven't really spoken in years, except for the casual greeting at the New Year's party or a "hi, how are you" at a random friends and family get together. Yet here he is, right when I need him.

I step into my bedroom and shut the door. Josh is spread out on my pink lace coverlet, his arms behind his head, and his legs crossed—the picture of relaxation.

He was on her bed.

He's in his standard outfit, faded jeans and a tight T-shirt depicting some obscure graphic novel character. His black hair needs a trim and he has at least two days' worth of dark stubble on his face.

Even though I'm indifferent to him as a person and I know for a *fact* he's not my type, my lady parts still clench. He's *that* good looking.

He smirks at me, like he knows the effect he's having. Here's the thing about Josh, he's completely unable to take life seriously. It's like the whole universe is a funny joke to him, and he's just living his life so he can be amused.

When he graduated from high school he was voted the most likely to succeed. He was captain of the football team, the basketball team, homecoming king and the valedictorian. Everyone thought he was going places. Especially me.

After he graduated from college he took a job at a tech start-up, worked his way up the ranks to VP, and then according to my brother, he just woke up one day and decided to quit. He walked into the office, took a box out of the supply closet, packed up his desk, and walked out. Ever since then he's been doing his web comic thing. But I guess if he's living with his dad again, it's not going all that well.

I look him over. The thing is, I'm not sussing him out as a prospective husband, I don't care about his career goals, how big his paycheck is, or whether he lives in his dad's basement. I don't care about his potential or non-potential as a life mate. I'm thinking about his genetics. And his genetics are just fine.

I close the door with a sharp snick.

"What are you doing on my bed?" I ask.

His eyes, always full of sharp intelligence, take in my sauce-covered dress and the blush still lingering on my cheeks.

"What are you doing covered in barbecue?" A small smile flits over his lips and his forehead wrinkles as he takes in my appearance.

My outfit from earlier is folded in a neat pile and sitting on my dresser. Josh starts to stand up.

"Stay there. I need to talk to you."

I decide that rather than risk him leaving while I change, I'll talk to him covered in sauce.

"Alright." He scoots over and pats my bed.

I give him a look and he shrugs. "Sorry. I was up all night finishing a storyboard. Whenever I stayed the night with Dylan, your mom would always give me your bed to sleep in. I didn't think, it just seemed natural to..."

He trails off when he sees the expression on my face. I'm not sure how I feel about the fact that Josh has apparently been sleeping in my childhood bedroom for years.

I look at my dresser and realize that my teenage diary is in the top drawer hidden under my underwear. My skin prickles with, yup, that's embarrassment. I look at the dresser then at Josh, but he doesn't seem any different than usual. Maybe he's not a snooper. Probably, yes, probably he never read it. Because if he had...errr...my teenage self was not shy about fantasizing about him.

I settle onto the mattress next to him.

He clears his throat and scoots over. "So what's up?"

Oh God.

Am I really going to do this?

Can I do this?

It seemed perfectly reasonable and normal when I was planning it out after my doctor's appointment. I looked more into donor sperm and weighed the benefits and detriments of donor versus Josh. Every way I looked at it, Josh came out on top.

He gives me a funny look. "Gemma? What's up? You alright?"

"I need your sperm," I blurt out.

Josh starts to choke, then he coughs. His face turns red and he hits his chest.

Oh no. I've killed him.

He coughs and his eyes water.

I slap his back and he shakes his head.

Maybe I shouldn't have just blurted it out like that, but I was nervous and I didn't think.

Finally, he takes a wheezing breath and says, "Come again?"

"I...I need your sperm?"

I smile at him. The look he gives me makes my hand fly to my mouth in an effort to contain the laugh bubbling up from my chest. Oh jeez, I've lost my brain. I should've written talking points or a speech or something.

"You want to have sex?" Josh asks. He looks really confused. "Gemma. You really have to work on your pick-up lines."

I shake my head. But he's already starting to lift his shirt up. I catch a glimpse of rock-hard abs. "If you want to, we can. But we'll have to hurry. The New Year's Resolution reading is soon. We have maybe ten minutes. Not that I can't blow your mind in ten minutes."

I scoot back and make a strangled sound.

He takes in my expression and starts to snicker.

"Kidding. Gemma, I'm kidding," he says, and he drops his shirt.

I nod and blow out a long, mind-clearing breath. "Sorry, I didn't say that right. What I meant to say was, ummm, we've known each other a long time."

"Twenty-four years," he agrees.

"Right. We grew up in the same town. Went to the same school. You're my brother's best friend. You come to our holiday parties, birthdays. You're always around."

I scrutinize his face to see if he gets where I'm going. Unfortunately, he just looks confused.

"I feel like I know you pretty well. I can say that you're a decent guy."

He frowns. "Thanks."

"If I ask you something, do you promise not to tell Dylan, or anybody?"

Josh leans back and studies me. "Gem, I don't think we should have sex."

I close my eyes. "No. No, jeez. Obviously. Ugh, did it once, got the T-shirt."

I open one eye and look at him, then I open the other.

He grins at me. "The T-shirt huh?"

I shrug and roll my eyes. "You remember when I had surgery for that ruptured ovarian cyst and the surgeon said I'd never have kids?"

At twenty-two I already had stage four endometriosis. Like

Greg Butkis said, my abdomen looks like a grenade went off and my tubes are completely blocked. For a lot of women, there's pain with endometriosis, but I never felt anything, never knew anything was wrong. Even today, I wouldn't know anything was off, except for the fact that the doctors can see the damage.

Josh swallows and sits up straight, the joking smile fades from his lips. "Sure. I remember."

I look at his expression and realize that maybe Josh doesn't always take everything in life as a joke.

"I went to see an infertility doctor. I'm going to have a baby."

An emotion flashes in Josh's eyes that I can't decipher, and the dark brown of his irises goes even darker. "You're...you're what?"

I nod. "I'm going to have a baby. The doctor said that I can't get pregnant naturally, but I can through IVF. That's in vitro fertilization-"

"I know what it is." His voice is terse, and I can't tell what he's thinking.

I clasp my hands together to keep from fidgeting. "The doctor said women either use their partner's sperm or donated sperm. And I..."

Oh jeez. Sitting in front of Josh, watching the expressions move across his face, makes this conversation a lot harder than I thought it'd be.

"You're pregnant?" he asks. He looks at my abdomen.

My hand flies to my stomach. "No. Not yet. That's why I wanted to talk to you."

"Okay?" Then the confusion fades and I can tell he understands. "You want me to...you want my—"

"I want your sperm."

"You want to have my baby?" he says at the same time.

"No," I say.

"No," he says.

"No," I say again. "I don't want to have *your* baby. I don't want you to have any responsibilities or anything like that. She'll be my baby, not anybody else's."

Josh makes an affronted sound in his throat.

I stand and start to pace. The horrible orange skirt climbs up my thighs so that my underwear is nearly visible. I yank it back down and the dried barbecue sauce flakes off my chest. Ugh.

"Okay. None of that came out right. I'm going to start over."

"Sure." Josh puts on his the-world-is-here-to-amuse-me smile that I associate him with and settles back on my bed to listen.

"I'm tired of waiting for some fairy prince to come along, sweep me off my feet and give me a family to love and kids to dote on. I'm thirty-two, it could be years before he arrives, if ever. In fact, seeing as how the last few years have gone, I'm banking on never."

"Alright," he says. "I'm with you so far."

I let out a surprised huff. "You know, that's what I like about you. You don't judge."

He nods and takes the compliment.

I continue, "I want kids. Ever since I first held Sasha in my arms and she grabbed my finger with her tiny little hand I—" My voice cracks. "I realized I wanted to be a mom."

I know it's not a modern sentiment, that I should be happy with my career, my single life, my autonomy, but darn it, can't I be a successful, modern woman and still want someone to love? A family to love? Can't I excel in my career and also want to hold my baby to my chest and wipe her tears or give her love?

"Alright, but what does this have to do with me?" Josh asks.

I stop pacing and pull down my skirt. The top dips lower on my breasts. To his credit, Josh's eyes never leave my face. Come to think of it, he's one of the few men outside of my family whose eyes have never strayed below my face.

"I could pick a sperm donor from a database. It tells you basic things about the donor. But that kind of freaked me out. I thought...I figured, if I'm going to have a baby, I'd like to know more about the father. So, I made a list."

There, see, I did make a list.

I hold up a finger. Josh stares at it. "First. I wanted the father to be smart. You're smart."

That's a bit of an understatement. Josh isn't just smart, he's brilliant. He got straight A's in high school and he graduated magna cum laude from an Ivy League.

I hold up another finger. "Second. I want the father to be..."—how to phrase this—"okay looking."

Josh raises an eyebrow. I wave my hands at his face. "You know. Your nose is straight, your teeth are straight, and you have a nice chin."

"A nice chin?"

"Yeah."

I hold up a third finger before he can say anything more. "Third. I want the father to be athletic, to make up for my complete and utter lack of coordination."

"You are pretty clumsy," he agrees, referencing, I'm sure, the sauce all over me.

I shrug and take his agreement as a good sign.

"Four. I want to know the father comes from a healthy, robust family." But, come to think of it, I don't know that about him. "Does your family have any history of disease? Cancers, diabetes, heart disease, you know all those things they ask you on the family history form at the doctors."

He lets out a disbelieving huff of air. "My grandpa had ulcers. And my mom's brother had arthritis. My grandma had adult-onset diabetes."

"Hmm. Okay. No, that's alright. Every family has something."

Josh raises his eyebrows. "So, that's it? I met your qualifications. I'm your perfect sperm donor?"

"Exactly. I mean, I've known you all your life. I know you're a good guy. You have really good genes." He raises an eyebrow and I shrug. "You're already like a member of the family. I'm not asking you to be a dad or anything. If you don't want the baby to know you're the father, that's okay. If you do, then we can make an agreement where you have a weekend a month or..." I trail off at the look on his face.

"For crying out loud, Gemma. This sounds like a divorce without the benefit of the honeymoon sex."

Oh. Wow. Okay.

I look down at the pink rag rug covering the wood floor.

Josh has never divorced, but I have. And now that he puts it that way, it does sound crazy/horrible asking him to be a sperm donor. There's nothing, absolutely nothing in it for him. Not even honeymoon sex.

I take a moment to think his words over then look up. "Okay. No, you're right. It was really stupid of me to ask. I just thought, you know, if I had to pick anyone to be a donor, I'd want to pick someone like you."

I feel myself flush. It's not like I've been pining after Josh freaking Lewenthal for twenty-four years. I'm indifferent to him. He's always been around, sort of like that potted plant in the corner that you don't notice until someone points it out. We don't really talk or interact, he's just there.

Suddenly I feel really bad. "Sorry. I didn't think through how crazy this would seem to you. Why would you want to donate your sperm to anyone, right? It's not like I could pay you more than a thousand dollars anyway."

Josh chokes on another cough. "You were going to pay me?" he asks incredulously. Actually, he looks really offended.

I try to play it off. "It's no big deal. The going rate is fifty dollars, but I figured you needed the money since you're living with your dad again."

I take a step back at the glower on his face.

"I'm not living with my dad. My apartment is under construction. It's temporary."

"Oh. That's good. I'm glad you have a place in..."

He scowls at me. "In Williamsburg."

I imagine the kind of place Josh would be able to afford on his web comic proceeds. It's a crumbly brick warehouse with rusty pipes and drafty walls. I picture a mattress on the floor, a desk with an old computer and a flickering lightbulb with a pull chain.

"Sounds nice."

"Is that all you wanted to ask me? The sperm thing?" He moves to the edge of the bed, like he's ready to head downstairs.

"Yeah. Yeah that was all."

He nods and stands up. My childhood bedroom, decked out in pink fabric, teen heartthrob posters, and white furniture, suddenly seems incredibly small. There's only a foot between Josh and me. He's a half a foot taller than I am and has wide shoulders. I check the urge to take a step back.

"Alright then."

"So, it's a no?" I ask. I feel incredibly, horribly, insanely stupid, but hey, like Ian says, success is ninety-nine percent perseverance.

"It's a no." Josh gives a firm, final nod. "I'm not some horse you can put out to stud. I'm kind of surprised, Gem. I never thought you viewed people like objects that you can use. I thought better of you. I'm a person, you know?"

Oh.

Ouch.

That hurt. And honestly, I'm mortified, so I lash out. "I didn't think it'd be that big a deal to you. You already made a sperm donation once. I didn't think it'd be a big thing for you to do it again."

He looks at me and his eyes go dark with emotion. He shakes his head and my skin itches with embarrassment.

"Thanks, but no thanks," he says.

And the way he says it reminds me of Greg Butkis, and how he said no to the idea of me as well. And it reminds me of Mort, and all the Mort-like guys before him.

"It's alright," I say. I put my chin up. "Sorry I bothered you."

Josh lifts his hand, extends it to span the foot between us. His fingers hover an inch above my arm. I shiver at the heat coming off of him. Then, he shakes off whatever he's thinking and pulls away.

"I won't say anything to anyone. You don't have to worry. You can tell your family when you're ready."

"Thank you." Then to make myself feel better I say, "No worries, Josh. Each of us steers our own ship of destiny by following the stars in our heart."

Josh's shoulders stiffen, then he turns and walks out the door, shutting it quietly behind him.

5

"The only limitations
we have are the ones
we place on ourselves."

ALL THE PARTY GUESTS ARE GATHERED IN THE LIVING ROOM. IT'S time for the official New Year's resolution roundup.

Sasha and Colin walk through the room handing out slips of paper and pencils.

Josh is across the room chatting with Dylan. Josh hasn't looked at me once since I came downstairs in my leggings and sweater. I mean, we don't usually look at each other, but this time it feels like he's purposely not looking. I didn't realize it before, but there's a big difference between not looking at someone and purposely not looking at someone. It's like I can feel his total attention even though he hasn't turned my way.

I guess the benefit of him not watching me is that I can look at him without him noticing. That way I can spend minutes rehashing our conversation with could-have-saids and should-have-saids while I wait for Sasha to give me a pencil and paper.

While I'm watching, Greg Butkis sidles over to Dylan and Josh and cracks a joke. I can't hear it, but Greg must think it's funny because he's laughing, gesturing at his chest and pointing at me.

Ah.

He's making a joke about me and my barbecue boobs.

I look at Josh to see if he's smiles or laughs. I imagine he might. After all, I did just embarrass him by asking for his sperm.

But wait. I tilt my head. Josh looks mad, really mad. He says something to Greg which makes Greg stop laughing and scuttle away, back to his mom. Dylan slaps Josh on the back in a bro-buddy gesture.

"Ugh, why is Greg Butkis here? Did Mom invite him for you?" I look over. Leah, my sister, has walked over and perched on the arm of the couch next to me. She's in a cute sparkly dress and has her hair in a high ponytail. She's my older sister by six years, but even with the gap we've always been close.

She rolls her eyes. "Eff it, Gemma. Eff all men. They're terrible mother effers, be happy you're single."

I look over at Leah. She used to swear like a sailor, but ever since she had kids she says things like "eff it" and "fudge" and "son of a biscuit."

She takes a long gulp of wine until the entire glass is empty. Then she wipes her mouth and says, "Eff it."

"What happened?" I ask. My sister usually has the ability to manage her four kids, her husband, and her job, like a circus master juggling monkeys—it looks insane, but she manages it with mad skill.

Her lower lip quivers and she shakes her head and blinks her eyes quickly, like she's trying not to cry.

"Leah, what?"

She shrugs. "Nothing. Just life. Being a mom of four kids is great, don't get me wrong, but cherish your single days, Gem. Revel in your bachelorette-hood. Cheese and rice, some days I envy you." She looks down at her wine glass and seems surprised to find it empty.

"Umm, okay. Here," I say. I hand her my glass.

She sets her empty glass on the coffee table and accepts mine. Then she takes a long swallow of the white wine.

"You sure you're alright?"

"I'm fine," Leah says.

Colin and Sasha skip up in front of us and Leah visibly pulls herself together.

"Hey sweethearts," she says.

"Here you go, Mommy. Auntie Gemma." Sasha says. Colin hands us pencils and paper slips.

"Thanks, kiddos," I say.

They skip off.

Because Leah looks so sad, I reach over and put my arms around her. It's awkward because she's holding the glass of wine, but I manage.

"Whatever it is, it'll be okay." Then I give her one of my favorite Ian quotes, "Everything in life happens for a reason, and it's always a good reason."

She gives me a sardonic look, then says, "Someday, Gemma, I think you're going to find that bull crap quotes can't make everything better."

I look at her in shock. "Seriously, are you okay?"

She twirls the wine glass in her hand. "I'm fine. It's just I know you believe there's always a bright side, but I don't think that's true."

"Of course it is," I say automatically. "Of course there's always a bright side."

She shrugs. "Maybe." Then she glances across the room at her kids, laughing and bringing around the bowl for everyone to drop their New Year's resolutions into.

She draws in a deep breath. "Let's write our resolutions, shall we? I'm going to take dance lessons. Alone time with Oliver. Romance."

"Alright," I say, and I don't push our conversation further. Leah still looks a little upset, but she's always been direct, and if something was truly wrong she'd tell me.

I kneel at the table and hold my pencil over the scrap of paper. I tap the eraser against the sheet and think about what to write.

When I came here today it was my goal to convince Josh to be the donor for my baby. That failed. I failed. But that doesn't mean I have to give up on my dream.

I can ask him again. Make a top-level presentation on why it would be a great thing for him to be a donor.

Or I can still, you know, ask someone else, or consider the donor database. And, really, what's so bad about an anonymous donor? Nothing. It's a great option.

There are no messy emotions with anonymity.

I'll find some brainiac type that looks like Thor or something. Or maybe an athletic type that volunteers as a mentor or builds houses for people after natural disasters. Or maybe a guy who has grandparents that lived to be a hundred and five. The options are endless.

As my latest Ian social media post said, *the only limitations we have are the ones we place on ourselves*. I included a gif of a sugar glider—because...flying squirrels. A few celebs shared the post, so I know it was a good one.

I'm not going to give up.

I look over at my sister. Her brow is wrinkled and she's

scrawling on her paper. She presses so hard a little bit of the paper tears.

I pretend not to notice and look back at my paper.

In small, precise letters I write out my resolution and make myself a promise.

Have a baby.

Make a family. Have a baby.

This year, I'm going to follow my heart and make my dream come true.

I drop my folded paper into the bowl with all the other resolutions.

My dad stands in front of the fireplace and pulls out the resolutions one by one and reads them in a loud voice.

There are the usual—get a promotion, lose weight, go to Fiji. I sit on the couch next to Leah and listen to the reading. We all laugh when my dad reads "convince my mom to get a puppy." Sasha definitely wrote that one. Everyone says "awwww" when Dad reads "convince the woman I love to marry me." There's a resolution to start taking night classes at the community college, and another to take dance lessons.

"And the last one," my dad says. He clears his throat and pulls the final slip from the bowl.

It's mine. I know it is, because he hasn't read it yet. I sit as still as a statue on the plastic-covered couch. Slowly he unfolds the paper. I hold my breath.

"Have a baby."

I wait for everyone in the room to turn and stare at me.

To point, or laugh, or shake their heads in amusement.

My skin prickles with dread at the knowing stares or side glances I'm about to receive.

"Aww, so sweet," says Mimi Butkis.

"Isn't it?" my mom asks.

No one looks at me.

No one realizes it was me that wrote it.

I let out a long exhale. Of course no one knew it was me. Why would they?

"That's it, folks," my dad says. "Good luck on your resolutions."

Everyone claps and my dad smiles and sets the bowl down on the mantle. Each of the paper slips has been tossed into the crackling fire. My dad, a romantic at heart, says the words are burned and sent as a wish up to heaven.

I relax back into the couch, grateful that my secret fear of everyone pointing at me and laughing was completely idiotic. No one, not a single person, realizes what I wrote.

Suddenly, my skin prickles with awareness. I look up.

Josh stares at me from across the room.

The side of his mouth turns up in a half-smile.

A flush spreads across my body and I feel the bright red blush that has to be working its way across my cheeks.

Well, I guess there was one person who realized it was me who wrote *have a baby*.

I hold Josh's stare, his eyes lock on mine and they remind me of the intensity he had all those years ago when we...

I clear my throat and the blush on my cheeks grows hotter.

Then, he lifts his wine glass toward me in the gesture of a toast, and I swear that he says, "To resolutions."

He lifts his glass to her. "To resolutions."

I raise my eyebrows, and he smiles.

"To resolutions," I say.

Josh nods, like we've just come to an agreement.

He drinks his wine and I feel like we've just sealed some sort of deal.

Except, I'm not sure exactly what we agreed to.

6

—————

*"Good things come
to those who wait."*

THE PIERCING RING OF A CELL PHONE WAKES ME. I WAS HAVING A
bizarre dream about dancing in a mountain of whipped cream
with Josh Lewenthal while I tried to convince him to marry me.
He kept saying no. Ugh.

I bolt upright in bed and then groan and grab my head. Oh,
ouch, hangover. Why did I drink so much boxed wine? Why?

After the New Year's party ended, my parents, my sister, my
brother and Josh (of course) congregated in the kitchen,
washed the dishes, and drank all the leftover wine. My mom
convinced me the wine would go bad if I didn't finish it.

So, I drank it.

Why, Mom, why?

The phone stops ringing and I breathe a sigh of relief. But
then almost immediately it starts up again.

I'm back in my apartment in Manhattan, a tiny studio above a noisy bar on Second Avenue. The curtains are drawn and my apartment is dark. The shrill ringing continues. I scramble across my bed and flip on the bedside lamp. The light floods the room and I shut my eyes against the stabbing pain.

I'm never drinking with my mom and sister again.

I grab my phone from the nightstand. Who the heck calls this early in the morning anyway?

"Hello?" I manage to garble into the phone.

"Gemma. For goodness sakes. Where are you?"

It takes a moment for me to place who's on the other end of the line. I swing my legs over the side of the bed and set them on the cold parquet floor.

"Lavinia? What is it?" I croak. I really, really need a glass of water. My mouth feels like I gnawed on a cotton ball all night long. I stumble across the room toward the kitchen sink. I startle when I see myself in the wall mirror. I'm in old sweatpants and a bra, my hair is sticking straight out from the side of my head and my mascara is running down my cheeks.

I stop in front of the mirror and give myself a shocked once-over.

"What do you mean 'what is it'?" asks Lavinia.

I wince at the shrillness of her voice.

"The marketing conference call started five minutes ago. They're waiting for you. Ian is waiting for you," she hisses. "Tell me you are outside the building."

Wait, what? What time is it? I squint at the clock on the wall. It's five after ten. Which means...

Oh no. Oh no, no, no.

I'm late for work. And I'm late on a day where Ian is on a conference call that I'm supposed to be on. I've never had a conference call with Ian before. This was my first and biggest opportunity to impress him. I've been preparing for it for weeks. I'm supposed to be leading the call, setting out our new initiative for social media marketing.

Noooo.

I hurry across the apartment to my work bag. "I'm calling in," I say to Lavinia. "I'll be on in two minutes. I'll be right there."

I can almost hear Lavinia rolling her eyes. But it doesn't matter. I tear my computer out of my bag, set it on my bed and power it up. I crouch in front of it and urge it to load faster. The conference call link is in my work email. I open my email, find the link and click it.

"I'm on the call. Thanks, Lavinia." I hang up my cell and squat in front of my laptop while the screen loads.

The call comes through. On the list of participants I can see the head of the consulting marketing firm, a few of his marketing minions, Lavinia, and Ian.

"Ah, here she is. What did I tell you? Good things come to those who wait." That's Ian, I can tell by his deep, buttery voice, and by the inspirational quote, of course.

"Sorry for the wait," I begin to apologize. But then I stop. Because instead of being a phone call like I thought, it's a *video* call.

The black screen with a list of names shifts to show the participants, all in little squares showing their faces. They're in business suits and dresses. You know—business attire. The neon green camera light on my laptop flashes. And then the screen on my laptop fills with a picture of me.

Well, not of me *exactly*.

Since, I'm crouched over my computer, which is propped on my bed, the camera actually shows a grainy image of my breasts.

I take half a second to see the entire horror show unfold in front of me.

My breasts, my bra with the word "juicy" written all over it, the bit of roll around my middle, it's all there, front and center.

My boobs are taking up the entirety of my computer screen.

I do the only thing that any reasonable person would do. I drop to the ground. I fall like a grand piano out of a second-story window and hit the ground with a crash.

I crouch on the ground, squeeze my eyes shut and hold my breath waiting for the inevitable uproar.

The "You dare show your boobs on a business call?!" shouts of outrage.

Or, "You're fired, you crazy flasher!"

Or, "Report to HR immediately!"

But none of that happens.

Slowly, I let out my breath, crack open my eyes and crawl forward on my hands and knees. I dodge the camera and come around the side of my laptop and peek at the screen. On the horrible, horrible *video* call I can see everyone in their little boxes. Their faces are expectant, but none of them show outrage, horror, or even amusement.

Ian has his usual I'm-too-sexy-for-my-inspirational-quotes look going.

Lavinia seems annoyed. That's her normal look though.

The head of marketing looks expectant. But no one looks like they just had a mid-morning flash.

"Gemma, are you there?" asks Lavinia in an annoyed voice.

"I'm here. Yup, I'm here," I squeak. "Sorry. My uh, my video isn't working."

Right now, it's showing a very grainy, darkened view of my far wall. Apparently, somehow, all the angels in heaven intervened and no one saw the two ginormous breasts fly across the screen.

"Shall we start then?" asks Ian. "Gemma can share her

screen so we can all see her excellent presentation. I for one can't wait to see what she has to show."

It's probably just me, but I sense a whole lot of innuendo in that last sentence. But I glance at the screen from the side and Ian has a perfectly normal business-like smile on his face.

"Of course. I'll just, umm, screenshare and get started."

Lavinia hands over control of the video chat to me. Very, very carefully I avoid the camera, open up my presentation on the laptop and share my screen. When the brightly colored picture loads I breathe a sigh of relief and begin the presentation that I spent weeks preparing.

Fifteen minutes later, after I've run through my five-point plan and recommendations, I ask if there are any questions.

One of the marketing firm minions asks about Ian starting a daily vlog. I mute my microphone. While he's talking I sprint across my bedroom, knock my ankle on the coffee table, curse the darn thing, limp to a pile of clean laundry and throw on a lime green cardigan. Then I rush to the sink, splash my face with water, and frantically rub off the mascara running down my face with a dishes scrubby. I check myself in the wall mirror. The day-old mascara that was running down my face is gone, and my cheeks are now bright red from the frenzied scrubbing. My hair though, still looks like the Eiffel tower sticking off the side of my head. I yank my hair into a top knot, grab a used chopstick off the counter and stick it through the bun.

Good enough.

"Gemma. How about we come back to video and close up the call?" says the marketing consultant.

I rush back to the laptop on my bed.

"Gemma?" asks Lavinia in a sharp voice.

"Of course," I say. Then I realize I'm still muted. I lunge toward the computer, unmute it, and then, "Of course. Excellent. Excellent," I say in a firm, all-business sort of voice.

Then I pick up the laptop and position myself in front of the camera.

When I turn the video back on, I see everyone on my screen. Including me, looking perfectly presentable in a buttoned-up cardigan with a stylish bun and chopstick up-do.

A huge wave of relief flows over me. The conference call is nearly over and I didn't get fired. Thank goodness.

I'm about to thank everyone and tell them I look forward to another successful year of social media marketing when the marketing consultant broaches a new topic.

"One last thing. I did want to speak shortly about the amount of resources we'll be allocating this year to the inner life mastery campaign."

Ian tilts his head thoughtfully. "Ah yes. The inner life, what's hidden underneath all our clothed exteriors. *Juicy* topic." Then, Ian looks straight into his camera and raises an eyebrow.

Holy crap.

My mouth drops open and I let out a little choked squeak. He's talking to *me*.

He saw. He saw my breasts flash the screen.

Oh no. What do I do?

I look at Ian's face, but he's giving everyone a bland business-like expression.

I take a deep breath. If there's one thing I learned from my ex-husband, it's this: deny, deny, deny. Even if you're caught porking on a tabletop, deny.

I keep my expression schooled. Maybe Ian isn't talking to me, maybe his word-choice was a coincidence. Maybe he didn't see anything.

"What do you think of using the e-book as a loss leader?" asks one of the marketing consultants.

"I think the idea has vision," Ian says. "Especially for those who can see past exteriors to the juicy bits underneath."

Oh no.

He saw.

What do I do?

Just as we're about to sign off, Ian sends a text over the office chat.

See me in my office at 6.

7

—————

"Fate finds you when you least expect it."

Seven agonizing hours later, I'm convinced that Ian is going to fire me. Gah.

It's only January 2nd and my hopes for the year have taken a hit.

Instead of Josh agreeing to my plan he said no. A hard no.

Instead of getting a promotion at work I'm about to be fired.

It's nearly six o'clock in the evening. I'm in Ian's office.

In the years that I've worked here, I've never ever set foot in Ian's office. It's sort of a sacred space that only top-level influencers and celebrities are allowed in. There's a tasteful waterfall and koi pond, a small putting green, a bar, and a seating area. Ian holds a golf club in his hand and putts a ball. It speeds across the green and lands with a soft clatter into the cup.

He looks up at me and flashes a bright white toothy grin.

I smile at him, but behind the smile I feel queasy. Getting fired isn't easy.

"Would you like a drink?" Ian asks. He tosses the putter onto a leather couch and strides toward the bar area of his office. His white shirt sleeves are rolled up and I can see a dusting of dark hair on his muscular forearms. "A martini? Whiskey?"

My stomach rolls at the thought of alcohol. I'm still recovering from this morning's hangover. "A sparkling water if you have it."

He looks over his shoulder at me and flashes another grin, showing off his chin dimple.

To be perfectly honest, I've spent years fantasizing about this man.

I know, I know, he's a "celebrity persona" and he only dates models and reality TV stars. Plus he dresses like a mannequin in a shop window on Madison Avenue. My sister claims that Ian is about as real as the mannequin. Meaning, he's as fake as they come.

She thinks he's a self-styled self-help guru that has made his way into the limelight by playing to the insecurities and neuroses of the masses. But I don't agree. He has a message that matters, he helps people, and he came from nothing and worked his way to where he is today. Sure, he only dates models and shallow reality TV stars, but maybe I can throw a cliché in here and say that he's merely waiting for the right woman to come along and love him for who he is. At least in my fantasies that's what happens.

Ian steps up to me, a martini in one hand and a sparkling water in the other.

He hands me the water with a smile.

"Cheers."

"Cheers." I raise my water to him and take a drink.

"I enjoyed your presentation today."

I blush and glance at him over the rim of my water. "Thank you. I worked hard on it."

Outside Ian's office the lights flicker off. Lavinia has left for the day. She's usually the last one out. Ian looks at the darkened space beyond the glass walls of his office then he looks back to me.

"You've worked here for six years."

Oh. Here it comes. The "you're fired" bit. I nod. "Seven next month."

What will happen to me if I lose my job? Right now, my health insurance covers fertility treatments, but if I lose my job, then I won't be able to pay for them. What then? Will my dream of having a baby with IVF end a day after it began?

Just as I'm about to rush into an explanation of why Ian shouldn't fire me, and why I love this job, and why it would be a mistake to let me go, he says, "Would you like to have dinner?"

Huh?

"Excuse me?"

He gives me a boyish smile that shows off the dimple on his chin. "Dinner. You. Me."

"Dinner?" I shake my head and try to do a mental three-sixty. "I thought you were going to fire me."

Ian chuckles. "Why would I fire you? You're the reason the last six of my online seminars went viral."

Well, that's true.

Relief washes over me. I'm not getting fired. No one but Ian saw the bra and boob show on the conference call. I get to keep my job.

And speaking of my job, is this a work dinner or is Ian asking me out on a date?

This is probably a work dinner. Most definitely...probably... definitely a work dinner.

Although it might be a date.

But the thing is, I can't start dating Ian when I'm preparing to undergo IVF and have a baby. Except. Unless. Maybe, this is fate. Like Ian says, "Fate finds you when you least expect it."

There's only one way to find out if this is a work dinner or if it's the hand of fate.

"I'd love to have dinner with you."

IT WAS A DATE.

And, we had wild, amazing, mind-blowing sex.

Okay, fine, the mind-blowing sex was in my imagination—played out in vivid detail while we ate steaming bowls of bibimbap and talked about the future of Ian Fortune, Live Your Best Life Starting Now Enterprises.

But, yes, it was a date.

8

"You should always believe
the universe is going
to give you good things,
because sooner or later,
it will."

I SPENT THE LAST SEVEN DAYS IN A STATE OF EUPHORIA. I FELT LIKE one of those anime characters with my feet floating inches above the ground and stars in my eyes. Ian "accidentally" met me at the little coffee stand outside the building six times in the past week. We had take-out sushi when we both stayed late at the office one night. And another time he stopped the elevator, brushed my hair back and pushed aside my cardigan "just to check" that I was wearing his favorite bra.

He also sent juicy chats and inspirational messages written just for me.

Like, even the worst days are better for having you in them.

And, I didn't realize what was right in front of me all this time.

Or, I've been waiting for you so long.

I know.

I know I said that I don't need a man to make my dreams come true. And I don't. I'm pursuing my dream of a family with or without a man. But, after my divorce and diagnosis of infertility, I found Ian's website, and his quotes were like a lifeline. When I started working for him I realized he's as amazing as his quotes. I've had a thing for him for seven years. He saved me from a load of pain and now he's taking me out to sushi and meeting me for coffee. How can I not live in this moment and enjoy it for what it is?

Today is a great day. Every day is a great day.

I've spent most of the past six hours going over web traffic and lead generation, mixed with covert glances at Ian's office. I have a hunch that Lavinia knows something is going on. She's been sending me the stink eye more than usual. And the last time I came back to my desk with a coffee, exactly two minutes after Ian came back inside, she sniffed at me then sniped that I ought to water the drooping plants.

When my vision starts to go fuzzy from looking at my computer screen for too long, I log off. I grab my purse from under my desk, slip on my wool coat and wrap my scarf around my neck. Lavinia looks over and purses her lips.

"I'm going to pop down to the coffee stand in case anyone swings by asking for me." Then, because it's a great day, "Need anything?"

Lavinia looks past me to Ian's glass-walled office then back to me. "No. But dump the shredder on the way out. You've filled it up again."

I haven't. I don't print paper. Lavinia, middle-aged tree killer, has filled it up.

"Sure, no problem," I say.

Not even Lavinia's mood or dumping five pounds of shredder paper in the recycling room can dim my happy mood. I ride the elevator down twelve floors and walk through the marble-floored lobby toward the wall of glass doors.

Then I step out of the heated office building onto the slush-covered sidewalk. To be honest, Midtown New York during winter is one of the uglier sites in the world. The ground is covered in black and brown slush and melting snow, crunchy salt pellets, trash bags piled high, and random splotches of yellow snow from dogs peeing on the curb. But today, I don't notice the dirt or the exhaust-perfumed air, I just see the sliver of bright blue sky and the little glitter of tiny snowflakes floating in the air.

The shiny metal siding of the coffee cart attracts me like a bee to a fat-headed flower. I walk across the salt-strewn sidewalk, through the slush to the metal cart.

"Milk and sugar?" asks Zamir. His breath puffs out in front of him. He's in a fluffy coat, a fuzzy hat, and fingerless gloves. Zamir is one of two brothers that runs the cart. He and his brother are from Iraq and they each take a twelve-hour shift serving up buttery egg sandwiches and milk-and-sugar-loaded coffee.

"Thanks. You know me."

When he hands over the blue and white coffee cup, I take a long, happy sip of the overly sweet, creamy coffee. Then I take a moment to just stand and watch the taxi cabs, the cars, the delivery bikes and the people rush by. Sometimes, if you stand still, it's like you're in the middle of a tornado with all of New York swirling by. You can stand like that for hours.

The beauty of it is that no one notices you, the tragedy of it is that no one notices you.

I sigh and start to turn back to the office when I feel a hand press into my back.

"I thought I'd see you down here. Ah, coffee, the drug of lesser mortals."

I turn and smile coyly at Ian.

"Are you calling me a lesser mortal?"

"Never," he says, and he puts a hand to his heart. "I'm the lesser mortal. How about throwing pity my way and getting a few drinks with me tonight?"

A little flame of happiness glows in my chest and warms me against the winter cold. I look down at the coffee in my hands. This thing, this...whatever it is...between Ian and me is becoming more serious. At least to me it is.

And tomorrow I have my second appointment with Dr. Ingraham.

I look back up at Ian. He's cool and confident in his suit coat, aviator sunglasses, and artfully styled glossy black hair. The mass of people flows around us, like a river around a stone. No one pays us any mind.

"Before I say yes," I start, then I stop and bite my lip.

"Gemma, you should always say yes to life's opportunities."

I huff and shake my head at his quote of the week. Then I smile and say, "I'm serious. I have to tell you something."

He nods and gestures me to walk back toward the building with him. I step over a puddle of slush and then I turn to him and say, "Whatever it is we're doing, I think you should know, before it goes any further..."

How do I say this?

"I'm going through IVF to have a baby."

He frowns and his winged eyebrows come down. "With your boyfriend?"

I shake my head. "No. I'm single. I mean..." I glance over at him from the sides of my eyes.

He tilts his head.

"I'm using a donor. I just thought you should know, it may not be just me for long. I might be a package deal. So...um... what do you think?"

I look away from him. I'm not capable of looking him in the face while he decides whether or not he wants to continue pursuing whatever *this* is.

"I think..." He stops walking.

I take a few steps then stop too.

"Gemma, look at me."

I do. He flashes me his blindingly white smile.

"I think you are the epitome of a strong, independent woman who doesn't require a man to get what she wants. Let's have drinks."

I smile back at him.

"Okay."

IAN TOOK ME TO DANIEL, THE FAMOUS, ULTRA-CLASSY FRENCH restaurant on the Upper East Side, where they served cocktails with large spherical ice cubes suspended in liquor, and other frothy concoctions. I felt incredibly out of place in my black leggings, chunky shoes, and nubby knee-length sweater.

Note to self—must buy cuter clothes for dates at posh, la-di-da restaurants.

Ian asked me about my decision to pursue IVF. When he asked who my donor was, I told him I'd hoped to do it with a family friend but was going to go with an anonymous donor instead.

"You know Josh Lewenthal, don't you?" he asked. "Your brother is Dylan Jacobs?"

"Yeah. I know him. You do too?" I was surprised that Ian of all people would know Josh, but not really excited to talk about him with Ian, or really, with anyone.

"You don't think much of him?" asked Ian, picking up on my disinterest.

I shrugged. "We have history," I said and left it at that.

Ian winced sympathetically. "Sorry. But I can't say I'm surprised."

"What do you mean?"

He leaned in over the candlelit white tablecloth and the shadows played over his face. "Just that Josh has a habit of disappointing people. If you know what I mean."

"Oh. Yeah. I guess so," I said, although I didn't know what he meant at all.

After that, the topic turned to the online conference we were prepping for. It was two months away and we had a load of work to do. The project was my baby and I was determined to prove myself. I'd even be introducing Ian as a speaker and hosting a Q&A session.

After the date, at the door to my apartment, I held my keys in my hand and slowly inserted them into the lock.

Ian stilled my hand and turned me to face him. The patrons at the rowdy sports bar on the first floor of my walk-up apartment cheered as some team scored a goal on the TV. I smiled, because they echoed exactly how I felt.

"I've dreamed of kissing you since the first time I saw you," Ian said.

Tiny snowflakes swirled down as he slowly turned me

toward him and kissed me. His lips were cold and I shivered in the frosty night air.

He pulled away after a few seconds, then grinned at me, his chin dimple deepening at his expression. "You should always believe the universe is going to give you good things, because sooner or later, it will."

I smiled back. "You're right."

~

BACK IN MY APARTMENT I CHANGE INTO A WELL-LOVED PAIR OF cozy flannel pajamas with my favorite snowflake print and climb into bed. I put my phone on the nightstand and set my alarm. It's then I notice a missed call.

Josh.

I look closer. He called at nine thirty. Right about when Ian and I were talking about him. Mandar, I swear he has man radar.

I open my phone and check to see if he left a message. There's nothing.

Then, thinking about what Ian said about believing the universe is conspiring to deliver good things, I hit redial.

I pull my comforter around me and wait for Josh to pick up.

He doesn't, the call goes through to voicemail.

"This is Josh. Who calls anymore? Send a text. Anyway. Leave a message."

I smile and lean my elbows on my knees. "Hey. Josh. It's me, Gemma. Umm, I saw you called. I thought, maybe you'd changed your mind about the donor thing? Or not. I don't know. I still stand by what I said, I feel like you'd be great, soooo...right, anyway, my next appointment is tomorrow. If you want to come, you can meet me there. It's at four o'clock in Midtown."

I give him the address and then say, "Sorry, if I made you feel like an object. Or if you were offended. I don't think of you like an object. I think you're a good guy. Like maybe, we could be friends. You don't have to be friends only with Dylan. You could be friends with me too, you know." I realize that I'm rambling and his voicemail will probably cut me off soon, so I say, "Alright, that's all. I hope I see you tomorrow. But if not, I understand. That's okay, too. And thanks for not telling anyone. I'm not quite ready for my family to know yet."

I hang up.

For a good five minutes I sit cross-legged in my bed and stare at my phone's display waiting for Josh to call back.

He doesn't.

Finally, I put my phone down, turn off my light, and try to go to sleep.

Tomorrow.

Tomorrow is another day, another step forward.

9

"Always say yes to the opportunities the Universe presents you."

I CAN'T BELIEVE IT. IT'S QUARTER TO FOUR, I'M WAITING FOR THE crosswalk light to change, and Josh freaking Lewenthal is leaning against the stone wall of the doctor's office. He hasn't noticed me yet. His shoulders are hunched and his hands are in his pockets. He looks out over the traffic, his eyebrows drawn down, his mouth curved in a pensive frown.

"Josh. Hey!" I wave, but the traffic noise covers my shout. He doesn't see me, but the woman standing next to me gives me a sharp look. The crosswalk light still hasn't changed.

I bounce up and down in my snow boots and try to get a better view of Josh. I can't believe he came. When he didn't call back or text I thought for sure that his call from last night was a butt dial or a fluke.

I was ninety-nine percent prepared to march into my appointment today and tell Dr. Ingraham I'd be using an anonymous donor. But Josh is here.

The flood of relief and happiness that flows through me makes me realize just how much I wanted a familiar face to help in this.

I watch as Josh takes a breath and lets out a long sigh, then he shakes his head like he's arguing with himself. He pushes off the wall and starts to walk away, shoulders hunched.

Is he leaving?

"Josh!" I shout.

The woman next to me glares.

Josh stops, turns back around, and leans against the wall again.

Thank goodness.

Finally, the traffic stops and the crosswalk signal changes. I slosh through the winter slush and hurry toward Josh.

When I'm a few feet away I see him take a deep, steadying breath and then run his hand over his face.

I stop next to him and shift on my feet, suddenly, I feel incredibly awkward. I bite my lip and clear my throat to let him know I'm here.

Josh looks over at me in surprise, and I watch as the worry line between his brows vanishes and he gives me his devil-may-care/life's-a-playground smile.

"Hey. You came. I didn't think you would. I..." My throat feels thick with tears and I realize how scared I really was to go down this path, but Josh being here, giving me his isn't-this-amusing smile makes everything okay. On impulse, I rush him and throw my arms around his neck.

He lets out a surprised grunt and stumbles a bit, then

stands awkwardly as I squeeze my arms around him. He's as stiff as a statue.

"Hug me back, you ding dong," I say, and I press my face into the warmth of his coat.

He lets out a rumbly chuckle that vibrates in his chest. Then he shakes his head and wraps his arms around me. "You're a strange one, Gemma Jacobs."

"Thank you. Thank you. Thank you." I squeeze him harder and bounce up and down, keeping my arms wrapped around him. Finally, I pull away and take a good look at him.

His nose is pink from the cold, he must've been standing outside waiting for me for a while. His hair is ruffled from the wind, he has a day or two worth of stubble, and he looks more tired than usual. Even though he's giving me his usual smile, there's a hint of something else in his eyes. Maybe doubt, or worry, or...I don't know, the emotion is like a snowflake that has landed on warm skin, there for a moment, and then gone.

A thought occurs to me. "Are you, um, did you come to be a donor? You did, didn't you? I mean, I just assumed, with that whole hug thing. But maybe you aren't actually—"

"Gemma. Relax." He shakes his head and looks at me with amusement.

"So, it's a yes?"

He gives me a rueful smile.

"But...why? Why'd you change your mind?"

At first I think he's going to tell me something profound, something serious, but then he says, "You know, I figured, you should always say yes to the opportunities the universe presents you."

I sigh. He gave me an Ian quote. "I really wish you wouldn't quote my boss. It's weird."

"What?"

I hold up my hands, "It's one of Ian's most famous quotes."

Josh scowls.

"Never mind," I say. "I just wondered why you changed your mind."

Ugh. I could almost kick myself. What next? Am I going to try to dissuade him from helping?

Josh gestures for me to walk closer to the building, I do and we both lean against the cold stone, our shoulders touching. "Why did you really ask me? Tell me that and I'll tell you why I changed my mind."

I wrinkle my brow.

"Come on, Gemma. Sure, I'm smart. I'm healthy. I'm good looking." He wags his eyebrows at me and I sniff at him. "But be honest, why'd you actually ask me? It's not like we're close. Usually people ask friends. We're not friends." He gives me a sardonic look and I assume he's quoting my voicemail from last night.

There's a tightness in my chest, something I don't want to look at too closely. I brush the feeling aside and turn my head to look at Josh. The winter wisps of our breath fills the cold air between us.

"We should be friends," I say. "We could be."

He raises an eyebrow, like he's challenging me to say more.

"Fine. Maybe...maybe I asked you because you've always been there. You're like a fixture."

"Really?" he drawls in a tone that's completely unimpressed.

"I mean. Ugh. No, look. I didn't want this to be wrapped up in emotion or drama. I don't need a boyfriend baby daddy or another husband. That's not the point of this. The point is bringing someone into this world that I can love with my whole heart. I thought, it sort of feels like, other than my family, you've always been in my life. Like, if I'm earth rotating around the solar system, then you're the Kuiper Belt, sort of on the fringes, stuck out there with Pluto."

Josh gives a surprised laugh. "That's the worst compliment I've ever received."

She said, "You're like the Kuiper belt, out there with Pluto."

I smile at him and shrug. "That's all I've got. You're already a constant in my family's life, in my life too. If you want to be a part of the baby's life, then you can be, easily. And if you don't, if you just want to watch from afar, then you can do that too. But, regardless, after twenty-four years of watching you be a decent enough human being, I can say that my baby would be proud to have you as her donor dad. With the database it's a gamble, the dad could be some psycho that burned ants with a magnifying glass as a kid, or collects vintage doll's eyes, or I don't know, has freezers full of feet. But I already know you and the worst thing you ever did was collect the panties of every girl you ever came across." I shake my head at him and drawl out, "Casanova."

Josh gives a short laugh. "Good enough, Gemma. Good enough."

He wraps his arm around my shoulders and we walk toward the front door of the doctor's office.

"So, now you tell me. Why'd you change your mind?"

Josh looks down at me and smirks, "I figured if I did, you'd throw some pity sex my way. Pay to play, Gemma. Pay to play."

I gasp in outrage and send a side punch into his kidney.

He grunts and then, "Kidding. Jeez. That's some right hook. What, did Dylan teach you that?"

"Tell me."

We stop in front of the glass front door.

I don't think he's going to answer me, but then Josh says in a quiet voice, so low I have to lean in to hear him, "You're not the only one who's been waiting for someone to love."

I'm stunned, but before I can respond, he starts to chuckle.

"You should see your face. I'm kidding, Gemma. I'm kidding."

Unbelievable. Of course he'd be kidding. "Don't you ever take anything seriously?"

He lifts his eyebrows at me and smirks, then he pulls open the door for me and holds it wide. "Come on, we don't want to be late for our date."

I step into the building lobby. The heat settles over me and nips at the chill in my cheeks. In a surprising gesture of solidarity, Josh takes my gloved hand and gives it a squeeze.

I smile at him in gratitude.

It's time to get to the business of baby making.

10

"If you want something bad enough, you'll do whatever it takes to get it."

Dr. Ingraham looks down at the history and physical form that Josh filled out, then back up at us. He scratches at his round, bald head and frowns.

"It says here you're single, but Gemma indicated that you were partners," Dr. Ingraham says.

I resist the urge to look over at Josh. I can feel myself blush. Josh sits next to me in a blue vinyl padded chair, mine is green vinyl. We're scooched so close together our knees nearly touch. Dr. Ingraham sits behind his desk. He's half hidden by the stacks of paper and journals surrounding him.

I noticed Josh raised his eyebrows at the pile of plastic anatomy models on the doctor's desk when we walked in, but other than that one change of expression, he hasn't seemed fazed.

"I only ask," Dr. Ingraham continues, "because it makes a difference in the process."

"Gemma and I are friends," Josh says. "I'm acting as her donor."

I try not to squirm in my seat. "Friends" is a far cry from "partner with super-awesome amazing winner sperm." But Dr. Ingraham doesn't even blink at the change of status.

"In that case, once you produce your sperm sample, we'll have to quarantine it for six months before it can be released."

"I'm sorry. What does that mean?" I ask.

I look over at Josh, and he shrugs at me and shakes his head.

"When you aren't sexually intimate with your donor, the FDA requires a six-month quarantine. The anonymous donor sperm has already gone through the quarantine process, but if you two aren't sexually intimate then the six-month quarantine is required," Dr. Ingraham explains.

I stare at the doctor. We have to wait *six months*? I can't think of anything to say, I can only think...six months?

I can feel Josh looking at me, but I'm too embarrassed to look back. It has to be obvious to him that I told the doctor that he was my partner, not just a guy I happen to know and convinced to give a donation. He must think I'm such a creep.

"We're friends," says Josh.

I squeeze my eyes shut.

"With benefits, is what I meant to say. Friends with benefits."

Both of my eyes fly open and I glance over at Josh. He gives me a smile that says, "come on, play with me" and slowly nods his head.

"Yup." I nod in time with Josh. "That's right. Josh and I just had sex before we got here. Three times. And once again when we got here in that slightly dirty bathroom in the lobby. You know, 'cause that's what we do. Have lots and lots of sex." I nod again. "Because we are two, physically intimate friends, doing the sex."

We are two, physically intimate friends, doing the sex.

Josh's eyes go wide and I can tell he's trying not to laugh.

I can't look at him when his lips quiver and his eyes light up like that.

I turn back to Dr. Ingraham.

He stares at me with a slightly bemused and sort of disturbed expression on his face. That's right. I disturbed a doctor that trained as a gynecologist and has probably seen and heard some of the weirdest stuff on the planet. His round face is red and he clears his throat.

I watch as he pushes aside a pile of manila files to reveal his desk phone. He picks up the receiver and hits a few numbers.

Both Josh and I sit silently and watch Dr. Ingraham hold the phone against his ear. Finally, a woman on the other end picks up.

Dr. Ingraham gives me a polite smile.

Oh no. We've broken some sort of IVF law and we're about to be kicked out of the practice.

"Yes. Dr. Ingraham here."

I squeeze my eyes shut. What is he going to say?

"Mhmm. Yes. Please send someone to clean the lobby bathroom."

What? I open my eyes.

"Yes. *Apparently*, it's slightly dirty."

Josh makes a choking noise and I look over at him. He's desperately trying not to laugh.

Jeez. *Jeez.*

I mock kick his ankle and he grins at me and wiggles his eyebrows.

Dr. Ingraham sets the phone back down and looks at us both. I school my expression.

"Now, where were we?"

"Sperm collection," Josh says.

Dr. Ingraham frowns. "You were never turned down at a high school dance, right?"

"Uhhh…" Josh looks over at me like it's a trick question. I shake my head.

"No?" he says.

"Darn. Every time. That's what they say *every* time."

Josh looks over at me with a confused expression. I shake my head, not able to explain that the good doctor has a real hang-up on sperm quality and high school dances.

Dr. Ingraham abruptly stands.

I snap to attention.

"Well, let's get to it then. Gemma, you're first, we're doing an ultrasound to see what's under the hood. Then Josh'll do his part."

~

When Dr. Ingraham said "ultrasound" I thought he meant the kind where you squirt some goop, rub a little device over your abdomen, then watch some blurry pictures show up on a screen.

Ultrasound. No big deal.

That's not what he meant.

That's not what he meant at all.

I glance over at Josh. He's sitting in a plastic chair next to the head of the freezing cold medical table my bare butt is plastered on.

I'm in a little paper gown, my legs are up in the stirrups.

Because...yeah.

When Dr. Ingraham asked if I wanted Josh to be there for the ultrasound, I said sure. Because an ultrasound is no big deal.

Josh doesn't look at me. In fact, I don't think he could turn his head if he wanted to. The lights of the ultrasound room are dim. There's a tray with a mobile computer screen on it turned toward us. Dr. Ingraham is in his long white coat and blue rubber gloves.

Josh watches him with an expression that I can only describe as growing dismay, possibly horror.

Dr. Ingraham holds up the ultrasound device. It looks, okay fine, it looks just like the dildo that my sister's maid of honor brought as a gag gift to Leah's bachelorette party. Because... surprise! It's a transvaginal ultrasound.

"Now, there'll be a little pressure as I move around to get a good look-see."

Oh. My. Gosh.

The saline ultrasound apparently involves inserting a good old-fashioned speculum like during a pap smear, then sending in a catheter, pulling out the speculum, sending in the ultrasound probe and flushing saline solution into my uterus.

Yeah.

But, like Ian says, if you want something bad enough, you'll do whatever it takes to get it.

Dr. Ingraham grabs a tube of goopy-looking lube and squirts about a cup and a half up and down the ultrasound probe. Which, I kid you not, is wrapped in a condom. He rubs the goop up and down its length.

I look at Josh to see how he's taking it.

And you know what, for the first time ever, Josh Lewenthal does not look amused. He looks like he has absolutely no idea what to do with himself, where to look, or how to act.

"How you doing over there?" I whisper.

Josh leans toward me and then shrugs. "Not so great."

"Why?"

"I'm feeling really insecure in my manhood. Have you seen the size of that thing?" He nods at the ginormous strangely penile probe in Dr. Ingraham's hand. "That's gotta be an XXL Trojan at the very least."

I can't help it, I laugh, and then cover my mouth with my hand and try to hold it in. Josh smiles at me, and suddenly, this moment isn't nearly half as awkward as it could be.

Dr. Ingraham starts the ultrasound and describes everything he sees in detail.

"This is your uterus, it tips forward. See that? Some uteruses tip backward. Hmm. Your lining looks appropriate for where you are in your menstrual cycle. That's good. I don't see any fibroids or problems with the uterus muscle."

I look at the screen and then back at Josh. He's watching me, avoiding looking down at the ultrasound end of the room. When he sees me turned toward him he smiles and winks.

Dr. Ingraham continues. "Over here is your ovary. These

little black circles are follicles, the special cysts that contain eggs. I can count them...let's see, twelve. Good. That's in the range I'd expect. This area here is a cyst which looks like endometriosis...."

He keeps talking as he probes around, describing everything. There's my ovaries. My uterus. Some follicles. Evidence of endometriosis.

Every now and then I sneak a glance at Josh. For the whole ultrasound he keeps his face turned toward mine. Which, you know, for Josh, really is kind of sweet.

Finally, Dr. Ingraham, pulls the ultrasound probe and the catheter out.

"That's that. Everything looks good. Your swimming pool is ready for a swimmer. We can start IVF at the beginning of your next cycle. That's depending on the quality of sperm, of course." He turns to Josh. "It all depends on you, champ."

It's my turn to look at Josh and give him a reassuring smile.

I SIT IN THE LOBBY WHILE I WAIT FOR JOSH TO FINISH UP IN "THE Production Room."

I cross and uncross my legs, shifting impatiently as I glance at the clock. What's taking so long? He's been back there at least fifteen minutes.

After the ultrasound, Dr. Ingraham ran over my bloodwork and urine. Everything looked good, my AMH, my thyroid, my STD tests, everything was normal. Josh had his blood taken for STDs and then a nurse with a pixie cut and sequined glasses led him away to produce a sample.

I glance at the clock. That was seventeen minutes ago.

Two couples have been called to the back.

There are only three other couples left in the room and a

woman sitting by herself in the corner. She has a magazine held in front of her, and she's wearing a wig, a baseball hat and huge sunglasses. In New York City, the only thing that can mean is she's either a fugitive from justice, or she's anywhere from mildly to wildly famous and doesn't want to be spotted by the autograph-seeking masses around her.

I try to ignore everyone. I tap my foot and stare at the big Georgia O'Keeffe painting on the far wall.

When I've nearly decided that the painting is one hundred percent definitely a flower, not part of the female anatomy like I thought last time, my phone buzzes.

I open my purse and look at the screen.

It's a text from Josh.

Josh: *I'm in the production room.*

I stare at the phone, mystified as to what I'm supposed to say to that.

Gemma: *Okay?*

Josh texts a picture. It's of a room. I'm guessing it's "The Production Room." Unfortunately, it's also the saddest, most depressing-looking room I've ever seen. It's about six foot by four foot. The walls are stark white and the floor is old gray tile. There's one of those wall collection metal shelves for the sample jar, a tissue dispenser in the wall, a garbage can, and printed instructions taped to the wall. That's it. No color, no decoration, no dirty magazines, no flat screen TV playing porn to get a guy in the mood. Nothing.

I text Josh back.

Gemma: *Is that the production room?*

Josh: *Yeah...*

I wait. Josh is typing another message.

When it comes through I stare at my phone in surprise.

Josh: *It's not working.*

I look around the waiting room, and I'm sort of surprised

that no one is staring at me in shock. Did Josh Lewenthal just tell me that he can't produce a sample?

The news plays on a muted TV near the scheduling desk. All the other couples are either watching it, looking at their phones, or reading a magazine. No one is paying me any attention. I quickly type back.

Gemma: *What's not working?*

Josh: *It's a lot of pressure. I need some inspiration. This room sucks.*

I blow out a breath.

I mean, I get what he's saying. It would be hard to get in the mood in a room that looks like a Russian prison cell. The tissue is for you to weep into.

I shift back into my chair and try to think of a solution. Ah, got it.

Gemma: *Look up porn on your phone.*

I blush and pull at the winter scarf around my neck. I can't believe I just wrote that.

Josh: *I can't believe you just wrote that.*

Ha. I write him back.

Gemma: *Well?*

Josh: *It's not working. Send me a pic of some skin.*

Excuse me? Did he just ask me to send him a dirty picture? Of myself?

Gemma: *No way.*

Josh: *Come on. I need help.*

I close my eyes. Fine. *If you want something bad enough, you'll do whatever it takes to get it,* even text dirty pics to "The Production Room."

I stand up and stride to the desk.

"Can I have the key to the bathroom please?"

The same scheduler that was completely disinterested in me last week tosses the key at me.

"Thanks," I mumble, terrified that she somehow has mind-reading powers and knows exactly what I'm about to do.

I shut the bathroom door behind me. Surprisingly, the bathroom's really clean. They must've actually sent someone over to clean it after Dr. Ingraham called. Huh.

My phone buzzes again.

Josh: *They're knocking on the door, Gemma. The pressure is a bit much here. Skin?*

I snort. Then I try to think of the least embarrassing place I can take a picture of that may elicit some sort of reaction.

Ah, got it.

I lift my leg up and set my boot on the toilet. Then I pull up my pants and take a snapshot of my calf. I hit send.

I yank my pantleg down and wait for Josh's reply.

Josh: *Seriously?*

I smile. Hey, I tried.

What else, what else?

Well, no one in the history of ever, complained about my breasts, soooo.

I pull off my winter coat, lift up my sweater over my head, dip my camisole low and take a cockeyed cleavage shot of my breasts. As I try to pull my sweater back down I stumble over the trash can and fall back onto the toilet. I hit with a thud and the trash can rattles, making a racket.

I wait a second. My heart beating hard.

There's a knock on the door.

"You alright in there?"

Oh jeez. It's the disinterested scheduler.

"Good. Fine. Just...busy."

Oh lordy. Busy?

I hit send on the photo of my boobs. Then I try to pull myself back together.

My phone vibrates.

Josh: *Not a breast man.*

Are you kidding me? Not a breast man? I sent him a deep cleavage shot that should have soared him into boner territory.

Gemma: *Then what?*

I scowl down at the phone.

There's another knock on the bathroom door.

"Just a minute," I call. "I'm busy in here!"

I stare at my phone as I wait for Josh to reply.

"Come on..."

I pace back and forth in the small space. Finally, Josh starts to text. Deletes it. Starts to text again, deletes it.

Gemma: *Come on. What?*

Finally his text comes through.

Josh: *Just send a shot of your bare shoulders, or your back.*

What? What the weird? Fine.

I pull off my coat and scarf, strip off my sweater, camisole, and bra, and stand with my bare back to the mirror. I look behind me. My hair is down and falls over my shoulders in a straight dark line. My shoulders are narrow, and my back shows the exaggerated curve of my figure. I never noticed or thought about it before, but looking at my smooth skin, the gentle flare of my hips and the curve of my spine, there's something strangely erotic about a woman's bare back. I take a shuddering breath. My nipples go hard from the cold air. I look over my shoulder at myself, there's a strange look in my eyes. I don't think about it. Instead, I lift up my camera, and snap a shot of my back in the mirror.

It's a half-blurry shot, my head is turned away, and my back is exposed. You can just barely see the edges of my breast under my lifted arm. It's almost...erotic.

I stare at the photo for a moment, and then I hit send.

Gemma: *Show this to anyone and I will kill you.*

Josh doesn't write back.

I throw on my bra, my cami, my sweater, my coat and my scarf, and then I splash ice cold water on my face. I wait a few minutes for Josh to text back, but he doesn't.

Another knock comes at the door.

"Hang on," I call.

I take a deep, steadying breath and open the bathroom door.

"All yours," I say to the woman waiting.

Then, I look toward the reception desk.

Josh is already there. He's leaning against the counter talking to the scheduler.

A full body flush rushes over me. I don't want him to look at me. I'm embarrassed...I'm...sure okay, yes, we've already had sex, but that was eons ago, a slam-bam-thank-you-ma'am job in my parents' garage, for crying out loud. And this, well, it was nothing. Just some pictures. But still. I don't know why, but it feels different.

I stay at the edge of the waiting room, afraid of the moment that Josh turns around and realizes I'm here.

Then he does.

The scheduler points at me, and Josh turns.

I hold my breath.

I don't know what I expected, but nothing out of the ordinary happens. Josh is just his usual self.

He looks me up and down, winks, and gives me his devil-may-care smile. Then he pushes away from the counter and strides toward me.

"Hey."

I shake out of my embarrassment. "Hey yourself. Did it work?"

He smiles down at me. "Consider it done."

I sigh in relief.

"Come on," he says. He nods toward the exit and slings his

arm over my shoulders. When we walk out into the cold early evening air, I shiver and lean closer to him. Rush hour is here and the car headlights and office windows light up the darkening sky. I shift and start to pull away from him.

"Well, thank you. I mean...I can't tell you how much this means, I'll keep you in the loop, I—"

"Hey. Isn't it a rule, that when someone puts out they at least get dinner?" He looks down at me with raised eyebrows.

"What?" I squeak.

He shrugs. "I just put out. The least you can do is buy me dinner. It's a long, hungry train ride back to my dad's."

I shake my head. He's so irreverent. So...Josh.

Although, it is a long haul back north. And I don't think he has much money. And this part of the city really does have some excellent restaurants.

I think of the Korean place Ian took me to last week, then I frown. If Ian and I start to date exclusively, then I shouldn't be going out with Josh.

"Or not. I can take a rain check," Josh says, studying my expression.

"No. It's not that. It's just, we're friends right? We can be friends?"

Josh studies me, and he's so still and quiet that I don't have any clue what he's thinking. The sounds of rush hour traffic, the cold of the air, and the smell of New York City in the winter —exhaust, snow and food stalls—fills the air. I wait for his answer.

"Friends with benefits?" he finally asks.

I smile and let go of the tension that had quietly and suddenly filled me. Of course he'd answer that way. "Just friends. No benefits."

He chuckles and elbows my side. "What's good to eat around here? I'm starving."

11

*"Love is the best gift
I've ever had the
privilege to give."*

WHEN YOU'RE IN A CITY FULL OF CULINARY DELIGHTS, CUISINES from around the world, and international markets, what would you choose to eat? If you're Josh, you choose pizza.

We're in a tiny, standing room only pizzeria that is basically a no-frills to-go storefront on the corner of a busy intersection. If it has a name, I don't know it, the sign out front just says PIZZA in big glowing block letters. There's a cooler for drinks, a long glass-covered pizza counter, and a cash register.

Josh looks down at the pizza counter, it's filled with trays of freshly baked pizza that you can buy by the slice. The crust is crispy, the cheese is bubbling and the smell of yeast, herby sauce and spicy meat fills the air. The pizzeria is nice and toasty from the wood-fueled heat coming off the brick oven. I rub my gloved hands together and press them against my cheeks.

"I'll have two slices of the grandma pizza," he says.

I grin. "That's what I'm getting."

Grandma pizza is delicious square pizza, covered in tomato and cheese. It tastes just like it came out of some nonna's kitchen in a little village in Italy.

"Anything to drink?" asks Josh.

I point to the cooler and the row of flavored sparkling water. "Want one?"

He nods and I grab two bottles of lime-flavored sparkling water from the cooler.

The worker hands over two paper plates, loaded up with our grandma pizza. The cheese is still melty and droops over the edges.

"Fifteen dollars," he says.

I dig in my purse and pull out the money.

"I got it," Josh says.

I shake my head. "No, you put out—"

But he's already paid.

The worker snorts and shakes his head at me and Josh. I scowl at him. I grab my paper plate and bottle of water and hurry after Josh. He's headed toward the door.

He holds it open for me and I step back into the bustle of the city. After the warmth cranking out of the pizza oven, the winter air feels even colder. I shiver and let the warmth of the pizza seep into my hands.

Josh takes a bite and groans in pleasure. "Now this is good pizza. I'll get off for you anytime if you promise to take me out for pizza more often."

I laugh and roll my eyes. But the smell of fresh mozzarella, tomatoes, and crispy golden crust is enticing.

"Deal," I say.

Josh's mouth is full of pizza but he manages to grin at me.

I pick off a bit of browned cheese and pop it in my mouth. To be honest, there's something about the way the smell of subway steam, traffic exhaust and city grime mixes with New York pizza to make it insanely delicious. I take a big bite and luxuriate in the flavor.

Josh starts to walk down the sidewalk, heading east. He ambles at a slow enough pace to take bites of the pizza as he walks. I walk next to him and pick the mozzarella off the top, popping it in my mouth.

"The only problem with places like that is there's nowhere to sit," I say.

Josh eyes me in surprise. "That's not a problem. That's an adventure."

I raise an eyebrow. "What's that mean?"

He tucks his drink into his jacket pocket and nods his head at the intersection. "We eat while we walk, and the mission is, we have to find a dessert place before we finish."

"Seriously? You do this kind of thing often?"

He nods. "Sure. I'm a risk-taker. I eat standing up, sometimes I don't tie my shoes. It gets me in a lot of trouble."

I shake my head at him.

"Come on," he says. "This is what friends do."

So, we keep walking down the crowded sidewalk. The sky has shifted to the dusky purple of a night filled with city lights. It's rush hour and we're close to a subway stop, so the mass of people squeezing against us is even thicker than usual.

"Let's go this way," I say and I turn onto a less busy cross street. I take another bite of my pizza. It's delicious. Really, delicious. Maybe I should eat pizza while walking through the city more often.

Josh seems relaxed. His gait is easy and he's taking happy

bites of his slice. I decide I could broach the more serious topic of *what next.*

I clear my throat and look around. We're on a pseudo-residential side street, the light is dim and there aren't many people around.

"So, I think we should have a contract for what happens next," I say. I've been reading a lot online and it's what all the experts suggest. It makes sense.

Josh glances at me and lifts an eyebrow.

I shrug. "It'll keep everything clean. We can sort out whether you want the baby to know you're the dad. Whether you want visitation rights."

"Yes, and yes," Josh says.

I look over at him in surprise.

He shrugs. "I like kids."

I study him. The sexy, fun-loving, devil-may-care image of him that I have doesn't exactly mesh with this information. "I didn't know that," I admit.

"You don't know a lot of things about me, Gem."

He quirks an eyebrow at me in challenge and I bristle, because it's not like after twenty-four years I haven't learned a few things.

"I know plenty about you."

"Really?" he drawls.

We come to another intersection. To the left, I see what looks like an ice cream shop. I turn toward it.

"I know you collect Godzilla models."

He gives a grunt, like knowing that isn't anything special.

"I know you like pizza." I gesture at the nearly finished slices on his grease-stained paper plate.

"You're failing, Gemma," he says.

I narrow my eyes at him. "Fine. I know that you have a lot of sex. Like, a lot, a lot."

He makes a buzzer sound, like the noise you get on a gameshow when you say the wrong answer.

"What does that mean?" I ask.

"It means I'm in a dry spell."

"Please. Two weeks or whatever doesn't count as a dry spell."

"Two years," he says.

I stop walking and stare at him. Josh turns around and looks at me, and I think there might me a blush on his cheeks, but it could just be the cold.

"Did you say two years? Two years? What happened?"

He shakes his head and says sadly, "I was in a terrible accident. A hot dog vendor cart fell on me in the park. The doctors said I'd never have sex again unless I did years' worth of physical therapy involving zero gravity, plasma pools and—"

"Oh, for crying out loud." I elbow him and start walking again. "You're ridiculous. Just admit it. You lost your mojo. You lost that magic man-fairy dust that made all the girls drop their pants for you. You lost it, buddy. Admit it."

The infamous hot dog cart.

He shakes his head. "Fine. There was no accident. Two years ago..."

"Yes?"

"I realized if I was ever going to win the girl I wanted to marry, I better start acting like a man for her."

"Really?" I ask, feeling sorta starry-eyed for his romantic notion.

Josh shakes his head. "No, Gemma, that one was even more fabricated than the hot dog cart crushing my balls."

I laugh. "You are such a freak." Then, "Speaking of. What kind of guy gets off from a picture of a girl's naked back?"

Josh stops and gives me a look that's so hot, his eyes so full of dirty suggestion that I forget all about the fact that it's so cold outside that there's snow on the ground and frost on the windows.

I clear my throat and look away from him. There's no way I'm feeling all hot and bothered for Josh Lewenthal. He's not my type. Not at all. He makes a joke of everything, he creates web comics in his dad's basement, he's a nice guy, but he's not...he's not...

Well, Ian.

For instance, Ian has an international business, he inspires millions with his quotes, and he dresses in tailored suits instead of jeans and anime T-shirts.

Getting emotionally involved with Josh would be a big mistake. He's the perfect donor, but not anything more. We're keeping everything platonic, friendly, and contractual. In fact, we should lay out a contract covering the future as soon as possible.

"There's an ice cream shop up ahead. We found dessert in time," I say. My voice is tight and the transition is super awkward, but I start walking again.

At the corner, I drop my paper plate into a garbage can. Josh throws his in too. He takes another sip of water and puts the bottle back in his pocket. I haven't even opened my water yet, it's still tucked in my purse.

The silence between us is heavy, I glance at Josh, but he's not looking at me. Instead, he's staring to the side, seeming lost in thought.

I push open the door of the ice cream place. The bell on the door tinkles and the smell of waffle cones and sugar greets us. It's a tiny shop, there are two barstools at a narrow counter at the window, and a glass case full of eight ice-cream flavors. The shop is empty of customers, although that's not surprising since it's after dark and below freezing outside.

I order a waffle cone covered in gummy bears and two scoops of lime sorbet.

Josh gives me a funny look. "You and your love of lime."

I shrug, but I wonder how he knows I love lime. The only time I eat it around him is when I gorge on my mom's lime Jell-O salad mold at the New Year's party every year. It's not like he's been watching me.

He remembers she likes lime.

"What do you mean my love of lime?" I ask.

"You ate two slices of key lime pie and three bowls of lime Jell-O at my high school graduation party," he says off-handedly.

"That's an oddly specific thing for you to remember.

Especially since that was sixteen years ago." Then I blush, because that was also the day he deflowered me in the garage, apparently right after he got turned on by my mad lime Jell-O-eating skills.

Josh ignores my comment and orders a sugar cone with a scoop of chocolate ice cream.

The older woman behind the counter hands us our cones. "Eleven fifty."

Josh pays again.

"You can't keep doing that," I say. "I'm supposed to be paying for this." Honestly, he can't have much money to spare, living in his dad's basement, drawing comics.

"Don't worry about it."

He holds open the door for me, and I shiver as we step back out onto the sidewalk. It's freezing. I turn back toward the shop —there were two barstools inside after all. But Josh shakes his head.

"Ah ah, the whole point is to walk and eat."

He takes a bite off the side of his ice cream scoop. I lick mine. There are bright green bits of lime zest mixed into the ice cream. It's tart and sweet on my tongue. It's delicious, but my lips start to feel like they're going numb.

"Never again will I suggest eating ice cream when it's below freezing. This is probably my worst idea ever." I give an involuntary shiver and the ice-cream cone shakes in my hand.

"It's g-g-good," says Josh.

And I laugh, because he's literally shaking so hard he can't talk. He takes another big bite of the chocolate ice cream. Apparently, he's a biter/nibbler, not a licker.

"Keep moving, it'll keep you warm," he says.

We start walking north, toward Central Park. The wind has picked up and the night is really, really chilly.

Josh looks over at me. "Your lips are turning blue."

"It's the price you pay." I take another lick.

He takes a huge bite of his cone and then drops the last bit in the trash. I look at my ice cream and back at the trash can. I should throw it away, it's too cold, but...

"Here. I'll fix it," Josh says. He unzips his down-filled coat and holds it open.

"What?"

"Get in here."

He's got that laughing spark in his eyes. I step up close to him, so close I can feel the heat coming off his chest, then he wraps his down-filled jacket around me.

"Now you can eat your ice cream."

I lean into his warmth and take a long lick of my cone. "Mmm. That's good."

"That's what they all say," Josh says.

I laugh and keep licking my ice cream. It's actually really, really nice standing in the warm, insulated stillness of Josh's arms. He looks down at me with an amused expression on his face as I gulp down my ice cream cone.

"It's sort of horrifying how you devour all those gummy bears," he jokes.

I lick my lips and grin at him. Looking up at his wry expression, I realize that this is the perfect ending to the day. There was so much pressure, so much potential stress, but having Josh with me, and then ending with pizza and ice cream...it's like he knew I needed this, needed to keep everything light. I pop the last of the cone in my mouth and crunch down on the sweetness. Then I wipe my mouth and look expectantly at Josh. He smiles at me.

"Good?"

I nod. "You know what, you're a really good guy."

He hums an acknowledgment.

"Thank you again. For agreeing to be my donor." And

because it feels safe, and sort of like we're friends sharing secrets in the quiet hush of the night I say, "I'm so glad you came."

"It's no big deal." He frowns and opens up his jacket for me to step out of.

"Right." I step back and shiver at the wind and the chill.

I look around and check the cross streets. We're not far from my apartment, maybe a ten-minute walk. "Do you want to come up to my place and have some coffee before you catch the train?"

Josh gives me a funny look. "For what?"

I shake my head, confused at his question, then I remember what he said at the New Year's Party. *I don't think we should have sex, Gemma.*

I flush and start walking. "I just figured you might want some coffee before a long train trip back north. No big deal."

"Okay, sure."

I look over at him in surprise. "Really?"

"Really."

Josh's phone starts to chirp. He frowns and pulls it out of his pocket. The display says *Dylan*. My brother. Josh sends it to voicemail and pops it back in his pocket.

"You can answer it," I say.

Josh shrugs, but then the phone starts to ring again. He pulls it out. Dylan's calling again. He looks at me and I gesture for him to answer.

"What's up?"

I hear Dylan on the other end but can't make out what he's saying.

"No, I'm in the city."

Josh listens for a minute, then, "Just getting dinner." And, "What do you mean, with who? No. No."

I give Josh a bemused smile. My brother sounds like a mother hen.

"I'm with Gemma. Yeah. Your sister Gemma," Josh finally says.

Then Josh frowns and holds out the phone. "Your brother wants to talk to you."

I take the phone and put it to my ear. "What?"

"Why are you out with Josh?" he says in an annoying big-brother voice, no preliminaries whatsoever.

I look at Josh and open my eyes wide. I haven't told my family anything about my decision to do IVF, and if it's not successful then I probably won't tell them ever. Sometimes, when you have a dream, it's too precious or too fragile to share with anyone. You have to keep it in the dark, like a seedling, and nurse it and let it grow before you share it with the world.

"Gemma?"

"What? I ran into him in Midtown at a pizza place. Why are you so nosy? Gah, you're a worse busybody than Mom."

"Gemma, you're my kid sister. I do not want you messing around with my best friend."

My mouth falls open. I cannot believe he just went there. "Dylan. First off, I'm thirty-two years old, I run my own life. Second, this is not some cheesy made-for-TV movie where I have an overprotective brother that dictates my life. Third, screw off, and I mean that in the nicest way possible."

Josh is watching me and I can tell he's trying not to laugh.

I hear my mom in the background, shouting something about pot roast to my brother. Dylan calls back, "No, Ma, he's in the city with Gemma, he can't come."

Then he says, "Whatever, Gemma. Obviously you and Josh aren't hooking up. You're not his type, and you're all about that Ian dude anyway. I'm just saying, hang on, Mom wants to talk to you."

I hear the phone rustle as Dylan hands it to my mom. Josh raises his eyebrows at me. "My mom," I mouth.

He smothers another laugh.

"Gemma, sweetie. I dry-cleaned the orange dress for you. You should pick it up this weekend when you babysit for Leah."

Oh blah. The pumpkin dress.

"Sure, Mom. I will."

"Good, sweetie. And tell Josh that he forgot his coat here the other day and I sent it to the dry-cleaners as well. He can grab it tomorrow."

"Okay, Mom. Will do."

Then Dylan's back on the line. "Let me talk to Josh."

I smirk and hand the phone back to him. He looks at it like it's a snake, but takes it. "Hello?" he asks cautiously. He listens for a full minute. I wrap my arms around myself and try to stay warm in the evening chill.

Then Josh says, "Yeah. I know. No. It's too late. No. I'll crash in the city at my place tonight. Yeah. See you tomorrow."

He drops the phone back in his pocket.

We've been walking at a good pace for the entire phone conversation and we've made it to my apartment.

"Well..." I clear my throat and gesture at the brick walk-up. "We made it. Home sweet home."

I put my keys into the lock and open the door. The fluorescent light in the entry buzzes. My walk-up is similar to thousands of others in the city. Mostly brick or stone five-story buildings from the 1800s and 1900s, segmented into small apartments joined by a dimly lit stairwell. There's a narrow entry with mailboxes in the wall, slightly grimy tile floors, and cracked plaster walls.

"I'm on the second floor," I say, and I lead Josh up the creaky stairs.

I unlock the deadbolt and the door lock, then swing open the thick wood door and flip on the lights.

"Here it is," I say, somewhat self-consciously.

Then I look around and try to see what my place would look like to someone seeing it for the first time.

It's a five-hundred-square-foot one-room studio with high ceilings. When I moved in I painted the walls light blue and stenciled in big scripty letters on the far wall my favorite saying from Ian: *love is the best gift I've ever had the privilege to give.* The only other decorations are the curtains that I sewed from some lacy fabric.

I kept the furniture minimal. There's my bed, a dresser and night stand, my futon, a coffee table, and that's it. My kitchen is a row of three cabinets, a small countertop, a sink, a tiny oven with a countertop stove, and a mini fridge. There's a dirty pile of laundry next to the bed and a couple of books on the floor next to the futon. Otherwise, thankfully, it's clean-ish.

"Well?" I ask, meaning, what do you think?

Josh doesn't say anything. I turn to him and realize that he's staring at the quote on my wall.

"What's that about?" he asks.

I blush then start to take off my coat and unwrap my scarf. I hang them on the coat rack by my door.

"I like Ian's quotes. Obviously. I've worked for him for almost seven years." I hold out my hands for Josh's coat.

But Josh wrinkles his brow, then, "Actually. It's getting late, I think I'm going to head out."

I frown. Something Josh said to my brother sinks in. Josh said he'd crash in the city. At his place. I imagine it, the crumbling walls, the old mattress on the floor, the construction debris. It sounds too depressing for words.

"I was thinking," I say. "You were really nice today, and the least I can do is let you sleep on my futon." I gesture to the futon under the wall quote.

Josh shakes his head.

"So you don't have to take the train all the way to Williamsburg," I quickly add. "My futon's not comfortable, it's got this nasty metal bar in the middle, but I mean, it's better than a dusty construction site. You told my brother that you'd sleep in Williamsburg, but that sounds depressing, so..."

He still doesn't say anything so I say, "Besides, we need to talk about how we're going forward from here."

"Thanks." He gives me an amused smile. "But as tempting as your not-so-comfortable futon sounds, I need to get going."

"Oh," I squeak, and even though I feel a weird sort of disappointment, I try not to let it show. "That's alright. Like I said, I'll keep you updated on everything. I can text you after the transfer when I get my results. Plus, we need to sort out the contract but we can do that through lawyers."

"Gemma." Josh reaches out and puts his fingers to my chin.

I stop talking.

He moves his thumb and drags it across my bottom lip. The room spins a bit and I feel slightly short of breath. The callous on the tip of his thumb rubs over the fleshy part of my mouth.

What? What the...?

My lips part as I draw in a breath and then Josh pulls his hand away.

He clears his throat and then, "You had lime zest on your lips." He holds out his thumb, and sure enough, there's a bit of lime on the pad of this thumb.

An image of me sucking it off his thumb flashes through my mind.

My lady parts clench.

Gah. Why?

"The contract," I blurt out. "We need to sort out the details."

"Let's catch up this weekend," he says.

Strangely, my heart thunders in my chest.

"Okay," I say over the thundering in my ears. "Thanks again. Thanks for everything. You have no idea."

He looks at me then turns, walks out, and shuts the door with a quiet snick.

I walk over to my not-so-comfortable futon and sit down with an exhausted flop.

What a day.

12

_"A friend is someone
who accepts your past,
loves you in the present,
and believes in
your future."_

I'M AT MY DESK, CLICKING MY MOUSE TO THE BEAT OF A POP SONG playing over my headphones. Today, I'm working on finishing up a social media story about the power of friendship. I worked with a designer to create this cute animation following the friendship of a fox and a rabbit. You'd think they wouldn't be friends since foxes eat rabbits, but Ian's quotes create a storyline that has friendship budding in only seven installments.

I don't want to brag, but it's kind of awesome.

I smile at the cute fox and fluffy rabbit on my screen, then I look across the room toward Ian's office. It's dark. He's been in LA for the past few days and I haven't heard from him. Not that that's unusual. When Ian is on media tours he works twenty-hour days and no one at the office hears from him unless it's an emergency.

I sent him a text yesterday: *Hope you're having a good time in sunny LA, you lucky dog.*

He didn't write back. Which is fine. Obviously. He's busy inspiring millions.

And I'm busy inspiring myself.

I've spent my nights logged into the fertility forums reading old posts and lurking on new posts. I also ordered about nine thousand books on infertility covering every topic imaginable from growing awesome super-fertile eggs by avoiding BPA to the raw food fertility diet to maintaining the proper mindset. The only thing the books don't cover is how to navigate an evolving relationship with Josh Lewenthal.

That's what I should've typed into the bookstore search engine.

Book title: How to make a baby and have an uncomplicated, platonic relationship with Josh Lewenthal while pursuing your career, finding fulfillment, and dating your incredibly sexy boss, self-help guru Ian Fortune.

Author: No one. Ever.

Right. So, that's that. The stack of books by my futon has turned into a mountain and I'm confused about what happened with Josh. Which I don't need. I asked him to be a donor for many reasons, one of which was that I'm not attracted to him/interested in him.

But spending such an emotional day with him was...nice.

Fine. More than nice.

He texted this morning. All it said was: *How's Friday night?*

I wrote back: *I babysit for Leah on Fridays.*

He wrote: *See you then. We'll do our thing after.*

Honestly, what kind of guy wants to babysit kids on a Friday night? I mean, yeah, he's living at his dad's, which is only five minutes from Leah's house, and he does know the kids and my sister and her husband, obviously, but...doesn't he want to hang out with his guy friends, or go on a hot date?

So I texted: *Don't you usually have a hot date on Fridays?*

He wrote back: *Haha.*

Then: *That hot dog stand was a real tragedy for my dating life.*

I sent back an emoji rolling its eyes.

And that was the end of it, I'll be seeing him tomorrow night for babysitting and contract talks.

I frown at my computer screen and readjust the text covering the graphic of the fox and rabbit. Then, the words of the quote sink in. A friend is someone who accepts your past, loves you in the present, and believes in your future.

That's it. There's nothing strange about what I felt the other day. I already know he's able to charm the panties off a nun, so of course I'd feel some attraction on close proximity, but the connection, that was friendship.

That's it.

We're becoming friends.

It's fun to hang out with friends.

Friendship is okay. Friendship is good.

My desk phone rings.

Lavinia glances over at me. She's been in a sourer mood than usual the past few days. So much so that I've stopped pilfering sparkling water from the break room fridge.

"Are you going to answer that?" she asks in a pinched voice.

I pull out my headphones and check the caller ID. It's Dr. Ingraham's office.

"Of course I am," I say and smile blandly at Lavinia.

I grab the phone, "Hello, Gemma speaking," I say in a business-like tone.

Lavinia frowns at me and narrows her eagle eyes on me. I swivel my chair around to face the quote wall.

"Hi Gemma. It's Joy, the scheduler at Dr. Ingraham's office." I raise my eyebrows. I hadn't realized the bored, couldn't-care-less scheduler was named Joy.

"Yes?" I ask, keeping my answers short, knowing that Lavinia is listening. The rest of the staff likes to work with headphones in, but for some reason Lavinia doesn't.

"So, Dr. Ingraham mentioned the fertility support group, right?"

"Uh, yes. He did mention it."

"Mhmm. Well, the fertility support group is a benefit we offer all patients as part of our advocacy for mental well-being."

Joy sounds like she's reading from a script. I've never heard someone so disinterested in what they're saying. She continues listing off the multitude of benefits to joining a group of women going through the same process.

"Are you interested in joining a support group for the duration of your fertility journey?" she asks in a bored monotone.

I stare at the quotes on the wall and think about the hours I've spent trawling the online forums, the books, and all the questions I still have. I think about how nice it would be to meet women who are going through the same thing I am. Women who won't judge, or question, who will understand.

"Yes. I'm interested," I say with a happy smile. "Very interested."

Joy gives a long-suffering sigh. "Fine. I'll add you to the Thursday night group. They meet weekly at seven o'clock in the basement of Clive's Comics on East Fourteenth Street. It's a real dump. Have fun."

"Um. Okay. Thanks? Wait. Thursday, that's today right?"

"Uh, yeah," she says, then she hangs up.

I hold the phone to my ear and smile at the quote wall. I can feel Lavinia still watching me, waiting for my call to end.

So I say, "Of course, yes. I'm very interested. Thank you, Mr. Berners-Lee, you've been a real help."

I turn around in my chair and place the phone back in its cradle. Then I look at Lavinia and smile.

"Mr. Berners-Lee again?" she asks.

I grin. "Real nice guy."

Lavinia rolls her eyes and turns away, but I swear she has a ghost of a smile on her lips. Good things are happening.

Josh is decidedly in the friend category.

I'm starting my IVF cycle in only three weeks.

Soon I'll meet my baby. Hold her in my arms.

And tonight I'm going to meet a group of wonderful, supportive, amazing, like-minded woman who want to share their journey.

Everything is looking up. It's going to be great.

13

"The true value of something isn't based on what it looks like, but what it has inside."

CLIVE'S COMICS IS A DUMP. IT'S A CLUTTERED, MUSTY-SCENTED shop with cockroach traps sticking out from under the shelves. I tiptoe around a cluster of the traps and a dead cockroach lying on the grimy tile floor. The lighting is fluorescent and overly bright, showing off all the grime, disrepair and clutter. There are stacks of comics in plastic sleeves, those collectible figure things, and bins of monster trading cards.

I walk to the back of the store and spin in a slow circle. There was no one at the cash register near the front door, and I don't see any sign of a basement or a fertility support group.

"Hello?" I call out. "Anybody here?"

My shoulders slump a bit when no one answers. I look down at my watch, it's already a few minutes past seven. I'm late. I left work with plenty of time to spare, but the subway was so crowded that I had to wait for two different trains before I could shove, elbow and forcefully squeeze myself onto the car. Even then, I stood for a good five minutes, smashed in the crowd, with my nose pressed into a big guy's salami scented armpit.

So, anyway.

I start to walk back toward the front door and let out a short sigh of disappointment. I guess I'm at the wrong place. I can call Joy tomorrow morning and ask for the exact address.

I look up when the bell on the front door rings. A small, bony man, with a large nose and a swagger walks in.

He stops when he sees me, and although he's so short he should be looking up at me, he makes it seem like he's looking down.

"What d'ya want?" he asks in a thick Brooklyn accent.

I open my mouth to say something, but I'm not sure how to respond. Is this Clive? Or...

"Um. Are you...? Is this...I'm looking for the fertility support group? Is that here?"

Clive grunts then turns back around and pushes open the front door. I stand still, not sure what to do.

He turns back and scowls. "Come on, then."

Oh. I hurry after him, my chunky heels clicking on the tile floor. He sees I'm following and starts walking down the street. He rounds the corner, and I take quick steps and try and catch up.

"Thank you. They said the group was in the basement, but I didn't see an entry, and there weren't any signs, and..." I stop rambling when the man stoops down and opens up one of those metal cellar doors built into the sidewalks all over the city. You know, the ones that look like old-fashioned cellar doors in Kansas that people dive into when a tornado is coming.

The man holds his hand out like "ta-da!" and gestures to the dark, stone steps leading down into the basement.

Hmm.

I look around. There are plenty of people walking by on their evening commute home. Nobody's screaming, "don't go in there! He'll take your skin!" But I'm feeling really uncomfortable.

"The fertility group is down there?" I ask, and then I lean forward and try to peer down the stairs into the dim basement.

The man grunts, "Go on then. I don't got all day."

I shake my head. Nope. Not doing it. *Not doing it.*

Just then a woman with frizzy copper hair, freckles and a drab gray business suit steps up next to me. She takes a long draw of a cigarette and blows a cloud of smoke out.

"Real crap hole, isn't it?" she asks.

I turn to her and take a closer look. Even though her hair is bright and her freckles could be considered cute, she holds herself in a way that shouts, "do not mess with me, or I will use your face as an ashtray."

She's waiting for me to respond so I say, "The true value of things aren't based on what they look like, but what they have inside." And then I inwardly cringe because...honestly, what the heck am I talking about? Who says that kind of thing to a stranger?

She snorts and then flicks her cigarette to the sidewalk. "Great. Another Pollyanna. Just what I need."

The man, who had been standing by the cellar doors lets out a long sigh. He swaggers away, calling, "Shut the door behind ya."

"Screw you, Clive," shouts the woman after him.

I look from Clive's retreating form back to the woman.

"You're here for the fertility support group, right?" she asks. She pulls a pack of cigarettes out from her suit pocket and lights one. She takes a long draw and then slowly blows it out.

"Yes?" I say.

She grimaces at me, taking in my bright red winter coat and my hesitant smile.

"Well, come on then. You first. I'll shut the door."

I hesitate, but then I hear female laughter from the basement. Real, happy, full-belly kind of laughter and I think, maybe my stupid rambling quote to this woman was right. The true value is found within, and I won't find it unless I *go in*.

So, I walk down the uneven stone steps into the basement of Clive's Comics.

The metal door clatters shut behind me. The woman steps next to me. The entryway is dark, most of the light comes from the glowing tip of her cigarette.

"It's down there." She points to a shaft of light coming out of a doorway down the hall. "I'm Brook, by the way."

I smile. "Nice to meet you. I'm Gemma Jacobs."

"Alright," Brook says, then she leads me down the dark, old stone-walled hallway. "Watch out for rats. They bite. And their piss will give you some freakish disease, so don't lick the floor."

I give her a quick look, certain she has to be joking, but she takes another puff of her cigarette and then steps into the doorway of the brightly lit room.

I stand behind her. The room is low-ceilinged, painted dark pink, and there are boxes full of comics shoved against the far wall. In the middle of the room a group of six folding chairs have been set up in a circle. Only two of the chairs are occupied.

There's a glossy blonde-haired woman with bright blue eyes who looks elegant and poised, like she could be a model on the cover of *Vogue*. She's talking in a clipped British accent to another woman who is listening to her and nodding her head intently.

The second woman has long, brown wavy hair that nearly reaches her hips and warm light brown eyes. She's in a shirt and long skirt that look like they were hand dyed, and hemp sandals, which wow, must be cold in the winter.

Brook clears her throat loudly and both women turn to her.

"Hello, darling," says the blonde woman.

"Brook, will you please put that out? My energy worker said that all your smoking and negative energy is blocking my chi," says the wavy-haired woman.

Brook snorts, but she drops her cigarette to the concrete floor and steps on it.

"We've got another one," Brook says. She pulls me into the room. I stumble to a stop in front of her and smile at the two women.

"Hi," I say and give a small wave.

Brook steps up next to me. "Her name's Gemma. She believes in never judging a book by its cover, has terrible fashion sense, and is routinely late."

"What? I am not, I—"

"She wants to have a baby, clearly. And she's delighted to make our acquaintance," finishes Brook.

I give her an incredulous look. Who *is* this woman?

"Delighted," says the blonde, she stands up smoothly and holds out her hand.

"This is Carly," says Brook. "She's a former model. Check out her nudies online." Brook whistles and Carly gives a smile. "She married a kazillionaire and never has to work again. Unfortunately, she's old, so her eggs suck."

Carly shrugs and gracefully sits back in her folding chair.

I look at her and wait for her to deny any of Brook's bio, but she just says, "That's all true."

"I still don't understand why we can't meet in your penthouse instead of this dump," says Brook.

"Because I like this dump," says Carly. "The pink reminds me of a uterus ripe for action."

"You are one sick Brit," Brook says.

The brown-haired woman covers a laugh with her hand. Then she stands and walks up to me. I smell lavender and maybe sandalwood? "I'm Hannah, it's wonderful to meet you."

I hold out my hand, "Gemma. Wonderful to meet you too."

"Right. Hannah is a crunchy granola type, if you couldn't tell. She likes almond butter, weaving her own shoes, and connecting with the energy of Mother Earth. Nobody knows why the hell she can't get pregnant, so she spends gobs of money on weird crap like fertility crystals and magic fruit pills from the heart of the Amazon."

Hannah rolls her eyes and sits back in her chair. "They're legitimate supplements, Brook. And I happen to like wearing rose quartz and moonstone." Then she looks at the expression on my face and starts to laugh. "You should sit down," she says.

I walk to the circle and take a seat next to Hannah in one of the rusty folding chairs. Brook comes and sits across from me.

"Perfect," says Carly, I look at her and try not to picture her naked. Why did Brook have to mention those photos? Brook grins at me like she knows what I'm trying not to think of.

"Since we're all here, I'll call to order the weekly meeting of the Fertility Support Group," Carly says. "The first item on the agenda is welcoming our new member. It's good to have you, Gemma."

Brook unzips her bulky canvas briefcase. "No. The first item on the agenda is wine." She pulls out two bottles of screw cap wine and a sleeve of plastic cups. "I had a helluva week.

Hannah, I brought you organic pomegranate juice harvested on the light of the full moon or some crap like that. So stop looking at me all disapprovingly."

"Wow. Thanks, that's really nice of you," Hannah says.

Brook opens the drinks and starts to pour. She hands Carly some white wine and Hannah a glass of juice.

"White or red?" she asks me.

"Um...red?"

She shakes her head. "You're not on cycle right?"

"Not for three weeks."

"Red it is." She hands me a clear plastic glass full to the brim with fruity-smelling wine.

Brook holds up her glass. "Cheers, ladies. To old eggs, blocked tubes, and bum sperm. May bad wine, okay-ish company, and the pink uterus room lift our spirits."

"Cheers," Hannah says, and she knocks back her juice.

"Salut," Carly says.

I hold up my glass and take a small sip. Maybe...maybe this wasn't such a good idea. I thought I'd be coming to a meeting of like-minded people, a supportive group of friends, but this isn't that.

Like Ian says, tell me who you associate with and I'll tell you who you are. Or was that Confucius? Huh.

Regardless, maybe it's time to go. I set my wine glass on the empty chair next to me and stand. "It was nice meeting you all, but I think I'll be going. I, um, have somewhere to be." I smile at them.

Carly tsks. "Brook, shame, you scared her off. I told you after the last one to stop doing that."

Last one? Have others left after the first meeting too?

"Don't go," Hannah says. "Really. Please don't. You have great, positive energy. Your aura is a nice canary yellow—"

"Not helping, Hannah. She's freaked out by us," Brook says.

"That's not it," I say. "I just realized that I don't actually need a support group. I'll be done with this whole process in a month and that's that. Easy peasy. It's better if I don't waste your time, or wine." I'm rambling, as usual. I start walking toward the door.

Brook blows out a long breath. "Stay. Please."

I stop and look at her. Instead of the cynical expression that she's worn since I met her she has a different look on her face. Embarrassment, maybe?

"Well...I..." I pause in the middle of the room.

Carly clears her throat. "We aren't bad once you get to know us. The problem is, we've all been doing this for a long time. I'm on cycle number seven."

I stare at her and try to compute what that means. She's gone through seven IVF cycles? *Jeez.*

Brook holds up her hand. "Number four."

Hannah says, "I'm on two."

I don't know what to say. When I said that I'd be finished with IVF in a month, I meant it. I didn't think that it might take seven tries. Or more.

"It's nice to have friends going through it with you, whether you get pregnant on your first cycle or not. You should stay," Carly says.

"You should," Hannah says. "If you do, I'll bring you some of my husband's honey. He's a beekeeper. And Carly gives really nice presents. Last Christmas she gave us Cartier tennis bracelets. And Brook, well, she's not always this annoying, so there's that."

Brook snorts.

I look at them all, at the rusty folding chairs, at the uterus-pink room. Then I walk back to my chair and sit down. "Okay. Sure. I mean, every journey is made easier with someone to share the load."

Brook laughs again and rolls her eyes. "Glad you're staying, but honestly, what's with the quotes?"

∿

AN HOUR LATER THE WINE AND THE POMEGRANATE JUICE ARE gone and I'm glad that I stayed. I got a rundown of all the fertility acronyms I need to know—CB is a cycle buddy, DI is donor husband aka Josh, then there's others like 2WW or two-week wait, BD which is baby dance (aka sex), and gross ones like CM for cervical mucus, or EWCM for egg white cervical mucus. Hannah literally pulled a stapled document out of her bag with all the acronyms on it.

"So my PGT results are garbage. Only one embryo is normal, maybe," Brook says. She's been talking about her week. Which sounds like the week from hell. When she described her job as a public defender as "just like living in Dante's Inferno," I asked her why she did it. She just looked at me and said, "I'm the best shot they have. If I don't help them, who will?"

"What do you mean the embryo is normal, maybe?" I ask.

"PGT is a genetic test. All the embryos were no-gos except one, which was mosaic. Basically, in laymen's terms, that means 'maybe it's normal, maybe it's not.' Which as a lawyer, I find really offensive."

"I'm not doing PGT," says Hannah. She shrugs at me. "Call me old-fashioned."

"Or an Earth Mother," Brook says. She waves the thought aside. "Anyway. I'm stressed. Worried. And slammed at work." She looks at us all. "Damn, I want a cigarette. Ugh, I hate that I want a cigarette. I'm going to quit. Starting now."

"Try hypnotism, I heard that helps," Hannah says.

"Will you do the transfer?" Carly asks.

"I don't know, we might try another retrieval first," Brook

says. Then she blows out a long breath and rubs her hands through her bright copper hair. "You know, why can't my husband have had superman sperm? I told him all that biking would crush his nads and kill his sperm. But did he listen? No. And all those hours in the hot tub. It fried them. And who wears tighty-whities? They should call them the sperminators, cause that's what they do, they eliminate sperm. I swear, it's hopeless. If I had neon lights pointing to my eggs his little buggers would swim the other way. Enough about me, let's talk about you."

Everyone turns and looks at me.

"Me?" I ask in surprise.

"Sharing is caring," Brook says.

Carly crosses her legs and then says, "You don't have to if you don't want to."

I shake my head. "No. That's alright. I'm...I have stage four endo, tubal factor, and I'm single, so I'm using a donor." I look at the understanding expressions on the faces of the women around me and decide that I don't need to hold back, "I've been waiting years for Mr. Right to help me make a family, and on New Year's I decided Mr. Right isn't coming and I'm done waiting, I'm moving on. I want a baby, a family. So here I am." I hold out my hands, encompassing me, sitting in the basement of Clive's Comics at the fertility support group.

"I'm definitely bringing you honey. And a rose quartz pendant," Hannah says.

Brook rolls her eyes at Hannah, and Carly says, "Good for you. What sort of donor did you choose? Tall to match your height? Good job? What sort of information do they give you again?"

A light blush covers my cheeks as I think about Josh in "The Production Room."

"Well, um, I didn't use an anonymous donor. I asked my

brother's best friend." I watch as all their expressions shift from surprise to interest.

"Did you blackmail him?" asks Brook.

"What? No!" I say. "Why would you think that?"

Brook shrugs. "If you aren't blackmailing him then is he blackmailing you?"

"What?"

"Oh my gosh, Brook, seriously? He's obviously also her best friend or in love with her. Clearly," Hannah says.

"No." I shake my head. "Not really. We were never close."

"Huh," Hannah says.

Brook studies me with a frown.

Then Carly says, "He has a fertility fetish."

"Yes. That's it!" Brook says.

"What's a fertility fetish?" I ask.

Carly nibbles on her pink glossy lips and doesn't answer, so Brook says, "A fertility fetish is what you call those guys who are constantly donating sperm to the sperm banks. They get off on the idea of having, like, three hundred kids. Or those guys who have twenty kids by six different women. Or like that fertility doctor who switched his sperm for the husband's sperm in all his patients and had like a thousand kids."

"You're kidding—"

"That's a fertility fetish," she says.

"He doesn't have that," I say.

Brook holds out her hands as if to say *then what?*

"He's just a nice guy," I try to explain. "I've known him almost my whole life, he knows my family, and he's a nice guy. He just wanted to help." Something in my expression must give away the fact that there's something inside me that doesn't quite believe this explanation. Josh never did say why he'd changed his mind. Why did he?

"No man is *just* a nice guy," Carly says.

Brook nods in agreement. "After twenty years in the legal system, I can vouch for that."

Carly continues, "Male female relationships are transactional by nature. Men want sex, women want protection, or money, or love. I married my husband because I wanted loads of security, and he married me because I'm beautiful. It was a transaction. Both of us were mature enough to acknowledge that up front."

I stare at Carly. Sort of dumbstruck. "But then what happens if you're no longer beautiful, or if he loses all his money?"

She tilts her head gracefully. "That's what prenups are for."

Brook starts to laugh. "Being a model was wasted on you, Carly. You should've been a lawyer. You've got balls of steel."

I pick up my wine glass and try to take a drink, only to realize that it's empty.

Hannah smiles at me and scoots closer. "If it means anything, I don't agree with Carly. I'm really happy for you that you know such a good man. My husband is that way too. He doesn't have a selfish bone in him. He'd give a stranger the coat off his back. It's why I fell for him."

Brook lets out a long sigh.

Carly lifts her cup in a toast and drinks down the last of her wine.

"Next time we meet, you'll have to tell us if anything's changed," Brook says. "My money is on blackmail. Or, hmm, he wants something. You have a contract, right?"

I look at her in surprise, then remember she's a lawyer. "Right. Yes."

At least, tomorrow I'll have one.

"Good." Then Brook looks down at her watch. "Well, time's up. I've got a ton of work to do tonight." She stands abruptly.

I stand up too and pull on my coat and scarf. Hannah steps

close and sticks her arm through mine. "So, you'll come back next week, right?"

I give her a smile. "Yeah. I'll be back."

With Hannah's arm looped in mine and Carly and Brook behind us, we leave the bright pink uterus room in the dingy rat-and-cockroach-infested basement of Clive's Comics.

When we're back on the sidewalk, Brook shuts and locks the cellar door with a padlock key.

"Do you own Clive's Comics?" I ask in surprise.

Brook scoffs. "No way. Clive's my second-cousin, he's a real douche. But I gave him some free legal advice last year so he owes me. Thus, we get the pink palace for our meet-ups."

"It's a lovely place to meet," Carly says.

Brook shakes her head, "I'm waiting on the penthouse invite, Carly."

Carly smiles. "Night, ladies. Ta."

"That means thanks," whispers Hannah.

Then Carly pulls out of her purse a wig, a hat, and large sunglasses. I gasp. "You're the wig lady. From the waiting room."

Carly lifts an eyebrow. "And you're the bathroom girl."

I blush. Right...

"Bad wigs and ugly hats. The trials of the semi-famous," Brook says. "Goodnight everybody." She lights a cigarette and then starts to walk away.

"You're supposed to be quitting," Hannah calls.

"Tomorrow," Brook yells back. "Night."

"Bye," I call.

"G'night," Hannah says.

I take my time getting home. When I'm finally there, I change into my fuzzy flannel PJs, brush my teeth, wash my face of the subway and city grime and then climb into bed. After thirty minutes of tossing and turning, thinking about contracts and babies and fertility, I turn on my phone and type a search into the browser.

Then—

Brook was right.

Naked Carly is hot.

I quickly shut the browser and slam my phone down on the dresser. I can't believe I just looked up a nude photo of Carly.

Jeez.

I force myself to go to sleep. When I finally drift off, I dream of sending naked photos to Josh and sperm trapped in tighty-whities running away from my eggs.

14

"Life is full of surprises,
accept them for the
gift they are."

IT'S FRIDAY NIGHT AND I'M IN MY SISTER'S KITCHEN POPPING popcorn for the kids. It's my weekly babysitting night, where I get to spoil my nieces and nephew for four hours straight. Josh texted an hour ago to say he was running late. I've already played nine rounds of snakes and ladders, three games of Chinese checkers, and a half-hour game of hide and seek. By unanimous vote, we've decided to have homemade kettle corn while we watch one of those adorable talking dog movies.

The kitchen is at the back of the house, well-lit, and wallpapered in an amazing pattern of chickens and daisies. It was on the walls when Leah moved in and she thought it was so hilarious she swore she'd never take it down. Twelve years later, the kitchen is still plastered in clucking chickens. While the rest of the house is modern, the kitchen is all farmhouse.

I have to admit, I like it. The kids have even named some of the chickens. For instance, the one over the oven is called Sir Clucks-a-lot.

"Auntie Gemma," Sasha calls from the living room. "Josh is here."

I quickly look up from the stove, like I can see the front door, which I can't.

I hear a bunch of shrieking and tumbling and I shout, "Let him in."

I'm currently stuck at the burner shaking a steaming pot of melting sugar and popcorn kernels, so I can't get the door.

"Josh, yay," the twins, Mary and Maemie yell. "Come play Go Fish with us."

"No, play Chinese checkers with me." That's Sasha, she's in a Chinese checkers phase.

"But I want to play chess. No one ever wants to play chess." Poor Colin. He's right.

"Hey guys, where's Gemma?" I hear Josh ask, and then I hear the closing of the front door behind him.

I smile and picture the mass of kids surrounding Josh demanding that he play with them. They can be pretty overwhelming if you're not used to them.

"Hey. I'm in the kitchen," I call.

The kettle corn has started to pop in earnest, the kernels are jumping up against the lid, bright white and covered in glossy caramelized sugar. The scent of warm, browned sugar rises to me.

Josh steps into the kitchen and gives me an amused smile.

All day at work I kept having thoughts of Josh having a "fertility fetish" or some weird motive for agreeing to be my donor. I search his expression, but there's nothing different in the way he's looking at me. It's the same look he's been giving me for years. It's the same Josh. The same nonchalance and irreverence.

"Question," I say.

"What's up?" He leans against the entry and puts his hands in his pockets.

"Err. Well. Have you ever donated sperm before, do you have any children, and/or do you have a fetishized fantasy of producing hundreds of children with your sperm?"

For a second, he just looks at me, then he lets out a sharp, choking sound and I realize it's a horrified laugh.

Alright, so there's my answer. I knew Brook and Carly were full of it.

Josh finally gets himself under control. "Gemma, what the heck? What the heck?"

I shrug. Then, I think, *oh well, may as well get it all out of the way.* "Okay fine. One more question. Were you planning on blackmailing me anytime in the future?"

His chin tilts down and he gives me a *look*. Then he says in a low voice, "And what would I blackmail you about?"

My heart skips a beat and I give the popcorn pot a hard shake. "Well, hmm. Never mind."

I squirm under his direct stare and say, "So, hey. Nice to see you. Feel free to forget everything I just said." I keep shaking the pot full of corn. Then, to break the tension I say, "Thanks for not freaking out. Like they say, life is full of surprises, accept them for the gift they are. And hey, at least I didn't ask you if you burned ants with a magnifying glass as a kid."

He looks at me for a moment and then shakes his head. "So random, Gemma. So weird." He peers over the counter at the popping corn.

"Do I get some of that?" He nods at the pot. It's full now, the lid is starting to come off from the excess amount.

I sigh in relief. He's changing the topic. That's another point to add in his favor—he doesn't judge and he lets things go.

I give him a bright smile.

"Well, it depends."

I flip off the burner, open the lid and dump the corn into a big bowl. Little strings of sugar swing through the air and the smell of kettle corn fills the kitchen.

"On what?" he asks.

"On whether you're willing to watch ninety minutes of a talking dog movie with me and the kiddos."

He looks at the ceiling like he's seriously contemplating the question. "Talking dogs, kettle corn, talking dogs, kettle corn, huh." Then he looks back at me and says, straight-faced, "Deal."

At that, the twins rush into the kitchen and grab Josh's hands.

"Come on, we have to play Go Fish before the movie starts," Maemie says. She and Mary tug Josh back down the hall. He looks over his shoulder at me with a self-deprecating, laughing expression in his eyes. Then he shakes his head at me and chuckles and I know he's thinking of my questions.

I wave him off. Then I give a small smile and grab a large serving tray from the cupboard. I lay out the bowl of popcorn, napkins, juice boxes for the kids, and sparkling water for Josh and me. From the living room, I can hear the girls giggling and Colin explaining to Josh why his Go Fish strategy is bound to fail.

When I walk into the living room, I find everyone seated on the floor around a fierce game of Go Fish.

"You're getting trounced," I say.

Maemie has a long row of pairs, and Josh only has two matches.

"Do you have a whale?" asks Maemie.

I set down the tray on the coffee table and peek at Josh's hand. I watch as he plays, and I realize quickly that he's purposely throwing the game. He looks over at me and winks.

I let out a small, surprised huff. The game ends and everyone climbs onto the long, plush couch in front of the TV.

Somehow, it ends up that Colin and Maemie are on one side, then Josh and I next to each other, and Sasha and Mary are on my other side. It's so crowded with six people on the couch that Josh and I are squeezed tight. I'm practically on his lap. My thigh is plastered against his and the edge of my breast brushes against his arm. I can feel my heartbeat in my throat. My breast is sensitive and heavy. I take a quick look at him and then turn away.

He stares straight ahead at the movie, seemingly unaware of how close we're sitting, or the fact that our legs are pressed together and my breast is against his arm. He laughs at the movie, throws popcorn at the screen with the kids, and then apologizes and promises to clean it up. The entire movie he seems engrossed in the storyline, the popcorn and the kiddos. Me, on the other hand, I can't concentrate on anything except for the fact that after the kids are in bed and my sister and her husband Oliver are back, Josh and I will be going out, alone.

It's nearly ten o'clock when Josh and I finally leave Leah's. I thought we'd go to a quiet bar or restaurant, but Josh said he needed to swing by his dad's.

He unlocks the front door with his key and holds the door open for me.

I step into the entry. The lights are low, but I can hear the TV on in the living room.

The layout of the house is nearly identical to the house I

grew up in. The only thing that's different is Josh's dad hasn't updated the décor since the early nineties. Hunter green carpet, burgundy walls, track lighting and big, bulky furniture. It makes me sort of nostalgic for what my house looked like when I was a kid. My mom went on a decorating frenzy a few years ago and updated everything, so my childhood home is almost unrecognizable.

Josh walks toward the living room and I follow. His dad is sitting in a plush recliner, nodding off, with a tank of oxygen next to his chair. He looks a lot like Josh, just older and thinner, with a pair of wire-rimmed glasses.

"Hey Dad," Josh says.

His dad jerks fully awake then coughs into his hand. "Josh, you home?" Then he sees me. "Well I'll be," he says with a smile. "If it isn't little Gemma Jacobs. I haven't seen you since Josh's high school graduation."

"Hi, Mr. Lewenthal, I hope it's okay that I came by with Josh?" I try not to blush. Clearly Josh's dad doesn't know what happened at his son's graduation party.

"Sure it is. I was just watching some medical drama garbage and doing my sudoku."

"Did you get dinner yet?" asks Josh.

His dad looks up at the ceiling and frowns. "Huh, guess I forgot."

Josh starts to walk to the kitchen. "I'll get you something. Be right back, Gemma."

He disappears down the hallway. I stand at the entry to the living room and shift awkwardly from foot to foot. I wonder if Josh told his dad anything about us.

"You may as well sit down," he says. Then he covers his mouth and lets out a phlegmy cough. "Don't worry, it's not contagious."

"Oh, no. I wasn't worried." I move to the overstuffed couch next to him and sink into the cushion.

He tilts his wire-framed glasses and gives me a searching look. "So, Gemma. What are you up to these days? Your reprobate brother never talks about you."

I fold my hands and picture how this conversation could go... *"Well,"* I'd say, *"your son agreed to donate his sperm so I can have a baby. He had a few problems producing it, so I sent him sexy photos. In a few weeks, I'm going to get my eggs sucked out, and your son is going to have to donate a fresh sperm sample. He might need some help then too. I haven't ruled out sending more photos, but I'm not sure."*

I imagine nice, calm, Mr. Lewenthal choking on a cough and wheezing, *"You did what? He did what?"* Before whacking me over the head with his sudoku book or clubbing me with the TV remote.

I clear my throat and smile at him. Does he know? Has Josh told him?

"Well," I say, "I live in the city. And I work for Ian Fortune, the famous self-help guru. He's amazing. Really an amazing person."

In the kitchen I can hear the sizzle of Josh sautéing something on the stovetop, it smells like onions and butter.

"Ah, so that's what's what," Mr. Lewenthal says, and the skin around his eyes crinkles when he smiles. "How many dates has he taken you on?"

At first I think that he's asking about Josh and I'm about to deny everything when I realize that he's actually asking about Ian.

"I mean...we're not actually..."

Mr. Lewenthal starts to wheeze, then he pulls out a tissue and coughs into it. When he's put the tissue aside, he says, "Don't deny an old man the pleasure of young love. Josh is a hermit, I don't get anything out of him. You'll be my only amusement all year. Come on then."

I laugh and shake my head. Then I count up all the times I went out with Ian for dinner, or to get a drink before he left for LA. "Seven, no eight. But we also get coffee sometimes, just for a break from work."

Mr. Lewenthal sighs and leans back in his recliner. "So you and Ian Fortune are dating. Is he as suave as he looks on TV?"

I laugh, and when I look up I see Josh in the entry, holding a steaming plate of food and a glass of ice water. It's clear that he came in just as his dad asked the last question. And for some reason the look on his face makes me squirm on the couch and shift uncomfortably. Then he looks away from me and walks over to his dad.

"Onion and cheese omelet and toast," Josh says as he places the plate on the side table next to his dad.

"Thank you, son. Appreciate it." He turns to me, "I forget to eat. Josh here keeps me in line." Then he looks back to Josh and says, "Did you know that Gemma here is seeing Ian Fortune?"

For some reason, I hold my breath while I wait for Josh's response.

But he merely raises his eyebrows and then shrugs. "She didn't mention it."

"Didn't you go to college with Ian?" his dad asks.

Josh nods. "Sure did." His dad seems to be waiting for him to elaborate, but Josh doesn't say anything more.

"We're going to head downstairs. You alright for now?" Josh asks.

His dad nods. "Go on then. I'm fine."

I follow Josh through the house. He doesn't say anything as he leads me through the kitchen to the basement door. I'm waiting for him to turn around and growl at me, "Ian *Fortune? What the heck? Why don't you ask him for his sperm?*"

But he doesn't say anything at all. He flips on the light and we descend down the plush carpeting of the stairs to the basement.

When Josh turns on the overhead lights, I let out a surprised exhale. It's actually really, really nice. There's thick white carpet, a comfy-looking couch and chairs, a TV, a small kitchen, a drawing table strewn with sketches and scraps of paper with handwritten notes, and a desk with a computer and three large screens. Basically, it's a second home. There's even an open door where I can see a spacious bedroom and I'm presuming an en suite bath.

"When did you do this?" I ask.

"Ian Fortune?" he counters. He leans back against the couch and puts his thumbs in his pockets.

Okay. Fine.

I shrug and lean against the couch too. "He's asked me out for dinner and drinks a few times. I didn't think it was relevant."

"Relevant?"

"To this." I gesture between us. "We're not dating. We're not in a relationship. I'm not holding you back from dating or you know, shagging whoever you like."

For some reason I expect him to argue, but instead he shakes his head and gives me a smirk. "Shagging?"

I throw up my hands. "Boinking, whatever."

"I think you forgot that I'm in a drought. No shagging or boinking happening over here."

I roll my eyes and walk across the room to his sketch table. He has dozens of sheets of paper with pencil and ink sketches. He walks up and stands behind me as I take in his drawings.

"These are really good." I look at him in surprise. "I didn't know you could draw."

He lets out a chuckle and shakes his head. "Gee, thanks."

"Okay, that was stupid. I mean, I know you have a web

comic, but I didn't know you were actually good. How long have you been doing this?" I run my finger over the fine details and the ink lines of his drawings. There's so much emotion in them.

"Nearly my whole life." He looks over the sketches on the table. "My dad says I used to finger paint stories and I picked up a crayon and started drawing as soon as I was able."

"How didn't I know this about you?"

He gives me a funny look and asks, "Were you looking?"

Oh.

That's fair.

I haven't really paid too much attention to him over the years. Which is probably why I often compared him to a house plant that you don't notice but is always just there. I had an image of him and maybe my image was wrong.

I bite my lip and think, what else don't I know about him?

Amidst the sketches for his comic series, I notice a drawing that's different than the others. It's done in pencil, with a lot of shading. I realize suddenly that it's a portrait of his dad, he's resting in his recliner with an oxygen mask on. The detail in the drawing is remarkable, but there's something in the curve of the lines that makes me extraordinarily sad.

"He's really sick, isn't he?" I ask.

Josh looks toward the drawing I point at. I think he's surprised that it's there, like he didn't realize he'd left it out for anyone to see.

"Sorry, I didn't mean to suggest—"

"He's dying," Josh says.

I stare at him, stunned by the rawness I heard in his voice. We're standing less than two feet apart, and I ache to reach up and put my hand to his arm, comfort him. But then, he gives me his laugh-at-the-world smile, and says, "It's what you get when you smoke two packs a day for fifty years."

"I'm sorry."

Josh shrugs.

"When did you find out?"

He looks away from me, at some distant point across the room. "January fifth," he says. "Helluva day."

I think about how at first Josh said no to my donor request, and then, it seemed like out of the blue, he changed his mind. It was shortly after January fifth. And if that's the case, then none of this is right, he shouldn't be my donor because he's grieving for his dad.

"Josh. If this is why you agreed—"

"No."

"What?"

"It's not. It's not why. Forget about it."

When he looks back at me his jaw is tight and his eyebrows are drawn. It looks like he's trying to contain a storm of feeling.

"Then why?"

He's quiet for a moment and then he gives me a half-smile. "Funny thing. You've got a big family. But me, I've only got my dad. He's the one person alive that really knows me. That remembers me when I was two, and drawing on the walls, or when I was four, learning to ride a bike. He remembers when I first tied my shoes, and he read my first comics. You, you've got lots of people to remember that. But me, when my dad's gone, all of those memories are gone with him. It's just me. There's no one else. Just like that, I'm the only one to remember him. I'm the only one left alive that loved him. There's no one left to share that with. Just me. Alone."

I stare at Josh and try to take in the profound loneliness of the future he's describing. And I realize that even though there's been a hollow space in my heart, waiting for a child to love, I'll always have my family. Josh is right. When his dad's gone, he'll be alone.

"I'm sorry," I say again.

"Don't worry about it. Every ending is a new beginning." He gives me a flippant smile.

I shake my head. He's quoting Ian at me. "Josh…"

"Seriously. Don't worry. I can see my future and it's bright. I'll adopt a three-legged dog from a shelter and name him Tripod, then I'll donate loads of sperm to sperm banks around the country so I can have hundreds of children and essentially be immortal. In a few years, I'll go a little crazy, possibly cut off an ear like Van Gogh, and then I'll draw bad comics in my warehouse for the next fifty years. Eventually I'll die from eating too many of those delicious chocolate cherry liquor candies you can only get at Christmas-time. Trust me. Life'll be grand."

I try to hold back a smile but can't. "Your picture of the future is so appealing. Just wondering, by any chance, do I or our possible child have any role in this hallucination?"

"Sure. You brought me the cherry candies."

"I'm the agent of your imaginary death?" I ask in mock outrage.

"Then you become a multi-millionaire from my estate, which is worth soooo much money. Because everyone wants a piece of my original work."

She'll bring him cherry chocolate candies.

I shake my head and smile, but I can tell, this joking is for Josh, because right now, I think he can either laugh or cry, and to Josh, laughing is always the better option.

"Speaking of estates," he says, "I contacted a lawyer in Brooklyn. They helped draw up a standard contract for us, we can go over it, you can send it to your own lawyer. Whatever you need."

"Oh," I say, surprised at the change of topic. Except, the contract is why I'm here, isn't it? "Right."

Josh grabs a document from his computer desk and leads me to the couch. We spend the next hour and a half going through it. This time, we sit on opposite ends of the couch, no touching at all.

Which is good.

Excellent.

Because we're friends.

15

"Every day is an opportunity to make it your best."

I'M AT MY DESK, WORKING ON CONFIRMING ALL THE SPONSORS FOR the Live Your Best Life online conference, when I hear the elevator door open. It's just past lunch. Usually at this time the mail guy comes and delivers letters and packages. But, by the sudden silence, frantic clicking of keys on keyboards, and people shuffling papers and trying to look busy and important, I can guarantee that Ian is back.

I force myself to keep clicking my mouse and then type some random words into my open document. I won't turn around and look. Especially because Lavinia has her eagle-eye stare going on and she's looking between the elevator and me with great interest.

That's when I know for a fact that Ian is back.

Finally Ian is there in my peripheral vision. Wow, Los Angeles was good for him. He's a little tanner, his glossy black hair is tousled, and his tie is loose in a casual, I'm-too-sexy-for-my-suit kind of way. Everyone is pretending to be *extremely busy* and productive as he strides toward his office. I'm watching him from the corner of my eye while I type nonsense into my document. Right when he's about to pass my desk, he stops mid-step and tilts his head like he's just remembered something.

Lavinia narrows her eyes on me.

Then Ian swivels on his foot, turns toward me, and strolls to my desk. I can feel every single person in the office watching while pretending not to watch.

"Ah Gemma, I've been meaning to ask," Ian says.

I close my document, look up and give Ian a business-like smile. "Yes?"

He smirks at me. "Have you lined up the sponsors for the conference?"

I don't know if anyone else can see it, but the level of heat he's sending my way is off the charts. Or maybe that's just my imagination. But I swear he's peeling off my top with his eyes.

I nod and squirm in my seat. "Mhmm. Just finished," I say, and then I clear my throat because my voice came out high and squeaky.

"Bring the document to my office, will you?"

"Will do."

Then Ian seems to notice the rest of the people in the office. He gives the room a bright smile and says, "Hello, everyone. Every day is an opportunity to make it your best. Shall we?"

"Hi Ian," a number of staff call and then, "Yes." It's no secret, basically everyone that works here worships the ground Ian walks on.

I stand at the office printer waiting for the document of all the confirmed sponsors to print. Behind me I hear the sharp click of Lavinia's heels on the wood floor. She stops at the paper shredder next to the printer and jams a fistful of documents in it. The whir of the shredder fills the air.

She looks over at me, then says, "I wouldn't, if I were you."

"What?" I ask, "I emptied the shredder yesterday. It's fine."

She purses her lips, "I mean Mr. Fortune. I wouldn't get involved if I were you."

I stare at her, a bit shocked to be honest. She's never said anything remotely personal to me before.

"I'm not."

She snorts. "I've lived in New York long enough to smell when a salami sandwich is being made."

What? "Excuse me?"

She shoves the last of her paper into the shredder, then turns to me and frowns. The paper stops halfway down. "The shredder's full. You shouldn't use it so much."

I shake my head and then grab my document out of the printer tray.

"I don't use it. The shredder and I aren't involved."

I hurry across the open office space to Ian's door. I knock on the glass and listen until I hear a muffled, "Come in."

The glass is soundproof, and as soon as I close the door it's like I've entered another world. This is Ian's sanctuary. The office is about three times the size of my apartment and has sort of an eastern philosopher meets modern New Yorker vibe.

The sound of the indoor waterfall bubbles through the room and I look over to the koi pond to see a flash of orange and gold. Behind the pond is a wall of foliage with sweet-smelling flowers in bloom and a meditation rock garden.

Beyond that is Ian's desk, a large custom sculpted piece made from driftwood and blue resin. He has a sleek computer and an aerodynamic chair. He isn't at the water feature or his desk. I walk farther in. My thick heels let out a thump on the soft cork floors as I head toward the bar area. Finally I see Ian. He's against the wall of floor-to-ceiling windows that looks out over Midtown. The afternoon sun lights a halo around him as he squares himself up to putt a golf ball across his putting green.

The ball makes a sound as he hits it, and I watch as it speeds across the green and clatters into the cup. Ian looks up at me and grins.

"Hello." Ian sets his club against the window and then walks with loose-limbed grace to me. He stops next to the seating area by the bar.

"Hi. I brought your document." I hold it out to him.

He takes it, looks at it, then tosses it onto the low velvet divan. "I missed you."

I open my eyes wide. Okay. So that's the direction this is going.

"Did you? Because I was just a text or a phone call away. You know, there's this funny little thing called a telephone. Back in the 1800s there was this guy, Alexander Graham Bell, who invented it, it's a nifty device, you might try it sometime."

Ian smirks at me. "Is that so?"

I shrug. "Might be worth a shot."

He steps forward and puts his fingers under my chin. "Some say Alexander Graham Bell stole his ideas from Elisha Gray."

"Alright?" I say, my voice a little wobbly.

Ian's eyes grow hooded.

"History is full of stolen credit. Edison stole from Tesla. Zworykin stole from Farnsworth."

"Who? What?" I'm not really paying attention to what he's saying, because he's looking at my lips like he's going to kiss me, right here, right now.

"Success goes to those brave enough to ask for it. Come to dinner with me tonight." He takes his fingers from my chin and steps back.

I swallow and try to shake out of my Ian-induced stupor. He gives me a charming, I'm-sorry-for-not-phoning smile.

"So, you had fun in LA?" I ask.

"It would've been more fun with you."

A little bubble of pleasure rises at that and I give him a smile. Ian Fortune, the man I've dreamed of for years, wants *me*.

"Alright. What time?"

He winks. "Not soon enough."

IAN TAKES ME TO THE PREMIER SUSHI RESTAURANT IN THE CITY. It's been written up in all the magazines and is impossible to get a table at.

"Are you trying to butter me up?" I ask. "I already work for you, you know."

He pours more sake into my hand-painted pottery cup.

"Hmm, so you do," he says. "How's the planning coming for the conference?"

"Really well. Really good."

He uses his chopsticks to pick up another piece of sashimi and pop it in his mouth. I grab a bit of edamame and nibble at it. I already downed two beautifully designed rolls that were more art than food and I'm full.

"The schedule is in place. The speakers are lined up. The sponsors are in order. I've launched the pre-sale campaign and tickets are selling-"

Ian leans closer. "Come back to my place."

My breath catches in my throat and for a moment I can't think. The noise of the restaurant, the people around us, it all disappears. I know what Ian is asking, I'd have to be a moron not to. I look at his face, the expression in his eyes, and for some reason, my mind flashes to Josh and how he looked sitting next to me on the couch the other night—relaxed, happy, joking.

I hesitate long enough that the expression on Ian's face shifts and he says more self-consciously, "Too soon?"

I let out a sigh and the rest of the restaurant comes back into focus. "A little. I kind of have a lot going on right now."

He gestures to our waiter and I hunch my shoulders. Is he seriously going to ask for the bill after being rebuffed? My dream image of Ian Fortune has been permanently destroyed.

"Yes, sir?" the waiter asks.

Ian looks at me and raises an eyebrow. Then, "Could we see the dessert menu?"

I look at him in surprise, and then a smile spreads over my face. He's not a horrible douche, thank goodness. I can keep my years-long opinion that Ian Fortune is awesome.

I get the soba ice cream and Ian orders the sorbet. When it arrives I let the flavor coat my tongue. Even though I was full, I have a rule, "one is never too full for ice cream."

As I'm licking the last of the ice cream from my spoon, a glamorous blonde in a tight sliver dress comes up to the table. I assume she wants to speak to Ian, but instead she smiles at me and says in a crisp British accent, "Gemma, darling, is this the FF? You chose well."

It's Carly. Holy cow, I didn't even recognize her. I blush, thinking of the nudie photo I looked up.

"Carly. Hi. Hi." Then I realize by FF she probably means the fertility fetish. She looks between me and Ian and wags her eyebrows suggestively. Oh no.

"Um. No. Carly this is Ian Fortune, my boss, the world-renowned self-help guru."

Ian stands and holds out his hand for Carly to shake.

"Ian, this is Carly..." My mind blanks and all I can think of is "sexy nude model that I met in the pink uterus room."

"Erm. Carly is a former model and my friend."

"Enchanted," Ian says.

"A pleasure," Carly says. She holds her hand out in that delicate non-shake that looks like she wants someone to kiss the back of her palm.

Ian takes it and gives her a suave smile.

Carly winks at me and I can tell she's having a lot of fun and that everyone is going to hear about this at our next meet-up.

"Are you having dinner?" Ian asks.

"La. We're finished. I'm here with my husband." She waves across the restaurant toward a man in his mid-forties. I take a second to study Carly's kazillionaire. He has brown hair streaked with silver, he's wearing an expensive business suit and is glowering down at his phone. He'd be handsome if he didn't look so serious.

"That sounds nice," I say and look back at Carly.

She lifts one shoulder in an elegant shrug. "It's Tuesday. We always have sushi on Tuesday. It's our chef's day off." She wrinkles her nose. "Someday, I'm going to ask for a pastrami sandwich."

Across the restaurant her husband looks up from his phone. He searches the room and when he sees Carly his glower deepens.

"Ah, my husband calls," she says dryly. "Laters, darling."

"Bye," I say. For a moment I watch her elegantly glide across the room. She slides back into her seat and gives her husband a bland smile. He shakes his head and looks back down at his phone.

Ian sits back down at our table. "How do you know her? She looks familiar."

"Oh. Through a mutual acquaintance," I say, keeping it vague.

Ian looks back to me. "She's lovely. But I prefer the woman I'm with."

I raise my eyebrows.

"So, what's an FF?"

I cough into my hand and shake my head.

"Femme fatale? No, that couldn't be it." Ian studies me. "Family friend? Hmm? No? How about, fortunate friend?" He watches my face and zooms in on my embarrassed expression. "Definitely friend something."

I shake my head no and take a long swallow of ice water. When I set my glass down he's still watching me.

Then Ian changes the subject and says, "Tell me about this 'a lot going on right now.' What's keeping you from pursuing the pleasure of two souls meeting as one?"

I let out a small, choked laugh. "Is *that* what they call it these days?"

Ian leans toward me with a smile. "Among other things."

I take a moment to think about my answer. "Well, like I told you earlier, I'm going through IVF. I'm not really interested in a fling."

Ian shakes his head, considers me for a moment and then asks, "What makes you think this is a fling?"

We end up back at his place.

16

"Never be sorry for expressing your inner truth."

"KEEP YOUR PANTIES ON, WE DIDN'T HAVE SEX." I'M ON THE phone with my sister Leah. She called to say that she wouldn't need me to babysit tomorrow and then asked about life. Somehow, my date with Ian came up. Probably because I wanted to avoid talking about Josh and why he came over to babysit with me last week. If she thought it was important, she'd be on it like a bloodhound on the scent.

"Gemma, are you kidding? What are you thinking getting involved with that Ken doll? Wait, I take it back, a Ken doll is less plastic than Ian Fortune."

A taxi driver lays on his horn, a long, irritated blaring, as I cross the street in front of him. I send him a friendly wave and hop up on the curb on the other side of East Fourteenth Street.

"I'll have you know, Ian has never had plastic surgery. He comes by his good looks naturally."

Leah scoffs. "I'm talking about his insides. The man is as fake as a Nada, you know, those bags you can buy on the sidewalk that are supposedly Pradas? Or the Nolex, the sidewalk Rolex."

I weave through the busy rush hour crowd at a fast clip. "What's your problem with him, anyway? I've never understood it."

I slow my pace and sniff the air. Over the exhaust I smell something delicious. Something really delicious, like cinnamon and honey and butter. I look around at the food carts and all the first-floor businesses. Leather repair, thrift store, bodega, laundry, candy store, deli. Wait, under the letters Candy Store are the words *egg cream* and *fresh beignet*. My stomach growls.

"I don't have a problem with him, I just don't think he's good enough for my baby sister," Leah says.

Huh. Alright.

I push the door open to the candy store and am rewarded with the scent of fried dough and sugar. "Three dozen beignets and four chocolate egg creams," I tell the older man behind the counter.

"Where are you?" Leah asks.

"I don't know. Getting delicious food."

"Are you with Ian?"

"Why would I be with Ian?"

"Who knows? Why are you getting so much food? Hang on. Mary! Stop vacuuming your sister's hair. Maemie, put the Kool-Aid down...don't you spill it, don't you do it. So help me, Mary, pull the vacuum away."

"Thanks," I mouth as I'm handed a warm bag of beignets and a cardboard container full of drinks. I head back onto the street. I'm only a few blocks from Clive's Comics.

"Maybe I do need you to babysit," jokes Leah.

I chuckle. "You guys having fun?"

"Mhmm. Speaking of...what's this I hear about Josh coming by the other week?"

I wrinkle my nose. Leave it to Leah to ask about this.

"Eh. He's bored at his dad's place, I guess. He'll take whatever company he can get."

She makes a disbelieving noise. "I guess. I didn't think you guys were close—" She lets out a gasp, and then, "Mary are you vacuuming Maemie's Kool-Aid out of her glass? That is *not* a safe choice! Sorry, Gemma, I gotta go. I cannot wait until Oliver gets back from his business trip. Lord, give me patience."

I stifle a laugh. "Okay. Bye, give the kiddos kisses for me."

I let out a sigh of relief. Saved by the proverbial bell, aka the twins at the height of mischief making. I'll have to bring them an extra-special present next week.

Leah hangs up, and my phone earbuds start to play music again. But I've made it. I'm at the sidewalk cellar door to Clive's Comics.

The beignets and egg creams were a hit. The pink room is filled with the scent of fried sugar and my stomach is happy. I lean back in my metal folding chair and lick the sugar from my fingers.

"So, explain to me how this works," Brook asks. She scowls at me, but the effect is ruined by the dusting of sugar on the tip of her nose. "You're dating Ian Fortune, he says he wants a serious relationship, and he doesn't care that you're using another man's sperm to have a baby."

"Correct," I say. Then I take another sip of my delicious chocolate egg cream. Ian and I talked about it last night at his place. He said that he respects my modern sensibilities and my refreshing view on relationships. I have no idea why after so many years working for him Ian has finally noticed me, but I'm not going to question the intervention of fate.

"And your FF," Brook continues, "doesn't mind that you're dating Ian Fortune, sleeping with Ian Fortune—"

"I'm not sleeping with him—"

"And possibly having a long-term relationship with Ian Fortune. Explain that to me," Brook finishes.

"Easy," I say.

Carly and Hannah put down their beignets and turn to listen too.

"My *donor*," not FF—FF according to Carly means Fertility Fetishizer—"is, like I said, a good guy. You guys were full of it. He doesn't have a fetish, or hundreds of sperm donations floating around the country, and he isn't planning on blackmailing me—"

Carly raises her eyebrows and Hannah covers her mouth to smother a laugh.

"You asked him?" Brook asks. "You actually asked him if he has a fertility fetish?"

I wince in embarrassment. It wasn't one of my better moments.

Carly starts to laugh and Hannah joins in.

"Obviously you guys got to me. But never again." I shake my head. "I'm on to you now and I realize you're all totally full of it. My FF, my donor, is a great guy who is doing this as a friend. He's not upset about Ian, because he and I are friends. Neither of us has an opinion about the other's love life."

Brook shakes her head, and I watch the sugar on the tip of her nose. "Ian Fortune, he's that self-help guy right?"

"That's right," I say.

"He's sexy," Carly says.

Brook interrupts, "sorry to burst your bubble, sunshine, but the self-help ones are the craziest of them all. I've represented a few therapists and the things they did would keep you up for weeks."

"Don't tell us that crazy barrel story again," Hannah says. "You got that from a true crime show. I saw it too."

Brook scoffs. "Did you ever think that maybe the true crime episode was based on my case?"

Hannah gives the ceiling a beseeching glance, then looks at me. "If you want to date a life coach then you can date a life coach. I bet he has a really well-developed sixth chakra. And maybe he does tantra. Yeah...wow." She looks a little dazed at the thought.

"What's tantra?" Carly asks.

"Cosmic orgasms," Brook says.

I gesture at her to dust her nose off. She gives me a look and shakes her head. I dust my nose harder but she ignores me.

"Are you starting your IVF cycle soon?" Hannah asks, changing the topic.

I nod. "My period's due next week."

"Well, then it's our duty to get you ready for the rollercoaster," Brook says. "Sit down, strap in, and listen to the instructions."

"Are you doing fertility acupuncture?" Hannah asks.

I shake my head no.

"You should, it'll help thicken your lining."

Brook sighs and rolls her eyes.

Hannah grabs her quilted fabric purse and digs through it until she pulls out another stapled document.

"Here's my holistic protocol." She flips through the pages. "Acupuncture twice weekly. Herbal supplements, I can get you the names. Daily fertility meditation. Energy work. I've got my crystals. There are a few teas that are good. I bought grounding sheets for this time, I think living on the fifteenth floor is preventing me from connecting with the energy of the earth. Also, I've cut out dairy, sugar, and gluten, and am increasing intake of liver—"

"I thought it was herring?" asks Carly.

"No. Liver," Hannah frowns and flips through her sheet. "And coconut oil." She flips the pages to the end, "Oh. And pomegranate seeds. And this time, after the transfer, I'm going to give my husband a...you know what and I'll swallow. That's supposed to help too."

Carly coughs into her hand. Brook just shakes her head.

"Isn't that to induce labor?" I ask. I think I remember Leah telling me about that during her last pregnancy.

Brook snorts. "Yeah right. I call BS. That's a rumor made up by men to get desperate women who just want to go into labor to give them one last BJ before the baby comes. A woman at forty-plus weeks will try anything to induce labor."

"How do you know?" Hannah asks. "It could work."

Brook just gives her a hard look, but the effect is ruined by the sugar smeared on her nose.

"I'm still going to try it," Hannah says. "Unlike you, I'm interested in improving my chances by whatever means necessary. You won't be laughing at my herbs and crystals when this time next month I'm pregnant."

Brook sighs and brushes her copper bangs out of her eyes. "You're right. I'm a bitter, chain-smoking lawyer with a glass-completely-empty kind of perspective. Sorry."

Hannah shrugs and sets her purse down. "No worries. As soon as your husband starts taking maca, your worries will be over."

"I'll bet," Brook says.

Then Carly clears her throat. "I've had my transfer. I'm in my two-week wait."

"You have?" Hannah cries. "Do you feel pregnant?"

Carly lifts a shoulder in her elegant version of a shrug. "We had one embryo. A girl. We'll see."

"But do you feel pregnant? Are your breasts tingly? Do you have an increased sense of smell? Any nausea?" asks Hannah.

"It's been one day," Carly says. "Also, during each of the last six two-week waits, I've had every early pregnancy symptom possible and I've never been pregnant."

Everyone is quiet. Carly's mood is sober. I realize it must be a lot safer not to get your hopes up, especially after so many tries. "Let's hope she sticks," Carly says, and there's a thick, sad note in her voice. "My husband would like a baby girl to dote on."

I think about Carly's scowling, tense-looking husband, and I can't imagine him doting on anyone. She gives me a self-mocking smile, as if she knows what I'm thinking and she agrees.

"Baby dust to you," Hannah says.

"Thank you, darling."

"So, Gemma." Brook turns to me. "A few days after your period starts you're going to be put on some meds. Listen to me carefully."

I look at her. "Okay?"

Brook smiles. "You get to stab yourself daily with needles and inject some wonderful hormones."

"Right. FSH and hMG," I say. FSH stands for follicle stimulating hormone and hMG means human menopausal gonadotropin. Basically I'm going to be loading myself up with hormones to make my follicles grow so that I can get some good eggs.

"Mhmm. That's right. And they'll either make you crazy angry, angrier than you've ever been in your life—"

"Yeah. Brook stabbed one of her clients with a fork," says Hannah.

"I missed," Brook argues. "The fork got stuck in his chair, which he was cuffed to, so the fork was a good reminder not to be a chauvinistic ass."

Holy cow.

"And she pushed a man into the path of an oncoming bicycle to get a cab," Carly says.

I give her a shocked look.

Brook nods. "It's not pretty. Anyway, if the injections don't make you crazy angry, they'll make you insanely horny, so get your vibrator or your man ready."

I widen my eyes and look at Carly for confirmation.

She shakes her head. "Don't look at me. I haven't had sex in months. The most action my eggs get is in a petri dish."

"Sad, Carly, sad. All that money, all those good looks, yet no sex," Brook says.

"IVF has taken the passion out of it." Carly shrugs.

"I hear that. My husband doesn't even want to have sex anymore, he says it's too much pressure. Especially since he knows that he's basically shooting blanks. He'd rather get off in the privacy of the shower than come near me," Brook says.

Hannah raises her hand. "Sad guys. Really sad." Then, "I'm the horny one. I jump my husband at least three times a day. And if we're not supposed to do it, then I have to, you know, take care of it other ways."

"Wow." I can't say anything else. I'm imagining Josh saying it's "too much pressure" and sending him photos to help him along. I'm thinking of BJs after transfers to help fertilize. And I'm wondering what I'll do if I become insanely horny and need it three times a day.

"Or you may become a sobbing emotional wreck," Brook continues.

Carly nods. "That's me. I sobbed when I saw a hot dog commercial last week. Or that advert with the old couple." Her lips start to quiver and she wipes at her eyes.

"Case and point," Brook says. "No matter which way it goes, you're in for a ride. You ready?"

"Of course," I say, "of course I am."

Carly blows her nose into a tissue. "Sorry, it was a really sad advert."

"It's okay. Never be sorry for expressing your inner truth," I say, quoting Ian. Then for some reason I picture him as a Ken doll, being represented in court by an angry, fork-wielding Brook. I shake the image out of my head.

"Well, best of luck this week. We're here for you," Hannah says. "Let me know if you want to borrow any crystals."

"Okay. Thanks." I smile at them all.

When we're on the sidewalk, everyone says goodbye, and see you next week, and thanks for everything.

"Aww, screw off, all of you," Brook says.

Hannah elbows my arm. "Should we tell her about the sugar all over her nose?" she whispers.

"I tried," I say.

Hannah nods. "Sometimes we've got to learn from our own mistakes."

But then, Carly who has donned her wig and hat, turns to Brook and says, "Come here, you bitter old hag."

Carly pulls her into a hug, and when she does, she rubs Brook's nose against her dress.

Brook pulls away. "Ugh. Gross. Feelings." She looks at us and when she does I see that the sugar is gone. I glance at Carly. She's brushing the sugar from the shoulder of her dress. She winks at me. I smile back.

"Have a good night," I say.

"Bye."

"Screw off."

"Laters, darlings."

Once I get home, I lay on my futon, the hard metal support digging into my back, and I try to read a book about improving egg quality. But the words blend together. I wonder what Josh is doing. I wonder how his dad is. I wonder if he's ready for next week. I wonder if I'll get my hopes up only to have them let down.

17

"*Wow.*"

I DON'T KNOW HOW IT'S POSSIBLE, BUT I'M ANGRY, SOBBY, AND mega-horny all at the same time. It's like the days before my period times nine hundred thousand.

I've been injecting the FSH and hMG into my abdomen for seven days now, and I've had ultrasounds every two days to monitor the growth of my follicles. Today, after work, I'm heading in for another ultrasound and to start another medication, an antagonist, to prevent ovulation.

I told Brook, Hannah and Carly that I was ready, but wow, these hormones are something else.

I drum my fingers on my desk.

Lavinia looks up and glares. "Do you mind?"

Ugh, she's in a mood today.

I stop and shift in my seat. When I do, my zipper rubs

against my area *down there*, and I let out a choked-off moan. I cross my legs, but that only makes it worse. All day, every move I make sends a zip of need through me. I uncross my legs and let out another moan that I cover with a cough.

"Honestly, Gemma. Do you mind? I'm trying to complete the quarterly budget," Lavinia says tersely. "You've been coughing half the day."

I blush, then, "Sorry. I've got a tickle in my...throat." I clear my throat to emphasize the problem. Lavinia frowns at me and turns back to her computer monitor.

I shift and try to sink down in my seat so there's no friction or rubbing happening *down there*. Now I see why Hannah jumped her husband three times a day. Heck, I'd jump a stranger, or possibly a coat rack if it'd help me get off.

I look over at Ian's office. He's out for the day, doing a press event in Soho. I squirm in my seat and another zing zips through me.

My cell phone vibrates loudly and I dig it out of my purse. It's Josh.

"Hello," I say in a quiet voice.

Lavinia glares at me.

"Hey, Gemma. It's Josh. What're you up to?" He's voice sounds a little tinny, and I can hear a lot of street noise in the background.

"I'm at work," I whisper. "What's up?"

"I'm at my place in Williamsburg. I thought I'd call and see how it's going." The sound of his call gets clearer and his voice comes across all deep and rumbly. And I'll be darned if it doesn't hit me right *there*.

I let out a little squeak, then cough to cover it. I glance at Lavinia but she's ignoring me.

"It's going. It's fine." I press my lips together.

"Do you want to hang out tonight?" he asks, and the tenor of his voice vibrates through all the places down there.

"Just a sec," I say. I stand quickly, look around the office, then take quick, mincing steps toward the bathroom. Each step my thighs rub together and there's a little jolt of pleasure. When I get to the bathroom I shut the door and lock it. "You're in the city?" I ask him. I lean into the sink and look in the mirror. My cheeks are flushed and my eyes are horny.

"I'm in Brooklyn. Do you want to do something tonight? I figure the transfer's soon, we could hang out before—"

"I've got an ultrasound appointment today. Do you want to come?" I ask. Then I look at my reflection in surprise. "What are you doing?" I mouth to myself in the mirror. I just look back at myself, completely unapologetic.

Ridiculous. These hormones have made me insane.

Josh pauses, then, "Yeah. Okay." Another pause, then, "Hey, you sound kind of funny. You sure you're alright?"

I run the cold water and splash it over my face.

"It's been a day. Can you get here in like twenty minutes?"

"No problem. See you soon."

FIFTEEN MINUTES LATER I'M STANDING OUTSIDE MY OFFICE building waiting for Josh. I wave to him when I see him down the block, just past Zamir's metal coffee cart. It's the end of January, and still bitterly cold. Dirty gray snow is piled on the curbs and large salt crystals interspersed with slush coat the sidewalks. The exhaust from a city bus chugging by hangs in the dry cold air, then disappears on a rush of wind.

Today, Josh has on his winter coat, hat and gloves. His pace picks up when he sees me and he lifts his hand in hello.

I smile at that and pull my coat around me a little tighter.

He grins when he gets to me, "Playing hooky? It's only three o'clock. Or am I rubbing off on you? All hail freedom from the nine to five." I cross my legs and try to ignore the pulse of pleasure that thrums through me at the deep rumble of his voice.

"Hmm?" I ask, when I've got my reaction under control.

"Hooky?" he asks, and I take in his unshaven jaw and the messy hair sticking out from under his winter hat. Before, as in, less than a month ago, I would've taken his appearance as proof of his devil-may-care, generalized slackerness, but now I'm not so sure. Maybe his air of not caring, and finding life a joke, isn't how he feels at all, it's just an image he shows the world.

"What are you doing in the city?" I ask.

His eyes light up, "I was checking in on the construction at my place."

"It's coming along?"

He nods and puts his hands in his coat pocket. "Should be done soon. What about you? Why're you playing hooky? Not that I object."

If he only knew.

"Let me tell you about my day. You know the medications I have to take to stimulate my follicles?" I ask. Then I look back at the entry to my office. "Can we walk and talk?"

He nods and holds out his arm. I reach out and even through his thick coat and the sweater he has on underneath I can feel the muscles of his bicep. I stifle a soft moan.

Get a grip.

"They've made me...angry," I say.

He turns and raises an eyebrow in question. We start to walk down the block, past Zamir's delicious smelling cart (he's cooking an egg and cheese sandwich) and head toward Central Park.

"Angry? I doubt that," Josh laughs. And his laugh sends sparks of pleasure through my abdomen.

"I threatened a database techie today over the last lime sparkling water in the breakroom fridge," I admit.

"Well, I mean, that's fair. You do like lime."

I level Josh with a stare. "I told him that if he touched the water I would infect his computer with a virus so horrible that it would haunt his grandchildren. For your information, he's twenty-five and doesn't have any kids yet."

"What?" Josh starts to laugh. Then, "But you got the water, right?"

I smile then say with a shrug, "Of course I did."

"Good. Is that it? Because even on a normal day you do crazy things for lime."

I do not. But... "I told the office intern that if he kept omitting SEO from his blog posts, I'd curse him with the pain of ten thousand paper cuts."

Josh looks over at me and grins. "Ouch."

He isn't taking this seriously. Except, now that I'm telling him about it, neither can I. "The hormones are also making me cry. At work, I tried to put together a post with a kitten hanging onto a tree limb, and I cried in the bathroom for twenty minutes."

He snorts and then coughs to cover the sound. I jab him in his side with my elbow. He pretends to be hurt but then starts to laugh harder.

"Is that all it takes for you to play hooky? Paper cut threats and kitten videos?"

We stop at the crosswalk at the southern edge of Central Park. A row of horses and carriages lines the other side of the street. A horse stamps his feet and blows out a long breath. Steam rises from his nostrils. I look at the horses, the art installation at the corner of the park, and a vendor with a table selling books. I completely and totally avoid looking at Josh.

Because...

"There's something else?" he asks. I can feel him closely inspecting my face, but I don't look at him.

The entire walk north, there were little zaps of pleasure down there, every single time Josh spoke/laughed/breathed, I felt a zing. I thought getting out of the office might make my predicament better, but it's only gotten worse. Much worse.

The crosswalk light changes and the crowd of pedestrians flows around us, but I don't move.

"What else?" Josh asks.

I flush and start forward. Once we're across the street, I take a curving sidewalk into the park. I glance at Josh from the side of my eyes, he's not watching me anymore. Instead, he's making sure we don't slip on a patch of ice. I grip his arm more tightly and take smaller steps. My zipper rubs against me and I let out a small moan.

"There's a problem," I tell Josh.

"What?" he asks. "You can't do the transfer?" He looks over, and surprisingly he looks worried for me.

"No. That's not it. I'm..."

He stops and pulls me aside so that the people behind us can pass. I look at his face. It embarrasses me even more to see how concerned he seems.

I look farther into the park, at the upcoming bridge where a man plays an erhu under the glittering stone archway. The two-stringed fiddle echoes and sends out a sweet, longing melody.

Josh squeezes my arm and looks down at me. "Hey. It's okay. You can tell me. I won't laugh."

I let out a long sigh, then, "Okay. I'm...I'm...horny."

At first it seems like he doesn't understand. Then, suddenly, it's like a dam breaks.

Josh snorts, coughs, then stifles a laugh.

I shove at him. "You said you wouldn't laugh!"

He pushes his lips together and I can tell he's trying his best to hold back his laughter.

"It's not funny. Being horny isn't funny." I push away from him. His shoulders jerk with the effort of trying to restrain his laughter as he wipes at his eyes.

Unbelievable.

Finally, he gets himself under control. He puts on his "serious face" and says, "I'm sorry, did you say your problem is that you're...horny?"

I cross my arms and try to ignore the party going on in my pants.

"Josh Lewenthal. You promised you wouldn't laugh. And for your information, it's torture being this horny." I point across the sidewalk at one of the green benches that line the walkways of Central Park. "I'd dry hump that bench if I didn't think I'd get arrested. Heck, I'd rub myself off on a tree this very second if you'd make sure no one was watching."

For the first time in my life, Josh Lewenthal is speechless. He opens his mouth, but nothing comes out, and then he just stares at me. Totally shocked.

I let out a long sigh.

"I'm telling you. It's torture. I walk, I'm horny. I go pee, I'm horny. You speak, I'm horny."

"Not sure being jammed in there with peeing and walking is a compliment," Josh finally manages.

I scowl at him. "My appointment is in one hour. I do not want to go in there for my ultrasound *like this*." I gesture at my lower region.

Josh's eyes light with understanding.

Then he looks taken aback. "You need my help?"

I blush and shake my head. I don't know what I need. I'm

not thinking clearly. "I don't have a vibrator," I admit. "And I've never been able to...you know...take care of it on my own."

Josh looks around the park. Just ahead is the Swedish Cottage where they put on the marionette plays. Behind the cottage is a sweet little garden.

He grabs my hand, and I can tell by the look on his face he's taking charge.

"Come on." He pulls me forward.

"What? You're not planning on..." I clear my throat.

"Your phone vibrates," he says in a logical tone.

"Um, yes?"

"Well, I'll keep calling, so it vibrates continuously until you get...relief."

I stare at him, but he refuses to look back at me. I let out a long sigh. It's crazy, it's insane, it's...brilliant.

At the garden, we choose the most secluded space we can find, a little area behind a tree with a low rustic wooden bench. The day is so cold and gray that there aren't any people loitering or taking in the tourist sites.

We're alone.

Josh pulls me close.

"You all ready?" he asks.

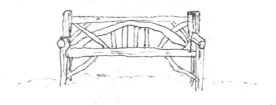

He finds a bench in a garden.

I give him a careful look. Then I pull my phone out of my purse and change its ring setting to vibrate. I can't believe I'm about to do this. But the horniness, it's driving me out of my mind. And I can't imagine facing the ultrasound probe at the doctor's office like this, there's just no way...

I stare straight ahead at the dark wood and arched windows of the Swedish Cottage as I slowly take my phone and press it firmly against my zipper.

"Ready," I whisper.

Josh wraps his arm around my shoulders and gives me a squeeze. A bird still here for the winter gives a short call from the tree over us and the wind rattles the branches. Other than that there's no sound, at least there isn't any sound until Josh presses the call button.

Oh.

Holy.

Cow.

The phone buzzes against me. I jerk back, but hold it in place. It pulses, vibrates, and my eyes nearly roll back in my head. I'm so sensitive, so overly sensitive, that the vibration feels like a thousand volts pulsating against me. The display of my phone lights up with the name Josh.

Holy. Freaking. Josh.

"Is it working?" he asks. I'm overwhelmed by sensations, but I think his voice is stiffer, tighter than usual. Deeper.

"Yeah, yup," I gasp out. "Working."

The ringing stops and the call goes to voicemail. "Again," I demand.

My skin tingles and everything in me aches.

Josh lets out a huff and presses call.

The vibration starts again and I arch my back and tilt into Josh's side. "Sweet, vibrating phone," I breathe.

The vibration licks across my entire body. I've never been so horny in my life. For the past few insanely long days I have walked around needing this. Exactly this.

The phone stops buzzing and I let out an involuntary cry of frustration.

"More."

The phone starts up again.

"Thank you," I whisper. My toes curl in my shoes and my breath starts coming in shorter bursts. There's a spring coiling tighter and tighter inside me and any moment it's about to burst into an orgasm of epic proportions.

I look over at Josh and I'm too far gone to be embarrassed. I half lay against him, my hips arch up, and my lips fall open to let out little moans of pleasure.

Josh's eyes are as dark as night and completely unreadable. In their reflection I can see myself, a black-haired wanton, getting off on a bench in Central Park.

"Hell. Gemma," Josh swears.

The phone stops buzzing. And I'm almost there, I'm so high, so close that I grab his thigh with my free hand and beg, "Please."

The buzzing starts again. Except, Josh didn't press call. His eyebrows crinkle and I look down.

It's my mom.

"Ack," I shriek.

My mom is calling!

Ack.

I yank my phone away and sit up. There's pain, there's actual pain from the interruption.

"Crap," I shout. I try to hang up on my mom, I paw at my phone and fumble with it. But you better believe instead of hanging up I hear my mom over the speaker.

"Gemma? Are you there? Gemma? Hello?"

I hold the phone out in front of me, complete and utter

horror floods through me replacing every other feeling.

I close my eyes and hold the phone away from me like it's radioactive. This *cannot* be happening.

"Gemma?"

I avoid looking at Josh. He sits stiff as a board on the bench next to me. His arm is heavy across my shoulders.

Slowly, ever so slowly, I pull the phone to my ear.

"Hey, Mom. Hi. I can't talk right now." My face heats with embarrassment and I can feel the sharp needles of a heated blush.

"Gemma. What in the world? Do you have a cold? Your voice is all scratchy. I was calling about Valentine's Day. I know you don't have a date, so I asked around and found—"

"Mom. I gotta go. Talk-to-you-later-bye."

I hang up and drop my phone like a hot potato onto the bench. It clatters then falls still.

I put my hands in my lap and stare straight ahead at the snow, the cottage, and the tree branches screening Josh and I from the view of anyone walking by.

After a good five minutes of raging embarrassment and repeated thoughts of *I can't believe, what was I thinking, holy cow, Josh, phone, what???!* I take a deep breath and turn to Josh.

He raises both his eyebrows and gives me a half-smile full of amusement and laughter.

"So. That happened," he says. Then, "How'd I do? Are my skills up to par? As good as you remember? Or have I upped my game?"

Oh my gosh. He's teasing me. He's unbelievable.

I hold back a sharp, hysterical laugh. "If you ever tell anyone—"

"Yeah, sure. But is the problem solved?"

I pause and take in how I'm feeling. Embarrassed, ridiculous, but...not horny. And not angry, and not sobby.

A huge smile spreads across my face.

Josh grins back and his shoulders shake with laughter.

"Unbelievable." I drop my head into the crook of his shoulder and smother my laughter in the warmth of his coat. It's soft and smells like soap, and ink, and...Josh. I hold on to him and close my eyes and wait for the ridiculousness of the moment to pass.

Finally, I come up again and I'm able to look him in the face without blushing.

"So, erm, my appointment is in thirty minutes. You still want to come? You don't have to, obviously."

He quirks an eyebrow, then stands, grabs my hands and pulls me to my feet. "Wouldn't miss it. Everything that could go wrong has already happened today, so we're in the clear for an easy go of it."

I groan. "Don't say that. Now you've jinxed it."

He just laughs.

18

*"You have to
pick your battles."*

HE JINXED IT.

"What do you mean you quadruple booked my appointment time?" I ask Joy, the scheduler at Dr. Ingraham's office. It's nearly six now, and I'm starving, the angries are back, and I nearly cried at a hemorrhoid advertisement in the grubby waiting room magazine.

Joy rolls her eyes and sighs. "Technically, I septuple booked, mmm, no, what's the word for fifteen? Fifteen tuples?"

Josh clears his throat. "It's quindecuple. You quindecuple booked her."

I give him a "what the heck" look, and he shrugs. "She asked."

"Right. I quinde-whatever booked you. Except, it's first come, first serve—"

"And we were here before you," the woman behind us snaps. She's in a shiny gold unitard, has amazing hair and is at least six foot two. "So sit your skinny little butt down, 'cause we were here first, and we'll get served first."

Skinny? I look down at my backside. I usually call myself curvy, or pleasantly proportioned. I've never gotten "skinny" as an adjective. Unfortunately, I think it's supposed to be an insult.

I ignore the woman, who is about as friendly as a wolverine, and turn back to Joy. "They weren't here first. They got here five minutes ago. We've been waiting for more than an hour, and two couples that came in after us have already come and gone."

"Hey, bony butt, me and my husband watched you walk in. Sit down, it's our turn." The woman in gold snaps her fingers at her husband. He's reading a car magazine, but when he hears her snapping he drops the magazine and stands.

"You ready to go back, baby?" he asks.

I look at Joy and hold up my hands. "Really? You're okay with this?"

She shrugs. "First come, first serve. You know, most practices book ultrasounds in the morning, but for some reason this *amazing* place books at night. Super fun times," she says sarcastically.

The nurse holding open the door to the back taps her foot. "Doctor's waiting," she calls.

"We could race," Josh says to me. "I bet we're faster."

This is ridiculous.

The woman in gold has gathered up her purse. Her husband is in workout clothes and has arms that are veiny and almost as big as my mom's annual Christmas ham. I'm not sure we could beat them.

Plus, I think the woman has the same reaction to the hormones as Brook. It's entirely possible she has a fork in her purse and she's waiting for an excuse to stab someone.

"Nah. Let them go, we'll go next. Besides, you have to pick your battles. Some just aren't worth fighting."

Josh and I sit back down, this time closer to the door to the back. I stare at the Georgia O'Keeffe painting and tap my foot. My stomach growls.

"Hungry?"

"No." Because if I ignore the hunger, maybe it'll go away.

My stomach growls again.

Josh snorts, then he digs through his pocket and pulls out a bar of chocolate. "Here. I saw it earlier today and thought of you."

I take the bar, it's dark chocolate with lime zest. My eyes widen and my mouth starts to water. How have I never heard of this? "Josh Lewenthal. You are my hero."

He chuckles and leans back in his seat. "That's what they all say."

I'd roll my eyes at him, but I'm too busy stuffing my face with the most delicious chocolate bar I've ever eaten. Between mouthfuls, I manage to say, "Who needs vibrating phones when you have lime-flavored chocolate?"

Josh chokes back a laugh as the door to the back opens and the nurse calls for the next patient in line.

DR. INGRAHAM HURRIES INTO THE ROOM AND STARTS THE ultrasound with no preamble. His round bald head is cherry red and a little sweaty, he looks harried, probably from the end-of-day ultrasound free-for-all.

By now, I know what to expect, and there aren't any surprises. As Dr. Ingraham studies my follicles I look over at Josh.

"How you doing?" Josh whispers.

I give him a grateful smile. "Good. You still feeling inadequate compared to you know what?" I nod in the ultrasound's direction.

He raises his eyebrows, then, "Nah. Now that I've got phones and chocolate in my arsenal I'm unbeatable."

I snort and shake my head. Then I look back at the ultrasound machine. I can see some blurred images on the monitor, but I can't really make out what I'm looking at. Dr. Ingraham clicks around and makes a few satisfied noises as he studies the image.

I press my feet into the stirrups, smooth down the paper gown and try not to shiver from the chill of the cold room air.

Finally, Dr. Ingraham clears his throat. "Well, good news, Gemma."

"Yes?" I perk up, then smile over at Josh.

Dr. Ingraham nods. "Very good news. Your ultrasound looks like a kid's Easter basket."

"Uh, what?" I ask, completely confused.

"So many eggs."

"Wow." Josh coughs into his hand and says, "Wow. That's egg-cellent, doc."

Dr. Ingraham chuckles. "Good man. I've always wanted to use that joke."

I look at Josh and mouth, "Are you kidding?"

He grins at me, completely unrepentant.

"How many eggs are there?" I ask.

Dr. Ingraham frowns. "Well, I'd count them, but I'd rather wait until they hatch."

Josh snorts and then covers it with a cough.

"Have you considered stand-up?" Josh asks.

Unbelievable.

"No. No. I find humor breaks the tension of medical procedures. Don't you agree?"

"Not really," I say, but then I feel sort of bad, because Dr. Ingraham looks like a sad French bulldog that I just beat with a rolled-up newspaper. "I mean, yeah, it totally does. Egg-ceptionally so."

I send Josh a pleading look, so he puts on his serious expression and turns to Dr. Ingraham. "Right. As much as we love humor, could you give us a little more info?"

Dr. Ingraham starts to shut down the ultrasound. He clears his throat and transforms back into his *serious medical persona.* "Well, Gemma, it looks like your follicles are growing nicely. At this stage, if left unchecked your follicles will ovulate, so we need to start the antagonist today. This medication blocks ovulation but also may slow down the growth of the follicles so you should increase your dose of the hMG to compensate for that. Alright?"

I nod. Then I sit up and swing my legs over the side of the exam table. Dr. Ingraham has finished the ultrasound, and I'm ready to get dressed and go get a real dinner. And possibly another lime chocolate bar.

~

I'm at Joy's desk in the reception area, waiting for my patient instruction print outs, when I hear a shriek of outrage. I turn around and see the tall women in the gold unitard.

"You...you..." Her face twists from shock to anger and back to shock. She holds up her cell phone. On the display there are a series of medical test results. "You gave me an STD!"

My mouth drops open. I glance over at Josh. He shakes his head and nods for me to back closer to Joy's desk.

"You turdy little rat, what does this say? What does my phone say? This says you dipped your prick somewhere nasty and gave me a disease. I'll kill you. I will kill you," she shrieks.

I'm really glad I didn't stand up to her before, because when she's mad, she's scary.

"I didn't, I didn't do it—" Her husband holds up his hands.

The lady yanks off a high heel and chucks it at him. He ducks and it hits the wall, punching a hole in the plaster.

"Oof, that hurts," Josh says.

The lady pulls off her other shoe and slings it at her husband. "You think you can reach into any old cookie jar?" The shoe flies through the air and hits her husband in the gut. He lets out a yelp and bends down.

"I didn't do it," he yells.

"Oh yeah? Yeah? Prove it," the woman snaps. She lifts her handbag, and I'm assuming she's about to thwack him with it.

"'Cause I don't have an STD," he shouts.

The woman stops. Her purse is suspended in midair.

"Well, that does prove it," Josh says.

I look over at him, and hiss, "Shhhhh."

Because before this moment, the couple hadn't noticed that we were in the waiting room with them. In fact, before this moment, I imagine they thought they were alone. It's just Josh and me at Joy's desk, and them.

But now, the tall lady and the ham-armed husband look over at us.

I squeak and shake my head. "Uh, ummm." Yeah, I've got nothing.

The husband takes us in, the unwilling audience.

"You've been with your boy toy again," he says.

Ms. Unitard scowls at him. "He's not a boy toy. He's a man."

She looks back at Josh, and darn it, if there had been *one* occasion in his entire life not to use the I'm-Josh-Lewenthal-and-I'm-a-suave-lady's-man smile, this would've been it.

But no.

He has to give her his devil-may-care smirk.

I sigh and slap my hand to my head.

The husband stiffens and the veins in his arms bulge. "Are you the boy toy?" he asks. Then, "Is this the boy toy?"

Oh jeez. If he were a bull, he'd be pawing at the ground.

Josh scoffs. "I'm not the boy toy."

"He's not the boy toy," I agree.

Gold unitard lady looks Josh up and down and obviously she likes what she sees (who doesn't?) because she says, "He *could* be the boy toy."

"Oh yeah?" the husband asks. Then, "You think you're the boy toy?"

What?

Josh laughs. The *idiot* laughs.

"Joy, call security," I hiss. Up to now, she's just been watching this unfold like it's the best episode of her favorite soap opera. I haven't seen her this interested in anything, ever.

"What? Why? This is awesome," she says. Then she rolls her eyes and picks up her phone.

"He's definitely a boy toy," Ms. Unitard says. "Yeah. He is. He's the boy toy. And he tried to steal our spot in line."

"What?" I squeak. "Are you kidding?"

"Whoa, whoa, whoa," Josh says. He holds up his hand. "I've never been a boy toy." Then he stops and I nearly slap my head again because he thinks for a second and then clarifies, "Actually, okay, I have been a boy toy. Quite a few times. But not with you. I'm not really into...gold. Okay? All good? Not the boy toy."

I stare at Josh, my mouth hangs open, because there are no words. None.

The unitard lady gasps, like she's been insulted. Then, thank goodness, the front door flings open and the building security guard runs in.

"What's going on here?" he demands.

But it's too late.

Because Mr. Ham-Arms has yanked the Georgia O'Keeffe painting off the wall. It's at least four foot by six foot of stretched canvas over a wood frame.

And from this angle, I can confirm the painting is of lady parts, definitely pink-uterus-room-colored lady parts.

"You think my wife's not worth your time? You think my wife's not beautiful? You don't think she's worth your boy toyness? Is that right? Huh, buddy?" The husband lifts the painting over his head and swings at Josh.

And I swear everything happens in slow motion.

Josh turns toward the husband. The painting descends like the hand of God about to smite all that boy toy wickedness. Josh looks up with a stunned expression on his face.

Then the center of the flower/female anatomy crashes over Josh's head. The canvas breaks, tears with a splitting sound, and the painting clatters to Josh's shoulders.

Holy. Crap.

Josh stands stock still. His head sticks out of the center of the "flower." He looks around the room with a stunned expression.

Then, the gold unitard lady stalks up to Josh and kicks him right where it counts.

I gasp and Josh falls to the floor.

He lets out a pained grunt.

"I'm done with you, boy toy," she snaps.

"Come on, baby," the husband says.

"Are you kidding me?" I cry. "That is *not okay*."

The couple runs toward the exit.

I look over at Josh, he's squatting on the ground, rocking back and forth, the Georgia O'Keeffe painting hanging around his shoulders.

He's not a boy toy.

And all of that hormonally charged anger that vanished when Josh "called" me in Central Park is back, full force. The unitard lady dares to kick my sperm donor? My Josh? My definitely-not-a-boy-toy Josh?

I run across the room and grab one of the woman's high heels. I chuck it after them as hard as I can. It flies through the air, hits the ground, and then spins across the floor after them. "What's wrong with you?" I shout. "Are you crazy?" I grab the other shoe and fling it at them. It clatters across the floor.

The security guard hurries after them. "Hey. Sir. Ma'am. Get back here!"

Yeah, good luck with that. They ignore him and move faster.

I jog forward and grab the shoe again, there's actually something immensely satisfying about throwing shoes. I chuck it after them. "He's *not* a boy toy! Not a boy toy. And next time, don't steal our spot in line. You hear me?"

I watch as the high heel hits the ground and slides after the couple.

As they reach the door, the woman turns to Josh, holds up her hand in a phone gesture and mouths, "call me."

Unbelievable.

"Not a boy toy," I shout.

The door slam shuts after them. The security guard is out the door a second later.

I turn back to Josh, my chest heaving and my face hot.

He's still kneeling on the ground, trying to get the painting off. He looks up at me, takes in my expression, then looks down at the blooming "flower" around his neck.

He lifts his eyebrows, then he says, "Do you think there's a metaphor here?"

I bite my lip and try not to laugh at how ridiculous he looks. I shake my head and say, "No, but forevermore, if I ever get chocolate or flowers, I'm going to think of you."

He grins. "Exactly what I was hoping for."

I walk over and help him tug the painting over his head. He stands up and together we hold it out in front of us. There's a circular head-shaped rip in the middle.

"You're going to have to pay for that," says Joy from behind her desk. She's peering over her partition at the damage.

I turn and scowl at her. "Are you kidding? The other guy swung it at him."

Joy shrugs. "Yeah. But his head broke it." She says this with utter seriousness.

I look back to Josh and I'm not surprised to see his eyes light up with humor. "In that case, I'm taking this baby home. I'll hang it above my bed. I'll call it Boy Toy and the Venus Fly Trap."

I let out a shocked laugh.

Then Josh pulls out his wallet and tosses cash on the counter.

We leave the office, the large painting held between us. As we walk down the sidewalk, avoiding the crowds, I say to Josh, "You really did jinx us."

He looks back at me and lifts an eyebrow. "Seriously, Gemma? Today's the most fun I've had in years."

He turns back forward and by silent agreement we keep walking toward my place. But all the while I stare at Josh's back and think *me too*.

Which scares me.

A lot.

19

"The contents of your heart shine through, and I see your beauty."

So, Josh and I are officially "friends." He confirmed it when he left the other night. He made sure I got to my place safe and sound and when I said thanks he said, "What are friends for?"

"Friends?" I'd asked, like the idiot I am.

He just grinned at me and said, "What else, Gem?"

I scowl at my computer screen and put the finishing touches on the latest marketing campaign. What else is right.

The quote on the screen blurs together until the words are all jumbled up. It's not yet eight in the morning, but I've already been at work for two hours since I need to leave early for my retrieval. I stopped all the medications and took my hCG nearly thirty-three hours ago for my 10:30 am retrieval, aka egg collection.

Or, as Josh dubbed it in honor of Dr. Ingraham, *the Easter egg hunt*.

I take a long sip of my decaf coffee and close my eyes. I'm not going to get any more work done, I may as well head out. Maybe Josh will be here early.

"You got coffee without me?"

I jump a little in my seat. Jeez. I'd thought the office was empty. I swivel my desk chair around.

"You scared me," I say.

Ian is only a few feet behind me. He's wearing a trendy suit and an open cashmere jacket dusted with melting snowflakes. "Did I?" he asks, then he gives me a smile full of simmering heat. "I was hoping you'd be here early."

His long, elegant fingers stroke the open length of his cashmere jacket as he stares at the low vee-neck of my dress shirt. I get warm at the look in his eyes and wonder if he's about to ask me into his office.

For some reason, the thought gives me a funny feeling in my stomach.

"Did you...want to talk about something?" I ask.

He raises an eyebrow. "I always like talking to you. Do I need an excuse?"

"Um, no?"

He chuckles and tosses his head so that the last drops of snow spray out of his hair. For years, I've idolized Ian and fantasized about dating him. For crying out loud, he's *Ian*. But now, when he's standing in front of me, looking like a male cover model, giving me a look that could ignite wet wood, all I can manage is "um...no?"

It has to be the hormones, they've been so crazy all over the place that I can't trust anything I think or feel anymore. Exhibit

A, for the last two nights I've had erotic dreams about Josh involving weird combinations of shoes, flowers, and cosmic orgasms. Exhibit B, I'm not over the moon that Ian Fortune is pursuing me. I mean, I should be over the moon.

He's a saint. He's a superstar. He's gorgeous. He's kind. He wants me.

Okay, that one is a little weird. I've worked for him for nearly seven years, so why is it that he's only noticed me now? Were my "juicy" breasts really that enticing?

"Why do you like me?" I ask.

But at the same time he says, "Will you go with me to the Hamptons for Valentine's weekend?"

I stare at him in shock. "The what?"

He smiles his bright white smile. "The Hamptons. I have a little cottage there and I thought you might like a romantic escape from the city."

Holy crap.

My stomach rolls and I grip the arm of my swivel chair.

"Did you just ask me to the Hamptons?"

"Yes." He nods.

"To stay with you?"

"Yes." He gives me a bemused smile.

"For Valentine's Day?"

"Again yes."

I stare at him, unable to think of an answer.

He lets out a low chuckle as he waits.

This isn't just fancy dinners and coffees and heavy petting back at his place, this is serious. This is the next level.

"But why?" I blurt out.

Ian slicks his thick hair back from his face and gives the low vee in my shirt another steamy look. "Because the contents of your heart shine through, and I see beauty."

Oh.

Ohhh.

He's not looking at my breasts, he's looking at my heart. That's actually really sweet. Then, I remember what a good guy Ian is, how he's been upfront about where he wants our relationship to head.

I think about Josh.

Josh.

My friend.

"What else, Gem?" he'd said. What else?

I don't know about what anyone else thinks, but it's pretty clear to me that Josh and I are meant to be friends. Maybe co-parents. But mostly friends.

Not more.

And that's okay.

Really.

Haven't I always said that I'm not interested in Josh Lewenthal? Hasn't that always been true?

I sigh.

Life's complicated.

"Well?" asks Ian. "What do you think?"

"Yes," I say. "I'd love to go."

IT'S NEARLY TIME FOR MY EGG RETRIEVAL. JOSH AND I ARE IN THE waiting room at Dr. Ingraham's office.

There's a large rectangular space on the wall with slightly darker paint where the Georgia O'Keeffe painting used to hang. I've been staring at the wall for the last ten minutes.

For some reason I'm horribly nervous. Like, feel-like-I'm-going-to-throw-up nervous.

Joy is making phone calls behind the desk, completely ignoring us and the other patients in the waiting room. The TV in the corner is playing a survival show marathon. I focus on the wall and try not to fidget.

Josh leans over and presses his shoulder to mine. He dips his head close and says, "You okay?"

I don't turn toward him, instead I keep staring at the wall. "I'll be alright."

He gives a slow nod and says in a quiet murmur, "Don't worry, Gem, I'm nervous too."

Finally I look away from the wall and glance at him. "Really?"

He leans forward in his chair. "Heck yeah. Think of the pressure. I've got to produce another sample in 'The Production Room,' and since you'll be conked out on anesthesia you won't be able to send me any kinky photos. What do I do if that visual of you getting off to your phone in the park just doesn't carry me through?"

I let out a surprised laugh and shove him away. "Pervert."

He smiles and his eyelids lower until they remind me of what he probably looks like when he's lying in bed, about to make love.

I shake my head. "I can't believe you."

"Yeah, but it's a valid concern. All you have to do is lie there, I actually have to perform."

I press my lips together to hold back a smile. I'm not nervous anymore. I don't know how he does it, but he's able to make everything easier.

He's still looking at me with a woeful, pity-me sort of expression, so I say, "Ahhh, the misery of man, your untold woe over the centuries. Even your stone age ancestor lamented his lot. Me, Kral, do all work, woman just lay there. No fair. Kral not happy."

He starts to grin, then laughs when I do my stone age voice impression.

"Who's Kral?" he asks.

"Your alter ego."

Josh snorts. "Really?"

I nod. "Mhmm."

"Well, Kral could use some inspiration for 'The Production Room.'"

I roll my eyes. "You've got your photo. You're not getting another."

Josh grins at me then asks, "Still nervous?"

"Not anymore." I lean into him and nudge him with my elbow. "Thank you."

"Anytime."

We're quiet for a moment and then I wonder about what he said. "Are you really going to have trouble?" I mean, the room was sterile and ugly, and it *is* a lot of pressure.

I study his face. He looks tired, the hollows under his eyes are darker than usual and it looks like he hasn't shaved in a few days. He sees my concern and smiles at me.

"Don't worry about it. I'm alright."

I'm not sure if he means he'll be alright in "The Production Room," or if he's alright in general.

"Is your dad okay?"

Josh nods, but he looks away from me and he doesn't say anything.

Oh.

I sigh and lean into him.

He pats my arm and then leaves his hand on my coat sleeve. He rubs his thumb up and down my arm. I look over at him, but I don't think he realizes he's doing it.

Finally I break the silence. "This waiting sucks."

Josh sits up straight then looks down at his watch. "They should call you back in a few."

"Are you sure you still want to do this?"

I know it's a weird time to ask this question, but this is just about the last time he can back out. Even though we've already signed the contract, the IVF consent forms, all the legal documentation, everything...still.

He looks over at me and I see that shadow of seriousness in his expression. "What do you think she'll be like?" he asks.

I look at him in surprise. "The baby?"

He nods.

I get a warm, happy feeling in my chest. "I don't know," I admit. Then, "For years, I've dreamed about having a family. A baby. But I never thought about what she'd be like, or what she'd do. It's more that I imagined the feeling. When I imagined her I didn't picture hair color, or personality, or likes and dislikes, instead I imagined the feeling of her. And it's like...hmm..."

I look at him to see if he's going to laugh, or make fun of me, but he's leaning toward me and his eyes look almost hungry. So, I continue, "When I was little, we used to spend Sunday afternoons in the park having family picnics."

"I remember."

I nod. I'm sure he does, he was invited to many of them.

"The thing I remember most about those picnics is the feeling. We were all there, sitting on our plaid blanket in the warm grass. Sometimes we'd crawl through the grass and hunt for four leaf clovers or we'd suck out the nectar from honeysuckle blossoms. Or sometimes we'd run barefoot through the grass and play tag. Me, Dylan and Leah would run, and wrestle and laugh. Sometimes we'd fight."

"Sometimes?"

I snort. "Yes, sometimes. But then, we'd always finish with my mom's fried chicken, and potato chips, and carrot sticks, and lime Jell-O. And then we'd all lay down in the grass. I'd be in my mom's arms or my dad's. And Leah would hold my hand

and Dylan would pull my hair. And then we'd watch the clouds, every single time, we'd watch the clouds and we'd tell each other what we saw. I'd always smile up at the sky and my heart would feel so big. And the feeling of that moment, the love, the belonging, the happiness, the warmth of the sun and the smell of the grass, the sound of Leah's laughter and my dad telling my mom he loved her, all that is wrapped up together."

I look over at him and he's watching me with an unreadable expression. I shrug, afraid I've shared too much. "Anyway, you asked what I thought she'd be like. I've always imagined she'll be like that feeling. Even when she's crying and colicky, or a teenager yelling at me that I'm parenting her wrong, or a young adult off on her own, I've always imagined, I'll love her as much as any human possibly could love another."

Josh is so quiet that I start to get uncomfortable. "Too much?" I ask him.

He shakes his head. "No, Gemma. Not too much. I'm glad I'm here."

Then, before we can say anything more, the door to the back opens and the nurse calls my name.

I WAKE UP IN THE RECOVERY AREA. DR. INGRAHAM SAID THE retrieval would only take fifteen minutes. He put me to sleep with an anesthesia drug and also gave me an amnesiac. He said I'd forget everything that happens for about thirty minutes after the drug was administered. That means I'd forget things even after I woke up.

I look at the clock hanging on the wall across from my bed. The numbers are a little fuzzy, but I manage to calculate that I still have about fifteen minutes of forgetfulness. I giggle. Then, I stop, because why am I giggling?

"Hey. You're awake."

I look over and blink until Josh comes into focus. I feel a little loopy and sort of fuzzy, like I'm still coming out of a really long, really deep sleep.

He's sitting in a chair next to me, his elbows propped on his knees. I blink again. But Josh stays a blur of messy hair, strong shoulders, and chiseled jaw.

Mmm Josh.

"Do you know how good looking you are?" I ask, which isn't actually what I meant to say at all. "You're like a fairytale princess."

"Uh..." He clears his throat and looks around the small curtained area. "Dr. Ingraham said you might need a few minutes before the amnesiac wears off."

"I'm fine. It's worn off," I say, feeling irritated. "Did he vacuum up all the Easter eggs?"

Josh rubs at his chin and gives me a look full of skepticism. "He said he got six."

Then I remember what Josh was supposed to be doing while I was under anesthetic. "Did you orgasm?"

He lifts his eyebrows, and when he goes fuzzy again a little part of my mind realizes that I'm still loopy from the amnesiac, that I probably won't remember any of this.

"We're all good," he finally says.

I smile at him and want to tell him thank you, but instead what comes out is, "I probably love you."

Josh stiffens and his face closes off. He looks away from me, up at the clock. His side profile is serious and almost...unhappy. There's nothing of the joking, relaxed, life's-a-lark Josh in him.

"What's wrong?" I ask.

Finally, he looks back at me, his expression upset. He gently runs his finger down the side of my face. "Gemma, let me know when it's not prob—"

"I never thought I could love a houseplant." I smile up at him. I used to think of him as a houseplant, always there but never noticed. I don't think of him like that anymore. "Houseplants are so nice."

She said, "I never thought I could love a houseplant."

He stops talking and stares at me, a stunned expression on his face. Then he takes what looks like an incredibly painful swallow.

I stare at the way the fluorescent light shines down on his skin. There are little sparks of light that catch and reflect off the strands of his dark hair. His eyelashes are long and darker than his hair, and for a second I'm fascinated by how long they are. Unfairly long.

He's taken his finger away from my face and I turn my head into the pillow. He's going in and out of focus again. He's wearing a T-shirt today with a character on it that looks familiar, I think it's from one of his drawings. Maybe it's one of his own characters. I smile at the slashes of color and look back up at Josh.

He's staring at the far wall and it almost looks like he's berating himself for something stupid he's done. Or did.

"What did you do?" I ask.

He shakes his head and then looks down at me. "What?"

I stare at him. And the way he looks at me makes my chest ache. Makes it hurt so much. I try to think back to the last thing we were talking about. It was just a few seconds, maybe minutes ago, something about houseplants? I try to grasp onto it, but it falls away from me like water running through open hands. I can't remember.

There's only flashes, like skewed reflections in a mirror of what was.

I lick my lips and try to blink myself back into reality. I push myself up onto my elbows and glance at the clock. It's been thirty minutes since the retrieval. I feel fine. I feel good.

Then, I remember, the retrieval.

"Did Dr. Ingraham say he got any eggs?"

Maybe that's why he looks so upset, maybe none of the eggs were good quality.

Josh frowns. "What?"

"Did he get any eggs?"

Josh gives me a careful look. "We already talked about this. Remember?"

I shake my head, and am rewarded with a bit of dizziness. "No. Um." I try to think back and just get strands and flashes of haziness. "Not really. Did it go okay?"

"You don't remember?" he asks, he gives me a searching look.

I frown at him, mostly because it's really frustrating to not be able to grasp ahold of the conversation we just had. I wrinkle my brow and try really hard. "Maybe...we talked about princesses? And houseplants?" Then I shake my head. "No. That's too weird."

Josh closes his eyes for a moment, and when he opens them all the seriousness is gone, and that spark of amusement is back. But this time, that amusement makes me feel sad.

"Don't laugh," I say.

He smiles and holds out his hands. "Maybe I'm laughing at myself."

Oh.

"We're you able to do your thing? In 'The Production Room'?"

He gives me a superior, full-of-himself look. "Of course. Did you doubt Kral for even a second?"

I give a short laugh. "And I had eggs?"

He nods. "Six."

I let out a long, relieved sigh. I reach over and take his hand, link my fingers through his.

"Thank you," I whisper, my voice thick with tears, and worry, and hope. "Thank you for being here. For being my friend."

He doesn't say anything, just nods, and stays still, his hand wrapped in mine.

20

"The surest way to be seen as beautiful is to make someone else laugh."

IT'S THURSDAY, AND INSTEAD OF MEETING AT CLIVE'S COMICS, Brook called to tell me to meet the group at an address in Tribeca.

"Wear a dress, something hot. Not your usual ugly sweater sack thingy. Carly is hosting," she said.

I frowned and looked down at the caterpillar green sweater I was wearing. "What's that supposed to mean?"

I was asking about the ugly sweater comment but Brook said, "It *means* Carly's hosting. At her place. It'll be like an episode of *Lifestyles of the Rich and Famous* times ten thousand. Trust me. Wear a dress. Oh, and she said to bring a date."

"What? Why?"

But then Brook was sniping at someone on the other end of the line about mandatory minimums and hard-ass judges and then she said, "I'm due in court. See you at seven."

I was still at work when she called, so I sent Ian an email asking if he was up for going out tonight. *Sorry, babe,* he wrote back, *I'm in Philly today.*

How hadn't I known that he was out of town?

"Did you know Ian was in Philly today?" I asked Lavinia.

She just gave me a flat look and said, "Do I look like a calendar?"

Back at my place, I'm in my bra and underwear rifling through a pile of clothes.

"Green sweater. Maroon sweater. Gray sweater." I toss clothes from the floor onto my bed. "Sweater, cardigan, shawl, sweater." Okay, maybe Brook has a point. When I get to the bottom of the pile I see a flash of bright orange.

"Pumpkin dress," I say. I pick it up and hold it out in front of me. It's still as tiny and orange as ever. But my mom did have it dry-cleaned so at least it isn't dirty.

"Pumpkin dress or 'ugly sweater sack thingy.' Pumpkin dress or…" I sigh and pull the dress over my head. One of these days I'm going to get a slew of new dresses and they'll be perfect for all the ritzy restaurants I go to with Ian and for all the nights I spend at Carly's.

The door buzzer to my apartment goes off. I squeak and pull the dress down my thighs. I run to the door intercom and press the button.

"Yes?"

I don't know who it could be. The only time my buzzer rings is when I'm expecting a delivery of mandarin chicken and fried rice or a few (okay, a dozen) cookies from the bakery down the block.

The intercom crackles.

"Gemma? It's Josh."

I hit the button. "It's unlocked."

I hear the door to the street bang shut and then Josh takes the steps two at a time. I pull open the door. He stops halfway down the hall when he sees me. My hair is a staticky mess, I'm barefoot, and the dress is doing that ride up the butt ride down the boobs thing.

A slow grin spreads over his face.

"Whatcha doing?" he asks.

I humph and yank at the skirt. Then I turn around and head back to search for a pair of heels. I call over my shoulder, "I'm going to a party for the rich and famous. What're you doing?"

He lets himself in and shuts the door behind him. "I was at my dad's. Your mom stopped by and asked me to bring you this lime Jell-O mold on my way through the city. She thought you looked stressed last time you were home."

I turn back to him and finally notice that he's holding a crystal bowl full of delicious looking cloudy lime Jell-O and suspended fruit bits. My mouth starts to water at the sight of it.

"You are the best thing that's happened to me all day."

Josh grins. "Why thank you."

"I'm talking to the Jell-O."

He laughs, "I know." Then, "What rich and famous?"

I slip on a pair of three-inch black heels then stalk over to him and peer into the bowl. There are carrots in there and tiny cubes of apple. I peel back the plastic wrap and the scent of nose-tickling lime rises up to me.

"Are you going to have any of this?" I ask him.

He shakes his head no. So I take that as permission to dip my fingers in and scoop out a jiggly glob. Then I stick it in my mouth before it can fall off. I roll my eyes in happiness at the tart flavor and the crunch of the carrot and apple.

When I look back at Josh he's laughing at me.

"What? You know this about me," I say. I take the bowl from him and walk across my apartment to my tiny fridge. I throw out a container of three-day-old fried rice to make room for the bowl. "Thank you for bringing it," I call over my shoulder.

"Sure. No problem." He looks around my apartment from the mess of clothes on my bed to the pile of fertility books to the quote on my wall. Then he rolls his shoulders and says, "Well, I should probably head out. Have fun tonight."

He turns to go and then I remember that Brook told me to bring a date.

"Wait," I call after him.

He turns, an eyebrow raised.

"Are you busy tonight?"

THE TRIBECA ADDRESS IS A TOWERING GLASS BUILDING THAT glows like a blue roadside flare lit up at night. It's an office building, not an apartment building or a townhome like I was expecting. Inside, the lobby is cold white marble and mirrors, and devoid of any furnishings except the sleek guard desk and a bank of mirrored elevators. The sound of my heels clicks on the marble and Josh's shoes scuff softly on the stone.

The guard stares at us from the desk, and I decide he definitely isn't the warm, friendly type.

"You sure this is the right place?" Josh murmurs to me.

I glance down at my phone and look at Brook's text. The address is the same. "I think so."

Josh smiles down at my phone and I flush at the memory I see on his face. He's thinking of the park bench and the vibrating phone calls.

Geesh.

I clear my throat when we reach the guard desk and tell him my name. He runs his finger down a list attached to a clipboard, then asks for our IDs. We hand them over and the guard scans them into his computer.

Josh puts his thumbs in his pockets and stares at the thirty-foot-tall glass windows and the handblown glass chandelier. For a second I think he's going to start whistling or calling "helloooo" to see if the empty lobby echoes. But then the guard hands us back our IDs. He takes our coats, puts them in a closet behind his desk, and hands us a coat check ticket.

"This way," he says.

Josh raises his eyebrows at me and I shrug. The guard walks purposefully toward the back of the lobby, around the elevators, and then escorts us to a marble stairway leading down.

"Take them to the bottom," he says gruffly. Then he turns back to his desk.

"Thank you," I call after him.

So, I guess this is Carly's place, or her husband's office building, or...something. When I realize we're headed to another basement I hold back a smile. Brook sure is going to be disappointed. This definitely isn't the penthouse she's been longing for.

"Thanks for coming," I tell Josh. "I don't really know what to expect. My friend just said to wear a dress."

He looks down at his scuffed jeans, his old T-shirt, and his much-loved sneakers, then he glances back at me, a whole lot of amusement on his face. "So, this is a fancy dress-up kind of party?"

He rubs his hands through his messy hair and I laugh at his self-mocking expression.

"Don't worry about it, it's just a few of my friends from the fertility group." How dressy can it be, honestly?

I grab the cold brass railing, and my heels click on the marble stairs as Josh and I walk down the steps. The walls are plaster and there's a beautiful glass mosaic on the ceiling with tiles the color of lapis lazuli, and light blue and inky night blue all backlit with gold shimmer. As I study the ceiling, I realize it's not just a pretty abstract picture. "Is it just me or is this mosaic the River Styx?"

Josh points to a cloaked ferryman in his boat in the corner of the mosaic. "Apparently, we're descending into the underworld," he jokes.

"Huh."

I wonder if Carly's husband owns this building and if he commissioned this piece. Is she the beautiful Persephone, stolen to the underworld for the pleasure of her grumpy, scowling Hades? I hope not. Persephone never seemed happy. Come to think of it, I doubt Hades was very happy either.

Music drifts up the stairs. It's a low bass beat that echoes around us. When we reach the bottom, the room opens up before us. I have to consciously keep my mouth closed. This is one of those moments where I'd really like to let my mouth fall open and just stare.

Josh lets out a low whistle.

I take it back, Brook is probably ecstatic. Or at least as happy as Brook gets. She wasn't kidding when she said it'd be like an episode of *Lifestyles of the Rich and Famous*. I stare at the over-the-top, opulent space.

"Who invited you to this shin dig again?" Josh asks.

I smile at the way Josh says "shin dig," all long and enunciated, like he means "party thrown by the Maharaj of Sultanville" in some bizarre-o alternate reality.

"My friend Carly, from the fertility group," I mumble, and then I seriously consider grabbing Josh's arm and hauling him back up the stairs and out the door.

The room reminds me of the center of Grand Central Station. The ceiling is domed and there's a beautiful mural of the constellations painted on the ceiling. There are towering white columns extending from the tall ceiling to the marble floor. The space is cavernous, with enough room to hold at least two hundred people.

It's decorated with swaths of sheer purple fabric, ottomans and pillows on the floor, and buffet tables full of sculpted foods, precarious-looking dessert towers, and a full service bar. Positioned among the guests are a dozen gorgeous, nearly naked models covered in glittering gold paint posing as living statues. I take another scan of the room and see a trio of contortionists twisting into an impossible shape in front of a cupcake table.

There are at least seventy-five, maybe a hundred guests. The men are wearing tuxes and tailored suits and the women are wearing dresses that I've seen in the windows of Madison Avenue. I look down at my pumpkin dress.

"You look beautiful," Josh says.

I give him a side-eye glance. "I wasn't worried."

"Let's find your friend." He holds out his arm and I take it. We move into the sea of people. I wonder why in the world Carly invited me to this party. In fact, I don't even know what it's for. Clearly, it has nothing to do with fertility.

The music grows louder and I notice a DJ set up in the corner of the room. I scan the faces of the people but can't find Carly, Brook or Hannah. It's sort of hard to look, though, because I'm trying to avoid looking at the paint-covered mostly nude models. It's not that I'm a prude, but their nipples are bare and painted gold, and they look cold, and they aren't allowed to move and rub them warm or anything.

A man in a black tux grabs Josh's arm. "Excuse me. Get me another scotch?"

"What?" Josh asks.

"I'd like another scotch. The Laphroaig ten year." He holds a twenty-dollar bill out. Josh stares at the money.

"Hurry up," the man says.

Are you serious? I have the urge to kick the guy. "He's not—"

Before I can say, he's not a waiter, Josh smiles at the guy and takes the cash. "No problem. Laphroaig?"

The man nods. "The ten year."

"What are you doing?" I hiss at Josh. He puts the cash in his pocket and pulls me away.

"Getting him a drink."

He pulls me toward the bar.

"Are you kidding?" I ask.

This is ridiculous.

Josh shrugs. "Why not? I'm thirsty. You're probably thirsty. That guy's thirsty." He jabs his thumb in the general vicinity of the man in the tux.

At the bar Josh orders a soda, a sparkling water with lime, and a Laphroaig. I can't help but smile because the lime is a nice thought.

We wander back toward the scotch drinker and I sip my water. When we find him, Josh hands the guy his drink.

"Here you go, buddy," Josh says with a grin.

The guy grabs the drink, but otherwise ignores him.

"Why do you let people do that? You could've just told him you aren't a waiter," I say. "I mean, you don't even look like one. The caterers are in suits, you're in jeans. It's ridiculous."

Josh raises an eyebrow. "Who's having more fun right now?" he asks. "Me or that guy?" He points from himself to the guy in the tux.

He said, "Who's having more fun?"

Josh's eyes twinkle, and I can tell he's finding this entire experience to be one of the more ridiculous things he's ever done. Meanwhile, the guy in the tux is trying to look bored and impress the people he's with all at the same time.

"Don't you ever take anything seriously?" I ask. But as soon as I say it, I realize that it was a stupid thing to ask. He takes a lot of things seriously.

"Not if I don't have to," Josh says.

I take a drink of my lime water to hide my frown. The tart fruit flavor bites at my tongue. I look over at him and note the laughing pleasure on his face as he takes in the opulent circus-like atmosphere of the party. I don't know any of the people, but I imagine we're surrounded by a lot of the movers and shakers of the city. Ian would love this party. I imagine he would've showed up in a tailored suit or a tux. He would never have been mistaken for a waiter. In fact, he'd be more like the tux guy, surrounded by a group of people, handing out quotes like gold alms to the poor.

I feel sort of deflated at the thought.

"I'll grab you another water," Josh says, interrupting my thoughts.

He takes my glass. Apparently, I drained it without noticing.

"Be right back."

I watch him go. He strides through the glittering crowd, completely at ease in his jeans and T-shirt. He nods at people and says hello in such a confident manner that people stare after him, wondering, I'm sure, who he is and if he's important.

Nope.

He's just Josh Lewenthal.

I let out a long sigh. We should leave. This is weird.

"Is that Josh Lewenthal?"

I turn toward the shocked voice. It's Brook. I stare at her for a second. One, because she's in a glamorous sequin dress, makeup, and her hair is in a high, elegant twist and two, because, how does she know Josh?

"Um, yes?"

"Josh Lewenthal? *The* Josh Lewenthal?" She drops her chin and emphasizes *the*.

And then I get it. Josh got around. A lot. Especially back in high school and college and, well, however long after. Brook is probably one of his former flames. Which...ewwww.

"Yeah. That's him," I say tersely. I don't really want to talk about him with her.

"He's your date?" she asks, and she has this calculating, lawyer-type look on her face, like she's running through arguments and counterarguments.

I shrug. I take the fifth.

Then she looks at my outfit and cringes. I could be offended, but I have the same reaction every time I look at myself in this dress too.

"You told me to wear a dress," I say.

"A dress, Gemma. Not a construction cone."

I choke on a laugh, and then, I do laugh, because I'm glad Brook is here, and I'm glad I'm not the only one that hates this dress.

"So, what is this party?" I ask. "I wasn't expecting...this."

Brook wags her eyebrows at me and gives a conspiratorial smile. "It's Carly's husband's annual investors ball. Basically, it's a bunch of Class-A jerkholes with too much money, masturbating to their own awesomeness and then cleaning up the jizz with hundred-dollar bills."

I stare at Brook, stunned but not stunned by her crassness.

She shrugs. "Long day in court. My filter's gone. Anyway, Carly wanted to skip this party for our weekly meeting, but apparently her husband wouldn't let her, so she invited us here instead. She's over there."

Brook points and I follow her finger. I'm surprised I missed Carly before. She's standing on an elevated platform with her husband and it looks like they're holding court. She's in a gorgeous sparkling blue princess gown, with a tight bodice and a skirt that looks like it's studded with a thousand diamonds. Her husband is holding her hand, but he's stiff and he doesn't look at her. You'd think that if your wife was as beautiful as Carly you'd stare at her all the time, but I guess he's immune.

"Yes. Those are real diamonds on Carly's skirt," Brook says. "I asked, because I have no class."

I hide my grin.

"Anyway," continues Brook. She points around the room. "I'll give the scoop. Recognize that guy over there? He does the reality show circuit, semi-semi-famous. Avoid him, he's a flasher, in and out of court all the time. That lady over there, she's on her sixth husband, they keep dying and she keeps getting richer. The latest is still in probate, it'll take years in court, some nasty battle. That couple, they're related to some royal family in—"

She goes on about more of the guests and the crazy things they've been involved in.

I look through the crowd for Josh. He's still standing in line, waiting for more drinks. He must feel my gaze, because he turns back to me, and when he sees me looking he gives a little wave and a smile as if to ask "you okay?" I nod and wave back.

"My husband's over there," Brook says.

I look to where she's pointing.

"Yeah. The grizzled cop in the suit. Nice, right?" I'm surprised to see she has a sappy look on her face. Brook loves her husband, like, really, really loves her husband.

"He looks nice," I say.

Brook snorts. "Yeah. I don't do nice guys, my husband is a hard-ass." She grins at me. "You see the guy he's talking to?"

The man next to her husband is tall, tanned and outdoorsy looking. He's wearing a linen suit and has a beard. "That's Hannah's husband. He's currently telling my man how icing his testicles three times a day for six months straight will send his sperm count through the roof."

"Really?" I look at the two men. Now that Brook mentions it, her husband does look like he'd rather be chewing on a lead pipe than having his current conversation.

"Really. I left when my husband growled something about icing his balls when hell froze over. He's pissed. I guarantee you that tonight we'll be having a fight. Then hopefully the cuffs will come out and I'll finally get some hot sex."

I look between her and her husband, then back to her again. "Uhhh."

She snorts. "I told you we'd been having a dry spell. We used to have the best sex. All that stern cop, naughty lawyer role play. Yeah. I miss that." She sighs. "You're lucky you're not having sex. You're not, right?"

I give her a look that says *none of your business*.

"So Josh Lewenthal, huh?"

"I don't know what you mean," I say. Or how you know him, I don't say.

She holds out her hands and the sparkles on her dress reflect the light of the chandeliers. "He's the FF right?"

"Who's the FF?" Hannah asks as she joins us. She has a tall glass of juice, with slices of orange and strawberry on the rim. Her hair is in a braided coronet on top of her head and she's wearing a beautiful flowy Grecian-style gown. Apparently, everyone had a fancy dress but me.

"Josh Lewenthal," Brook says.

"Really?" Hannah asks. She turns to me with a look of surprise.

"I didn't say he's the FF," I say.

They both stare at me, identical expressions of disbelief on their faces.

This is ridiculous. "Are you two serious? How do you even know him?"

Hannah gives me a surprised look. "What do you mean? He's famous," she says, like it's obvious.

Brook gives me a funny look and says, "Duh."

I look back at Josh, thirty feet away. He's made it to the front of the line, he's chatting up the bartender, and I can see his shoulders shaking in a laugh. I'm just making sure he's still Josh because I don't know if we're talking about the same person.

"That Josh?" I point at him. The Josh that grew up down the street, took my virginity, is my brother's best friend, and loves my mom's pot roast...that Josh? "He's not famous," I say.

"If he's not your FF, he should've been," Brook says. Then she frowns. "Do you even know him? Are you here with him?"

"Yes, I know him," I snap, suddenly feeling irritable and exasperated, because why is she looking at me like I don't know him at all and why does that bother me so much?

"Maybe they just met," Hannah says. "Have you seen his aura, all orange and yellow and full of creativity. Just like I thought it'd look."

Brook gives me a hard stare and I imagine she's cross-examining me in her head.

But before she can say anything, Josh walks up and moves in next to me. "Got you more, double limes." He hands me the sparkling ice water. The outside of the glass is already dripping with condensation.

"Thanks," I say slowly. I study him and try to see what the heck Brook and Hannah are talking about.

Josh gives me a funny look. "What? What is it?" He brushes at his cheek. "Something on my face?"

I shake my head and he gives me a smile.

He turns to Brook and Hannah. "Hi. I'm Josh."

"We know," Brook says. "You did a signing at my douche cousin's shop. There was a line half a mile long. All those freaks in their costumes, waiting to get their comic books signed."

Oh. Ohhhh. That's how they know him. He did a comic book signing at Clive's Comics. That makes sense. The world hasn't been turned upside down and inside out. Josh is still Josh.

Even though I only learned recently how good he is at drawing, at least I knew this. That's why they think he's famous.

I look over at Josh to see if he's taken offense at Brook's description of his fans as freaks in costumes. He doesn't seem to mind, in fact, I think he finds her funny.

"My husband and I love your work," Hannah says. "Especially Grim. His unrequited love for Jewel, it's amazing." Hannah leans forward and I'm surprised at the hero-worship expression she has. "I know you probably can't say, but will they ever get together? I mean, it's been years."

It looks like Hannah is holding her breath, and even Brook edges closer to hear the answer.

Josh gives them his devil-may-care, the-world's-my-playground smile. "I'll let you know when I figure it out."

"You don't know," Hannah says. It's crazy, but she actually sounds upset. "I thought you knew what happens. It's been so long."

Josh shakes his head like he's sorry to disappoint, then he glances at me, and for some reason the way he looks at me makes me feel as naked as the models in their sparkly gold paint.

I frown at him. "Don't look at me, I don't read your comic. I can't tell you the ending. I don't even like comics."

Josh laughs. "Someday, Gemma. Someday you'll read it."

"And you'll like it," Hannah says. "Won't she, Brook?"

But Brook is looking between Josh and me with narrowed eyes and a pucker between her eyebrows. Ugh. I don't want to hear more about the FF.

"I'm going to go say hi to Carly and thank her for inviting me." I turn to Josh. "Do you want to come?"

"Please don't," Hannah says, "I actually have more questions about Grim. And I was wondering about the upcoming civil war."

I wave them off and head through the crowd toward the platform on the other side of the room. The music has shifted to a more raucous beat and the party is beginning to have even more of a bacchanalian feel. The contortionists are twisting their limbs together, there's a trapeze artist twirling from the ceiling and I see that a few belly dancers are making their way through the crowd. A number of couples have settled down to lounge on the plush floor pillows. A woman in a gorgeous billowy black dress leans back on a pillow and sips from a glass of pink champagne. As I pass, she glances at me and quickly dismisses me as no one of importance. In fact, that's the general impression I get here. The people see my pumpkin dress, and decide that I'm the pumpkin, not the carriage, and definitely not Cinderella.

But as Ian says, the surest way to be seen as beautiful is to make someone else laugh, make someone else smile, then no matter what you look like, you'll always be beautiful.

I frown, because, come to think of it, that sounds like something Josh would say.

Weird.

I make it to the platform and catch Carly's eye. When she sees me, she leans in to her husband and whispers something in his ear. He looks at her disapprovingly, then shrugs. She gives him a bland smile, lifts her skirts and steps down from the platform.

"You came," Carly says. She kisses the air next to my cheeks. "Hello, darling. Let's walk, I hate standing on that bloody platform." Her British accent is more pronounced, and I think it's because she's upset.

She threads her arm through mine and we walk toward the stairwell and a relatively empty section of the room.

"I'm going to take you shopping. Your dress is hideous."

I try to hold back a laugh and only just manage. "That's what everyone says."

"How do you expect to keep that sexy Ian if you can't dress yourself properly?" This sounds so much like something my mom would say that I'm almost offended, except I can tell that Carly isn't even thinking about what she's saying, instead she looks like she's trying not to cry.

"Are you okay?" I ask in a quiet voice.

I look around. There are a few people watching us. Carly is beautiful, she actually looks like Cinderella in her blue sparkling dress. I think no matter where she goes people watch her. She realizes it too. She looks around, then back at her husband still standing on the platform. He tilts his chin up and glowers at her.

She turns back to me. "I need to visit the powder room."

We walk at a sedate pace down a long, tiled hallway until we come to a door with a brass knob. She turns the handle and we step into a large, carpeted room with cushioned chairs, vanities with mirrors, china vases with floral arrangements, and at the far end, bathroom stalls. The room smells like lemongrass and gardenias.

"I'll just be a moment," Carly says.

I lean against one of the vanity counters while she uses the bathroom. While I wait, I stare at myself in the mirror. I realize that I don't look at myself very often, that I haven't really looked at myself since my divorce. To be honest, I've been afraid that if I looked good and hard, I'd see why Jeremy left me. That if I looked long enough in the mirror I might see why I wasn't good enough. I'd see the woman that everyone in my hometown sees, the desperate charity case that can't get a date. I'd see a disappointment.

But in the gardenia-scented, hushed room, I finally gather enough courage to have a good look.

Funny enough, nothing earth-shattering happens. It's just me, in a horrendously ugly dress, my hair in a messy ponytail, a slightly bemused expression on my face. I stick my tongue out at myself and wrinkle my forehead.

Nothing happens.

I give myself a smile.

Still nothing happens. It's just me. Slightly older, slightly less sure of myself than I was seven years ago, and slightly more hopeful about my future. Because, this face, the face I see in the mirror, someday, hopefully soon, she'll have a baby to look down at and love. I'll make someone laugh, I'll make someone smile, and they'll find me beautiful.

At the other end of the powder room, the bathroom stall shuts and Carly comes out. She washes her hands, slowly pats them on the thick paper towels, and then walks to the vanities.

When she reaches me she stops. Her face is bone white and her expression is pinched.

"Are you alright?" I ask. She really doesn't look well.

Her hand shakes as she smooths down a strand of hair. Then she lowers her hand and shrugs. "I've started bleeding."

I pull in a sharp breath, that means...it means she's not pregnant. Again. Her seventh try failed.

"Carly. I'm so sorry." I reach out and touch her hand.

She shrugs. "No matter." Then she gives herself a smile in the mirror. It's a brilliant, model-worthy smile. In fact, it's worth the cover of a magazine for how much she shines. But I can see her eyes and they're as bleak and dry as a desert.

"I'm truly sorry," I say again.

She turns to me. "Why should you be sorry? Like Brook says, I'm beautiful, I'm rich, I..." She trails off, swallows and tries to continue. "I..." Her lower lip quivers. "Excuse me for a moment."

Then she stands and walks to a china vase full of flowers. She carefully removes the flowers and sets them on the vanity, takes the vase to the bathroom sink and empties out the water.

She walks back into the lounge area, the large vase cradled in her arms. The delicate blue and white china pattern matches her dress perfectly.

"I'm beautiful. I'm rich. Right?"

I nod. I'm not sure what she needs right now.

"I...shit," she says. "Shit. Shit. Shit."

Then Carly lifts the vase and throws it across the room. It soars through the air, past the vanities, past the bathroom stalls, and smashes against the far wall. The vase shatters in a loud burst and more pieces shatter as they hit the floor.

Carly's chest heaves and she stares at the broken bits of pottery.

"Shit," she says again. Then, she looks at me. "Once more."

"Alright," I say and I nod.

I grab the vase on the vanity nearest me and hand it to her.

"Thank you."

Then she sends the vase, water, flowers, everything and flings it. It hits with another loud crash. The pottery shatters and the water and flowers fall down with the shards. Carly stands still, and stares, transfixed by the mess.

Then, like the water spreading over the floor, she closes her eyes and tears fall down her cheeks.

"Carly," I say.

She shakes her head, so instead of talking I reach over and put my hand on hers.

"He doesn't love me," she finally says.

"Who?" I ask, then I realize who she means even before she answers.

"My husband."

She opens her eyes and gives a scornful laugh. "That was the deal, wasn't it? I bring the beauty, he brings the money. Feelings had nothing to do with it. But stupid, stupid me, I went and fell in love with him."

"That's a bad thing?"

She uses the back of her hand to wipe the tears from her cheeks. Her makeup smears and she lets out a sigh. "Love has made my marriage intolerable."

"I don't understand."

She smiles and sniffs back the last of her tears. "Do you know what my husband will say when I tell him I haven't conceived?"

"No?" And I'm fairly certain I don't want to know.

She puts on a low dismissive voice. "'Try again then, if it makes you happy.'" She clears her throat. "And that will be the end of it. He won't mention anything about this again, and neither will I."

"Do you...will you try again?"

Carly looks down at her sparkly, diamond-covered princess gown. "What does all the beauty and money in the world matter, if I can't get the one thing I want most?"

I don't know whether she means a child or her husband's love. She turns to me and smiles and I imagine she knows what I'm thinking.

"No. I don't think I will. It's time I gave up. On a baby and on my marriage." She crumples the dress in her hands. "Ever since you first came to our meetings, I've known I need to change. If you can face the world on your own, find your own way, so can I." She tilts her chin up. "So can I. No matter if it hurts."

I rest my hand on her arm. I don't have any Ian quotes to give her about plucky futures and gold pots at the end of rainbows. Her IVF cycle has failed and she's decided to leave her husband. What sort of thing do you say to that?

Except. "Have you tried telling him you love him? Maybe you should before you leave?"

She gives me another photo-shoot worthy smile. "That, my darling, would take more guts than I have. I told you I was a masochist, trying so many cycles and failing, but even I have my limits."

I sigh and look at the shattered pottery strewn over the tile floor. "Should we clean up before we go back out?"

Carly nods. "Thank you. I'd rather no one know that I rage-threw the privy flowers."

It doesn't take long to scrape the large chunks of pottery and the flowers into the trash. I sop up the water as best I can.

Before we exit the bathroom, Carly gives me a swift hug. "Thank you. And good luck Saturday."

I wrinkle my brow, and then I remember, Saturday is my transfer. The big day.

It's only been twenty minutes when I make it back to Josh,

Brook and Hannah. They're still talking about Grim and Jewel. It's as if the world outside stood still while the world for Carly fell apart.

I look back at her. She's on the platform again, standing next to her husband. Except this time I look more closely. And I see it. She watches him when he isn't looking. She leans closer when he speaks. She loves him, and he has no idea.

Hannah and Brook have stopped asking Josh questions. He takes the opportunity to lean closer to me.

"How you doing?" he asks.

I lean into him. The music is getting louder as the night goes on. "I'm alright."

"You were gone a while." He looks down at me and his eyes grow cloudy, "I was about to come looking for you."

"I guess I'm just getting worried about Saturday."

He studies my face and his brow wrinkles. "Do you want to go?"

I look over at Hannah and Brook, they're busy arguing about some new supplement. They've completely turned away from Josh and me. That's good.

"Maybe we could get some pizza?" I ask.

A slow smile spreads over his face. "And dessert?"

I give him an answering smile. A funny little feeling grows my chest. "Do you realize we have expensive foods and desserts right here, but we'd rather have street food?"

"And....?"

"I'm just saying, I'm glad you know what makes you happy."

"That I do," he says. Then he grabs my arm and steers me out of the "underworld," back up the stairs, through the glass and marble lobby. We grab our coats from the security guard and walk into the night streets of Tribeca.

"Which direction? I'll go where you go," Josh says.

I give him a funny look. Because the way he said it

reminded me of Carly. She loves her husband, but won't tell him, because she's not that brave or that masochistic. I study Josh's expression. Does he...?

He lifts his eyebrows. "Well? Where to?"

No, I decide. He doesn't.

There's no way Josh Lewenthal's been carrying a torch for me all these years.

I point in a random direction down a likely street, and we walk into the night.

"We're friends, right?" I ask, just to make sure.

He looks down at me and scoffs, "What do you call this? Jeez Gemma. Sometimes I wonder about you."

I shove at him playfully and he laughs. Then, we keep walking down the icy cold streets of the city. As friends.

In two days, I'm having my transfer, and maybe, maybe, if I'm lucky, I'll get pregnant. But right now, all I need to worry about is finding a slice of pizza, and ice cream for dessert.

21

"The worth of a person is measured in the fruit of their actions."

THE SCENE AT THE DOCTOR'S OFFICE IS ALMOST DÉJÀ VU. ONCE again the nurse called to remind me to have a *very* full bladder. So, on the way I chugged a bottle of water and a decaf latte. Now, once again I'm crossing my legs, feeling like if I don't pee soon I'm going to explode.

So, all that's the same.

But there's one huge, massive difference.

I look at the seat next to mine.

Josh is here.

Before, I was alone. This time, Josh is here.

He's drumming his fingers on his leg, but when he senses me looking at him he turns to me and gives me a weak smile.

"How you doing?"

"Good," I say. I cross my legs the other way and shift in my chair. Unfortunately, I've been giving myself progesterone shots in the butt for the past five days and my cheeks are welt-ridden and bruised and sitting is majorly uncomfortable.

"Nervous?" Josh asks.

I shake my head. "No." I squirm a little more.

He swallows and nods. "Me neither."

"Uh huh."

He goes back to drumming his fingers on his leg.

Jeez. This moment feels as awkward as Dr. Ingraham's fictional high school dance.

It's Saturday morning and we're in the waiting room, about to be called back for my transfer. You know, that moment when Josh's sperm and my egg, the day five embryo, gets placed inside my uterus.

It feels like we're about to have sex for the first time (again), except...not.

I take another quick look at Josh, then look back ahead at the spot on the wall where the Georgia O'Keeffe painting used to hang. He's still drumming his fingers nervously.

I bite my bottom lip and squeeze my thighs together.

"Thanks for coming," I say, trying to break the awkward tension that has sprouted between us ever since we walked in this morning.

"Of course." Josh shrugs. Then he clears his throat and goes quiet.

Okay, this is ridiculous.

Josh Lewenthal is never quiet.

This moment is more awkward than teenage boners and training bras. The only way to stop the awkwardness is to pop it like a balloon.

"So. Since I'm about to be impregnated, you wanna give me some dirty talk?"

Josh coughs and then straightens in his chair. "Excuse me?"

I cross my legs, "I mean, since this feels as awkward as having sex for the first time—"

"Wait. You thought it was awkward?" he interrupts. There's a genuinely surprised expression on his face.

"Umm. Really?"

He gives me an affronted look. "What was wrong with it?"

I stare at him in shock. He wants to talk about this now? "Well, uh...it was on the garage floor."

"Yeah," he says, and he sounds like he's reliving a particularly pleasant memory. I jab him with my elbow.

"It was hard and cold," I say. Except, honestly, I barely remember the floor, all I can really remember is his mouth and his hands and how he groaned my name. I shake out of the thought.

"Was it?" he asks.

I flush, because his voice has that low, deep reverberation that makes my insides quiver. I try to get back to my point.

"There was lime Jell-O all over me. That was awkward." When I was cleaning up I'd accidently spilled a bowl on my shirt, it was sticky and wet and—

"Mmmm," he says. "I remember. You like lime Jell-O."

Wow.

I feel a little hot, and a little bothered that his eyelids are lowered and he looks like he's envisioning making love to me again. A picture of us on the floor, naked, rolling in lime Jell-O flashes in my mind.

What the...

I cough into my hand and my bladder pinches in protest. "Yeah, no."

Josh looks over at me with a mock-affronted expression. "So

that's why you never looked at me again. It was awkward." He says "awkward" with a heavy emphasis.

I scoff and shift in my seat again. My bum is really sore, and jeez, can't they call us back already so I can go pee?

I blow out a breath, and just in case Josh actually feels upset I say, "It wasn't terrible."

I peek from the side of my eyes at him. He's staring at me like I've just said the looniest thing on the planet. Then his expression shifts and it looks like he's taken my words as a personal challenge.

"Oh no," I say. "I didn't mean to imply that lots of other women didn't enjoy it. I'm sure they did. I'm not saying that your two-year drought has anything to do with your lack of finesse or..."

Heat travels across my chest and my cheeks.

I lean back in my chair and look at him as carefully as you would a tiger stalking close to the bars of its cage. I feel like if I lean in he's going to bite. I stare at the sharp angle of his jaw and the firm lines of his face. How have I never noticed how masculine he is? How was I fooled by the messy hair and the T-shirts? Looking at him now all I can see is his solid jaw, his wide shoulders, the six-pack I know is under his shirt, the strength of him and the heat of him and...I try not to fan myself at the sexual awareness that is licking at me.

He takes in the look on my face, then he narrows his eyes, "I'll do it."

I shake myself and pull out of the sticky, Jell-O thick lust that just rolled over me. I clear my throat. "Do, ummm, what?"

He smiles at me and his eyelids lower in a hooded, predatory gaze.

Oh no.

He's turning on the once-famous, rip-off-your-panties, Josh Lewenthal charm.

"I'll talk dirty to you."

My lady parts clench and I re-cross my legs and squeeze them together.

"But—"

"Your friend Hannah told me if you orgasm after the transfer you're more likely to get pregnant."

What?

"She said what?"

He smiles and nods.

She also said that giving BJs and wearing crystal bracelets would improve your chances, but before I can tell him so, the door to the back opens and the nurse calls my name.

I LEAN BACK ON THE EXAM TABLE AND THE PAPER COVERING crinkles beneath me. I'm in the usual get-up, the itchy hospital gown that ties in the back and leaves my bum exposed, and my legs are up in the stirrups. I still have to pee and the draft running over my needle-bruised bum is not pleasant, but...

I turn my head and smile at Josh.

He looks back at me with a serious expression on his face. Which is really un-Josh-like. He's perched on a chair near the head of the exam table. The room is small and sterile and smells like nose-tickling antiseptic and cold stainless steel.

My heart knocks hard against my chest, sharp beats that thump nervously against my breastbone. I swallow and rub my clammy hands against the paper covering the table.

Dr. Ingraham stands at the foot of the exam table. He confirmed that I'm receiving my embryo, verified the chain of custody, etcetera, etcetera, we're ready to go.

Josh lets out a long breath and leans toward me.

"You good?" he asks in a quiet voice, just for me.

I nod, because for some reason I can't speak beyond the hard lump in my throat.

Dr. Ingraham clears his throat. "Alrighty. We're ready to go. I'm going to insert the speculum now. I'll wipe off the cervix, then place the catheter through the cervix. I'll use the ultrasound to observe the catheter placement. Then, I'll send a smaller catheter through the outer catheter and place your embryo inside the uterus. All set?"

I glance at Dr. Ingraham. He has everything ready to go.

I nod and say, "Mhmm." That's all I can manage.

Josh wrinkles his brow and looks more closely at me.

I blink quickly, because for some reason, there are tears pressing at the back of my eyes. Why the heck would I cry now of all times?

Josh scoots his chair closer to me and then, instead of whispering a joke like I think he's going to do, he reaches up and takes my hand.

My stomach does a little flip. His grip is firm and his hand is warm and comforting. When he runs his thumb in a circle on my palm, my stomach twirls around with it. I take in a long, shaky breath.

Dr. Ingraham starts his thing. The ultrasound goop is on my belly, cold and slimy. It's an abdominal ultrasound this time. He runs the device over my stomach and presses down on my abdomen to get a clear view. I can feel a weird pinchy sensation down below when he inserts the catheter, but otherwise, the biggest feeling is the urge to pee and my sore tush.

"Everything looks good. I've placed the catheter," Dr. Ingraham says.

I keep my eyes on Josh and look at his familiar face, his dark eyes, his long eyelashes, his permanently upturned lips. He keeps ahold of my gaze, and just like his grip, his eyes are warm and reassuring.

He nods at me, as if to say, "it's okay, you're doing good."

I blink back the threatening tears. We made a baby.

Josh and I made a baby.

All the hoping, all the wishing, it's right here, right now.

"Okay, I'm placing the embryo in your uterus."

Josh's thumb stops circling my palm.

I hold my breath.

Please God, please God, please let this baby stick, let this work, let me meet her someday.

Let it work, let it work, let it work, let it-

"All set," Dr. Ingraham says.

I let out all my breath in a rush and draw in air.

"Okay?" Josh asks me.

I nod and he gently pulls his hand from mine. I frown, because it doesn't feel as okay now that he isn't holding my hand anymore.

I turn my head away from him and lick my dry lips.

"You're welcome to empty your bladder now, then the nurse will take you to the recovery area and you can put your feet up for twenty minutes," Dr. Ingraham says. He pulls off his gloves and tosses them into the medical waste bin.

"Thank you," I say, which is the first thing I've managed to say since Dr. Ingraham came into the room.

Peeing is sweet, sweet relief, even though I'm terrified that somehow peeing will dislodge the baby (anatomically impossible), or walking will shift it around (also anatomically impossible), or that I should've worn Hannah's crystals to work some metaphysical energy mojo to help the baby stick (anatomically improbable?).

I lay back on a cot in the recovery area. Josh and I are in the same curtained area where I recovered after the egg retrieval. There are at least six beds and curtains separating each. This is a busy medical practice. I smile when I remember the wall quote—ten thousand babies and counting. I hope that mine is including in the "and counting."

"So, you ready for the dirty talk?" Josh asks.

I scoff. "Not necessary."

He leans forward in his chair and rests his palms on the edge of the hospital bed. A lock of hair falls over his forehead and I stop myself from reaching up and pushing it back.

The serious, reassuring Josh that was there in the embryo transfer is gone. His usual expression of perpetual amusement is back. And also, a stubborn look that reminds me he felt challenged when I said that sex with him "wasn't terrible."

"Look, I didn't mean to offend your man-sensibilities. I'm really sorry. Sex with you was A-OK. It was perfectly adequate. You don't have anything to prove." Oh lordy. I almost smack my head. What am I talking about?

He gives me a look that tells me I'm spouting nonsense.

"Gemma, this isn't about proving anything. Your friend said you need to orgasm after the transfer to increase your odds. I'm going to help you out."

I cough into my hand.

"Ready?" he asks.

I shake my head no. There are other women only a few feet away, laying on their own cots, separated by flimsy curtains. There are nurses, medical assistants, doctors, and who knows who else walking through. We could be interrupted any minute.

I'm not ready.

And...and...Josh and I aren't a couple.

I'm going to the Hamptons with Ian, I'm something, not exactly dating, but something with Ian.

Josh and I...we're...

"I'm going to rub lime Jell-O all over you."

What?!

I snort and cover my mouth with my hands.

That is *not* dirty talk. Unless messy eating is dirty.

Josh has on a smile that's dripping sex and he's looking at me with the steamiest expression I've ever seen. The patterned curtain behind him flutters and another couple enters the cot beside ours. Josh doesn't notice, he just leans closer to me and says, "And after that lime Jell-O is slathered all over your body I'm going to take a straw and suck it up."

I start to giggle.

I can't help it, he's ridiculous. He's so ridiculous.

He leans in and puts his lips close to my ear, so close that when he starts talking my hair flutters from his breath and I can feel the vibrations of his voice all the way down to my core.

"When I can't suck up anymore, I'm going to use my tongue, and I'm going to lick you, and suck you. I'm going to find all those nasty carrot bits and the chopped apples that shouldn't be in lime Jell-O and I'm going to lick them off you."

Oh lord. I'm laughing, but at the same time, the reverberation of his voice sends warm spirals of wanting all through my body. He's rumbling into my ear and he's so close that sometimes his lips brush against my earlobe, and when they do a zing of pleasure pulses through me.

I let out a huff of air and clutch the white sheets.

"All those fruit and vegetable bits, all that sticky lime Jell-O, I'm going suck on you, I'm going to suck so hard because there's whipped cream in there too. You love whipped cream."

My hips involuntarily tilt up and I stifle a moan. Because the way he says whipped cream, all low and deep and sexy, means he's not talking about whipped cream at all.

Gah.

I blink up at the bright light in the ceiling and clasp the white bedsheets. Josh leans in closer and his breath flutters my hair and his lips brush my earlobe.

A little sound escapes from my lips.

My eyes are closed. My body is aching and hot and my hips are tilted. There's a pool of warmth growing in me and all I need, all I need is for Josh to keep talking dirty to me.

Josh makes a noise of approval and then he says, "And when I've sucked and licked and eaten my fill I'm going to..."

"Yes?"

"To..."

I open my eyes. Josh stares down at me, his eyes are caught on my mouth. I lick my lips and I swear I can taste lime.

He leans forward, closer, closer. My stomach flips and I stare up at him, caught by the look in his eyes.

My word.

He's going to kiss me.

Josh Lewenthal is going to kiss me.

He draws closer and my heart thunders in my ears.

I want him. I need him. I—

"Boy toy? I heard that boy toy. Where is he?" A man booms.

Josh rears back and looks around the small curtained area.

My hand flies to my mouth and my eyes go wide.

Un-freaking-believable. It's the gold unitard lady and her husband.

"You heard nuthin'," the woman says.

Oh jeez. They're right next door. They're on the bed next to ours.

Josh sits upright and looks at me, his eyes full of shock and yes, laughter.

I put my finger to my lips and shake my head.

He better not start laughing. I scowl at him, because now that he's not about to kiss me I feel achy and deprived and really, really cranky that he got me turned on with his bull crap lime Jell-O farce.

"I did hear him. He was telling you he was going to suck you and lick you and eat your cream. Was he on your phone?"

Josh snorts and then cuts it short. I shush him and wave my hand for him to be quiet.

We are literally three feet from these crazy people with only a thin piece of fabric separating us. Didn't he learn his lesson last time? You can't reason with crazy.

"No, he wasn't on my phone. He ain't here."

"You told him to call you. I heard him saying he'd lick your cream. I'm telling you, baby, I'll punch that boy toy in the face."

Josh was trying to hold in a snicker, but when he hears the ham-armed husband threatening to punch him he stops looking amused.

"Is he here?" Ham-Arm asks.

"You're crazy," Gold Unitard says.

On that, we agree.

"I'm gonna find him," the husband says.

There's a shuffling noise and then I see black shoes stomping around on the other side of the curtain. I glance at Josh and you better believe he looks concerned.

He rubs his forehead and I think he's remembering the "private parts" painting smashing down on his head.

"Gemma," he whispers. He stands up and looks at the curtain.

I shush him and shake my head. Then I have an idea. I lift up the sheet. "Get under," I hiss.

He gives me a confused look.

"Get under there," I whisper.

He raises his eyebrows. Yes, I'm inviting him to climb in bed with me.

"Desperate times," I whisper.

And of course, of course, he can't let an opportunity for a

good joke to pass him by because he says, "But where's the Jell-O?"

I smack my head, and just at that moment the curtain that separates our bed from the one next to us rips back with a metallic screech.

Mr. Ham-Arm stands there with a triumphant look on his face.

"We don't got Jell-O. We just got knuckle sandwiches," the guy says, and to emphasize the point he smacks his fist into his hand.

Josh can't help himself, really he can't, because at the phrase "knuckle sandwich" he lets out a sharp laugh.

Ham-Arm isn't having any of it. "You tell my lady you want her cream? You don't get her cream. You don't get her Jell-O. You sick pervert. You stay out of my lady's business. She's getting pregnant."

Oh jeeeeeez. Why? Why?

Josh lifts his hands in a calming gesture.

But the guy roars and rushes forward like a bull. His big head's down, aimed at Josh to deliver a head butt.

Josh swiftly sidesteps him.

The guy has his head down, so he can't alter his course in time. Instead, his momentum carries him into my bed. He rams into the edge and flips over my legs. Then he crashes into the curtain and yanks the fabric down on top of him.

From her bed, the gold unitard lady screeches.

Ham-Arm rolls around on the floor and tries to get himself out of the tangle of curtain.

I look between Ham-Arm and his shrieking wife. Then I look at Josh.

He's not laughing.

He's stunned. And, bless him, he knows when it's time to make an exit.

"Come on. Time to go," he says.

I go to jump out of the bed, but he leans down and puts his arms under my knees and my back and scoops me up. I wrap my arms around his neck.

"You have to stay horizontal," Josh says. "Twenty minutes. For the baby."

There's the light in his eyes again, that glimmer of laughter. It's only been ten minutes. He's going to keep me horizontal come hell or high water. For the baby.

I give him a beaming smile, and Josh wastes a precious few seconds to just look at me, a stunned expression on his face, like he's never seen my smile before.

Ham-Arm has almost extricated himself from the curtain.

"Come on. We gotta go," I say.

Josh nods and hefts me closer to his chest. I can feel the hard beating of his heart. He starts to go, then, "Wait. My purse, my coat," I cry.

Josh grabs them from the side table, then he makes a swift exit from the recovery area. Shouts of "boy toy," "Jell-O" and "cream" follow us.

When we make it to the lobby, I see Joy at the desk. As Josh jogs by, I call, "You might want to send someone to the back. A couple had an accident."

Joy pokes her head out from behind her high desk. Her mouth drops open when she sees Josh running through the lobby with me in his arms.

"I'm not paying for it," he calls over his shoulder. "This time, *his* head broke it."

I start to laugh, then I can't stop. I bury my face in Josh's chest and laugh until I'm out of breath. As we pass through the lobby, the same security guard as last time rushes past us toward the fertility office.

Once we're out onto the sidewalk, Josh slows to a walk. The

crisp air bites at my cheeks and I blink at the brightness of the late morning.

We made it.

I wiggle in his arms. "You can put me down now," I say. I'm not exactly light.

He shakes his head and pulls me tighter against him. "Five more minutes."

I sigh and then lean my head against his shoulder and let him carry me through Midtown Manhattan. My coat is in my arms and acts as a sort of blanket against the chill. It's Saturday so there are window shoppers, couples, and families ambling down the sidewalk. Still, no one except curious little kids look at the tall handsome guy carrying a woman down the street.

I wrap my arms more tightly around Josh's neck and shoulders. They're solid and muscular, thicker than they were sixteen years ago. You know, the last time I was this close to him. His body is different. To be honest, a lot different. He was seventeen then, and he's thirty-three now. I'm sure...I know, a lot has changed.

I remember how much I'd idolized him. How much I fantasized about him as a teenager. Now I know, even then, I didn't really know Josh, I just fantasized about the idea of him.

It's sad to admit that you never really liked someone, that instead, you liked the *idea* of them.

And then, just as easily, I discarded the idea of him.

For all these years, I never, ever knew Josh.

Not a bit.

I sigh and lean my head against his warm chest and stare up at the winter blue sky.

The sounds of the city, the whoosh of the buses, the taxi horns, the screeching of the subway rising from the sidewalk grates, all of those sounds mix with the steady beating of Josh's heart.

Finally, he comes to the southern edge of Central Park. He heads down a path that leads toward the little iced-over pond. There's a green bench looking over a flock of geese that have found a small bit of water not yet iced over. He settles down onto the bench and sets me down so that my head rests in his lap. I bend my knees and put my feet on the bench.

Josh gives me a rueful smile. "Well?"

Then, I can't help it, I grin back at him. Because we did it. We did it.

"In less than two weeks we'll know—" I begin.

"What are you doing for Valentine's—" He stops, clears his throat, and then says, "I was wondering what you're doing for Valentine's Day?"

He asked, "What are you doing for Valentine's Day?"

Embarrassed heat flares over my cheeks and I look away. "Oh, um." I scramble up and sit upright on the bench, then shove my arms into my coat and zip it up.

Josh avoids looking at me and I realize that my reaction wasn't exactly what he was expecting. I cough into my hand and then shift uncomfortably, because darn it, my bum still hurts.

"Well," I say. Then I stop, because suddenly nothing makes sense anymore. Or maybe it wasn't sudden at all. But still, nothing makes sense. "I have a date."

Josh looks at me quickly, then away, back toward the pond and the geese flapping their wings at each other.

I swallow and rub my hands up and down my arms. It's cold out.

"No problem. I was only asking," Josh says, "because you'll find out the results around then, and I thought you might want company. Your mom said you didn't have a date." He still won't look at me.

I nod. "Okay. Yeah. No. I've got a date."

"Right. Good."

"Mhmm," I agree.

We sit for a minute, just watching the geese honking and being jerks in the water, and then I stand. It's too awkward. It's awkward again.

"Thanks for today, I'm going to head home." I pause when he looks up at me. His eyes are so dark that I can't read the emotion in them, but his lips curve into his usual laughing smile.

So, maybe the entire dirty talk thing was just a joke. The near kiss was just momentary madness brought on from the emotions of the situation. If Josh can laugh it off, brush it off, so can I.

"Who's the date with?" he asks. Okay, maybe he's not brushing it off.

I bite my bottom lip, then say, "Ian."

Josh gives me a look almost like I've disappointed him.

"He's a good guy," I say defensively, which was a stupid thing to say. So I add, "The worth of a person is measured in the fruit of their actions."

Josh stands up and puts his hands into his pockets. "True. Another Ian quote?"

"Yeah." Then, because I don't actually want to go, I ask, "Do you want to stay for the day? We could get lunch? I mean, I do owe you a meal or three. And I can't ever...I can't ever express how thankful I am to you."

Josh reaches up and tucks a strand of hair behind my ear. I shiver as his fingers trail along the sensitive edge of my skin.

I stare at him as he concentrates on smoothing my flyaway hair down. Finally, he pulls away and catches my expression.

"Your hair was all..." He makes a messy gesture with his hands. "From me carrying you around the city."

My heart thumps. "Do you think she'll stick?" I ask. In less than two weeks we'll know whether or not the transfer worked.

Josh pauses, thinks for a long minute, then, "Whether she does or not, she was loved."

I put my hand to my belly and nod.

Right now, there's a day five embryo knocking around in there, and if I'm lucky, someday I'll get to meet her.

"Come on," Josh says, "you're right. You owe me some pizza."

So, we walk out of the park and head toward the nearest hole-in-the-wall pizza joint and then we spend the day together just walking around the city, messing around, taking in the sights, being friends.

When I climb into bed that night, I stare at the ceiling and try to do one of Hannah's fertility meditations. I imagine my uterus as a fertile garden, ready to nourish and provide life. But halfway through the meditation I open my eyes and stare at the far wall.

It's dark, so I can barely make out the painted quote, but long ago I memorized what it says. *Love is the best gift I've ever had the privilege to give.*

I hold my hand to my abdomen and stare at the wall, at the words.

It's funny, I haven't truly let myself love anyone since Jeremy. The cheating, the divorce, the infertility diagnosis, it all broke something inside me, and I've never trusted myself to love again.

I thought if I had a baby, that I could love her without fear, but that's not true. Love always involves risk. It involves risking hurt.

No mother is guaranteed that her children will always love her, or that they'll never hurt her. In fact, I think the one thing they're guaranteed is being left behind. And being left behind hurts, even when you're happy that they're grown, it still hurts.

So, I guess loving is accepting that it's about giving and never about taking. If you expect something in return, then love becomes a transaction and it's not love anymore.

Maybe that's why I attached myself to Ian. There was never any chance of pain there. And maybe that's why I never accepted any of my mom's set-ups, or any other date, because I was too afraid. But now Ian wants more and I don't know what to do.

Because when I close my eyes at night I don't see Ian, I see Josh.

But I guess, in the end, I am a coward, because I'm too scared to admit that out loud. Or even really to myself.

Because what if I say something and instead of saying he feels the same way, Josh laughs. Because, ninety-nine times out of a hundred I think it's guaranteed that that's what he'll do.

Carly said I'm brave, but I'm not brave, I'm a coward.

I rub my hand over my belly and try to think of a fertile, happy, pink-uterus garden.

22

*"You never regret the
doing, only the
not doing."*

VALENTINE'S DAY IS HERE. I SPENT THE LAST WEEK IN A MANIC haze of symptom spotting. I told myself I wouldn't do it, but somewhere between the day of the transfer and the next morning I became obsessed with every single tingle, sneeze, or itch.

I kept a diary of symptoms in my phone's calendar. It reads like a hypochondriac's wet dream. Slightly congested morning after transfer, symptom of pregnancy? Web search—definitely, yes. Dry skin, chapped lips, symptom? Maybe, yes. Gassy after lunch on day four after transfer, symptom? Possible, yes, but three-day-old fried rice could be culprit. Spot on my chin on day six, symptom? Web search—yes. Vivid dreams, restless sleep. Symptom? Yes. The list goes on...tired, irritable, more thirsty than usual, craving salt, tingling breasts...according to the internet, someone somewhere has had each symptom that I've experienced and yes...chapped lips, zits, hiccups, accidently placing your keys in the freezer, and craving watermelon are all a sign of pregnancy. Since I've had all these symptoms and more, then I'm definitely, probably, maybe pregnant.

Soon I'll know.

I lean back in my office chair and the donut pillow under me squeaks. I gave in after too many miserable days of sitting on my needle punctured welt-ridden bum and bought a little ergonomic chair pillow. Lavinia raised an eyebrow the first day I brought it in, but otherwise, no one said anything.

I've decided progesterone shots are the worst. *The worst.*

Who decided it was a good idea to shoot yourself in the butt with a needle day in and day out? It bruises, it welts, it hurts, and then what? How are you supposed to sit?

I look around the office. It's nearly six and everyone is already gone for the day. I'm nearly wrapped up, Ian's virtual Live Your Best Life Conference is soon and I'm concentrating on making sure all the partner presentations are complete and on-message. I also wrote another draft of my remarks since Ian asked me to introduce him on the first day. Unfortunately, I had trouble concentrating.

I open up my phone, tap on my calendar, and write *trouble concentrating, symptom*?

When I look up from my phone, I see Ian. He's standing at my desk, smiling down at me. He looks good today. He's dressed in what I'd considered his Hamptons outfit, a dressy casual outfit that would work in a boardroom or on the deck of a yacht.

"Oh, hi," I say. I slide my phone back into my purse and bite my bottom lip. "How are you?"

Ugh. Brilliant.

Ian grins his bright, white toothy smile. "Ready for the weekend?"

I pat my suitcase, a little overnight bag that I put under my desk this morning. Ian said we'd be leaving from the office.

"Yup. All set, mhmm." I fidget with the hem of my new dress. I went out with Carly over the weekend and she helped find outfits that "showed off my assets." I'm in an Audrey Hepburn-inspired dress, with a silk scarf tied in my hair. It's a long, long way from my usual chunky sweater and legging get-up. It makes me look sophisticated and elegant, so I'm not sure why I'm so uncomfortable.

"Shall we?" Ian asks. "The car is ready." He holds out his arm. I hesitate for a moment, then Ian says, "I've never regretted the doing. Only the not doing."

I tilt my head. "Is that a new quote?" I haven't seen that in any of his books or materials before.

"Hmm. Let's just say, I felt it fit the moment." He holds out his hand, and when he does, the fluorescent lights of the office shine down and hit him just right. There's a glow around his black hair, like he's been anointed by the angels. I'm reminded that he's Ian Fortune, the man that pulled me out of my self-loathing and hurt after my divorce. He's Ian Fortune, guru extraordinaire.

And he's reminding me to live my best life.

He's right, you never regret the doing, only the not doing.

Josh hasn't called. Josh hasn't texted. Josh hasn't...

I stand and put my arm in his.

"Happy Valentine's Day," Ian says.

～

THE CANDLELIGHT IS LOW, THE RED ROSES ARE BEAUTIFUL, AND the music is romantic. Everything about dinner in the Hamptons is perfect. Except...I keep waiting for that spark, to feel that unfurling of love or even lust (remember the mind-blowing sex fantasy?), but it's not there.

Don't get me wrong, Ian is attentive and charming and easy to talk to, but...

He's not Josh.

I regret the doing.

I shouldn't have come.

The waiter clears away our dessert dishes and presents us with a silver coffee service. Decaf for me. I take two scoops of sugar and stir them into the steaming liquid. I pour cream, and keep my gaze down, giving myself time to think. I'll have to take a bus back, or a taxi or...I think Carly said she was coming out here for the week to get "some space." Maybe I could call her.

"So, Gemma, is your brother still friends with Josh Lewenthal?"

I quickly lift my head and look at Ian. It's strange he'd mention Josh. Especially when my thoughts have been drifting to him during the entire eight-course meal.

Lime zest shavings in the curry soup—Josh.

Julienned carrots in the salad—Josh.

Oregano and basil on the lamb, tastes like pizza—Josh.

Ice cream and profiteroles for dessert—Josh.

Abstract flower paintings on the walls of the restaurant —Josh.

Gah.

"Why do you ask?" I manage to say without showing too much interest. At least, that's my hope.

Ian lifts a shoulder in a shrug. "We went to university together, then we were at the same start-up. Let's just say, I'm curious what became of him."

I lift my eyebrows, "I didn't know you were at that techie start-up. And here I thought you were always a guru."

He chuckles and then I watch as he spoons sugar into his cup and then pours a small drizzle of cream so that his coffee turns a caramelly brown. His fingers are so long and elegant, his movements so precise. A month ago, I would've fantasized about his hands. But now...nah.

"So what is he up to these days?" Ian asks when he's done taking a sip of his doctored coffee.

What to say. What to say.

"He has a web comic, I think it's popular. I don't know, I haven't read it."

Which I should. I really should.

Ian lifts a winged eyebrow and says, "Still not a fan? We share that sentiment, I suppose. Although not many people do."

I take a sip from my coffee to cover my frown. When I've swallowed I ask, "What do you mean?"

Ian looks around the elegant restaurant, at the tables nearby, but not too near, at the other guests, and then he leans forward and says in a quiet voice, "I've never told anyone outside of the start-up about this, but when we worked together, Josh stole my work. I had a book full of essays and quotes that I'd spent years working on. It was the concept I built Live Your Best Life Starting Now around. He found it in my desk and stole it. Attempted to make a business out of it. That break of trust nearly ruined me. It took years for me to recover from."

I stare at Ian, at the hurt expression on his face and the betrayal I see written there. And I don't know what to say. Josh...Josh did...

"Is that why he left the start-up?" My voice sounds funny to my ears. I clear my throat.

Ian nods. "After the theft was discovered, he left. Like I said before, he has a habit of disappointing people."

"Oh. Right." I take another sip of my coffee, but now instead of tasting sweet and like toasted nuts, it tastes bitter.

Was I wrong about Josh? Have I been wrong all this time?

What do I really know about him anyway?

I've been building him up in my head again, maybe even, if I admit it to myself, falling for him. But what for? If what Ian is saying is true, (and why would he lie?) then Josh isn't the decent, stand-up guy I thought he was.

"I wondered what he was up to nowadays. If he ever got over it all. He was angry he got caught, but I say, let bygones be bygones. Let it go and live your best life." Ian leans back in his chair and gives me a charming smile.

Josh has never said anything about Ian, but I've always gotten the feeling he isn't his favorite person. Apparently, this is why. Maybe he's just embarrassed he made a stupid mistake. After all, it was years ago that this happened.

I twist the napkin in my lap and smile back at Ian. "I wouldn't know. Sorry."

After dinner, we stroll down the quaint sidewalk. I'm feeling deflated, incredibly, horribly deflated. Not even the cute, brightly lit shops and Ian's company can lift my spirits.

I'm only half listening to Ian as he's talking about some big-name celebrity he knows that owns the house next to his when he cuts off and stops walking.

"Well, I'll be," he says.

I turn to look at what's caught his attention.

And there, not twenty feet from us, walking down the sidewalk with a box of pizza in his hands, is Josh. He's in scuffed jeans, an old winter coat, and sneakers, and if I didn't know him I'd think he was the pizza delivery guy. He's holding a cardboard pizza box in his arms and looking down at the sidewalk as he walks toward us. I hold my breath. I don't want him to look up. I don't want him to see me in my Audrey Hepburn-style dress holding Ian's arm outside of an expensive la-di-da restaurant.

I really, really don't want him to look up.

But of course, in life, things don't always happen the way you want them to.

When he's only a few feet away, Josh glances up from the snowy sidewalk. At first, I can tell, he doesn't recognize us. He's about to pass us by, like the strangers we could've been. That only lasts for a split second. As he's passing he focuses on my face and suddenly, his eyes catch mine. And he realizes we aren't strangers.

That it's me.

With Ian.

At first Josh looks surprised and then maybe... uncomfortable? Upset?

He gives a hard swallow as he pauses in front of us. "Hey."

My heart gives a hard thump.

I step away from Ian.

"Josh, hey. What're you doing out here?" I give a bright smile, because the amount of tension that just sprang up around us is intense.

For a second, I don't think he's going to respond, but then he shakes himself and his old life's-my-playground smile lights up his face.

"Hey, Gem. Ian. I'm just..."—he holds up the box of pizza —"getting some dinner. You know me and pizza."

Oh.

Oh Josh.

Anyone else would've been fooled. I'm sure of it. I would've been fooled a month ago. Josh looks like he doesn't have a care in the world, like life's a lark and it's no big deal running into me and Ian in our Valentine's Day finest.

Ian chuckles, "Right. You never did appreciate the finer things." He looks over at me and smiles, and I think, I *think* he's talking about me. But that doesn't actually make any sense.

Looking at Josh, I feel like the lowest, the jerkiest, the crappiest person.

"What are you doing out here?" I ask again.

Josh looks past us, like he wishes he were anywhere but standing outside a five-star restaurant holding a cardboard box of pizza. He turns back to me and gives me a light smile, "I thought I'd bring my dad out to see the beach. He was talking about how much he missed it. We used to come out here when I was a kid."

Oh.

Oh no.

I almost can't hold Josh's gaze, because when I look beyond his smile, I can see that drawing of his dad, the one where Josh is telling you with pencil and ink that his dad is dying. And I can hear him say, "when he's gone, no one will remember my first steps, my first drawings, and no one alive will mourn him like I do. I'll be alone."

Josh gives me a false, tight smile and to my shame, I look away.

"That's nice," Ian says. "I asked Gemma earlier how you've been. But it looks like you've landed on your feet. Dinner with your dad on Valentine's. The universe has a way of giving us exactly what we deserve, doesn't it?"

I look over at Ian in shock. I've never, ever known him to be cruel. But that was cruel.

Josh just gives a short nod, then starts to move past us, "Ian. Gemma, have a good night." His voice is light, but I can hear the ache beneath the words.

There's a big part of me, a huge part, that wants to grab Josh's arm and ask him if I can come and join him and his dad for pizza and a walk on the snowy beach. But that would be intruding. Josh brought his dad out here for goodbye. That much is clear.

So I don't say anything, except, "Have a good night."

But as Josh passes us Ian calls after him, "We will. Trust me. I've never regretted the doing. Only the not doing."

Josh's back is turned but he pauses and I can see his shoulders stiffen. Then, slowly, he turns around. There isn't amusement on his face anymore. In fact, this is probably the first time in my life that I've ever seen Josh look furious.

"What did you say?"

Ian smiles at him. "I've never regretted the doing. Only the not doing. There's a lesson there, don't you think?"

I look between the two of them.

Ian smiles with easy charm and the assurance that comes from the adoration of millions. He's in full guru mode.

There isn't an easy smile on Josh's face. In fact, by the absence of any amusement, laughter or smirk, I'd say that Josh is livid.

He stalks back to us and then he says in a low, hard voice, "Say it again."

Ian smiles and shrugs. "We're all friends here. It's water under the bridge. Let bygones be bygones."

Josh looks over at me, and I can tell he's trying to push down all the emotion that just came riding up. He sighs and seems to shake it off.

"Alright. Fine. See you later."

He turns to go, and when he does, Ian leans toward him and says something. It's too quiet for me to hear. But when he does, Josh stops walking. He turns back around.

"Gemma, hold my pizza."

He asked her to hold his pizza.

I frown at him. "What?"

"Hold. My. Pizza."

Oh. Okay. I hold out my hands and take the warm box. When I do, Josh gives me a small smile.

"Thanks."

"No prob—"

I don't finish because as soon as he lets go of the box, Josh turns to Ian and swings his fist.

He punches him right in the face.

There's a nasty-sounding thunk as his fist connects with Ian's nose.

I let out a squeak as Ian pinwheels back and falls into the snowbank.

A bright red splash of blood runs down Ian's face.

Holy crap.

"Josh, what the heck?"

He shakes out his hand and grins. "God, that felt good."

Ian moans and covers his nose.

I shove the pizza box back at Josh. "What's wrong with you? Are you insane? He was trying to give you advice. He's a self-help guru. It's what he does."

The smile on Josh's face slips.

Good.

I rush over to Ian. He's sprawled in the snow bank, trying to stop the blood running from his nose.

"Are you alright?" I kneel down next to him in the cold, icy snow.

Ian moans and I can't believe it, I just can't believe that Josh punched him.

"Think it's broken," Ian says, and his voice is muffled from the swelling that's already started

I swing back to Josh. He's standing there with the pizza box in his arms, and I'm so mad at him right now, I can barely think.

"What's wrong with you?" I say again.

He stares at me for a long, long moment. The hard snow scratches my knees and the cold starts to burn. I glare at Josh.

Finally he nods and says, "I'm sorry. I misunderstood."

"What's there to misunderstand?" I cry. Josh gives me a funny look and for some reason everything feels so wrong.

Ian groans and I lean forward and dab a tissue against his lip.

"Right," Josh says. "Right." Then he turns and walks down the dimly lit sidewalk.

I fight back the tears at the back of my eyes and give Ian a sympathetic smile.

"Are you alright?"

"Mhmm," Ian says. "But I'll be better when you take me home."

"Oh. Sure. Okay." I stand up and Ian follows. We wipe the ice and snow from our coats and I stamp my high heels and try to get some feeling back into my cold legs and numb toes.

Before we go, I take one last glance in Josh's direction, but he's gone.

~

IAN'S "COTTAGE" IS HUGE. IT'S A MASSIVE, BEACH-FRONT THREE-story home with gray shake siding and elegant lighting lining the driveway and the front porch. It looks like a house out of a fairy tale, including the landscaped bushes with mounds of white snow sparkling in the lights.

We're at the front door. I rub my hands together and try to warm up. The car ride wasn't long enough for the heater to get hot, so I'm still uncomfortably cold.

Ian fits the key into the lock. His nose has stopped bleeding, but there's swelling and it looks painful.

"This isn't exactly the Valentine's Day I had in mind," he says, "but we should never turn away the universe's gifts. And having your sympathy is definitely a gift I'm not refusing." He smiles and then winces.

"Don't worry about it, we'll find you some ice," I say. "Maybe we can relax. Watch a movie, or..."

I trail off.

Ian has opened the front door.

Inside, there are dozens of red rose petals and burning candles. The perfect seduction scene.

It's romantic.

It's lovely.

It's not for me.

Sprawled on a divan in the middle of a circle of rose petals is a very beautiful, very naked woman.

Ian looks at the woman, then he looks at me. Oh.

"Gemma," he says. He holds up his hands in a conciliatory gesture.

"Gemma?" the woman says disdainfully. "The frumpy divorcee from your office? Really, Ian? You want to screw the quote girl? You've officially hit bottom."

What?

What?

I look at the woman. She's even more beautiful than Carly in her nude photos, and that's saying something.

"Gemma," Ian says again.

I glance down at myself, the high heels, the cashmere coat, the Audrey Hepburn dress that isn't me, isn't me at all, and I see what she sees. Gemma Jacobs. Frumpy divorcee. Chubby Dimmy Gimmy. The pity date.

And also, the terrible friend that somehow managed to hurt Josh without knowing how, or why.

I look back at the woman.

This scene is Jeremy having sex on the dining room table all over again.

And that's when I know something is broken in me, because I'm not surprised and I'm not upset. In fact, I don't feel anything at all.

There must be something about me, something wrong with me that makes men treat me this way. There must be something in me that makes them think this is okay.

I turn back to Ian. "Thank you for a lovely dinner." Then I turn and walk down the sidewalk toward the driveway.

"Gemma. Where are you going?" Ian shouts after me. "Gemma, wait. There's no taxis Gemma, this isn't the city. Don't be an idiot. Wait!"

But I don't. I take off my stupid heels and I jog barefoot down the freezing cold driveway and keep running until I'm a quarter mile down the road, out of sight of Ian's ridiculously fabulous cottage.

By that time my feet are numb, I'm out of breath, and I have pinchy cramps in my abdomen. Sharp, painful, pinchy cramps.

"Stick tight, baby," I say and I rub my abdomen. "Stick tight."

Then I pull out my cell.

"Hello darling."

At Carly's voice, I start to cry, but I manage to say, "Carly, I'm in the Hamptons. Are you here?"

"Of course, I'm running away from my loveless marriage-"

"Can you come pick me up?"

She does.

23

"There are people who win in life, and there are people who lose."

MONDAY MORNING DAWNS BRIGHT AND COLD. IT'S THE BITTER sort of mid-February day, where the freezing weather seeps into your bones and doesn't let go. Instead of wearing one of the dresses Carly helped me pick out, I put on black pants and a long sweater and trudge to the office. In the subway car, there's a puddle of urine on one of the plastic seats, and the smell makes me gag. I would write in my calendar, *symptom(?)*, but the smell of old urine on the subway always makes me queasy.

I took the bus back to Manhattan on Saturday morning. Then I spent the whole weekend in my pajamas, lying around, feeling incredibly sorry for myself.

I sent Josh a text Saturday afternoon. It said: *Sorry about last night.*

He wrote back: *Don't worry about it.*

After fifteen minutes of staring at my phone I finally typed: *Friends, right?*

Then I banged my phone against my head, while I chanted, "Idiot, idiot, idiot."

The five minutes it took him to respond felt like five hours. Finally, he wrote: *Let me know when you get your results.*

It took me the longest time to write back: *Okay. Tell your dad hello for me.*

He didn't write back.

I stared at my wall, the looping cursive of the quote, mocking me. When Ian came up with that quote about loving, was he actually talking about the barrels of women he's seduced?

Ugh. Ugh. He's a creep. Leah was right, he's a fake, plastic Ken doll. Brook was right, the self-help types are the most messed-up of us all. Josh was right. I don't know why he punched Ian, but heck, he was right.

They were all right.

The fantasy that I created around Ian after my divorce was just as unrealistic as the fantasy I created about Josh as a teenager.

I didn't love him, I loved the idea of him.

I think I need to face the fact that I haven't learned, not in thirty-two years, to look past my own ideas of people. I never, ever look to see who people truly are. Not even the people closest to me.

In New York, when you sit in the subway or walk down the street, you never make eye contact with the people around you, it's like they aren't there, the people are just *impressions* of people. No one sees anyone. Not really.

I think that's how I've been living my life. Not looking closely at anyone.

New York City is the only place in the world where you can be surrounded by millions of people and feel completely, utterly unknown.

The subway doors whoosh open and I push my way through the crowd and climb the concrete stairs to Midtown and the biting cold wind.

On my way into the office I step into a twenty-four-hour laboratory to have my blood drawn. Today is the day.

I get to see if my baby stuck.

Pregnant or not pregnant. Pregnant or not pregnant. Today I find out.

I have to admit, over the weekend, I bought twenty, yes twenty, pregnancy tests. I chugged water, tea, and decaf coffee and peed on a stick every few hours. They were all negative. When I peed on the last one, and the negative showed, I looked at myself in the mirror with disgust.

"Honestly, Gem?" I'd said.

But honestly, I didn't know what I was asking myself to do differently.

Or why exactly I was so disgusted with myself.

But I was.

I slink into the office fifteen minutes late and sit down on my doughnut pillow. I turn on my computer and enter my password. When I type it in, the bandage covering the blood draw puncture pulls at my skin. The phlebotomist had to dig around with her needle to find the vein and I think it left a bruise.

But that's okay. Because in a few hours, I'll know. The pee on a stick method isn't as sensitive as the blood draw. All those negatives over the weekend mean nothing. Today my blood test will tell me.

Pregnant or not pregnant.

Pregnant or not pregnant.

I should've called in sick. I look around the office. The lights to Ian's office are still turned off. Thank goodness, I don't know how I'm going to face him. Every time I think about seeing him I get a queasy feeling in my stomach. What am I supposed to say?

He's my boss.

And I can't just quit my job. I've always loved working here. Truly.

I sigh and turn away from the door to Ian's office.

Lavinia is watching me. She gives me her sour, the-plants-are-wilting-and-the-printer-is-malfunctioning, it's-Monday-morning look. She's about to say something, but when she sees my expression she stops, frowns and then says, "The salami was bad? Don't say I didn't warn you."

Ugh.

Why?

It isn't any of her business, it really isn't.

"Lavinia, for your information, I don't eat salami. In fact, I loathe salami. Okay? I really, really loathe salami."

Lavinia's mouth purses, like she's sucking on a lemon. She looks over at Ian's office, then back to me, and shrugs. That's it. Just a shrug. Then, "The plants are wilting. You should move them to the sun."

I glance around the office and shake my head. There is no sun. Our loft-style, open-concept office space has four walls of brick, plaster and painted quotes. The only space with windows is Ian's office. He has a whole wall of them.

I'm about to tell Lavinia so when her eyes widen and her mouth puckers even more. I look behind me to see what's gotten her so worked up.

It's Ian.

I'd like to say that he has bags under his eyes, messy hair, and sloppy clothes. I'd like to say that he looks like hell.

But I can't.

Even with a slightly swollen nose, and a light purple bruise under his left eye, he looks just as gorgeous, just as prime-time-TV ready as ever. When he sees me at my desk, a happy smile lights his features and I swear one of the interns across the office sighs in appreciation of his man-beauty.

"Gemma," he says, and his voice carries around the open space.

I drop my head, and my stomach clenches into a tight nervous ball.

"Glad you made it. Can I talk to you in my office for a moment?"

I look down at the floor, at Ian's perfectly polished black dress shoes, and squeeze my eyes shut. I feel like I'm going to puke. Honest to goodness.

Symptom?

No.

Just my emotions finally catching up to me. Ian. The man I worshiped for seven years is a certified douche and now he wants to talk to me about it in private.

I'd like to say, "I'd rather not," but that would cause more gossip among my colleagues than getting up and walking nonchalantly to his office.

So I stand up and follow him.

Lord, let this be a lesson to every woman that has ever thought about getting involved with her boss. Don't do it. Just say no. It won't end well.

Because for the foreseeable future I have to show up at work and promote Ian Fortune to the world and pretend that he's an enlightened shining example of manhood. When, in reality, he's not.

When we're inside Ian's private domain, he strolls to the back of the space, farther from the door, toward the putting green and the large indoor koi pond. I follow after him, my stomach rolling around. I shouldn't have eaten those blueberry waffles with sausages and orange juice for breakfast. I really, really shouldn't have.

I press my hand to my stomach.

"I want to apologize," he begins.

"Alright."

"I like you, Gemma. I really like you."

I look closely at Ian. He seems sincere. In fact, he looks really broken up about everything.

He's about to say more, but I interrupt him. "Why?"

He rubs his thick hair back from his forehead. "Uh. Why what?"

"Why do you like me? And don't give me that crap about seeing my heart. You don't know me, not really."

Ian takes a step toward me. The cologne he's wearing is crazy strong, gag-worthy strong. It smells like Pine-Sol and musty wood shavings. My stomach rolls.

He gives me his guru smile, "Gemma. We're both incomplete souls, looking for the other half."

Oh jeez.

That's from his first book, chapter twelve, page one eighty-two.

What a tool.

I take another breath and my stomach rolls again.

"The first time I saw you," he continues earnestly, "I knew that you were imperfect, self-conscious, lacking. There are people who win in life, and there are people who lose. You're one of the losers, Gemma. Hell, me too, you've seen it, but together, we could win."

I stare at him in shock and press my hand against my abdomen.

"What do you say?" he asks.

He holds out his hand, and I stare at his long, elegant fingers.

"Gemma?"

I shake my head. The room tilts like a boat tossing in New York harbor. My skin goes clammy cold, and then I know, I know—

"What do you say?"

"I'm gonna be sick," I gasp.

And Ian must think that I'm talking about his speech, because he steps forward, as if to convince me otherwise. But that was a mistake, because right as he steps toward me I gag and that plate of blueberry waffles and maple syrup and that pile of sausage links and all that orange juice comes riding up and I spew all over Ian Fortune's perfect face.

It's like a scene from a horror movie. There are blueberries in the vomit, and it's bright orange and chunky from half-digested food. And it keeps coming. I keep gagging and every time I pull in another breath I smell Ian's cologne and I start up again.

He shouts out in shock and stumbles away from me. He wipes at his face, trying to clear off the vomit, but as he stumbles back, he trips over the rocks at the edge of his ornate indoor koi pond.

I've stopped gagging, there's nothing left in my stomach. So, I wipe my eyes and watch in horror as Ian cartwheels over the rocks and plunges into his fish pond. The water rolls over the edge and splashes onto the floor.

Oh no. Oh no.

I rush forward. But, oh, that makes my stomach hurt. I grab my abdomen and watch as Ian splashes around and then comes sputtering up to the surface of the shallow water. His expensive suit is drenched and a lily pad hangs from his shoulder. There's a bit of water weed in his hair, which is plastered to his head, and the koi fish have swarmed him and are starting to nibble at the blueberries stuck to his jacket.

I have to say it. Ian Fortune doesn't look sexy. He looks like a tool. A puke and pond weed-covered tool.

He shakes his head and the water flies from his wet hair and splashes against my sweater. Then he forcefully rubs the water from his eyes and his face.

"What the hell is wrong with you?" he snarls.

My face drains of blood, and I realize that I don't need any test results, because what's wrong with me, is...I'm pregnant.

I can't help it, the biggest, happiest smile breaks out across my face.

This is the best day, the absolute best day of my life.

I can't wait to tell Josh.

"What are you smiling at?" Ian grinds out through his teeth.

"I'm taking a sick day," I say with a beaming smile. I start toward the door and call over my shoulder, "Really sorry. Sorry about the fish and...stuff. Also, no thank you. I'm not a loser. The only way I'd be one is if I kept dating you."

I hear him smacking around in the water, swearing and snarling. But I can't be bothered to care. I'm pregnant, I think I'm pregnant, puking on your boss is a symptom of being pregnant, isn't it? I'm pregnant. I can't wait to tell Josh. I can't wait to get my results. I can't wait.

I can't wait to meet my baby.

24

*"Focus on the positive
and life will bring
you endless amounts
of joy."*

I CALL JOSH AS SOON AS I LEAVE MY OFFICE BUILDING. I BARELY feel the winter wind or the cold air. In fact, I can barely feel my feet hitting the sidewalk. I'm floating on a surge of pure happiness.

Like Ian (ugh) says, focus on the positive and life will bring you endless amounts of joy.

He may be a douche, but he has a way with words.

I let the phone ring and ring. I think Josh's voicemail is about to come on when he picks up.

"Hello?" His voice is thick and sleep-filled.

"Hey." I grin like a loon, even though he can't see me. A woman walking a pair of dogs sees my grin, frowns, and crosses to the other side of the sidewalk. Apparently, undiluted happiness is scary.

"Did I wake you?"

"Mmm. I worked late." I like the sound of his morning voice. It's deep and gravelly, sort of intimate. A picture of him shirtless, lying in bed, his hair messy and his jaw unshaven flashes through my mind.

Wow. I stop walking, and a heated flush rushes over me. It's freezing out, but I don't feel it.

I clear my throat.

"You okay? What's up?"

Right. Amazing, amazing things are happening. I start hurrying toward my apartment again.

"I puked on Ian."

I hear a sharp surprised laugh, then a cough, and then Josh drops his phone. I hear the rustling of his sheets, him jumping out of bed, and then putting the phone up to his ear. "Gemma? Did you just say you puked on Ian?"

"Yeah?" Maybe I shouldn't have started with that.

"Huh. Not what I was expecting." There's rustling and then his voice is muffled when he says, "Hang on. I'm throwing on some clothes."

I try to block my imagination from running rampant with that visual. It already ran wild with Josh's gravelly morning voice. But I can hear the cotton whoosh of a t-shirt and the zipping up of jeans and it's hard not to think what's happening on the other side of the phone line.

"I'm back. Are you alright? You sick?"

"No, no, I feel great." I'm a little surprised at that, but I feel completely fine. I haven't actually spoken to Josh since Valentine's Day, and before anything else is said, I need to clear the air. "Look, I don't know why you went all Hulk on Ian, but I trust you had a good reason."

He doesn't say anything, so I continue, "When we went back to his place there was another woman. She was naked and, well, I left. I won't be going out with him again."

There's a whole lot more pain behind last weekend than those three sentences can convey, but I try to keep it short and light.

He's quiet for a moment, and then he says in a low voice, "I'm sorry, Gem. You okay?"

It's funny. I realize that he could've said, "I told you so," or "I could've told you he was an ass." In fact, Leah probably will say that. Brook too.

But Josh doesn't. He just asks if I'm okay.

And him asking me if I'm okay rather than telling me I should've known better is enough to make me wipe at my eyes. "I'm alright. You know me, I'm a true believer that there's always a bright side, always something positive in every situation."

That's been my core belief, the mantra that has kept me afloat for years. It was the first quote I found on Ian's website all those years ago. I believe it with all my heart.

"That's true, but I do have one question," Josh says.

Oh. Here it comes, the "why couldn't you see Ian was a poser?" question.

"Yeah? What is it?"

I hold my breath as a city bus passes and kicks up a cloud of feather-light snow and city dirt.

Then Josh says with a smile in his voice, "I'm glad you're okay. But where in the heck does the puke come in?"

I let out my breath in a laugh, "Let's just say it was my form of a sucker punch."

I don't know how I can tell, but I know that on the other end of the line Josh is grinning. "The universe has a way of giving us *exactly* what we need."

I chuckle and then look both ways before hurrying across the street. That's one of Ian's most famous sayings. So much so that even Josh knows it.

I'm halfway to my apartment, passing one of my favorite bagel shops. Somedays I stop and grab a cinnamon and raisin bagel slathered with butter, but today, I just want to get back to my place and wait for the phone call that'll be coming anytime.

And wouldn't it be wonderful if Josh were there too?

"So anyway, the reason I'm calling is because I'm playing hooky again."

"Oh yeah?" he asks, and his voice has gone all low and warm. I blush when I realize that he must be thinking of the reason for the last time I played hooky.

"Right. Yeah. So, I was wondering if you wanted to come down?"

"Really?" he asks, and he sounds surprised.

My cheeks feel hot.

"Well, I mean, I'm going to find out the pregnancy results today and I thought...I thought..." Suddenly, stupidly, I'm nervous. I swallow the lump in my throat. "I thought it'd be nice if you were here too."

My chest feels tight as I wait for him to respond. I'm not sure why, but it's hard to take a breath, and when I do, the icy air pinches my lungs. Finally, I decide that I'm an idiot, and I shouldn't have asked, because this whole thing has been for me, not Josh, he's just tagged along because he's a friend, a nice guy, a—

"I'll be there in a couple hours."

I let out a whoosh of air and it fogs in front of me in a haze of relief.

~

FOUR HOURS LATER I OPEN THE DOOR FOR JOSH.

I spent the entire time he was on the train pacing around my apartment checking my phone for missed calls from Dr. Ingraham's office and scrolling through my symptoms list.

Pregnant or not pregnant.

Pregnant or not pregnant.

Josh looks at me expectantly. His hair is mussed as if he ran his hands through it for the entire train ride. He's wearing a well-worn leather jacket, a t-shirt and jeans and he has a bag with him that is usually full of his drawing pads and pencils. When I buzzed him in I heard him take the stairs two at a time. Looking at his face, the question in his eyes, I'm so, so glad that he's here.

I wave him in and then point at my phone. I'm on the line with the nurse. She phoned right when Josh arrived.

I nod and let her finish her instructions. My heart gallops around my chest like a wild horse trying to kick down a fence. Josh closes the door behind him, pulls off his coat, and then watches me with quiet intensity.

I don't remember him ever looking at me like this before. Like I'm the only thing in the whole world worthy of his complete and utter focus. I try to take in the nurse's instructions, try to hear everything she's telling me, but my mind is swirling around and my heart is still trying to jump out of my chest.

Lord.

Good lord.

My eyes are drawn to Josh's. I hold onto his gaze and for the first time in my life I don't think I could look away from him, not even if I wanted to. Because he's not smiling, not laughing, not amused, he's...he's...

I don't know what. But whatever it is, it makes my heart race harder and my body feel tingly and uncomfortable.

There's an intensity to him that I've never seen before, but that I suspect has been there all along.

Maybe I never noticed it, or maybe he's never shown it before. I don't know.

The nurse wraps up her instructions and I manage to say, "Thank you. Okay. Yes. Bye."

I hang up and slowly put down my phone.

Josh watches me, he doesn't say anything, I think he's waiting for me to speak. I lick my lips and his eyes finally leave mine to latch onto the tip of my tongue circling over my mouth.

My stomach does a flip and I let out a shaky breath.

Josh's eyes grow darker and I notice that his hands are clenched and he's holding himself still. His eyes move over my face, carefully taking in my expression, and then he gives a slight frown and his shoulders fall.

"You'll try again?" he asks.

I shake my head no.

"No?"

"No."

Then I can't take it anymore. I launch myself at him, and thank goodness he's quick because he catches me in his arms. But I've knocked him off balance and he thuds against the thick wood door. I wrap my legs around his hips and my arms around his neck and I hug him to me.

"I am," I laugh, "I am. I am. I am. We did it. We did it. She stuck." Then I'm laughing and hugging him and saying over and over, "We did it, we did it."

For a second, he stands stone still, then I think he takes in what I'm saying because he pulls me closer and then he's spinning me around and the world is spinning in a happy, beautiful blur.

We did it.

The biggest, happiest smile I've ever had travels all the way from my heart to my lips. I bury my face against Josh's shoulder and breath in the familiar smell of him and feel the rumble of his laugh.

Finally, he stops spinning me around and he comes to a stop.

He looks down at me and smiles.

My heart turns over in my chest. I'm slightly dizzy as I focus on him. My face is inches from his, so close that I can see his pupils dilating and feel his breath fall on my skin. My legs are wrapped around his hips and my arms cling to his shoulders. Suddenly, I'm aware of the heat of his hands gripping the space where my thighs and backside meet. I'm aware of my inner thighs wrapped around his middle. I'm aware of my sensitive breasts pressed against his chest. And I'm very, very aware of my lips only a breath away from his.

My body grows heavy and I sink further into him. My lips feel full and tingly. I lick them and move a little closer to him. Josh's breath hitches as he stares down at my mouth. There's nothing I want more than for him to span those few millimeters and press his lips to mine.

"Josh," I whisper.

His pupils dilate even more.

"Yes, Gemma?"

"We did it."

Then I can't take it anymore, I lean forward and press my lips to his.

For a long moment he doesn't move. He holds completely still as I take in the coolness of his mouth.

"Kiss me back," I say.

Then, a dam inside him breaks.

He spins us around and shoves me against the apartment door. The thick wood rattles in the frame and vibrates against my back. Josh closes his mouth over mine. There isn't any gentle coaxing or leisurely tasting. No. Not for Josh Lewenthal.

He bites my bottom lip, and when I gasp, he plunges in. His tongue licks at me, his teeth nip at me. He invades me. Never in my life have I experienced a kiss like this. He thrusts his tongue into my mouth and God help me I suck on it and try to pull him deeper.

I dig my fingers into his shoulders and lean into him. The way he's kissing me, like he's been waiting years to take my mouth, makes me feel disoriented and dizzy. I can't tell up from down, I only know that I'm in Josh's arms and he's right in front of me.

He tastes just like I remember, like sweet longing, laughter, and promised pleasure. My whole body lights up and I moan at the sensations building in me. His mouth is soft and hard, smiling and insistent, gentle and demanding.

His fingers dig into my hips and I rock into his length. I cry out at the sparks that light in my core. He starts up a demanding rhythm, the pace of his mouth matching the rocking of his hips. I reach up and grasp the length of his hair and tug, so that I can have more of him. More of his kisses. More of his thrusting. More.

"More," I say against his mouth. "More."

The liquid ache spreading through me has centered in my core and it's growing and growing. I rub myself over him and my entire body blazes in pleasure. I cry out.

That does it.

Josh swears and lowers me to the hardwood floor. I'm panting, my lips are swollen, my breasts are heavy and all I want is Josh to touch me everywhere. I ache for it. I ache for him.

He looks into my eyes and whatever he sees there makes him stop and stare.

"Don't stop," I tell him. Then, in case he needs encouragement, "I have lime Jell-O in the fridge if you need it."

He lets out a laugh and the look in his eyes has shifted into one I recognize. It's the same hungry, wanting look he wore the last time we were together on a hard floor.

"Not necessary," he says.

Then he pushes me down and spreads me out beneath him. He moves to my feet and takes off my socks. He presses a kiss to each of my ankles, then he grasps my pants and tugs them down my legs. The fabric scrapes over my bare skin and I shiver at the fibers running over my legs. His hands circle my calves and he pulls my pants off. Then he trails his mouth up my calves, along my inner thighs and up to my panties.

I can't help myself, I tilt up my hips. He spreads his hands over my hip bones and runs his fingers over me. The muscles inside me clench in response.

Then he takes my sweater and the cami underneath and pulls them gently over my head. I lean back to the hardwood, the coolness presses into my sensitized skin. I sprawl beneath him and luxuriate in the look in his eyes. It makes me feel wanton and beautiful.

I watch as he swallows and his Adam's apple bobs in his throat. He's...nervous?

Not possible.

I reach behind me and unlatch my bra. My breasts come free, and even though he claims he's not a breast man, his eyes grow dark and heated. Then I move to my panties and ever so slowly I move them down my legs until I kick them off. I'm completely naked beneath him.

I'm flushed and wanting and there's nothing more I need in the world than him to spread himself on top of me.

His eyes never leave me as he pulls off his shoes and socks, then his pants, and finally his shirt.

Goodness.

Everywhere that I'm soft, he's hard. His shoulders are bulky, his chest and abs muscular and defined.

While I'm curvy and soft, he's all long lines and strength. I pull in a breath. Only his boxers are still on and I can see him straining against them.

Then he slips them over his legs and he springs free.

I let out a sharp breath, then I hold open my arms, inviting Josh to the floor.

He gives me a different smile than I've ever seen him give anyone before. But I don't have time to think about it because when he lowers his body over mine all thought leaves my mind.

I can only feel.

His knees nudge my legs apart, and I open for him. He kisses his way up my neck, across my chin and to my lips. When his mouth takes mine, he positions himself at my core. I tilt my hips up.

"Gemma," he whispers into my mouth.

Then, he slides in.

I cry out and cling to his shoulders. I've never felt anything like this, never in my life. I clench around him and hang on as he starts to move.

My word.

Josh is inside me. He's making love to me, he's making me feel things I've never felt before.

Every time he thrusts, my entire body lights up and intense pleasure rides through me all the way from my head to my toes. I'm climbing closer and closer and closer. He's pulled my legs around him and his hands are cupping my breasts, my shoulders, clasping my hands. He's touching me everywhere, kissing me everywhere. I'm rocking with him, pulling him close. Then, I feel the moment he loses all control.

Because he grabs both my hands, holds me down, and

thrusts into me fast and hard. So hard that I toss my head back and forth and cling to him. All I can do is hang on, because I'm almost there. I've had a million little explosions of pleasure, and they're all building and building, then Josh shouts my name and pulls me closer and I can feel him losing himself inside me. He's thick and hot and he's saying my name over and over. And when he does, everything inside me unravels.

I'm lost.

I'm completely lost in him.

Me and Josh Lewenthal, making love on the floor.

WHEN I'M BONELESS AND SATED, JOSH TURNS ON HIS SIDE AND fits my back into his chest, spooning me on the hardwood. I can feel the thundering of his heart. He smooths my hair back from my face. I lay on my side and take everything in. I'm sore, sated, achy and happy. Josh trails his hand from my neck down my back, tracing the line of my spine.

I remember the text that I sent him of my naked back. I wonder if he's thinking of it. His fingers run leisurely over my spine and I tilt toward him. My breathing has slowed and I feel like I've almost come back to earth. So much so that the hardwood floor is becoming uncomfortable.

In fact, the hard coldness reminds me of my parents' garage floor.

A flicker of unease passes through me. The last time Josh and I had sex, we ended up on the floor. It was fast and dirty. Just like this time.

He moaned my name and...yes...stroked my back, just like this time.

And then he went to college and I didn't see him for six years.

Because, just like every other guy in my life, I didn't really mean all that much to him.

Oh.

Oh no.

The only thing different about this time than the last was that I initiated the sex this time. I jumped him and he seemed surprised.

He wasn't expecting sex. He didn't necessarily want sex. But it's been two years for him, hasn't it? He probably would've had sex with any woman who threw themselves at him like that.

Oh no, what have I done?

In my stupidity, I complicated things horribly.

When I started this whole thing I just wanted a sperm donor. A nice, uncomplicated, business-like arrangement with a decent guy. We had a contract, visitation agreements. No complications. None.

My body runs cold and I wrap my arms around myself.

Josh's hand stills on my back. "You okay?" he asks. "Were you not supposed to have sex?" He sounds worried.

I sit up and start to pull on my clothes. My pants and sweater are cold from the draft that comes in off the floorboards. "No. No. It's alright. I can have...sex."

I flush and turn my face away from him.

From the corner of my eye I can see him stare at me, a confused expression on his face. Then, he pulls on his boxers and his pants.

"That's good," he says, and he sounds relieved. "I made the baby her first comic. It's in my bag. You could check it out while we get some pizza. Or I'm up for lime Jell-O if you want to go that route." I can almost hear the suggestive laughter in his voice, and my stomach clenches in response.

The thought *what have you done, what have you done, what have you done*, repeats over and over in my mind.

I turn back to Josh and try not to stare at his naked chest. I can't think straight when I look at him.

"Hey," he says. He reaches out and runs his knuckles down my jaw, then he gives me that smile again, the one that I've never seen before.

My heart flips over and then I feel like I'm going to be sick.

He frowns and pulls his hand away. "What is it?"

I swallow and look down at my bare feet. I can't look at him. I don't want to look at him. But if there's one thing that Josh always deserves from me, it's the truth.

We shouldn't have done that.

It complicated things.

It complicated everything.

"What do you think about telling everybody at your parents' get together on Sunday?" he asks.

I look up at him and shake my head. What's he talking about? "What?"

"Your mom's post-Valentine's Day pot roast. We could tell everyone the news on Sunday."

I press my hand to my stomach. "I..." I shake my head. "You're going?"

He frowns and studies my face. "I thought I was. Is there a reason I shouldn't?"

I clench the hem of my sweater.

"I wasn't going to tell them until I'm showing. And..." Oh, this is hard. "I wasn't going to tell them you're the father until..."

His shoulders stiffen. "Until when?"

His face has wiped completely of any expression.

I swallow and then shrug. "I hadn't figured that out yet."

My chest tightens as he takes a moment to study my face. Then he says, "You don't think they'll figure it out when I bring her home for weekends? Or when I pick her up every other

Christmas? Or hell, when she comes out with my eyes, or my nose, or my dad's hair or—"

He cuts off. Then he gives me a look like he doesn't know me at all.

Heat rushes over me and I say, "It's not that I'm not going to tell them, it's just, I'm not going to tell them yet."

"Why? What are you ashamed of?" he demands.

I look around my apartment, at my bed, my futon, my wall quote about the gift of love. But I can't look at him.

I can't look at him at all.

"I see," he says in a quiet voice.

But I don't think he does, because honestly, I don't see.

I'm afraid of him. I realize that now. I'm afraid of Josh Lewenthal. Not because he's horrible, or a cheater, or a bad person, but because of exactly the opposite.

Because I could easily fall completely, totally, irrevocably in love with him.

Maybe I already have.

I flinch at the thought.

No. I haven't.

I chose Josh to be my donor because he wasn't marriage material. He wasn't even boyfriend material. I didn't think I was in any danger of falling for him. At all.

I figured, he's thirty-three, living in his dad's basement, writing comics, making a joke of life, there's no way I'd fall for him.

No danger of getting involved. No danger of getting hurt.

We'd be friends, and that's all.

I could have a baby to love, and never, ever get hurt.

Except.

Isn't this feeling hurt?

I put a hand over my heart. "I'm so sorry. I didn't mean to complicate things. You're not...I don't want...this was just a stupid mistake. If we could go back to the way things were, if we could just be friends…"

Finally, I look up at him.

He stands completely still, so much so that I wouldn't know he was here if I wasn't looking at him.

"Josh?"

Then, the smile I'm used to, the one that says *I'm Josh Lewenthal and the world is here to amuse me* appears on his face. And for some reason, when I see it, my heart starts to break.

He bends down, picks up his shirt and puts it on. Puts on his shoes. All the while the smile remains.

He sends it my way, full wattage turned on.

"I'm happy for you, Gemma. Really happy. But I don't think we can be friends."

The room tilts, and I watch, unable to say anything as he grabs his coat and puts it on. Then he opens the door to leave. Before he steps out he turns to me. "Do you mind if I tell my dad? I'd really like him to know and he won't be around long enough to tell anyone else."

I wrap my arms around myself and nod. "Of course," I whisper. "Of course."

"Thanks, Gem. See you around."

I want to tell him to stop, to stay, to…I don't know. What? I don't know. I don't know what to say. I've made a mess of everything.

Josh gives me a final nod and then he shuts the door with a quiet snick.

I kneel down on the hard floor and listen as his footsteps fade.

I press my hand to my abdomen, but instead of making me feel better, for some reason, I feel infinitely worse.

25

*"My world is a better
place because
you're in it."*

I WALK INTO THE PINK UTERUS ROOM FOR OUR THURSDAY fertility meeting. I have a paper bag of hot beignets and a tray of egg creams for everyone. It's a celebration after all.

My most longed-for dream came has finally come true. I'm going to be a mom.

Just like Ian always said, anything is possible if you put your mind to it.

Thanks to modern science and Josh Lewenthal, I finally get to meet my baby.

A spot in the center of my chest starts to ache. It's the same place that hurts every time I think about Josh.

But I'm not worried, there's always a bright side, always a

positive, always a silver lining. I just have to wait and the universe will bring good things.

"Hey everybody, I brought beignets," I call.

Everyone is already here. Hannah has on a long, flowy cotton dress. She's trying to give Brook a pink crystal bracelet. Brook is in a business suit, a pack of cigarettes in her shirt pocket, and she's adamantly shaking her head no. Carly watches them both with an amused expression.

When I wave the bag of beignets and the cinnamon sugar smell wafts in front of me, Brook and Hannah stop arguing.

"Beignets and chocolate egg creams," Brook says in a matter-of-fact voice. "That means the transfer failed. Comfort food."

Carly tilts her head. She looks tired, and her eyes have shadows beneath them, but her lips quirk into a smile. "For once, you're wrong. Beignets are for celebrations."

"Really?" Hannah asks.

Before I can say yes or no, Hannah jumps up. "Don't tell us, don't tell us. I've been dying to try this pregnancy test where you pee on an onion and if it turns purple then you're pregnant." She starts rooting around in her handbag.

"You have an onion in your purse? Specifically for peeing on?" Brook asks. She looks appalled but also slightly impressed.

I walk to the circle of folding chairs and set down the tray of drinks. I hold the bag of beignets out to Carly. I remember last time she devoured them.

"Thank you darling," she says. She reaches into the bag and pulls out the warm, sugar-covered doughy treat.

I sit down into the folding chair and it creaks beneath my weight. The fluorescent lights overhead buzz and I breathe in the musty smell of old cardboard and dusty basement as I wait for Hannah to finish looking through her purse.

Finally, Hannah yells, "Aha!" She triumphantly holds a wrinkled yellow onion in the air.

Gross.

"I'm not peeing on that."

Hannah frowns and lowers the onion to her lap. "Really? Not even a little?"

I shake my head. "There's no bathroom down here."

"So you'll go upstairs?"

"Errr. No."

Hannah sighs and puts the onion back into the depths of her bulky purse. Brook looks over the handbag with interest.

"You know," she says, "I could really use a bag like that. What else you got in there? Could it hold some bricks?"

Hannah gives Brook a surprised look. "Maybe three or four. Why?"

Brook has a thoughtful gleam in her eye. "That bag is like the clown car of purses."

"Ladies, have you forgotten? Gemma has *news*." Carly says, then she dabs her lips with a napkin and reaches for another beignet.

All three women turn to me.

I try to hold back my smile but I can't. "I'm pregnant."

Hannah jumps up and rushes to me. She pulls me to my feet and gives me a huge hug. "I'm so happy for you. So happy."

I hug her back. "Thank you." But my heart squeezes a bit, because I hear Josh's voice saying *I'm happy for you, Gemma. Really happy.*

"Hang on," Hannah says. She hurries back to her chair. "I have a bracelet for a healthy pregnancy in my purse. I've been saving it, but you can wear it."

While Hannah digs around in her handbag, Brook and Carly stand.

Carly gives me a swift hug and kisses me on both cheeks.

Then Brook pulls me in for a quick hug, and when she steps back I think that she's embarrassed to have shown so much emotion.

"So, you're pregnant. Knocked up. Bun in the oven. Congratulations," Brook says. She looks back at Hannah and Carly. "How did the FF take it? And that Ian guy?"

"He's not an FF," I say automatically.

Then Hannah bounces up and holds out a bracelet full of different colored crystal beads. "Here it is. There's amethyst, quartz, moonstone, garnet, aquamarine. They prevent miscarriage, balance hormones, ease tension, prevent heartburn, soothe stress—"

"And bring world peace," Brook says.

Hannah rolls her eyes. "Here you go."

"Thank you," I take the cold bead bracelet and slip it onto my wrist. "That's really thoughtful."

We sit down and pass around the drinks and the beignets. I take a bite and savor the taste of cinnamon and sugar.

"So, how did they take it?" asks Hannah.

I look over at Carly. She's the only one who knows about what happened on Valentine's Day. So, I take a minute to describe what happened with Ian on our weekend away and then what happened in his office on Monday.

"I knew he'd turn out to be a dick," Brook says.

Hannah frowns at her. "Well I didn't. I had high hopes for him. I like his books. I read them all."

Yeah, no matter how I feel about Ian as a person, his message of positivity is really good.

I shrug. "I guess it's easy to think you know someone when you really don't." Then I frown, because that's similar to something Josh said to me. That I didn't really know him.

"How's the FF?" asks Brook.

"Not the FF." I scowl at her.

She grins at me while chewing on her straw. "That's the man you need to be with. When you walked away from us at Carly's party he watched you like he couldn't wait to get you all alone, strip you down and donate some more sperm to the cause."

Carly snorts indelicately.

I flush. That's not the way Josh looks at me.

"That's not how he looks at me," I say.

Hannah shakes her head. "Sorry Gemma, but he did. He really did."

I stare at them, then down at my hands. "It doesn't matter. We have a contract. We're not in a relationship and we're not going to be. That would complicate everything. Can you imagine if we started dating and then realized we hated each other? Or if we got engaged and then he cheated? Besides he's not really a dating and marriage kind of guy." My chest squeezes painfully. "My relationship with Josh is best staying contractual and business-like."

They all stare at me like I've sprouted two heads, and I realize that I just let out three days' worth of pent-up frustration and justification in a thirty-second monologue.

Carly is the first to speak. "So your relationship with him is a transaction?"

"Exactly," I say.

Then Carly looks at me with something like pity and shakes her head.

I stare back at her and realize what she must think. "No. It's not the same. I'm not stupid enough to enter a relationship with him."

Unlike you remains unsaid.

Hannah gasps and Carly looks up at the ceiling and blinks rapidly.

A flash of guilt rushes through me. I've made her cry. "I only meant you married your husband and you shouldn't have, not if you're too scared to tell him you love him. And you keep trying to have a baby with him. Why would you do that? A baby isn't going to fix your relationship. It's stupid. Like Ian says, you can't get the right results from the wrong actions."

Carly sniffs and I think my explanation just made things worse.

She wipes at her eyes. "You know, I don't remember telling you my reasons for wanting a baby. I don't think you have them *quite* figured out."

Hannah sends me a reproachful look. "You shouldn't have said that. My energy worker says any negativity blocks your fertility channel. You should apologize."

I stare at Hannah and then at Carly discreetly wiping her eyes.

The thing is, what I said hurt, but it was the truth.

"I told the truth. I'm not going to apologize for telling the truth. For instance, somebody should've told you months ago, all of your crystals, and herbs, and woo-woo stuff, none of it is going to work. None of it."

Hannah gasps.

"Wow," Brook says. "I think you're more like Ian than we realized."

"What?"

Brook holds out her hands and shrugs. "He pretends to be a guru but he's really a lying prick. You spout positivity quotes and pretend you're courageous, but really you're a judgmental coward. I've seen enough of human nature to know a dickish judgmental coward when I see one."

When Brook stops speaking the room goes silent.

I look over at Carly, but she's still staring at the ceiling, refusing to look at me.

Hannah looks down at her purse.

Brook crosses her arms over her chest.

There's something inside me that's whispering, *she's right, she's right*.

I shake my head no.

"You're the judgmental one. You always blame your husband for being infertile. Well, how about you stop smoking? Don't you think that has something to do with your egg quality? Maybe it's more your fault than you care to admit?"

Brook abruptly stands up. The bag of beignets falls to the ground. "I think the meeting's done."

I stand too. "Fine. This is my last one anyway."

No one says anything.

So I grab my purse and walk out of the pink room, down the long dark dirty hallway up the stairs to the darkness of the city.

I don't need friends. I don't need Josh. I don't need Ian. I don't need them.

I've got myself, I've got my baby, I've got my family.

That's all I need.

∿

IT'S MONDAY.

I skipped babysitting on Friday and the post-Valentine's Day pot roast on Sunday. I couldn't face my family or the possibility that Josh would be at the meal. I couldn't face it. I feel scraped raw. Plus, I'm exhausted and have constant stabbing cramps that make it feel like my period is on the way.

I looked up cramping in the fertility and pregnancy online forums and almost everyone agreed—cramps are a sign of early pregnancy.

The Live Your Best Life Virtual Conference begins in a few minutes.

We're all set up with a large poster backdrop, lighting, cameras, microphones, the works. Ian is in a tall chair in the corner getting his makeup and hair done. The sound technicians have already done their checks and the cameras are waiting to feed to the live stream.

I've been here since five in the morning getting ready for our nine a.m. start. I check my computer and see that almost twenty thousand people are already logged on waiting for the feeds to go live and for me to give my introduction.

Nearly the entire staff is at their desks, helping with the Q&A, the chats, the loading of the presentations and making sure the day goes smoothly. Lavinia has been tearing around the room reprimanding interns, scolding junior staff members, and for the most part, acting like a banshee. Today, I appreciate it. Her iron fist is going to make sure this whole thing goes off without a hitch.

Ian gets down from his makeup chair and strides across the office. He comes and stands in the stage area beside me. I have to admit, he looks great, like the perfect self-help guru. He gives me his toothy, bright white smile.

"All set, Gemma? My introduction is in..."—he looks down at his sapphire-faced watch—"fifteen minutes."

I brush my hair back from my face and nod. I'm wearing one of my new dresses, a classic gray shift with a black belt.

"We aren't going to have any problems, right? All water under the bridge? Keep it professional." He looks at me from the side of his eyes as he smiles at the cameras. "Let bygones be bygones."

I glance at him in surprise. That's the same thing he said to Josh on the sidewalk. "Sure," I say.

We have little microphones attached to our collars, and I don't want to say anything, because I'm not sure whether or not the techs are listening. Lavinia is at the sound board, she's watching me with her usual lemon-sucking frown and eagle-eyed stare.

Oh well.

"How about you practice your introductory remarks one final time. I can give you last-minute pointers on your performance," Ian says.

"Alright," I swallow and try to let go of the nerves that have been jangling around inside me since I woke up at three thirty this morning.

Ian steps close to me so that our elbows nearly touch. He's wearing his usual cologne, and it still smells like pine-sol and musty wood shavings.

He leans in and says in a low voice that I used to find sexy, "Go ahead, Gemma."

I clear my throat. The professional lights are bright and hot. I wipe away the drip of sweat at my hairline. I've been dizzy for the last hour, but I pushed through. This conference is important. It's going to help thousands of people. A little dizziness can't get in the way.

When I take a deep breath and stare into the camera black dots dance in my vision. A sharp cramp stabs my abdomen. I shake my head and clear my throat again.

"Welcome to the Live Your Best Life Virtual Conference," I begin. My voice sounds like I'm speaking through a long tube. It's far away and shaky. Another pain stabs at my abdomen. I blink away the dizziness. "We are so pleased to welcome you to the biggest event of the year, where world-renowned, self-help..."

I gasp at a sharp stabbing pain.

Ian shifts on his feet and frowns at me.

"Self-help expert and..."

I press my hand to my abdomen. It hurts. It hurts more than my period. It hurts more than...it shouldn't hurt like this.

"Gemma," Ian says from the side of his mouth, "what the hell is wrong with you?"

My face drains of blood and I feel cold and hot at the same time.

Ian scowls at me. He takes my arm with his hand and gives me a little shake. "Wake up. Try again, will you?"

I see Lavinia at the sound desk glare at us, then narrow her eyes on Ian. She moves over to the computer controlling the live stream.

Another wave of dizziness hits.

"Something's wrong," I whisper.

Ian digs his fingers into my arm. "Pull yourself together. Do your job."

I press my hand into my abdomen and try to lessen the cramping.

I start again. "Welcome to the Live Your Best Life Virtual Conference. We are so pleased to welcome you to the biggest event of the year, where world-renowned, self-help guru Ian Fortune will help you become the best version..."

I gasp and look around the office.

Everyone is watching. The interns, the junior staff, the programmers, the videographers, they're all watching.

"The best version of your...of your..."

Ian looks at me with his teeth barred and gestures for me to continue.

"Of yourself. The best version of yourself."

I look around the room, at the walls covered in inspirational quotes, at the cameras and the lights, at my colleagues standing in a semi-circle, and at the monitors showing twenty-thousand participants waiting for the live stream.

My heart lurches, slows, and then gives a hard thud against my breastbone.

Then my whole body runs cold.

Because I'm bleeding.

There's blood running down the inside of my thigh.

I'm bleeding.

I blink at the bright lights.

"Gemma, what the hell? How hard is it to give a two-minute introduction?"

"I'm bleeding," I whisper out loud, forgetting about the lights, about the people, about everything except the fact that there's blood running down my legs. And that means...that means...

Does that mean?

"I don't give a shit if your arm is cut off and is a dangling, bloody stump. Pull yourself together and give me the introduction an effin' star deserves. Are we clear?"

The room spins and I press my hand harder against my abdomen.

Don't go, baby. Don't. Please.

"Gemma? Are we clear? What, you need a quote? Here you go: my world is a better place because you're in it. There ya go. Now pull your shit together."

I look over at Ian's face, but I don't really see him. The room is a blur.

"Thirty seconds and we're live," someone calls out. "Quiet, everyone."

"Don't embarrass me," Ian growls.

I barely hear him. There's blood trickling down my legs, underneath my black stockings. The tech begins the countdown, then holds up his fingers for the last of the count.

We're live.

I look at the camera. My face appears on the monitors.

It's bone white and there's a sheen of sweat on my forehead. My eyes are glazed. Ian smiles at the camera and digs his fingers into my arm.

I blink and put a bright, bright smile on my face as another cramp tears across my abdomen.

My baby. She's not...she didn't stick. She's not...

"Welcome to the Live Your Best Life Conference," I begin. "We are so pleased to welcome you to the biggest event of the year." Black dots dance in front of my eyes and I put on a smile that I've seen Josh give the world a thousand times. The one that says *the world is my playground, the world is here to amuse me, isn't the world grand?*

Ian clears his throat, and I keep on. "Where world-renowned, self-help guru Ian Fortune will help you become the best version of yourself."

Another cramp hits me and I smile, and I smile and I smile. "Because when you stay positive and believe that the universe will bring good things, the universe will comply. If you ask the universe for what you want, you'll get it. So, please give a round of applause for the man who has bettered millions of lives, because what he says is true, accentuate the positive and eliminate the negative. Because there's always a silver lining. What is meant to be will be, and it is good. Ian Fortune is a wise man and I'm grateful for his words: you choose how you respond to a situation, you choose whether or not something is positive or not. I choose to make life beautiful. I choose the positive. The world is a better place because you're in it. Thank you."

I stare into the monitor, at my dazed expression and my colorless face and lips.

"Thank you, Gemma, for the introduction," Ian says. He gives a wide grin and gestures for me to leave the stage.

I walk toward the edge of the room. My body is numb, the only thing I can feel is the blood running down the inside of my legs.

I barely notice the monitors full of hundreds of comments.

Lavinia hurries toward me.

"I'm going," I say in a choked voice. "I have to go."

She frowns at me. Then says, "I think that would be best. Good luck, Gemma."

I look back at Ian, he's in his element, giving one of his favorite talks to the cameras.

I grab my purse, my coat and hurry out the door. On the way downstairs I dial Dr. Ingraham.

～

"THE EMBRYO NEVER ATTACHED," DR. INGRAHAM SAYS.

He's looking at the ultrasound. I am too. I stare at the screen. I can't make anything out, only gray and black and white shapes that mean nothing to me.

"But the blood test said I was pregnant." My voice breaks, but Dr. Ingraham is kind enough to ignore that. I rub at my eyes. "Aren't I pregnant?"

He shakes his head no. "This is what we call a biochemical pregnancy. It happens when you have a positive blood test but not a positive ultrasound. This can happen with early detection in pregnancy. If you hadn't had the blood test, you would never have known this wasn't just a normal period come a few days late."

I stare at him in his white coat and his latex gloves, what he's saying isn't sinking in.

"I was never pregnant?"

He shakes his head and pulls out the ultrasound. "You were. It wasn't viable. I encourage you to look on the bright side. We now know you can get pregnant, next we'll have to work on you staying pregnant."

I stare at him. The air from the vent blows over my bare legs and the paper gown flutters. The exam table is cold against my skin.

"We can start another cycle as soon as you're ready," he says.

I blink and my heart thuds loudly in my ears. "I'm not pregnant," I say again.

He frowns and pulls off his gloves. "It's an early miscarriage. It will feel just like a normal period."

It will feel...just like a normal period? It will feel...normal?

The breath leaves my lungs, and there's such a heavy weight on my chest that I can't pull in any air.

"You didn't have any other embryos that made it to the blastocyst stage," Dr. Ingraham continues. "Your partner will have to come in again to donate another sample and you'll need another retrieval."

I still can't pull in a breath. There's no air in the whole room, in the whole world. I try to drag in another breath and finally I manage to work my lungs.

"All set?" Dr. Ingraham asks. "You can start again with your next cycle. Let us know when you're ready to proceed."

I swallow and nod, but I'm not able to talk past the burning tightness in my throat.

He leaves me to get dressed again. But for the longest time I'm not able to climb off the table. I just stare at the blank ultrasound machine and at the red spot of blood on the paper beneath me.

AN HOUR LATER I MAKE IT HOME. WHEN I CLOSE MY DOOR BEHIND me another cramp catches me off guard and I gasp. I press my hand against my stomach.

Then I pull my phone out of my purse. I need to call Josh. He should know.

I dial his number and hold the phone to my ear. After it rings and rings he picks up.

"This is Josh."

"Josh, hi, it's—" I start to cry.

"Who calls anymore? Send a text. Anyway. Leave a message."

It's his voicemail. It isn't him, it's voicemail. I sniff and try to pull back my tears. I can't tell him over voicemail, I can't, I don't even know how I'll tell him in person.

I close my eyes and say, "hey. It's me. I'm playing hooky again. Call me?"

I hang up and drop my phone to the coffee table. The beaded bracelet on my wrist clacks as I drop my hand. It's the pregnancy bracelet Hannah gave me. The one that's supposed to protect from miscarriage and guarantee a safe pregnancy.

I stare at it. Then I rip it off of my wrist and fling it at the wall. The bracelet breaks and the beads bounce around the floor.

I drop down and wrap my hands around my knees. The bracelet took a chunk of paint off the wall, right above Ian's quote.

The one that says, *love is the best gift I've ever had the privilege to give*.

"Bull crap," I say.

Tears run down my cheeks and I press my thighs against my cramping abdomen.

Love is bull crap.

What has it ever done for me? I loved Jeremy and he left me for his current wife and their three perfect children. I loved my job and all of Ian's positive mantras and that turned out to be a lie. I loved my baby girl, I really, really loved her, even though I only had her for a week, I loved her. How stupid is that? I loved her.

I had daydreams about what she'd be like when she was born. What she would look like, and what her favorite color would be. I dreamed about her first smile, and taking her to the beach, her first day of kindergarten and her college graduation. The second I learned I was pregnant, I loved her. I loved her with my whole heart.

I sent her all the love I had to give. Every last bit of it.

Isn't that what moms do? Love their children?

I lay down on the floor and stare at the wall. I hate that quote. I hate it. As my baby girl leaks from my womb, I stare at the quote and the thought of love hurts.

"I'm sorry," I whisper. "I'm sorry I wasn't able to hold on to you. I'm sorry I messed up. I'm sorry I couldn't keep ahold of you. I'm sorry."

Then, I'm quiet.

I lay on the hard floor as the light comes through my window, travels across the floor, moves from late morning, to afternoon, to dusk.

Josh never calls.

My legs go numb and my body aches.

I'm sorry.

It's all my fault.

I'm sorry.

Love is a terrible thing.

When my apartment is dark and I can't see the quote on the wall anymore, I finally admit to myself there's one other person that I loved. But I messed that up too. Because Brook was right. I'm a judgmental coward. I'm selfish and fearful, and I've used all those quotes and mantras to keep from facing the world and facing the truth.

I've not always been a good person.

I'm not as brave as I pretend.

The reason I'm alone is because I refuse to let anyone get close.

I judged Josh and used him and kept him at arm's length.

And I love him, but I'm too afraid to admit it.

Because what if he loves me back?

As the darkness grows deeper, I realize I've been wrong. Truly, deeply wrong. Because there is nothing good in this moment. There is no silver lining. There is no way to look on the bright side. Josh is gone. My baby is gone. And all the lies I told myself are gone too.

26

"Love is the best gift any of us have to give."

THE WEAK LIGHT OF TUESDAY MORNING SPREADS OVER THE hardwood floor and settles on me. I lift my cheek from the wood and open my eyes. They're grainy and itchy, and I feel exactly like you'd expect after spending the night on an old wood floor. I wince at the ache in my back and my hips.

I consider calling in sick and crawling into bed when my phone starts to ring.

Josh.

I scramble toward the coffee table and grab my phone.

It's not Josh, it's Leah. I frown. It's only seven in the morning, usually this is when she's in the mad morning rush of getting the kids off to school. She never calls before nine, not until after the kids are gone and she's had her coffee.

"Hello?" I wince at the croaky sound my voice makes.

"Gemma, hey. Did I wake you? Aren't you working today?"

"Uh," I clear my throat. "I'm awake."

She doesn't hear me because she's pulled the phone away from her ear and she's yelling, "You only get one fruit snack pack, Mary. Put that down. Sasha, take your homework out of the cat's mouth. No, I will not tell your teacher the cat ate your homework."

While she's corralling the kids I stumble to the kitchen, grab a glass of water and gulp it down. The wall mirror reflects my red-rimmed eyes with dark hollows under them. Beyond that, I look exactly the same as I always have. I turn away. It feels like I should look different, that I'd be able to tell just looking at myself that everything has changed, but no.

"Anyway," Leah says, "Mom asked me to call you, because she's been so busy making all the food and everything and helping Josh organize. The "poor dear comes from a broken home" and all that. You remember. Kids, you've got five minutes to get in the car!"

I blink and try to understand what Leah's saying. My mind feels sluggish and fuzzy.

"Sorry. What are you talking about? What about Josh?"

Do they know? Did Josh tell them after all? Is my mom busy making her favorite party foods, mini gherkins on toothpicks, mini sausages on toothpicks, pimento olives on toothpicks, and lime Jell-O molds to celebrate me and Josh having a baby?

I wrap my free hand around my stomach.

That doesn't make any sense though, not even to my groggy mind.

"Oh right. You haven't heard. Josh's dad died on Saturday. You remember Mr. Lewenthal?"

I reach out behind me and grab the edge of the kitchen counter.

"What?"

"I know, kind of a shock. I didn't realize he was sick. His funeral's tomorrow. You don't have to come, obviously, since you and Josh aren't close."

I blink and try to take in what she's saying.

Josh and I aren't close.

Josh's dad, Mr. Lewenthal, died.

I think about the look on Josh's face when he talked about his dad. About how much he loved him. How he brought him dinner at night, took him to see the beach in winter for goodbye, how he said that when his dad was gone he'd be alone. How he asked if he could tell him that we were having a baby.

That he wanted his dad to know he'd be a grandfather.

I press my hand to my stomach, the sharp cramps have faded to a dull, echoing ache.

I hope Josh got to tell him, I hope he told him while it was still true. I hope...

Leah is still talking. "Mom wanted me to call you, since she offered to do all the food for the funeral reception and she wanted to know if you'd come up and help her. She's all stressed out, elbow deep in dips and casseroles. You know how she gets, I'll be there, but she's stressed. And she said you make the best Jell-O molds, which apparently Josh loves and she said it'd make him feel better. Kids let's go, it's time for school! Call Mom, okay Gem?"

"I...Leah...I..." My fingers dig into the metal edge of the old laminate countertop. I'm about to tell her, to tell her everything. But then I realize the line is quiet, and that she's already hung up.

I stare at my phone and at my distorted reflection in its surface. My chest aches and I'm surprised when a tear drop falls from my cheek onto my phone's screen. I swipe at my cheeks and then scroll through my contacts to find Josh's number.

The phone rings, and rings, and rings. Until finally his voicemail picks up.

I swallow down the hard lump in my throat, "Hey, it's me. I just heard. I'm sorry. Josh, I'm so sorry. I'm coming, I'll be there soon. I..." I stop and press my hand against my stomach and draw in a shuddering breath, "I'm coming. I'm sorry."

I TAKE THE TRAIN UP AND THEN SPEND THE NEXT EIGHT HOURS IN the kitchen with my mom and sister making funeral foods. Creamy potluck potatoes, seven layer salad, five bean salad, savory meatballs, stuffed mushrooms, macaroni salad, potato salad, chocolate chiffon pie, Texas sheet cake, lime, lemon and raspberry Jell-O molds.

Every three to five minutes I glance out the kitchen window. It overlooks the front yard and the street. Josh is out with Dylan and my dad. They've been at the funeral home all day, and then, according to my mom, at the lawyers, and then back at Josh's dad's house, and then back at the funeral home.

I want to see him, I want to hold him, I want to tell him I'm sorry. But I'm glad that if I can't be the person he needs that he has my brother and my dad. They haven't let him down like I have, that's for sure.

Josh said he'd be alone when his dad died, but he's wrong. He has my brother, he has my dad, he has my mom and my sister.

He has me.

He has all the people in town that have stopped by to drop off flowers and cards and food. People care. More people than he knew.

Leah plops down a bubbling hot tray of spaghetti casserole onto the counter. It's one of dozens of dishes lining every surface. She arches her back and lets out a groan as she stretches.

"I'm beat," she says.

My mom clucks then dusts the flour off Leah's face with a kitchen towel even though Leah is going on forty and well beyond having her mom wipe her face down. Leah wrinkles her nose. "Thanks Mom."

My mom taps her finger on Leah's nose. "You girls were life savers today. Josh the poor dear, when he showed up on Saturday I knew something was wrong. He looked so lost. Luckily, your father was there, and Dylan too. You girls are lucky to have each other, don't forget it. It's hard losing a parent when you're an only child. No one to share the load. But that's why we're here."

Leah bumps her shoulder against mine and says. "Hear that, Gemma? We're lucky to have each other."

My throat goes tight and hot, so I turn and pretend to readjust the chicken casserole cooling on the counter. "That's right," I say.

I hear the front door open and voices coming in from the front hall. I quickly turn and look toward it expectantly.

"Oh good, they're back. We'll have dinner. Leah, I'll give you a Tupperware to take home to Oliver and the kids."

Dylan strolls into the kitchen, looking tired and rumpled. I look behind him, but there's no Josh.

"Where's your dad? Is Josh joining us?" my mom asks.

Dylan looks around the kitchen and then meanders over to the counter and grabs two meatballs from a cooling tray and pops them in his mouth.

"Dylan Michael, that food is for tomorrow," my mom scolds.

I bite my lip and wait for my brother to answer my mom's question. "Dad's getting changed," he says. Then he waits for my mom to turn back to the beeping timer on the oven and he grabs another meatball.

I wrap my arms around myself and look out at the front yard. It's dark out, dusk has come and gone.

"Where's Josh?" I ask.

Leah looks over at me, and Dylan frowns. "He went back to his dad's." Dylan shrugs. "We invited him for dinner but he said he had some things to take care of."

I imagine him alone in his childhood home, the quiet and the dark. I bend down and pull a Tupperware container from the cupboard. "I'll run over and take him dinner."

Dylan shakes his head. "He'll order pizza."

I start scooping spaghetti casserole into the container. Then I grab another plastic tub and scoop in fluffy lime Jell-O salad full of whipped cream and lime zest.

"He should have a homemade dinner," I say.

"Why do you care what he eats?" Dylan asks. "You haven't paid attention to him in decades."

I stop scooping, the metal spoon hangs in the air. "That's not true."

Dylan gives me his big brother, I'm always right look. "Oh right, you had dinner together in the city one night. So what, you're friends now?"

"You had a date with Josh?" my mom asks.

"Mom," Leah says, "please. Remember two years ago, when you had the harebrained idea to set Gemma up with Josh? Remember what she said?"

My mom's mouth turns down in concentration.

Dylan raises his hand, "I do. Josh and I were in the next room. We heard."

I flinch and drop the spoon back into the Jell-O bowl. I don't remember, but by the look on Dylan's face, I'm sure it wasn't nice.

"What did you say?" my mom asks.

I shrug and shake my head. "I don't know."

But Leah remembers. "Gemma said, and I quote, 'Me and Josh Lewenthal? Are you kidding? He's been with the entire female population of this town, he doesn't have a career or direction, and he thinks life is a big joke. Why would I ever date Josh Lewenthal? I'd rather date Greg Butkis."

My body goes cold. I have a vague recollection of saying that. We were in the kitchen making a Sunday roast and my mom was trying to find me a date for the New Year's party. She suggested Josh. And I...I judged him and rejected him.

"You forgot the part where she said that inspirational quote, the one about the gift of loving and that she wouldn't waste it on a guy like Josh," says Dylan. He gives me a dark look. "It wasn't cool, Gemma. So if you're just going to go over and tell Josh some positivity crap or make fun of his life choices, you can put the spaghetti down. He doesn't need that right now."

I look down at the food spread out across the counter, ready for the reception after the funeral.

"Ease off, Dylan. Gemma doesn't go around dumping on people. She's just trying to be nice. It's not her fault Josh heard her. There were plenty of times she voiced her opinion of him and he didn't hear. Remember the Fourth of July party the year Sasha was born? Josh was there and she said, 'Where did all his potential go? Remember when we all thought he was going to do great things? But like Ian says, 'It takes a great person to do truly great things.'"

I'm cold with shame.

"Okay, I won't try to set Gemma up with Josh," my mom says. "They wouldn't be a good fit anyway. Gemma needs someone who doesn't mind that she can't have children. And who doesn't care if she's a tad bit overweight or wears oversized sweaters and—"

I press my hands to my cheeks. They feel drained of blood. Then I turn to my mom and my sister and brother. "Mom, I'd appreciate it if you didn't ever try to fix me up again. Or fix me, period. I know you mean well, but it hurts me when you try it, okay? It makes me feel as if you don't think I'm okay just as I am. And I know I'm not as pretty as Leah, or as funny as Dylan, but that doesn't mean you have to fix me. Maybe you could just love me as I am?"

My mom gives me a stunned look. "But dear. I do love you as you are."

I look at her through watery eyes, and I realize that yes, of course she does.

"I'm sorry, Gemma. I was trying to be useful. It's hard to be useful as a mom when your kids are all grown and living their own lives." She reaches out and gently tugs on a lock of my hair, just like she used to when I was little.

"That's alright Mom," I say. "Don't cry."

She sniffs and dabs her eyes with the kitchen towel.

Dylan clears his throat. "Well, Mom, you could take care of me by letting me have that tray of meatballs. And maybe that chocolate chiffon pie? I also wouldn't mind you ironing my clothes like you used to."

My mom swats at Dylan with the kitchen towel. "Shame. That's not what I meant. You're thirty-three years old. Iron your own underwear."

Leah snorts into her hand. Then she steps closer to me and knocks my hip with hers. "You alright?"

I shrug. "I don't know."

She nods. "Me either. I haven't for a while now." She takes my hand in hers and squeezes it, then we watch my mom chase

Dylan around the kitchen while he tries to steal another meatball.

"I'm going to take these over to Josh." I grab the containers of spaghetti and Jell-O.

"I'll see you tomorrow," Leah says.

"Tell Josh I'll bring him a tie in the morning," calls Dylan through a mouthful of food.

I wave as I slip out of the noise and warmth of the kitchen.

No one answers the door, but it isn't locked, so I slip inside. The house looks exactly the same as the last time I was here with Josh, except his dad isn't in the recliner in the living room and the television isn't turned on to some "medical drama garbage."

"Josh?" I call out.

There's no answer. I walk farther into the house. It's quiet and dark and there's a sadness hanging in the air that wasn't here before. It's like a curtain has been pulled and the room has been shaded from laughter.

I stop when I see a half-finished sudoku puzzle on the seat of the recliner. I wonder how many half-finished things lie around the house, waiting for Josh to stumble on.

I clasp the containers of food to my chest and move farther into the house. There's a light coming from under the door leading to the basement. I turn the door handle and walk down the carpeted stairs.

I let out a shaky breath when I see Josh hunched over his drawing table. His back is to me, his shoulders are slumped and he's running his pencil over a piece of paper. I stop on the stairs. He looks so...un-Joshlike.

His dark hair falls over his forehead and blocks his face

from view. But the lonely tilt of his head, the darkness of the room, the tightness with which he holds the pencil, he looks so alone.

I must have made a noise, because suddenly he stiffens and then turns in his chair toward the stairs.

I pull in a breath when I see his face.

Oh Josh.

He looks...he looks like I did when I looked into the mirror this morning. At the time, I didn't think there was a difference in me, but now I know there was, because I can see it in him.

He tries to lift his lips into a smile, but it falls flat.

"Hey Gemma," he says. He sets his pencil down and stands. "What's up?"

The air I pull in burns my lungs. My legs are shaky as I walk down the rest of the stairs. I hold up the plastic containers. "I brought you dinner."

He stares at the containers, like he isn't sure exactly what they mean or what he's supposed to say. Finally he swallows and nods. "Okay. Thanks."

I set the food down on the edge of the drawing table. I catch a quick glimpse of what looks like a kid in a spaceship and planets and stars.

I turn back to him, try to smile and fail. "It's spaghetti and lime..."

He nods politely, distantly, so I trail off, then say, "Did you get my messages?"

He shakes his head. "I have so many calls I stopped checking. I didn't realize how much work it is to bury someone."

"I'm sorry," I whisper.

He pushes a hand through his hair and sighs. "Look Gemma. It's been a long few days—"

He's going to ask me to go. The back of my eyes burn. I

thought I couldn't cry anymore, but I think I was wrong. My throat feels raw.

I don't think, I close the three feet between us and wrap my arms around him. "I'm sorry," I tell him. "I'm sorry."

I bury my face against his chest and whisper it again and again. He stands unmoving and stiff. My heart breaks a little more. He wants me to go.

I start to pull away, but suddenly Josh moves, his arms come around me and he pulls me close and drops his face to my hair. Then, I feel his shoulders start to shake with choked tears as he silently mourns his dad.

His hands move over my back and he clings to my dress and pulls me closer. I hold him as tight as I possibly can.

We stand in the center of the darkened room holding each other. The only light is a small desk lamp illuminating the drawing table. I bury my face into Josh's chest and he drops his chin to rest on my head. Minutes pass. We don't speak, and I don't want to move.

But finally Josh pulls away. When he does I notice the chill in the room and wrap my arms around myself. He gives me a small smile that doesn't reach his eyes. "Sorry about that. I guess it hadn't really hit me that he's gone."

I shake my head. "It's okay."

He puts his hands in his pockets and takes a step back. "How are you?" He looks down at my arms crossed over my abdomen. "How's the baby?"

My skin goes cold and I turn my face to the side. I'm weak, aren't I? Because it's so hard to say this out loud. And I don't have any pithy quotes or positivity to make it better either.

"Gemma?"

I look back at him. He's a better person than I ever knew, than I ever gave him credit for. I wish I'd seen it two years ago, or two months ago, or heck, even two weeks ago.

"Did you get to tell your dad?" I ask. I hold my breath. I hope he at least had that.

Josh nods. "He was really happy. I told him you'd give her his middle name. Charlotte for Charles." He gives a wry smile. "You don't have to. Obviously he's not here to know the difference. But it made him happy to think you'd do it."

My heart beats a painful tune in my chest.

"I'm sorry," I whisper.

He shrugs and gives me the ghost of one of his former smiles. "No worries. Like I said, you don't have to—"

"She didn't make it." I hold my breath to keep from crying.

Josh stops and his brows lower in confusion. "What?"

I shake my head quickly and pull in a sharp breath. "I miscarried. I'm...miscarrying."

He stares at me, and the look he gives me makes me realize for the first time how much he wanted her. How much he cared.

He wasn't just a donor.

He wasn't just a friend.

He loved her too.

"How? Was it...?"

I shake my head. "No. We didn't cause it. Dr. Ingraham said it's common. That about twenty percent of all IVF pregnancies result in biochemical pregnancies. He said..." I stop, because I can't remember what he said. And it doesn't matter what the percentages are, because a percentage is just a percentage until it happens to you.

"You're bleeding right now?" Josh asks.

I look at him and nod.

He closes his eyes. His lips tremble, then he presses them into a firm line. After a moment he draws in a deep, shuddering breath. When he opens his eyes again, he steps forward and runs his finger over my cheek to catch a tear.

"I had that comic I wrote for her. Do you mind if I read it, before...?"

I look at the table and the papers laid out. "Of course. Of course."

He walks to the table and pulls off the top sheet. The one I saw with the girl and the rocket ship and the stars and planets.

We walk to the couch and he sets the paper down between us.

"Before you were born," he begins. His voice is deep and raspy, "your parents didn't know you, but they imagined you."

Before you were born, I loved you.

I listen as Josh reads the story of the little girl that builds an imaginary spaceship and travels the stars. Her spaceship is powered by her dreams and by her parents' love.

"I can't wait to see the heights you reach. And the people's hearts you touch. I can't wait to meet you in this big, wide universe."

Josh sets down the paper and looks up at me. "Okay?" he asks.

I nod. "Do you think it's stupid that I loved her?"

Josh shakes his head. "No. But if it was, we can be stupid together."

Josh takes me and pulls me across the couch to settle against his chest. He rests his hands over my abdomen.

"I'm not sure that loving anyone is worth it. You always get hurt, don't you?" I say.

Josh strokes his hand over mine. "Come on, Gemma. Love is the best gift any of us have to give." He says it with a slight smile in his voice that makes my heart give a little tug.

"You don't believe in all that Ian stuff."

Josh looks down at me and raises an eyebrow. "You'd be surprised."

I lay my head to his chest and listen to his heart.

"I'm sorry," I tell him again. "I'm sorry about your dad. And I'm sorry about all this. For dragging you into it, for using you—"

"Hey. You didn't use me. I wanted to do this. I went in eyes wide open."

I look up at him. "Leah and Dylan reminded me tonight that I've said some crappy things about you. I had the wrong impression for a long time. I'm sorry for that. It's hard to admit when you've been so wrong about someone. And I was wrong about you for a long time. For the record, I think you're the best person I've ever known. No matter whether you'd like to be my friend or not. I've got some things to figure out, I haven't been wrong about just you, but a whole lot of stuff. I doubt you were wondering, but in case you were, I like you, Josh Lewenthal. I like you exactly as you are and I don't think you should change a thing."

He lets out a short huff of air and makes a surprised sound. "I like you too."

I smile up at him. "Exactly as I am?"

"Maybe you could stop hogging all the lime Jell-O?"

I jab my elbow into his side and he gives me his first genuine smile of the night.

"Exactly as you are," he says.

Then he pulls me down into his chest and leans back into the couch cushions. Within minutes he's asleep. The warmth of his arms and the steadiness of his breath lull me and I fall asleep in his arms.

27

No more quotes

THE HOUSE IS MORE CROWDED THAN IT IS DURING THE NEW Year's resolution party. All the food that Mom, Leah and I made yesterday is spread out on the dining room table for the after-funeral reception. There has to be at least a hundred people here. My mom had my dad pull out the plastic coverings this morning to shield the furniture and the carpet.

"Have you seen Josh?" asks Leah.

She leans over the dining room table, grabs a plate and piles it with pimento olives.

"No. Not since the funeral."

My family sat next to him at the graveside service. Josh didn't look at me, or at anyone really, for the entire service. But during the last song, Amazing Grace, he dropped his hand, reached over and brushed the back of his knuckles against mine.

"I guess he wanted to stay a little longer," Leah says. Then she sees Mary and Maemie tearing through the living room chasing after a remote-control car. "Girls, not inside," she calls. She turns back to me. "About last night."

"Hmm?"

I left Josh's shortly after sunrise. I have to admit that when I woke up at five, I pretended to be asleep for a few moments so that I could keep lying next to him. But then he stretched and looked down at me and said, "You slept with me, Gem. Does that mean I get breakfast?"

I blinked up at him and realized that he was joking and trying his best to face one of the hardest days of his life. I made him chocolate chip pancakes, bacon and coffee. While we ate at the kitchen table he rested his foot against my ankle and stroked his arch up and down my calf. I looked up at him and flushed, but he just smiled at me and kept eating.

When I got back to my parents', I showered and put on one of the new dresses I bought with Carly. A conservative navy and black dress with heels.

"I've been thinking about what you said to Mom."

"Oh. Right." I shake myself out of my thoughts and focus on my sister.

"You're right. I'm sorry, Gem. I always thought Mom was the only one who thought you needed fixing, but I realized yesterday that I've thought it too. It's why I never really told her to stop. Truth be told, I was sometimes envious of you. It's hard having four kids. I've been feeling overwhelmed. It's hard, Gem. I've wanted to tell you but you're so busy with your job and your life in the city and sometimes I wish I had what you had. No concerns."

I give my sister a stunned look. As usual, she looks perfectly put together in a lovely black dress with her hair in a braided twist. I've always judged her as having the perfect life, being the perfect mother, I thought she had no concerns.

I was wrong about her too. My own sister.

Suddenly it hits me. Each of us, all the people in our lives, are like icebergs floating near each other. We only see the top of the icebergs, the faces we show the world, and the rest, all our inner lives and secret fears remain hidden underneath the surface.

I was judging based on the tiniest glimpse of a person, not what was inside.

But the thing is, Leah is wrong about me too. Because I haven't shared either. I was too afraid to share myself with my own family.

I look around the dining room. No one is nearby.

"I'm sorry, Leah, I didn't realize. Funny thing, I've always envied you. I'd love to have a big family." I bite my bottom lip and then decide to take the plunge. "I'm trying to have a baby."

Leah starts to choke on the pimento olive she was eating. She hits her chest and her eyes begin to water.

"Did you just say you're having a baby?"

I turn around. My mom stands behind me, a shocked look on her face.

"But Gemma, you're infertile. And single. Unless? What?" My mom stops talking and shakes her head in confusion.

I look around at the large number of people gathered in the living room. There's Mimi and Greg Butkis, Father Gibbly, a number of Mr. Lewenthal's former colleagues.

I grab Leah and my mom and pull them into the kitchen.

It's time.

I won't tell them about Josh's role, that's his decision, but it's time I told my family who I am, or at least, who I want to be.

When my mom and Leah face me, I say, "I had IVF. I was pregnant, but it didn't stick."

My mom's hand flies to her mouth.

"Mom. I know you want me to get married to some old guy

and follow the traditional route for life, but that's not how things have worked out. I might have a baby with IVF, and I might be single when it happens, and I hope that you'll love me and the baby just as much as you would if it happened in the normal way of things."

My mom takes a hard swallow then puts her hands on her hips. "What's normal, Gemma Louise? Normal, my behind. What kind of nonsense are you talking about? If this is what you want, if it will make you happy, then you go on ahead and do it. I'll love my grandbaby no matter how he gets here. What are you on about? Normal. Bah."

She pulls me into a hug and tugs on my hair. "There. Life is wonderful, isn't it? There, there, Gemma." She pats my back and I realize that I'm sniffling back tears.

"I lost an early pregnancy last year," my sister says. "It's why I was so down at Christmas and New Year's."

I pull out of my mom's arms. My mom nods at Leah. She already knew.

"It was hard," she says.

My mom nods again.

I look at them both. "Sometime soon, do you want to go out, all of us, just us? It's been years. I miss you."

My mom smiles and a little spark enters her eyes that I usually only see right before she's about to suggest another match. "You can tell us all about IVF."

A few minutes later Leah is called away by Colin, his remote-control car's battery died. Then my mom is called away to replace the seven layer salad and refill the punch bowl. I'm left alone in the kitchen.

I sit quietly for a moment and take in how much has happened.

I still don't believe in quotes, and I'm not sure about love, but I do know that I've been doing some things wrong, and I have work to do. First, I need to find a new job. Second, I need to apologize to my friends. Third, I need to ask Josh if he'll forgive me, and if he could possibly maybe want to try again. My heart thuds at the thought.

I'll give him time.

We both need some time.

I walk back toward the dining room. When I do, I see Josh in the living room talking to Father Gibbly. I stop and just watch him.

"Gemma. Wow. You look great."

I shake my head and turn to find Greg Butkis looking over my new dress and my figure appreciatively.

"Your mom mentioned at New Year's that you're looking to date. There's a new steak place in town, what do you think about—"

"She's not available," my mom says. She's carrying the punch bowl and pushing past us.

Greg turns to her and his mouth drops open. "Huh?"

"Buzz off, Greg. Gemma isn't for you."

I press my lips together and hold back a laugh.

"But, you said, my mom said—"

"Buzz off," my mom calls. She plops the punch bowl down and it sloshes over the edges. "What do you think my Gemma is, a buffet you can browse at your leisure?" She picks up her towel. "Shoo."

Greg looks at her like she's lost her mind. Which maybe she has. I hold back a laugh. My mom winks at me and then hurries back toward the kitchen, "Gemma, dear, I'm getting more barbecue sausages. If he bothers you, you can drop them on his shirt."

I cover my mouth with my hand. Because my mom knows about New Year's and Mort and all of that mortification. She saw and she's telling me, in her own way, that she's on my side.

I look out over the living room with a wide smile on my face.

At that moment, Josh looks up and meets my eyes.

My smile falters. I hope he's okay.

I mean, how can he be?

But I hope he'll be okay.

He says something to Father Gibbly and then starts to walk my way.

I twist my hands together and wait for him to reach me.

"Hey," I say.

He smiles. "Thanks for coming."

"Of course I came. Look at all the people that are here. So many people cared—"

"I meant last night."

Heat prickles over my skin as I remember the feel of his warm chest.

"Are you staying in town tonight?"

I shake my head but my chest pinches with disappointment. I wish I could stay. "I have to work tomorrow. And I have a lot of things to take care of in the city. Are you...are you staying up here?"

He nods. "For a bit."

He doesn't say anything more and my stomach drops.

"Oh..." I pause and look around the living room. At all the people in black and all the flowers brought back from the service. "Do you think...will I see you soon?"

Josh studies me, as if he's trying to read a code that he doesn't have the key to. So, I say, "I'd like to see you."

Josh closes his eyes for a moment, then he peers at me.

I shift in my heels and say, "Thank you for the comic you drew. It was beautiful. You can't know how much it meant to me."

He nods and starts to say something, but then one of his

dad's friends comes over to give Josh his condolences and in seconds Josh is surrounded by a group of people that doesn't thin up for more than an hour.

At that point in time, I have to head out if I'm going to make the last train to the city.

Josh looks at me through the crowd around him and gives me a half-smile. I hold up my hand and wave to him.

He really, really isn't anything at all like I believed.

When the taxi pulls up to the house I say goodbye to my mom, dad, sister and brother.

As I'm walking down the drive, the front door opens. I turn back and watch Josh jog toward me.

"What is it?" I ask, my heart in my throat.

He isn't wearing a coat. Tiny snowflakes fall around him.

"I wanted to say goodbye," he says.

"Oh. Okay. Goodbye."

"Bye, Gemma."

My heart falls from my throat to the sidewalk. You know what, there is no if, and, or but about it. I love Josh Lewenthal. I love him, really, truly love him. And for someone who isn't sure how she feels about love, that's a really awkward position to be in.

For all my realizations, I'm still as scared as ever.

"I probably won't see you for a while," he says.

"What? Why?"

He shrugs. Snowflakes dust his hair and his eyelashes. The taxi honks at me. I look over and hold up my finger in the "one minute" sign.

"I have to take care of my dad's estate. Then I'm going on tour."

"Tour?"

"To Europe. For conventions, signings, that sort of thing." He shrugs again.

I stare at him, unable to comprehend that Josh won't be around. He's always here. He's always around. I don't know what to say, I have no idea what to say to this. There are things I'd like to say, "don't go," "take me with you," "you can't leave," and "what about us" chief among them. But instead I say, "Wow. That's a big deal. Congratulations."

He gives me his smile, the life's-my-playground one, but this time I see past it.

Then he brushes my jaw with his fingers and leaves a trail of melted snowflakes.

"I'll miss you," he says.

I'm taken back to the time in my parents' garage when he told me he'd miss we while he was away at college and then I didn't see him again for six years.

"I'll miss you too," I say and my voice breaks.

He said, "I'll miss you." She said, "I'll miss you too."

The taxi honks again. I look at it, then at my watch. I have to go.

But instead of rushing to the taxi I wrap my arms around Josh and hold him in a tight, swift hug. And as I squeeze him through my winter coat I try to convey what I can't quite say, *thank you, I love you, I'm sorry, I love you, I'm sorry I'm afraid, I love you.*

Finally, I pull back. "Don't forget to write." I smile, even though my heart is breaking. "Isn't that what they say?"

Josh searches my expression and nods. "Sure is."

I press my fingers to my lips and then touch them to his mouth. "I...I'll see you soon."

He frowns, his expression solemn.

I turn and rush to the taxi. Josh stands in the drive, the snow falling around him. I watch him, my hand pressed to the window, as the taxi pulls away.

28

All the quotes

IT'S THURSDAY, THE MORNING AFTER THE FUNERAL. I WALK INTO the office at nine sharp, a steaming cup of coffee in my hand. I stopped at the coffee stand on the way up and Zamir gave me an extra-large, double cream and sugar on the house. He seemed to think I'd need it.

I spent the night sending my résumé out. By four in the morning, I'd applied for three dozen different social media marketing positions. Hopefully by this time next month I'll have a new job.

I look over the office. All the backdrops and lighting for the virtual conference are gone. The cameras are gone. I frown and stop walking toward my desk. I'd say only about a quarter of the staff are here. Most of the desks are cleared off of any personal possessions. They're empty.

What in the world?

Usually at nine, everyone is here, drinking their morning

coffee, starting on projects, gathering for team meetings. But this morning it's strangely quiet.

Lavinia is at her desk. She's pulling stacks of paper from her file drawer and tying them together with a rubber band. I walk over and set my coffee on the edge of my desk.

"Where is everybody?" I ask.

She purses her mouth. "You haven't heard?"

I look around, stumped. "Ian gave everyone a day off after a successful conference?"

Lavinia's lemon-pursed lips turn up into the first smile I've seen her give in seven years. I have to admit, it's really, really weird to see her smile.

"Well, that's good, I guess."

"He asked to see you as soon as you arrived. In his office." Lavinia waves at his glass door and then goes back to pulling folders from her filing cabinet.

I look around the office again. A few of the interns are openly staring at me and the database techie that I threatened over the sparkling water gives me a salute. I send an awkward wave back and then I pull off my coat and purse and hurry to Ian's office.

I have no idea what's going on, but I have a feeling it has to do with his introduction for the conference and then me leaving for the day.

I knock on his door and then slowly open it. Ian is at the back at his putting green. He's on the phone, talking loudly and pacing back and forth. When he sees me he gestures for me to come in then turns his back and continues his conversation.

I close the door behind me and wander slowly toward him. It sounds like Ian is in the middle of a heated conversation and won't be finishing anytime soon. I can't hear the words but his tone is *not* happy.

I stop at the koi pond and watch the orange and gold fish

swim to the surface and beg for food. But the koi pond reminds me of puking on Ian and realizing I was pregnant, so I turn away and walk toward Ian's desk. Just past it is an abstract painting that I can stare at while I wait for Ian to finish his phone call.

I'm only a few feet from Ian's desk when something catches my eye.

A book sits on the edge of his desk. It's open to a page near the center. That's not unusual. What's unusual is that the book is one of those thick, three-hundred-page, leather-bound drawing journals with unlined artist's paper and a silk ribbon to mark the pages. I lower my brow and step closer. The page that the book is opened to is filled with ink sketches.

I take a sharp breath and run my hand over one of the drawings.

It's me.

It's a sketch of me.

Or, at least me as I looked fifteen years ago. I recognize the T-shirt I was wearing, it was my favorite band, and I have on the thick-rimmed glasses I decided I needed to wear as a "fashion statement."

What is this?

The hair on my arms rises in goosebumps. I look back at Ian, but his back is turned away from me. He's looking out over Midtown, snarling into his phone.

I glance back at the journal.

Ian didn't know me when I was a teenager. He didn't meet me until seven years ago.

I look at the page again. Opposite the sketch of me are the scrawled words—*anything is possible if you put your mind to it.*

What is this?

Slowly I reach out and turn the page. It's a sketch of a

shaggy dog with floppy ears and a tongue that hangs from the side of his mouth.

I know this dog...it's Dodger. Josh's dog. He died almost fifteen years ago. Under the drawing of Dodger are the words *a friend is someone who accepts your past, loves you in the present, and believes in your future.*

My word.

Oh my word.

I bend over the desk and flip through the journal. It's full of Josh's sketches. Hundreds, no, thousands of drawings. There's a sketch of his childhood home, his dad reading a book, our school, Dylan laughing, me again, a landscape, a picnic basket. Every page, nearly every drawing has a quote under it. I recognize every single one.

Because Ian has used all these quotes in his books, on his website, in his marketing campaigns. My skin goes cold and clammy as I comprehend that the last seven years of my life have been based on a lie.

I turn the pages again and stop at a picture I see.

"What..."

I remember this day. It's the last time that my family went on a picnic in the park together. Leah had almost finished college, Dylan had just turned sixteen and liked to sulk, I was fifteen and feeling incredibly awkward. Josh tagged along for the picnic. I think Dylan invited him, or maybe my mom did.

After we'd eaten, my mom and dad called us all to come and lay in the grass and look at the clouds. Dylan and I both balked but finally gave in. So, for the last time (even though we didn't know it was the last time), we stretched out in the grass, held hands, and looked at the clouds.

Josh captured that moment with his drawing. Each one of us is looking up at the sky.

Except him.

His head is turned to the side and he's looking at me.

Underneath the drawing are the words, *love is the best gift I've ever had the privilege to give.*

My heart thunders in my ears and the world feels like it tilts on its axis, turns everything upside down, and then realigns itself.

Josh.

When I felt like I was broken after my divorce it wasn't Ian's words that pulled me up, it was Josh. When I felt that I couldn't go on after my diagnosis, it wasn't Ian who helped me, it was Josh. Every time I quoted Ian to Josh, I was actually quoting Josh back to himself.

Why didn't he ever tell me?

Why didn't he ever say anything?

"I didn't know that was you in the drawings until this year," Ian says.

I look sharply over at him. I was so engrossed in the journal that I didn't hear him walk up. He gestures at the picture. "Your looks improved with age. Lucky for you."

A hot anger rises in me. "You stole Josh's book." It's half-question, half-statement. Then, Ian smirks, and like a movie shown in replay, I remember all of Ian's questions about Josh, his gloating reaction to Josh outside the restaurant. I remember how Josh stared at the quote on my wall, how he seemed annoyed whenever I told him to stop quoting Ian, how I thought that some of the quotes sounded just like something Josh would say. I remember all of it. And all the missing pieces click together to make a new picture. "You lied. Josh never took your work. At the start-up, you stole his work. You made a company from his ideas. You're the thief."

I look at Ian with a whole new level of disgust. I'd thought he was a sleaze that knew how to write inspirational words, but no, he's a sleaze that steals other people's words.

"You're disgusting."

Ian lifts his eyebrows, then shrugs. "Unfortunately, half my fanbase agrees with you. The microphones were on during your practice introductory remarks and someone fed them to the live stream."

I narrow my eyes. What's he talking about? Then I remember. He showed his true colors and someone must have aired him to twenty thousand people.

I remember Lavinia glaring at us, sitting behind the sound board. There wasn't any reason for her to be there. Except...

"You know who did it," Ian says. His eyes narrow on my face.

"I don't," I say.

I turn back to the journal. "This belongs to Josh."

Ian shakes his head. "Actually. It doesn't. I had my lawyers copyright, trademark and legally bind it to me years ago. Josh would have a hell of a time proving ownership. Besides, he never tried, did he? He could've taken me to court. But he didn't. Instead he decided to quit and start a *comic*."

I stare at him in shock. "But you stole from him. You lied. Everything you've done is based on a lie."

Ian sighs and runs his hand through his thick hair. "Gemma. Grow up. Josh was never going to do anything with this book. It's a glorified sketchpad that he left in a desk drawer. I saw it and realized the potential. I took it and made a multi-million-dollar business that has changed millions of people's lives. What's wrong with that? Tell me. *The worth of a person is measured in the fruit of their actions.* My 'stealing' and 'lying' has given millions of people hope."

I'm so stunned by his logic that I can't think of anything to say. Because in a way, he's right. No matter what he did, no matter how rotten of a person he is, the words that he put out helped people.

I press my hand against my stomach. I feel slightly ill.

Ian lifts an eyebrow. "Don't tell me you're going to be sick again."

I shake my head.

Ian nods. "Good." He gives me a searching look. "So you understand me then? Josh has never been a go-getter. He's a living example of his own quote, *I never regret the doing, only the not doing.* He is an example of *not doing.* For example, it's clear he has feelings for you, but he hasn't acted on them, has he? He let me steal his work, and then he let me steal his girl."

I clench my fists together and resist the urge to punch him in the face. Now I understand exactly why Josh laid him out on Valentine's Day. I'd like to do exactly that. "You didn't steal me."

"Near enough," Ian says. "That's not the point. Here's the deal. Three quarters of my staff has quit in outrage because of the 'incident.' The media is having a field day tearing my carefully built image apart. I need you. You believe in this organization as much as I do. I need you to issue a statement that you and I were role-playing a situation of how not to talk to others and it was all in good fun. Then we can come out with a series of videos about self-esteem for women in the workplace."

I let out a disbelieving noise and Ian raises his eyebrows.

"Furthermore," he says with the confident smile that I once found attractive, "next month, you'll be promoted to vice president of Live Your Best Life Starting Now, where you will spearhead an overhaul of our image and the recruitment of new staff. With a commensurate pay raise, of course. Think of it, Gemma. You've worked so hard. You believe in our message. You can help me reach millions of people and get the credit you deserve. We can do great things together. We can make a difference."

I look down at the journal, at the drawing of my teenage self, staring up at the sky. I wonder what I saw in the clouds that day, what I dreamed of. I wonder what Josh was thinking when he lay there next to me, when he drew this picture.

Ian watches me intently. "You have to see the reality, Gemma. Remember what I told you before? If Alexander Graham Bell hadn't stolen from Elisha Gray we wouldn't have the telephone as we know it. If Edison hadn't stolen from Tesla, where would we be? If Zworykin hadn't stolen from Farnsworth we wouldn't have television. Imagine that, by your reasoning there is a lie, a crime behind every television in the world. But isn't it better to be on the side of progress and not limit that?"

I look at Ian and nod in understanding. I get exactly where he's coming from.

Ian took Josh's work and made it into something that changed lives.

"You're right. *The only limitations we have are the ones we place on ourselves*," I say.

He gives me his bright white, toothy grin that has wooed millions of hearts.

"I knew you'd see it my way."

I brush my hand over the pages of the journal. "I do."

I shut the pages of the book. Ian watches as I do.

Then I say, "The thing is, I don't think I want to be vice president."

"Really?"

I lift my chin. "I'd rather be COO."

Ian gives a low chuckle. "Second only under CEO? Directly under me? Quite the negotiator." His eyes flicker to the journal. "You have more balls than I thought."

I pick up the heavy book and feel the soft worn leather of the binding. "Right. I'd like to be Chief Operating Officer of Never Working With You Again. Because if I did, the limitation I'd place on myself would be becoming a grade-A ass for the rest of my life. So, no thanks, Ian. You can take your enterprise, your reputation, your promotion and your philosophy and you can shove it. I quit."

Ian's face turns an unhealthy shade of splotchy red. "That's a mistake, Gemma."

I back away toward the door. "I don't think so." I lift the book, "I'm taking this. It's not yours."

He bares his teeth, "I have digital copies."

I keep walking away. "Good luck in life. There's one quote that isn't in this book that I think you should know."

"Really?" he drawls.

I open his office door and say, "It goes like this, you're a jerk and a liar and a thief and I'd rather have a dead-end job posting sad kitten memes about hemorrhoids than work another second with you."

When I turn to leave I see that all the staff left in the office heard every word I just said. They all stare at me with wide, shocked expressions.

Then, Lavinia raises her hands and starts to clap.

I can't believe it, but the database techie joins her, then the interns, then the web designer. I let out a disbelieving laugh. I grab my coat and my purse from my desk, wave to everyone in the room and hurry toward the elevators.

They're still clapping.

I turn and look behind me while I wait for the doors to open. Lavinia nods at me and when I smile at her, she purses her lips more tightly, because, wouldn't you know it, she's trying not to grin.

As the elevator dings, Lavinia rushes over. She has a wilted potted fern in her arms. "Take this. The light here is terrible. It couldn't thrive. Anyway, I won't be here to take care of it, I've got a job offer at a law firm."

I look at her in surprise, then down at the plant. "Um, thanks Lavinia. I appreciate it. And...everything else."

If she hadn't turned on the mics the world may never have realized what a toad Ian is.

She purses her mouth. "Don't forget to water it."

I smile. "I won't."

Then I step into the elevator and watch as the doors close forever on Live Your Best Life Starting Now Enterprises.

29

"I've never regretted the doing. Only the not doing."

I STEP INTO THE BASEMENT OF CLIVE'S COMICS WITH AN ARMFUL of decaf coffees and a bakery box. I'm late for the meeting. Hannah, Carly and Brook are already seated and Brook is in the middle of a story.

"—couldn't believe the freaking ice worked. He iced his testicles for two weeks and his sperm count doubled. Hannah, I think you're crazy, but even crazy is right once in a—" Brook trails off when she sees me standing in the entry.

"Hey everybody," I say.

I shift uncomfortably. I didn't exactly leave them with the best impression of me, and I don't think they expected to see me again.

Brook raises her eyebrows. Carly bites her lip but doesn't say anything and Hannah looks down at her lap.

"So..." I begin, "I heard there was a fertility meetup down here every Thursday, and that it...that it had some nice people at it." I swallow nervously.

Hannah wrinkles her forehead in confusion, and Brook crosses her arms across her chest and frowns. Carly shakes her head.

Yeah. I messed up.

"So anyway. My name's Gemma. I used to judge books by their cover, in fact, I was a real jerk about it. I said some stupid things to people I consider my friends. Also, I have terrible fashion sense and I'm routinely late."

Brook straightens in her chair and focuses on me. I think she's realized that I'm reciting her introduction of me from all those weeks ago, with a few modifications.

Hannah starts to smile.

"I want to have a baby, clearly." I blink quickly and say, "And I'm delighted to make your acquaintance."

No one says anything, all three of them just stare at me like I've lost my mind, so I hold up the coffees and the box and I say, "I also brought coffee and some humble pie."

Then Brook snorts and shakes her head.

Hannah gives a full smile and Carly says, "Darling, I absolutely love humble pie."

I give a sigh of relief. "Thank goodness, because it would've been really awkward eating the whole thing on my own."

Everyone starts talking at once, but over the noise, Brook says, "I *told* you she'd be back."

We sit down and I cut into the caramel apple pie with crumble topping. I hand out forks, plates and jumbo pieces to everyone.

"This is so good," Hannah says. "It isn't on my raw diet, but it's good."

"Darling, humble pie is on every diet," Carly says.

Brook grunts and says around her mouthful, "So to sum up my iced testicles story, our embryos came back with the PGT results and we had a winner and now I'm pregnant."

"What?! Congratulations!"

"That's amazing!"

I get up and give Brook a quick hug. She grimaces at me, but I can tell she's pleased.

"I'm happy for you," I say.

She shrugs. "It's all thanks to Hannah."

Hannah blushes and tries to deny it, but Brook says, "Please, accept my thanks. Did I ever tell you about that case where the woman never accepted thanks and it turns out it's because she was collecting—"

"You told us," Hannah interrupts. "And I had nightmares for weeks. So there's no need for a repeat."

I grin at all of them.

"What happens when we've all moved on and don't need our meetings anymore?" Carly asks. "Brook is pregnant. Gemma too."

I look down. I haven't mentioned yet that I'm not anymore.

"Hannah will be soon, I'm sure. And me, I'm not trying anymore. I had the divorce papers delivered to Theo last night. So, that's it for me."

"Oh, Carly. I'm so sorry," Hannah whispers.

I look around the room at the group of women who have almost nothing in common with each other except for one thing, not infertility, but friendship.

"We'll keep meeting," I say. "Why do we need an excuse? We're friends. We'll stay friends. Just because we stop fertility treatments doesn't mean we have to stop being friends. We'll meet whenever we want, for as long as we want."

They all look at me, identical stunned expressions on their faces. Then Brook says, "Who is this woman, and why is she talking like a real person instead of spouting inspirational quotes?"

Carly covers her mouth and Hannah stifles a laugh.

I grin at them and am about to give them a quote when the sidewalk cellar door bangs shut. Loud footsteps rush down the stairs and then down the hall.

"Who is that?" Hannah asks.

We all turn and watch the door.

"Did I ever tell you about that guy, the cellar psycho?" murmurs Brook.

But then Hannah shushes her, because a large, brooding man fills the doorway.

Carly pulls in a sharp breath.

"Wow," Brook says. "That's some Heathcliff going on right there."

No one moves.

It's Carly's husband. And he looks...terrible. The last time I saw him he was in an expensive tuxedo, perfectly groomed, an arrogant, impatient, disapproving king of his domain. The last time I saw him I would've bet that Carly was right and he truly married her for her looks alone.

Now...

"Carly," he growls.

Carly stiffens and raises her chin. "Theo. I'm in a meeting. If you would like to speak, do so through my lawyer."

He draws in a deep, shuddering breath. His tie is loose, his suit wrinkled, his hair sticks up on end, and his eyes are bloodshot. He looks like a man that just found out he's lost his whole world and he has no idea what to do about it.

He strides across the room, steps over the box of pie and comes in front of his wife. Carly flattens her lips and shakes her head. "I know you don't like to lose, Theo. I understand that this is just like losing a merger or having a failing stock. It's a hit to your ego. It's intolerable. But don't look at it that way. It will be easy, I promise." She lifts her eyebrows and smiles. "You can get a newer, younger model. One who finds your terms of marriage acceptable."

Theo flinches and the lines around his mouth deepens. He looks around the room, at me, Hannah and Brook, then back at his wife. "What is this? I thought you met at the Ritz on Thursdays. It took me hours to find you."

Brook snorts. "The Ritz?"

Hannah waves at her to be quiet.

Carly crosses her arms. "No, Theo. I don't meet at the Ritz. I'm sorry. I lied to you. I meet in a dilapidated, rat-infested basement."

He raises his eyebrows and gives her a surprised look.

"There aren't actually that many rats," Brook whispers to me.

I shrug. I saw two last week.

Carly continues, "I also dislike six-hundred-dollar sushi and prefer six-dollar burgers. With fries." Then her voice softens and she says. "I'm sorry, Theo. I haven't been honest with you. I can't continue our marriage."

"Is there someone else?" he asks, and his voice sounds close to breaking.

Carly shakes her head quickly. "No. Of course not."

"Then why?"

"I just...I can't."

Theo shudders and then drops to his knees in front of her. "Is it money? Do you want more? Carly, I'll give you all my money. All of it. Just stay with me."

Oh. My. Word.

Carly shakes her head no. "I don't want your money," she whispers.

Brook leans forward. "I'll take your money."

"Shhh," Hannah hisses.

"What, he's giving out money," Brook says.

Theo looks around the room. He looks lost, confused, and nothing at all like the scowling, arrogant businessman I remember.

He turns back to Carly. "You don't want my money?" He sounds surprised, the idiot.

Carly shakes her head. "No, Theo. I don't."

"I thought you were happy with our arrangement."

"Not anymore."

Theo drops his head. He says in a low voice, "Did you know, I was terrified when you agreed to be my wife. I knew someday money wouldn't be enough. But I wanted you so much, I took the risk that you'd stay. I know I'm not a good bargain. I'm not what you deserve. But if there's anything I can do to convince you not to go, tell me. Please tell me. I'll give you the world."

"Holy shit," whispers Brook. "Ask for a Learjet. No, wait...an island. Ask for an island."

I kick her in the shin.

Luckily, neither Carly nor Theo heard her.

Theo reaches up and grasps Carly's hands, like they're a lifeline. I can see her fingers shaking in his.

She's scared.

I know she's scared, because I've felt exactly the same way. Wait, I still do. It's terrifying telling someone you love them.

She looks across the room and meets my eyes.

I nod at her, "Love is the best gift I've ever had the privilege to give," I say in a quiet voice.

And I mean it.

I realize that I mean it.

I thought if I stopped loving then I'd no longer hurt. But I had it wrong. In life, there will be times that you hurt no matter what, whether you love or not.

I press my hand to my abdomen. I'm glad to have loved.

I think of Josh, cradling me in his arms. I'm glad to have loved.

I think of my mom and sister, my brother and dad. I'm glad to have loved.

I think of Jeremy, of my broken heart, and I'm glad to have loved.

I look around the room, at my friends, and I am glad to have loved.

Carly takes a deep, steadying breath and gives me a small smile.

Then she leans forward and puts her mouth to her husband's ear. As she whispers to him, his shoulders straighten and his head tilts up. He looks at her with something like awe.

"You love me?" he asks in a stunned voice. "You love me."

Suddenly, he shakes himself off, stands, grabs Carly under her legs and pulls her into his arms like a groom carrying his bride over the threshold.

"I'm taking you home," he growls. Then he whispers something to Carly. Her face flames bright red and she looks over her husband's shoulder and smiles at us.

"Wow," Brook says.

Hannah stares at them with wide eyes.

"Ladies. Have a good night," says Theo. Then he swiftly carries Carly out of our pink uterus room. She waves at us from over his shoulder.

We stare after them in stunned silence. When the cellar door clatters shut, Brook shakes herself and says, "She really should've asked for an island."

Hannah starts to laugh and then after she wipes her eyes, she asks, "Was there any more pie?"

I grin at her. "There sure is."

We scoot in our chairs and eat out of the box, our forks scraping the bottom of the pan. While we eat I tell them about the baby not sticking, about Josh's dad, and the truth that I've not been able to face. That I've been misjudging people I care about, hiding behind quotes, and hiding from love.

"I knew you had a thing for the FF," Brook says.

I give her a skeptical look. "No you didn't. You thought there was blackmail involved or a fetish."

She holds back a laugh and shrugs. "Well, I never said I was always right."

"What are you going to do?" asks Hannah.

I look at my two friends, and I know that whatever I decide to do, they'll support me. Or they'll tell me they think I'm being an idiot. Either way, they'll be here for me.

"Well, his dad just died and he's mourning, that's not the best time to start a relationship," I begin.

"That's rough," Brook says.

"And he's headed to Europe for a tour."

Hannah nods.

"And for the past seven years, I've worked for the man that stole his ideas and pretended they were his own. And I continuously quoted that man to him and...I've really messed up. You know?"

Brook pops a bit of apple into her mouth and nods. "You have," she says around her mouthful.

But then I think about Carly and how she was brave enough to tell the truth.

"I'm going to tell him," I say. "I'm going to tell him the truth."

"I think you should read his comic," Hannah says.

I stare at her and shake my head. "What?"

She nods quickly. "It's really good. You should read it."

"You still haven't read it?" Brook asks. She's swiping her finger on the bottom of the pie plate.

"No." And I have to admit, I'm embarrassed by that fact. Why haven't I read his comic?

Brook shakes her head. "Gemma. Read his comic."

But I'm thinking about something else. "What if...what if he says that he doesn't feel the same way?" I voice my biggest fear out loud.

But neither of them have to answer, because I already know. I take a breath. "It's okay," I say. "If he doesn't, I'm still glad to have loved."

Brook pats her hand against my thigh. "Thatta girl. Also, I had a client once in a similar situation, she took a meat cleaver—"

"Brook!" Hannah stands and shakes her head. "I'm going home. The pie's gone and I have an hour of fertility meditations and fertility yoga before bed."

Brook and I stand too, and I grab the empty box and the plates and cups.

Hannah digs around in her purse while I do, then she makes a happy sound and holds a piece of paper out for me. "I printed this out the other day. It might give you courage."

I take the folded, crumpled paper and open it up. It's a computer print-out of a single frame comic, with Josh's signature and date at the bottom. It's from just before Valentine's Day. The panel shows a man staring into the distance. His expression is forlorn. The words say, *'I've never regretted the doing. Only the not doing.'*

My heart thumps in my chest.

Josh drew this right after my transfer.

And then Ian quoted it to him.

"Who is this?" I ask, pointing at the man.

"That's Grim. The main character in Josh's comic." She closes her purse and starts walking out.

Brook and I follow.

"You've read it?" I ask Brook.

She rolls her eyes. "Duh. I'm one of those freaks in costume, waiting to get my comic book signed."

I give a surprised laugh. Then I squeeze her in another quick hug. "You're going to be a good mom," I tell her.

She gives me a watery smile. "Obviously. I quit smoking, my husband has magic ice sperm, I won my last case. I can do anything."

I laugh.

Hannah calls from the stairs, "Come on. The rats are looking at me from the dark, it's creepy. Next time, we really should meet at the Ritz."

"Huh," Brook says.

Then, we all look at each other and say, "Nah."

Instead of parting ways, we walk to the subway together. It's nearly March and the weather is warming up. I tilt my face up to the night sky.

It's been a good day. I quit my job, got Josh's journal back for him, apologized to my friends and found the courage that I didn't know I had.

I finger the printed copy of Josh's comic in my pocket.

I've never regretted the doing.

30

"*Anything is possible if you put your mind to it.*" –Take 2

I SPENT THE ENTIRE NIGHT READING SEVEN YEARS' WORTH OF comics. And after nearly twelve hours of reading, three things are obvious. One, Josh is a genius. Two, he needs a social media marketing coordinator for his legion of fans. Three, he loves me.

He really, really loves me.

Halfway through the series I grabbed my purse and coat, hailed a taxi to Grand Central and caught the early morning commuter train north.

I stare at the last entry. Josh uploaded it last night.

The main character Grim is traveling across the galaxy, leaving behind any hope of being with the woman he's wanted for so long. He'll be gone for a year if not more. The last panel shows a picture of Grim and Jewel an entire galaxy apart.

I'm Jewel.

I'm the girl in Josh's comics.

When Hannah and Brook wanted to know if Grim would ever end up with Jewel and Josh looked at me and said he didn't know, it's because he was waiting on me to answer him.

He's been writing me a love letter for years, and I never knew.

I never knew.

The train slows to a stop at my station. I grab my purse and coat and jump to the platform. Josh's dad's place is only a half mile from the station, so instead of catching a taxi, I run. Because you know what? When you realize you love someone and that you want to spend the rest of forever with them, you want forever to start right now.

So, I run.

Josh doesn't answer. I knock and knock and knock, but he doesn't answer. The lights in the house aren't on and the door isn't unlocked (like usual). The spare key isn't under the mat. I knock some more. Then I pull out my cellphone and dial Josh's number.

It goes to voicemail.

"Josh. Hey. I'm at your dad's place. Are you here? Come answer the door."

He doesn't.

And he doesn't call back.

I start to text him, but I spin around when a car pulls into the drive. It's him, it's him, it's...Dylan.

"Whatcha doing in town, Gem?" he calls from his car

window. "Mom's making pancakes and bacon this morning, want some?"

I stare at Dylan. He works the night shift and when he's lucky, my mom pampers him with breakfast before he heads to his place and crashes.

"Gemma? I'm tired. You want pancakes or not? Stop knocking on Josh's door. He's not there."

My stomach drops. "Where is he?"

Dylan gives me a funny look. "He took the train down to the city this morning. Or last night. Dunno. He has a flight to London today."

I hurry over to Dylan's car and jump in the passenger seat.

Josh already left for his tour? He didn't say goodbye. Does that mean he'll be gone for a year? That he doesn't think there's any hope?

He didn't say goodbye.

"So, you're up for breakfast? Cool, sis, cool. I've been meaning to ask you—"

"Take me to the train station."

"Huh?"

"Dylan. If you care about your personal health and safety, put this car in reverse and drive as fast as legally permissible to the train station."

He looks behind him, then back to me, then behind him again.

"Dylan! Just drive."

Maybe if I can get back to the city in time I can catch Josh before he leaves.

"I can't," Dylan says.

"Why not?"

He gestures behind him.

I turn and look. Leah, Oliver and the four kids are loaded into one of those twelve seat rental vans. The kids wave at us from the windows. They're blocking the driveway so Dylan can't pull out.

"What the heck?" I jump out and run to Leah's window.

"Hey Gemma! We were going to come down to the city and surprise you. Mom and Dad were coming too. We're going to do Broadway and dinner."

"Hey Auntie Gemma," all the kids chorus from the back.

"Hey guys, hey Oliver," I say.

Dylan shouts out his car window. "I'm tired, Leah. I want Mom's pancakes. Move your creeper van!"

Leah rolls her eyes. "Anyway, what are you doing up here?"

My stomach flips over and my purse feels heavy with the weight of Josh's journal and print-outs of my favorite parts of his comics.

"I have to talk to Josh," I say.

"He's flying to London," Dylan calls. "Forget it. Let's have breakfast."

I grind my teeth. Brothers. Why?

"I need to go to the train station. I have to get to New York as fast as possible."

Leah frowns at me and then her expression clears. "You like Josh," she says.

I nod.

Then her eyes widen and fill with understanding and she says, "You *really* like Josh."

I nod again.

"Oh. Wow. Okay." She sends me a look that says she's here to help, whatever I need.

"Did you just say that Gemma likes Josh? My best friend, Josh?"

I turn around. Dylan has left his car and is standing behind me, his arms folded across his chest.

Leah glares at him and puts on her mom-of-four-little-kids voice. "Yes, I said it. Get over it."

Dylan stares at me, then at Leah, then he shrugs. "Fine. Whatever. Can we have pancakes now?"

Leah scoffs. Her phone rings, she looks down at it, then answers, "Hey Mom. No, we're on our way. We ran into Gemma. Mhmm. No, she has to catch the train down." Leah pauses and her forehead wrinkles. She says to me, "Mom says there's a four-hour delay on the southern route."

My chest squeezes and I shake my head. "When is Josh's flight?" I ask Dylan.

"I don't know, sometime today. He said he was going to stop by his place in Williamsburg first."

I blow out a breath. "Okay."

"Mom says we can all ride down in the van. It'll be faster than the train," Leah says.

"No breakfast?" Dylan asks.

Leah rolls her eyes. "Mom says she'll pack up the pancakes and bacon in Tupperware if you want to ride in the back and sleep on the way to the city."

"Cool. I'm in."

Leah gives me a searching look. "How about it, Gemma? Oliver won't speed, but we'll still beat the train. We'll help you catch Josh before he flies out. That's what you want, right?"

My chest expands. This is my family.

Oh jeez. This is my family.

Oliver drove by my parents' place and they climbed into the van. My mom had two coolers worth of food and drinks, to which Dylan and all the kid's cheered.

Dylan took five pancakes, rolled them up like tortillas

around his crispy bacon, ate them all in ninety seconds and then fell asleep in the back. He snores.

My mom can't stop saying, "Josh? Josh Lewenthal? I made this match, didn't I? Two years ago, I suggested it. And when you were little, I told you he was a good boy."

I cover my snort. She did *not*.

Then my mom gets a happy smile on her face, stares out the window, and then a few minutes later she starts up again.

Leah rolls her eyes at me in her mirror and I smile back. But it's a weak smile. Because I'm nervous. What if he's already gone? What if I was wrong and he doesn't love me and the Jewel in his comics doesn't actually stand for Gem? I shake my head, it doesn't matter, I'm going to tell him. I'm going to stop hiding.

As we cross the bridge, I stare at the glittering line of skyscrapers, at all of Manhattan sprawled out in front of us. Dylan lets out another snore and the kids start to sing for the thousandth time, "Josh and Gemma sitting in a tree. K-i-s-s-i-n-g. First comes love, then comes marriage, then comes a baby in the baby carriage."

I don't have the heart to tell them that their song is backwards.

Leah calls from the front, "I swear, if you kids sing that one more time, there will be consequences."

HE'S NOT HERE.

All ten of us are gathered outside of Josh's loft.

And wouldn't you know it, I had it wrong. When I pictured his place, I thought he was sleeping in a dingy, worn-down warehouse with a mattress on the floor.

No.

This place is a gorgeous, modern, brick-faced building, with large, bright windows and a huge entryway. It's big enough for all ten of us to crowd into. There are only three homes in the building, one per floor. Josh's place is on the first floor.

I ring the buzzer again. And again.

"Josh, Josh Lew-en-thal!" Sasha calls.

And then Mary and Maemie sing, "Gemma looooves you!"

My cheeks heat.

But I ring the buzzer again and all the kid's start shouting, "Josh, come out! Gemma's here!"

They're jumping up and down and shouting.

And even my mom calls out, "Yooo-hoooo! Josh!"

But no.

He's not here.

"He isn't here," Colin says, as practical as ever.

I have to agree. "You're right. He's gone."

I sigh and my shoulders fall. I missed him. He hasn't answered his phone or responded to my texts. Not any of Dylan's either. Which can only mean one thing. He's gone. He's either in the air or already in Europe.

I missed him.

"This is a beautiful home," my mom says.

"Not bad," my dad agrees.

"Yeah. He bought it after he got that television mini-series contract. It's not bad." Dylan shrugs.

All the grown-ups turn and look at him.

"What?" he asks.

I shake my head. I feel deflated. Hugely, unbelievably deflated.

On the first day of this year I told myself that I didn't care about Josh, that I just needed his sperm. Now, I realize that I've never been more wrong in my life. It's not about making a baby with Josh, it's just about being with Josh.

The two of us. Together. Come what may.

I reach up and wipe a tear from my cheek.

"Don't cry, Auntie Gemma," Sasha says.

"That's right," Colin says, "like you say, if at first you don't succeed, try, try again."

My lips wobble as I take my family in.

"Alright. Okay."

I walk out to the sidewalk and look around, try to consider my options. I could call Josh, tell him how I feel over the phone, but shouldn't something like this be said in person?

My family crowds onto the sidewalk.

A short copper-haired woman tries to push her way through. "Excuse me. Quit blocking the sidewalk, would ya? Move."

I grin. "Brook. Leave my family alone."

Brook looks at me in surprise then she takes in my family. "Why are they blocking the sidewalk? What are you doing out here?"

Sasha jumps up and down. "She came to find Josh Lewenthal."

"'Cause she loves him," says Maemie.

"Shhh," Leah says.

"But he's in London," Mary says.

My shoulders slump. "Yeah."

Brook narrows her eyes on me. "You read his comic?"

I nod.

She pulls out her phone. "I have an idea."

"Does it involve a Learjet?" I ask.

She smirks. "Not quite."

ONE TRAIN, ONE BUS, AND ONE PLANE LATER, I'M IN LONDON.

I'm at a spacious hotel and conference center in the outskirts of the city, this year's location for the annual United Kingdom comic convention. I hold the map and schedule out in front of me. Josh is doing signings in the northeast corner. I adjust the chin-length lime green wig on my head and pull at the spandex dress I'm wearing, trying to stretch it so it fits a little better. I'm a few inches taller than Brook and it's tight.

The convention is packed. Jam-packed. There has to be at least a thousand people here. Most everyone is dressed up in costume, carrying swag bags or books to be signed. I let out a breath and wade into the mass.

The convention hall is a huge space with high metal-beamed ceilings, bright posters hanging from the walls and the ceiling, and hundreds of decorated booths and tables. The concrete floor amplifies the sound of a thousand excited voices. At the back of the hall is an event stage with a huge movie screen playing loops of anime and comic art. I had no idea so many people would be here. I walk through the thick crowd and try to peer over people's heads toward the back of the hall.

Finally, I spot Josh.

He's sitting at a table, talking to a fan, signing a poster for them.

My heart clatters around in my chest and I feel so happy, so glad to see him.

I push through the crowd and walk toward his table. The person signing has left. "Josh," I call.

I'm only twenty or so feet away when a big, bearded guy in a security uniform stops me. "Whoa, lady. The queue's back there." He thrusts his thumb in the direction behind him.

I stumble a bit, then catch myself. I look to Josh. He's talking to another fan. "Huh?"

"Do you speak English? There's a queue. Back there." He

speaks slowly, then shakes his head, and says, "Always with the cutting here."

"But..."

"Queue," he says. He points and I follow his finger. There's a line. It has to be two hundred people long. Two hundred people holding posters, or drawings, or comic books, waiting to see Josh.

It'll take hours to get to the front.

My heart sinks. "But he'll want to see me. I'm..." Inspiration strikes, "I'm Jewel."

The guard scowls. "Yeah. And so is that lady, and that lady, and look, that lady too." The security officer points at a dozen different women wearing the same exact outfit as me.

My face heats and I realize how crazy this is. How stupid.

"No, I mean, I'm actually Jewel."

The man glares at me and reaches for his walkie-talkie.

"Did you say you're actually Jewel?" A teenager with a Scottish accent, in the same outfit as me, stops and looks me up and down.

"Yes." I nod my head quickly. "I flew a really long way to get here, and I need to see Josh. It can't wait."

The Scottish girl is with a group of half a dozen friends, all dressed up, looking like hardcore fans.

"You're shorter than Jewel," one of the guys says. "And a little more..." He waves his hands in front of his chest. One of the girls smacks him.

I shake my head. Unbelievable.

I look back at the security guard. His arms are folded across his very muscular chest. He's not letting me by. He scowls and points at the line. I turn back to the group of super fans.

"Look, please. I'm the real Jewel. You've been waiting to see what happens with Grim and Jewel, right? Well, it's happening right now. I'm here. Can you please help me get to him? Please?"

"Wowwww," one of the girls says.

The security officer turns on his walkie-talkie. "We've got a nutter here who thinks she flew in from outer space. I need some backup."

The Scottish girl wrinkles her brow and looks at my expression.

Then she nods. "Alright. We'll help."

"How?" a redheaded guy in a black leather cape asks.

"We'll make a scene," I say. "So big that Josh can't ignore us."

"Ma'am, I suggest you get in the queue."

I turn to the security guard and glare.

The Scottish girl says, "You're going to feel like a real wanker when you realize you tried to prevent intergalactic love."

He sighs and says into his walkie-talkie, "Hurry with the backup."

Then the group of teenagers behind me starts shouting, "Grim! Grim! Jewel is here. She's here!"

I jump up and down and wave at Josh.

"Jewel's here!" they shout. "She flew a really long way!"

The people in line look over at us. A little girl points at me.

I keep jumping up and down, waving my arms, trying to get Josh to see me. Finally, he looks up from signing a book. He frowns at me and wrinkles his brow. For a second, I think he recognizes me because he leans forward and his eyes widen, but then he shakes his head and turns away.

"Josh, look! I'm here!" I shout.

But the security guard keeps stepping in front of me. I'm twenty feet from Josh's table and he doesn't see me, he doesn't realize it's me.

"Josh! It's me! Gemma!"

"She's Jewel," the teens shout.

Then, the worst thing that can happen does. All the other women in line that are dressed as Jewel start shouting, "I'm Jewel! I'm Jewel! No, I'm Jewel! Me too!"

I can see Josh's face. He shakes his head and he looks like he's about to start laughing. Like life is the biggest joke. Like life is his playground. Like he has women pretending to be his Jewel every day of the week. Like he doesn't have a care in the world.

But he does. I know he does. I know him.

"Sir," the security guard shouts, "do you know this Jewel woman?"

Josh gives a laughing grin and shakes his head no. And then, he calls the next person in line forward to sign their comic book.

I can't believe it. I cannot believe it. I'm so exhausted, I haven't really slept for days, I'm worn out, and all I want is to hold Josh and tell him I love him. And I don't want to wait to do it.

"Ma'am, it's time to go. Back to Mars or wherever you flew in from," the security guard says.

That's it.

If you want something bad enough, you'll do whatever it takes to get it.

I reach down and yank off my shoe. Then I fling it past the security guard. It flies through the air and hits Josh's table with a crack.

She threw a shoe at him.

He jerks back and looks up in shock.

"Josh!"

I pull off my other shoe and chuck it at his table. It skids across the floor.

Josh stands up and sends a quizzical look in my direction.

"It's me," I call. But the noise of a thousand people packed into a conference center buries my voice and it doesn't reach him.

He frowns and looks toward me. Like maybe he realizes that no one else in his life but me would know that throwing a shoe at him would catch his attention.

Because, who throws shoes? Honestly?

I jump up and down and wave my arms, "Josh!"

"That's it, ma'am. You're being escorted from the premises," the security guard says. He starts walking toward me. Then I notice that there are three other security guards closing in.

This isn't looking good.

But, as the extremely sexy, world-famous quote-maven Josh Lewenthal once said, "*Anything is possible if you put your mind to it.*"

However, as I once said, you have to pick your battles. And

right now, I'm about to be tackled by a group of burly security guards.

I look to my left, away from the approaching guards. There's a space through the crowd, and something else, something that you better believe the universe provided just for this moment. I sprint barefoot across the floor toward the low stage with a microphone in the middle. There's a blonde woman at the microphone announcing a special event starting in only five minutes. When she finishes her announcement she sets the microphone back in its stand.

I run up the steps. "Excuse me. Sorry. I just...sorry." I grab the microphone. From the height of the stage I can see the security guards hurrying towards me. I don't have all that much time.

"Josh," I say, "it's me, Gemma."

We're a hundred feet apart, separated by a big crowd and four angry security guards. But when he hears me his head snaps up and he looks around the room.

I start inching down the stairs on the opposite side of the stage from the approaching guards, trying to delay my inevitable escorting out.

"You once said that love is the best gift we ever have the privilege to give, and for a long while I didn't believe you. I thought I did, but I didn't."

Josh comes out from behind his table and tries to look over the crowd to find me. He doesn't see me. The security guards have made it to the stage. My time's almost up.

"I was afraid. I'm sorry I didn't see you for who you were. I'm sorry it took me so long. I was scared to tell you. I was scared to say I love you."

The entire conference center has gone quiet. Everyone has turned toward the stage. Josh has finally seen me. He's stuck at the back of the crowd, trying to push his way through.

I look over at the guards, they're only a few feet away.

Well, this is it.

I look back at Josh. "You once said, fate finds you when you least expect it. I didn't expect to find you. Or to love you."

Even though we're far apart I focus on him, on the expression on his face. He's giving me that smile, the happy, quiet one that he only ever gives me.

"But I do. I love you."

The big security guard steps in front of me and holds out his hand for the microphone.

My time's up.

"Josh. If you feel the same, well, I'm about to be banned from the convention, so I'll wait for you outside. I know I took the long way to get here, the really, really long way to figure this out. But now that I'm here, I hope that I'm not wrong. That by following the stars in my heart, I found you."

"Ma'am," the guard says.

I nod and drop the microphone into his hand. My group of teenager friends start to clap and cheer. A few others join in.

Two of the guards take my arms and then guide me down the stairs. I've lost sight of Josh.

The guards escort me through the crowd and out the back exit. I'm banned. Prohibited from re-entry. Not allowed back inside.

I nod in understanding.

When they go back in I sit down on the parking lot curb and curl my toes under. It's really cold in London, in late winter, when you aren't wearing shoes.

I wrap my hands around my knees and shiver. The sky is a washed out gray, with a tiny patch of blue and a little stream of sunshine just breaking through. The pavement is still wet from a late morning shower and the air smells like wet grass and rain.

I pull my legs closer to my chest. It's cold.

I drop my chin onto my knees.

Then, I hear the metal door clang shut.

I turn and look over my shoulder. Josh strides toward me. My heart leaps into my throat.

"Hey." I smile up at him.

He lifts an eyebrow then sits down next to me on the concrete curb. He picks up a strand of my lime green wig and his eyes crinkle. "So random, Gemma. So random."

I give him an answering smile. "You don't like it?"

He shakes his head. "I didn't say that."

It's hard to take a full breath. "You didn't say goodbye. You left, and you're going to be gone a year and you didn't say goodbye."

His brows lower. "What? Who said that?"

"Grim. In your comic, he was leaving for a year and he didn't let Jewel know that he loved her and—"

"You read my comic?" Josh's grin spreads across his face.

I swallow. "Mhmm."

"What did you think?" He looks at me closely, his face only a few inches from mine. The mist from our breath mingles in the air between us.

"I liked it. I really liked it, but I think Grim should've told Jewel that he loved her."

Josh looks into my eyes, then he reaches up and runs his finger down my cheek. "Do you?"

My heart leaps at his touch. "I do," I whisper.

"Gemma." He leans forward.

"Yes?" I hold my breath.

"I only left for the weekend. I fly back on Monday."

"What?" My mind is fuddled with his mouth so close to mine.

"I canceled my tour. I'm staying in New York."

"Why?" I whisper.

He reaches up and places both hands on my jaw and strokes my skin with his fingers. "I thought we could try making a baby again."

At his words my heart starts to fill up with so much happiness.

He wipes a tear from my cheek. Then he leans forward and brushes his lips across my skin, over my cheeks, my nose, my eyes. His mouth is warm and gentle. I hold still under him as he trails his lips over my face.

I let out a small sound.

He pauses, his mouth hovering over me, his hands not moving.

"Josh," I whisper.

Then, he presses his mouth to mine. He sucks on my bottom lip, licks me, tastes me. He pulls me close and says, "I love you, Gemma. I love you."

And even though it's freezing out and my toes are going numb, my whole body feels warm and happy. I'm so happy.

I smile against Josh's mouth.

He takes my lips in his, kisses me, and in his kiss I can feel how much he wants me, how long he's loved me. Then he says, "Gemma, if you don't let me strip you down and make love to you in the next five minutes, you and I are going to have problems."

EXACTLY THIRTY MINUTES LATER I'M WARM AND WELL-LOVED, curled in Josh's arms in his bed at the convention center hotel. He strokes his fingers up and down the curve of my spine.

"You figured out I wrote all the quotes?" he asks. His voice is intimate and low in the soft confines of the down-comforter and the dimly lit hotel room.

I turn toward him and run my hand over his bare chest. I don't think I'll ever get tired of touching him. "I found your journal in Ian's office. I brought it with me."

He gives me a half-smile, then returns to stroking my back.

"Why didn't you ever say anything? Why didn't you fight him?" I ask. I shiver when he places a kiss between my neck and my collarbone.

Then Josh pulls back and says, "Why would I? He took something I made and shared it with the world. He made people's lives better. What more could I want? Money? Power? Recognition? If I wanted those things, it would stop being about making the world a better place and start being about me. That's not who I am."

He's right. It's not. He truly does just care about making the world better.

"But why didn't you tell me?" I ask. "Why didn't you tell me Ian was a thieving liar *and* that you loved me?"

His hand stills on my back. "Would you have believed me?"

Oh.

"No." I had a lot to learn.

He starts stroking my back again.

After a moment of quiet I say, "You don't have to cancel your tour, you know. It's a big deal." It bothers me that he'd give up such a huge opportunity.

He makes a low sound against the back of my neck. "Maybe you could come with me. It's three months. Paris, Prague, Budapest. Imagine the trouble we could get up to together."

I hide my face in the pillow and grin. Finally, when I'm able, I turn and look at him. "I like getting into trouble with you."

After a moment he says, "Gemma?" His fingers play with my hair.

"Hmmm?"

"You love me." His voice is low and raw and happy.

I nod. "I do. I really, really do."

He makes a sound and then flips over and pulls me on top of him.

"Do you know how long I've been waiting for you to say that?"

I shake my head no, then squirm a little until I'm settled comfortably on top of his chest. "How long?"

His eyes drift to my mouth and he smiles.

"Two years ago, exactly two weeks before New Year's, I heard your laugh. I'd heard it a thousand times before, practically my whole life. But for some reason, that day it hit me. Right here." He puts his hand to his heart. "That was it. I was a goner. I knew that I loved you, and it wasn't something that would go away. It was for good. Then your mom asked if she could set us up for the New Year's Party and I thought, *yes. Say yes.* But you—"

I bury my face in his chest. "Don't say it."

"You told the truth."

I look at him. He shrugs. "So, I started working on becoming the man you'd want to spend the rest of your life with."

My eyes widen. "The two-year sex drought."

His lips lift into a half-smile. "It was worth it."

I squirm on top of him and he runs his hands over my back.

"So, you didn't love me as a teenager? Those drawings in your journal?"

He shakes his head and looks chagrinned. "No. I was just a horny teen. Sorry."

I grin at him. "Don't be sorry. I liked the Jell-O bit."

He gives me a considering look. "Think we could recreate it?"

"Maybe." But then I search his expression. "I need you to know. When all this started, I thought it was just about making a baby, that I didn't need or want you, but...that's not what it's about. Even if it doesn't work out, that's okay. I'm just glad, I'm so grateful that I found you. That you're here with me. That we could do this together. I wouldn't want to do it with anyone else."

Josh nods. "I know."

"You do?"

He gives me his life-is-my-playground smile and says, "You love me Gemma. You can't help it."

I laugh and shake my head. I'm about to give him one of his quotes about loving and living, but he flips me over to my back and slips inside me and I forget everything that I was about to say.

Except, "I love you. I love you."

31

"Love is the best gift."

My mom's annual Fourth of July Punch and Pies party is this evening. But first, Josh and I have to finish up at Dr. Ingraham's. I look around the waiting room. There are four other couples here waiting to be called back by the nurse. Joy is behind the front desk, ignoring everyone. I stare at the new wall décor, an abstract landscape painting. I can't tell whether it's a skyscraper, or...no, it's definitely a skyscraper.

I just had my egg retrieval. Dr. Ingraham said that my eggs looked to be of "superb quality." Apparently three months in Europe with Josh was good for me. Or it's my new job, freelance social media marketing consultant. I have to admit, I love being my own boss.

I tap my foot against the low-pile carpet. What could be taking Josh so long?

My phone buzzes and I look down at the display.

I smile when I read the message.

Josh: It's not working...

Then he sends through a picture. It's a shot of The Production Room. The room is just as bare and depressing as the last time he was in there. This time Josh is in the shot too and he's sending me sad, puppy eyes.

I can't help it. I grin.

Gemma: Look up some porn.

Josh: Gemma...

I stand and hurry to Joy's desk. I clear my throat. She looks up and raises an eyebrow. "What?"

"I need to use the bathroom," I say.

She shakes her head and drops the bathroom key into my hand.

My phone buzzes again.

Josh: Inspiration?

I step into the bathroom and lock the door behind me.

Gemma: How about an ankle pic?

Josh: ...

Gemma: I could send you a pic of my stomach.

Josh: Gemma...they're knocking on the door. Little help here?

I grin at myself in the mirror. Then I prop my phone on the sink and hit the video call button.

Josh answers on the first ring.

"Gemma?"

His voice echoes in the tile bathroom. I put my finger to my lip and smile.

Then I whisper, "How's this?" I pull my T-shirt over my head. My hair comes out of my ponytail and falls around my shoulders. I stand in front of the camera in my bra and shorts.

Josh's eyes go wide, and he gets that look I recognize. The one where I have about five seconds to choose between the bedroom or the floor.

"Not a breast man," he says with a low growl.

I smile at him, then turn my back to the camera. I unhook my bra and let it fall away.

I hear his sharp intake of breath. But I don't stop. I unbutton my shorts and then slowly side them down my legs.

"Gemma..."

I push my panties down my legs, until I'm standing in front of the camera completely naked. Josh sucks in a harsh breath. I look over my shoulder and smile at him.

His eyes aren't focused on my bare skin, but on my face.

"I love you. Have I told you lately how much I love you?"

I shake my head no. "Not since this morning."

He gives me a surprised look. "Let me remind you then. I love you. I love that you're mine. I love you."

"I love you," I say back.

And that's when I know, everything is going to work out. Everything is going to be okay. Everything is going to be perfect.

Because when you believe the universe is going to give you good things, sooner or later, it will.

It's January first and all our friends and family are gathered at the annual Wieners and Wine New Year's Resolution Party. My parents' house is full to the brim with guests, even more than usual. There has to be at least a hundred people here. The plastic wrap is out in full force protecting all carpeting and furnishings from barbecue sauce and red wine spills.

I breathe in the happy, familiar smell of barbecue wieners, mini gherkins, and lime Jell-O. My mom bustles out of the kitchen with a tray of pimento olives on toothpicks. She lifts it up high as Sasha, the twins and Colin race under it after their new puppy, a little cocker spaniel named Chase.

"Kids, no running in the house," Leah calls after them. But she's distracted when Oliver grabs her hand, spins her around and dips her. Leah smiles up at Oliver, then he plants a kiss on her lips.

"Leah made her resolution come true," I say.

Josh looks at my sister and her husband. "Dance lessons?"

I nod. "And Sasha got her resolution." I point at the puppy that the kids got for Christmas. The girls are now huddled under the dining room table trying to pry Chase away from chewing up the table leg.

"What are we talking about?" Brook walks over with her husband in tow. He's a bulky, rough-looking New York City police officer with a tiny little newborn in his arms.

"You're Daddy's girl, aren't you?" he coos to her.

Josh looks over at me and smirks. Then he turns to Brook. "We're pointing out whose New Year's Resolution came true."

"Mine did," Brook says. Then she nods at Carly and Theo. "Carly's too. Did I tell you? He got her a Learjet."

I shake my head. "I don't think that was her resolution."

Brook nods sagely. "But it should have been."

Hannah comes over. She's in a long red velvet dress with a crown braid on top of her head. She looks like a fairy princess. She has the tiniest little baby bump, and I expect she'll have an announcement for everybody soon.

"Mini gherkins, I *love* mini gherkins," she says. She scoops a dozen of them onto her plate.

Brook looks over at me and gives me a wide-eyed stare. I wink at her. She turns to Hannah. "Pickles aren't on the raw fertility diet."

Hannah scowls at Brook. "I'm having pickles. Okay? And do

not tell me a crazy story about some random pickle crime boss or I will stab you with a toothpick. 'Kay?"

Brook gives a huge smile. "Sure, Hannah. Don't worry about it. Have as many pickles as you want."

I cover a laugh. Josh leans into me. "What's with the pickles?" he murmurs. "You never want pickles."

I wrap my arms around him and lean my head against his shoulder. "Yeah, it's all cantaloupe and steak for me."

He chuckles and then he gently rests his hand over my rounded belly. His hand moves in a slow, loving circle and I feel the baby give a kick.

"He's awake," I say.

"She," Josh says. He gives me a teasing smile and spreads his fingers across my belly. The protective warmth of him spreads through me.

We decided to wait to find out whether our baby's a girl or a boy. I think he's a boy, but Josh swears she's a girl. In four short months, we'll find out.

"What was your resolution?" Hannah asks.

I'm still looking at Josh, his expression is intimate and I'd like to take him upstairs to someplace quiet so that I can kiss him and...

"Gemma?"

I blink and shake my head. Josh chuckles. He knows *exactly* what I was just thinking.

"It came true," I tell everyone. I take Josh's hand and hold on to him. "And it was better than I could ever have imagined."

I never, ever could've guessed what fate had in store for me when I wrote my New Year's wish.

"Do you know," I say to Josh, "everyone in my family had their resolution come true. The kids got their puppy, Dylan got his promotion, my parents went to Fiji. But I never..."

I frown at Josh and wrinkle my brow.

"What?" he asks. He lifts an eyebrow and pulls me closer to him.

"I never asked what your resolution was."

Every year, when we write our resolutions and my dad reads them out loud and then tosses them into the fireplace, I imagine that there's a little bit of magic helping make our dreams come true. But I never asked Josh if his resolution came true.

The corner of his mouth lifts into a nervous smile and he shakes his head.

"What is it?" I frown.

"No, it didn't happen yet."

My chest pinches. He seems so uncertain. He swallows nervously.

"What?" I ask. "Can I help? What was it? I mean, this amazing guy I know once said, *anything is possible if you put your mind to it.*"

Josh chuckles, "Did he now?"

"He was right," Brook calls over her husband's shoulder.

Hannah's munching on a pickle, but she says, "I have a quartz on me if you need to manifest your intentions."

I grin at Josh, and his eyes light up with laughter. "I'm good," he tells Hannah. "I'm just about to get there, I think."

"Oh," I say in surprise. "That's good."

Josh nods. "Sure is. Want to hear it?"

"Yes. Of course."

Josh presses a kiss to my lips. I wrap my hands around his neck.

"That was it? A kiss?"

He laughs and shakes his head. "Not even close."

Since he's not talking, I think back to last year's reading. "Was it to take night classes?"

"No."

I laugh, "Go to the gym?"

"No," Josh growls.

I look at him and the expression in his eyes makes my heart stutter. "Save money? Travel?"

He slowly shakes his head.

I can't think of any other resolutions from last year's reading. In fact, the only thing I really remember is Josh lifting his glass to me, toasting me as if we'd just made a deal. My dad had read my resolution last and Josh had watched me and...

He watches my expression intently. "You want to know?"

"I do."

He smiles when I say those words.

"What was it?"

He leans close, presses his lips against my ear and says, "Convince the woman I love to marry me."

He made a resolution.

My heart gives a happy, joyful beat, then I turn my face to

him and catch his mouth with mine. I clasp my hands around his neck and kiss him.

"Wow, that's some resolution," Hannah says.

I laugh against Josh's mouth.

Finally, he pulls away.

"Last year?" I ask, "You made that resolution last year?"

He gives me a laughing look and then says, "I had high hopes." Then he drops to his knee in front of me and takes my hands in his. Around us, all of our friends and family realize that Josh is about to propose. The room grows quiet, and even the puppy stops misbehaving.

My vision goes blurry and I blink back tears.

He made a resolution to marry me last year?

"Gemma, I love you," he begins and he squeezes my hands. "We've known each other a long time." He grins and lifts an eyebrow.

A laugh bubbles up. "Twenty-five years."

He nods. "I think you can say that I'm a decent guy."

"Mhmm." I can't speak. I can't...he's so wonderful, so Josh.

"We grew up in the same town. Went to the same school. Your brother's my best friend. I come to your holiday parties, birthdays. I'm always around."

I start to laugh, I can't help it. But I'm also starting to cry. I love him so much.

"I have straight teeth, a nice chin. Healthy genes. I'm smart. Athletic."

"All true." My lips wobble as I try to smile.

A happy light fills Josh's eyes as he gazes up at me. "I thought...maybe you'd want to know me for another twenty-five years? And then, twenty-five after that. And then, many years more, for as long as we both live?"

My heart fills with so much joy, so much love.

"Marry me, Gemma. I love you. I'll keep on loving you. You're the star that guides my heart. Marry me?"

I try to hold back my tears but I can't. "Yes. Yes, of course, yes."

I drop to my knees and wrap my arms around him. He pulls me to him and presses his mouth to mine. I can taste tears of happiness, and love and joy. The baby gives a kick. Josh grunts in surprise and then pulls me closer.

"He approves," I say.

"She," Josh says.

I laugh, and then Josh is kissing me again, and my family is cheering, and my friends are laughing, and the puppy is barking, and our baby is kicking, and everything, everything is perfect.

Suddenly, I pull away from Josh. I've just thought of something. "What's your resolution for this year?"

He looks at me, then gives me that private smile, the one just for me, and he says, "I don't have one. I have everything I want."

"Everything?"

He nods and says with complete certainty, "Everything."

Then he pulls me back in his arms, and whispers in my ear, "Gemma, if you don't let me take you upstairs and strip you down..."

I laugh and then Josh has scooped me up and is hurrying up the stairs.

"But what about the resolution writing?" my mom calls.

"And the champagne?" says Leah.

"Carly, can they borrow your island for their honeymoon?" Brook says.

"Darling, I told you, I didn't ask for an island."

"Do you think they'll want a summer wedding?" my mom asks.

Josh grins down at me and I start to laugh. Then, I can't hear my family and friends anymore because Josh has made it up the stairs and he's looking at me like there isn't anyone or anything in the whole world except me.

And I know exactly how he feels.

"I love you."

He kicks open the door to my bedroom and gently drops me onto my childhood bed. "Kinky," I say.

He lifts an eyebrow, "I figured the garage would be too cold."

Hmm. "Maybe this summer? After the baby comes."

His eyes light up and he grins. "Deal."

I laugh, and he covers my mouth with his. He strips me down, and then he loves me and loves me and loves me some more. And me, I love him right back.

After all, everybody knows, love is the best gift, the best gift in the whole wide world.

The End

*ILLUSTRATIONS BY JOSH LEWENTHAL

A NOTE FROM THE AUTHOR

Infertility effects one in eight couples, and each of us or someone we know – a family member, a friend, a neighbor, the person behind us in line at the grocery store – is impacted by infertility. Even though it's so common, we rarely talk about it or share the effect it has on our lives. The struggle, the hope, the yearning.

Every infertility diagnosis is unique and every person addresses it with their own feelings, their own views, and their own hopes.

I wanted to write a book that opened up an experience so many women, men, and couples have, but that is so rarely shared. The diagnosis, the IVF, the miscarriages, and the will to keep trying, even though.

In this book, Gemma faces infertility in her own way. It won't be anyone else's way or anyone else's journey, it's hers. I believe that hard times are always best when faced with a smile. I hope Gemma's humor and courage brought a smile to you.

Sincerely,
Sarah Ready

ACKNOWLEDGMENTS

In case you missed the dedication, this book is for you. Yes. You. Thank you.

I don't know if you've ever had a book written for you before, if not, here it is. You deserve it and so much more. You are my inspiration.

It's always my greatest wish to give joy, happiness, and courage to others. I want to acknowledge two female writers who have done the same and inspired generations of women. Jane Austen and Helen Fielding. Thank you. Thank you from the bottom of my heart.

These brilliant women brought to the forefront of society universal questions that needed to be asked. Elizabeth Bennet in *Pride and Prejudice* asked: is it right to marry for money and status or can we marry for love? Bridget in *Bridget Jones's Diary* asked: can a woman have self-determination of her career and relationships? Both asked: what does it mean to be a woman today? I'm honored and grateful to these two writers to be able to reframe, recreate, and address this question in the pages of this book.

Josh and Gemma Make a Baby explores a new social commentary concerning so many of us today – fertility, family building, and choosing our own destiny as a woman. I hope that this book is worthy of the legacy of Jane Austen and Helen Fielding. Thank you for being an inspiration so that a new story highlighting women, our struggles, and our lives could be written.

On a note concerning advocacy, thank you to RESOLVE, The National Infertility Association, for your resources, acronym database, helpful information, and all the work and advocacy you do.

Thank you to the Reproductive Endocrinologists consulted, for your careful edits and suggestions, and your help in making sure Gemma's story was as accurate as possible.

I'd also like to acknowledge my good friend, after thirteen tries you succeeded — a girl! Your hope, belief, and strength were inspirational.

Finally, back to you. My greatest wish is that when you finish these pages you are filled with hope and love and a sense that anything is possible if you put your mind to it. Because it's true. Reach out, dare to dream, you have the whole world inside of you and all the love too. Take ahold of all your dreams and live them.

Thank you for your kindness and for being you.

Sarah

JOIN SARAH READY'S NEWSLETTER

Want more Josh and Gemma? Get an exclusive chapter from Josh's POV.

When you join the Sarah Ready Newsletter you get access to sneak peaks, insider updates, exclusive bonus scenes and more.

Join Today for Josh's Chapter

www.sarahready.com/newsletter

ABOUT THE AUTHOR

Author Sarah Ready writes contemporary romance and romantic comedy. Her books have been described as "euphoric", "heartwarming" and "laugh out loud". Her debut novel *The Fall in Love Checklist* was hailed as "the unicorn read of 2020".

Sarah writes stand-alone romcoms and romcoms in the Soulmates in Romeo series, all of which can be found at her website: www.sarahready.com.

Stay up to date, get exclusive epilogues and bonus content. Join Sarah's newsletter at www.sarahready.com/newsletter.